"ALL HANDS, T

Richter paused to t[...] been done to his submarine, ignoring [...] blood from his brow that already soaked his collar.

"We've just collided with a Russian sub and are taking on water in the engine room. We've lost our main engines and have conducted an emergency blow. We're at four hundred feet and headed for the surface. Everything's going to be fine. I want all stations to report any injuries and stow your spaces. We're in for a bumpy ride."

DANGER'S HOUR

"Submarine tales that live up to real life on the boats have been all too rare. Even rarer are gripping stories built around what men and machines can and cannot survive. *Danger's Hour* does both, and does it with a deployment that is as unforgettable as it is chilling."
—Sherry Sontag, coauthor of *Blind Man's Bluff: The Untold Story of American Submarine Espionage*

"Told by one who knows the strengths and the flaws in today's rescue systems, this utterly compelling book chronicles the reality of living for days in a sunken flooded nuclear hull. . . . All too true to life, this book haunts you long after you have put it down."
—Admiral Sir James Perowne, KBE, Royal Navy

"A gripping story . . . the medical/physiological aspects are beyond reproach, as would be expected from such an authority. And the meticulous chronological sequencing in the several time zones of the action at sea and onshore is very effective."
—Surgeon Vice-Admiral Sir John Rawlins, KBE FRCP, FRAeS

DANGER'S HOUR

James Francis

AN ONYX BOOK

ONYX
Published by New American Library, a division of
Penguin Putnam Inc., 375 Hudson Street,
New York, New York 10014, U.S.A.
Penguin Books Ltd, 80 Strand,
London WC2R 0RL, England
Penguin Books Australia Ltd, Ringwood,
Victoria, Australia
Penguin Books Canada Ltd, 10 Alcorn Avenue,
Toronto, Ontario, Canada M4V 3B2
Penguin Books (N.Z.) Ltd, 182–190 Wairau Road,
Auckland 10, New Zealand

Penguin Books Ltd, Registered Offices:
Harmondsworth, Middlesex, England

First published by Onyx, an imprint of New American Library,
a division of Penguin Putnam Inc.

First Printing, April 2002
10 9 8 7 6 5 4 3 2 1

Ⓡ REGISTERED TRADEMARK—MARCA REGISTRADA

Printed in the United States of America

This work
is dedicated to
the courageous people
of all nations who serve in submarines

ACKNOWLEDGMENTS

I could not have written this book without the help and encouragement of some wonderful people. In particular, I would like to thank both the serving and retired US Navy and Royal Navy submariners who have been so generous with their advice and encouragement. I'm also most grateful to our friends and neighbors for their constructive criticism of the manuscript at various stages of its development, and to Ed Stackler for his professional advice. I am also deeply indebted to my agent, Bob Diforio, for his tireless assistance and support. Above all, I would like to thank my wife, Veronica. She had to endure long periods of solitude when I shut myself away to concentrate on writing. She put up with my swings of mood from elation to depression as progress was either made or not and looked after me throughout. She read every draft and her imprint on the characters is indelible. Without her help and encouragement I would have never started this project, and would certainly never have finished it.

AUTHOR'S NOTE

This story was written before 118 lives were tragically lost when the RFS *Kursk* sank on Saturday 12 August 2000. As I watched the ill-fated rescue effort, mainly as reported by the British media, I couldn't help but note the similarities between real life and my fictional account of a submarine rescue in the Norwegian Sea. In particular, the substantial and unpredictable influence of the weather in those latitudes, even at the height of summer, proved to be as disruptive as I describe in the following pages. One big difference between this story and the events that surrounded the sinking of the *Kursk* is the way in which the Russian authorities provided consistently inaccurate and contradictory information to the media. The misleading of news consumers around the globe was compounded by the limited access the media were given to events as they developed at sea. While one can reasonably expect a Western government to provide incomplete information, particularly in the early stages of a breaking story, this is usually balanced by the disclosures of investigative journalists. For this reason, the quality and quantity of information given to the general public is far greater in this story than it was in real life.

The narrative is related in local time and the standard time notation has been used. Thus, times in Moscow are designated the "C" time zone notation that is two hours ahead of the "A" time zone that covers Norway and its adjacent seas. This is one hour ahead of the "Z" time zone in the UK that, in turn, is five hours ahead of the East Coast of the USA, which is in the "R" time zone.

CHAPTER

1

Thursday, 28 October

1145A, USS *Tulsa*

Commander Richter sat in his chair in the control room, close to exhaustion. After five weeks of constant surveillance of the target and the fitful sleep that is so characteristic of submarine patrols, it was only sheer professionalism that kept him, or any of his crew, alert. They had been listening to the *Uriy Dolgorukiy*, a new Russian submarine, undertake repeated diving and surfacing drills in the naval exercise area off Murmansk before the Russian had moved into the Norwegian Sea to conduct deeper trials.

"Conn, Sonar."

"Conn," replied Lieutenant Schwartz, the officer of the deck.

"Target's going shallow." Schwartz looked toward Richter for direction.

"OK, Harvey, follow him up." Richter switched his attention away from the fitness reports on his officers and once again evaluated their target. The RFS *Uriy Dolgorukiy* was the first new submarine that the Russians had designed and built since the Cold War. It was a project that had proceeded in fits and starts as the money had either trickled through, or had been choked off, by politicians. Despite the delays, this submarine was potentially a formidable opponent. The *Borey* class would represent the fourth generation of ballistic-missile submarines. They were somewhat smaller than the Typhoons, the largest submarines that the Russians, or anybody else, had ever constructed—but larger than the Deltas that had served as the backbone of the Soviet second-strike capability during the seventies and eighties. Once fully operational, the *Uriy Dolgorukiy* and her sisters, if they were ever funded, would hide at sea and serve as a threat to any nation that was stupid enough to attack the Motherland. Today, its mere existence was a tribute to Russia's desire to remain a serious player in the nuclear league.

The *Tulsa* had tracked the Russian submarine more or less continuously since it had left the base at Zapadnaya Litsa for its first sea trials. Richter's mission was to use the *Tulsa*'s highly sophisticated sonars to define the acoustic signature of the boat so that it could be identified and tracked in the future. He also wanted to get some idea of its operating envelope—such as how deep it could dive and its maximum speed. He was aware of intelligence reports that it was equipped with a new kind of propulsion system. In addition to a conventional pump jet, it could apparently employ a magnetic pump that uses the electrical conductivity of seawater to drive the submarine through the oceans. Having no moving parts, this had the potential for ultraquiet performance. When combined with the recent technological advances that the Russians had made in reactor cooling and hull insulation, the *Uriy Dolgorukiy* was potentially an extremely difficult submarine to find and follow.

To date, however, the challenge of the mission had not lived up to its billing. In fact it had been dull. The target had only employed its conventional propulsion, and even that at modest speed. There had been no full-power trial, no missile drills, no torpedo firings, and no suggestion of the "silent" drive being tested. It had been unexciting, yet nobody, least of all Richter, had been able to relax—just in case the Russians unexpectedly tried something new. The absence of missile firings was no surprise. The delay in producing adequate missiles for the boat was well-known and, as far as Richter understood, was still an ongoing problem. It had almost caused the program to be canceled.

Richter glanced back down at the fitness reports that would be due on completion of the patrol. Top of the list for his consideration was his engineering officer, John Dowling. It was also the most difficult. Richter was presented with a conundrum. Lieutenant Commander John Dowling was an excellent engineer. He ran a tight outfit and the maintenance, safety, and inspection record of his department was impeccable. By any professional standards, John would make commander, yet he was facing serious difficulty getting there. The problem? Well, there were two. He had been an occasional user of marijuana in his younger days, as had so many, and was lucky to have gotten away with a questionable random urine test soon after they were introduced in the mid-eighties. He'd learned his lesson and that was now ancient history. The more pressing problem was that John was not an exercise freak. That was, if anything, an understatement. He positively hated running and had been scared of water since a near-drowning incident in his childhood, so he wouldn't swim. Richter had often wondered why he had chosen the navy as a career. His choice of submarines was even more baffling. His dislike of exercise would not matter too much if it weren't for his passion for haute cuisine and a wife who enjoyed nothing more than pampering him in that department. The result was that John's figure was rather too full for the esthetic taste of today's brass, and he frequently had difficulty passing the physical readiness tests that he was obliged to take twice a year. The brutal fact of the matter was that Dowling could walk on water, feed thousands on a picnic for two, and turn water into wine but, unless he lost weight, it was his chances of promotion that were slim.

"Right 15 degrees rudder, steer 080," announced Schwartz.

"Right 15 degrees rudder, steady on 080, Helm, aye," replied the helmsman. Richter glanced over at the plot. On this course, the bottom would shortly shelve sharply from over three thousand feet to under one thousand.

"What's he up to, Mr. Schwartz?"

"Looks like he's headed back up over the shelf, sir."

"OK, stay with him."

Richter returned to Dowling's FITREP. What made the matter all the more galling was that he was a personal friend of many years' standing. John was more than that. Although John was five years younger than he, he was easily Richter's best friend, and that made the wording of his report so difficult. He had to appear dispassionate and objective when he was not. It would be wonderful if he could arrange for John's next appointment to be XO of a boat from which he could be promoted, and this report could clinch that. He casually began to wonder how John would pen his fitness report if their roles were reversed. This was much more difficult. Yes, he kept himself in shape and looked the part. He wore his thirty-eight years well, and only a receding hairline and the "laugh lines" that radiated from the outside corner of each eye betrayed that he was not in his first flush of youth. He was bright. That wasn't just vanity, it was widely recognized in the submarine fraternity. Nonetheless, he commanded the respect of his men more through affection than fear, although his occasionally abrasive remarks to those who performed at a lower standard than he considered acceptable meant that the affection was not unqualified. Ignorance among his men he was prepared to accept and rectify, stupidity he was not.

Richter's inability to tolerate fools was legendary. It was, perhaps, his most obvious fault and one that he had found impossible to fix. He also wished he had a better sense of humor. He had been told more than once that he took life and work rather too seriously. His intolerance and difficulty with relaxing had marred so many relationships that he was resigned to the fact that the navy was to be his one and only bride. Since the death of his younger brother in a motorcycle accident nearly twenty years ago, his father had relied on Richter to perpetuate the family name. It was the only expectation that he showed no sign of achieving.

1150A, RFS *Gepard*

"Please be seated, gentlemen," announced Commander Borzhov automatically as he entered the wardroom. "I've asked you to this meeting to tell you our orders and outline how I intend to carry them out." He briefly studied each of the officers who were gathered around the table. They looked attentive and even a little intrigued. "The situation," continued Borzhov, "is that an American submarine, an improved Los Angeles class boat named the *Tulsa*, has been shadowing the *Uriy Dolgorukiy* since she commenced her sea trials and so far she has been unable to shake the Yankee off her tail. So, gentlemen, it has fallen to us to do this for her." Borzhov glanced down at a piece of paper he had retrieved from his jacket pocket and then back up at his astonished audience. He raised his thick eyebrows momentarily and continued: "Now I don't think this is going to be as difficult as you might imagine. First of all, we will not have to find the *Tulsa* because the *Uriy Dolgorukiy* will bring her to us." He got up from his chair, unfolded a chart, and placed it in the middle of the table. "We are roughly here"—he stabbed the chart with his index finger, indicating a position to the southeast of Bear Island—"and the *Uriy Dolgorukiy* is roughly here, about forty nautical miles to the west of the island. She will be traveling east at about eight knots for the next two hours or so. I intend to maneuver close to this underwater rock formation here"—he stabbed at the chart again—"and there we will wait for the *Tulsa* to come to us. Is that clear?"

"Aye, sir, but what will we do when the *Tulsa* shows up?" The question had been asked by Lieutenant Meltzer, a fresh-faced officer whose youthful looks belied his advancing years, and whose seniority as a lieutenant disguised his lack of experience at sea.

"As soon as she has passed by us I'll wait until she clears her baffles and then approach her from astern and 'ping' her. A blast of active sonar at close quarters will put the wind up the sonar and control-room crews in no uncertain terms and serve as a signal to the *Uriy Dolgorukiy* to slip away." There were smiles around the table. It was an elegantly simple plan.

"What if it doesn't work?" persisted Meltzer.

"We'll cross that bridge when we get to it, but I am quite confident that it will. The captain of the *Tulsa* is a man called Richter. This is his first command. I don't think he'll want to hang around once he knows he's been detected. In fact, I expect he'll have a rather large laundry bill by the end of this afternoon!" The other officers round the table broke their silence and started to laugh. Borzhov waited until their mirth began to fade and raised a hand. "Any more questions?" Borzhov's eyebrows again rose expectantly as he glanced around the table. It was the navigator who spoke up.

"And once we have seen off that Yankee, what's next?"

"Our first task is to ensure that the 688 keeps away, then we will serve as a target for the *Uriy Dolgorukiy*'s first series of sonar trials. I expect we will be busy for the next two weeks at least, and maybe longer. I will promulgate the program as soon as I have it. Anything else?" Borzhov checked his watch. "Well then, it's time I relieved Mr. Zerchev. I believe you have the deck, Mr. Meltzer."

1350A, USS *Tulsa*

For the past two hours Richter had wrestled with the wording of Dowling's fitness report as the *Tulsa* trailed its target. He was having little success in making it look right, and the page in front of him had become covered in revisions embedded in a maze of circled text and arrows. Much more of this and it would be completely undecipherable, he thought. He rested back in his seat and rubbed his eyes. He would tackle it again after some sleep. In a few minutes the XO would relieve him, and he could get some rest. A speaker on the overhead broke the silence.

"Conn, Sonar," Schwartz reached for the MC.

"Conn, aye."

"I have a new towed-array contact close aboard in the starboard baffles. Believe this contact to be submerged."

"Sonar, Conn, aye," replied Schwartz. "Report the range to the new contact."

"Conn, Sonar, believe this contact is within two thousand yards."

"Sonar, Conn, aye."

"Where did he come from?" asked Richter.

"Looks like he just popped up from the bottom, sir. Must have been waiting for us." Schwartz turned to the tracking party. "Attention in the Section Tracking Party, we have a new submerged contact close aboard in the starboard baffles drawing forward. Set initial range at one thousand yards. This contact is designated Master-17 and is the new primary target. Track Master-17." Schwartz and Richter were both staring at the remote sonar display on the forward bulkhead.

"What's your plan, Mr. Schwartz?" The officer of the deck wrinkled his forehead, opened his mouth, and made to speak but instead looked over at the

plot. It was obvious that he was still trying to assess
the situation. Richter was thinking as well. This contact was obviously another submarine, and it wasn't
one of theirs. The chances were that it was another
Russian. What was it up to? The sonar chief had
sounded anxious, that was always a bad sign. "I'm
going to maintain my course and speed until we have
a CPA, sir," announced Schwartz.

"No, I don't think so. This doesn't feel right. Let's
get out of here."

"Aye, sir, but we may lose the boomer."

"Don't worry about that, we'll find him again," reassured Richter.

Schwartz slipped his hand into his pocket, withdrew
a tissue, and surreptitiously mopped his brow with it.
"All ahead two-thirds, left fifteen degrees rudder,
steady on course 350," he announced in his most
stolid tone.

"Left fifteen degrees rudder," replied the helmsman, "steady on course 350, my rudder is left fifteen,
all ahead two-thirds." Schwartz moved over to the
periscope stand to brief the Section Tracking Party.

"My intentions are to maneuver to the left away
from the new contact and open the CPA. On this leg,
our goal is to confirm the range to Master-17 and—"

"Conn, Sonar. Master-17 is classified as an Akula
II making 150 shaft revolutions. That equates to
twenty-eight knots. He's moving, sir!"

"Sonar, Conn, aye." Schwartz released the MC.
"OK, everybody, at twenty-eight knots he's probably
flying blind and hasn't even detected us. Once we're
steady on 350 . . ."

Richter had risen to his feet and was staring up at
the towed-array sonar screen as it suddenly went
blank. "Shit!" he muttered under his breath.

"Conn, Sonar. We've lost the towed array. Believe
the contact is now less than two hundred yards . . ."

The impact threw everyone who was standing to the
deck or against whatever was immediately aft of them.

Schwartz instinctively reached for the curtain rail that surrounded the periscope stand, ripping it off its brackets as he was thrown backwards. The quartermaster, who had been taking a reading from the fathometer, was hurled against the plotter and piled on top of Richter, who was apparently out cold. The boat was plunged into darkness for a moment until the emergency lighting took over. The echoes of the impact were replaced by the deafening screech of metal being torn and twisted out of shape, accompanied by thunderous crashes as the Akula scraped along the port side of the 688. The percussion suddenly stopped as the submarines separated. Harvey Schwartz rose to his feet and automatically screamed, "Sound the collision alarm!" Chief Petty Officer Hicks, the diving officer, noticing that the Chief of the Watch was sprawled over the deck, reached over and threw the red-colored alarm handle near the overhead. The boat was immediately filled with the shrill scream of the collision alarm. The noise almost drowned out the breathless announcement from back aft that crackled over the 4MC emergency circuit.

"Flooding in shaft alley! Flooding in shaft alley!" Schwartz noticed that the Chief of the Watch was still on his knees, clutching his head, and reached again for the 1MC.

"Flooding in shaft alley. Helm, all ahead full, Diving Officer, make your depth 120 feet."

The quartermaster rolled away from the captain. Richter gradually stirred and opened his eyes. His vision was blurred and his head ached, a sensation that worsened the moment he sat up. He noticed that the spot where he had been lying was now decorated with a puddle of blood and, as he felt the left side of his head, realized that it was his own. He reached into his pocket for a handkerchief and held it against a broad gash that extended from just above his ear to the edge of the eyebrow. In moments the handkerchief was soaked with blood. He blinked a couple of times to clear the crimson haze from his eye and, ignoring the stabbing pain in his head, began to focus on the problem at hand. His thoughts were interrupted by another announcement from the engine room.

"Conn, Maneuvering, abnormal noise in the reduction gear . . . stopping and locking the shaft."

"Maneuvering, Conn, aye," replied Schwartz, who was visibly shaken. He was pale, his speech was delivered in an unusually staccato tone, and his eyes flicked around continuously as he shifted his gaze about the control room. Richter realized that the time for analysis was over. His boat had obviously been damaged in the collision, probably seriously, and it was time to reach for the roof.

"I have the conn. Emergency blow," he announced in the forceful, yet controlled way that everyone on board knew meant delay was not an option. The Chief of the Watch was back on his feet and stabbed the general alarm handle. The warbling of the Klaxon momentarily drowned out every other sound until Chief Hicks reached for the two "chicken" switches located just above the ballast control panel. He hit them and released thousands of pounds of compressed air into the ballast tanks with a roar that could be felt almost as much as it could be heard. He then glanced over his right shoulder to the fathometer and started to read out the depth:

"412 feet . . . 413 feet . . . 414 feet . . ." Richter glanced at Schwartz and realized that he was frozen with terror. He was standing by the main periscope, his eyes bulging, gripping what was left of the curtain rail and wearing an expression of absolute panic. His forehead glistened with sweat. Richter rose to his feet and reached unsteadily for the MC.

"Maneuvering, Conn. Report the source and status of the flood in shaft alley."

"Conn, Maneuvering, the flooding is from the shaft seals. The engine room lower level watch is attempting to inflate the emergency shaft boot seal to control the flood. The engineer and watch supervisor are on the scene."

"Maneuvering, Conn, aye." Richter had a moment to think. The collision alarm would have resulted in the bulkhead between the forward and after compartments being sealed. It was a safety measure designed to limit the amount of the boat that would be flooded if the hull was damaged. There was no way he was going to risk his boat by breaking the rig for flood order. Oh God, he thought, unless John Dowling and his engineers can control that flood, they'll not be coming out of there.

"429 feet . . . 430 feet . . . 431 feet . . ." announced the diving officer mechanically. Next to him, the Chief of the Watch had donned his sound-powered telephone headset and was busily scribbling on a clipboard. He looked over his left shoulder at Schwartz.

"Sir, engine room lower level reports the flooding can't be stopped with the emergency boot. He's also reporting a rupture in the main hydraulics in shaft alley. The engineer recommends a shallower depth to reduce the flooding."

"What the fuck does he think I ordered the emergency blow for?" retorted Richter. "Making bubbles? Chief, have the engineer contact me over the growler." Richter was feeling unsteady on his feet and returned to his chair. A moment later, the sound-powered telephone beside him squawked and Richter lifted the receiver. "John! What the hell's going on back there?"

"452 feet . . . 452 feet . . . 451 feet," announced the diving officer in his characteristic monotone. "Looks like we're head'n up, sir."

"Conn, Sonar, Master-17—the Akula—appears to have slowed and is headed for the surface." Richter, with one ear to the telephone listening to the engineer, looked at Schwartz expecting him to acknowledge. Schwartz was still frozen to the spot just in front of the scope, so Richter reached for the MC.

"Sonar, Conn, aye." He focused once again on the

handset. "Sorry, John, what was that?" His concentration was disturbed once again as the Chief of the Watch announced:

"Captain, sir, all stations, with the exception of the engine room lower level, report they are rigged for general emergency and collision. The lower level watch is still dealing with the casualty in shaft alley. The engine room reports uncontrollable flooding from the after shaft seals. The water level is now above the deck plates in the lower level. The main hydraulic pumps have been isolated."

Richter nodded and concentrated once again on the handset. "OK, John, just do your best," he said, and returned the handset to its cradle. He then looked over to the Chief of the Watch. "Thank you, Chief."

Richter paused to think about the damage report he had just received from John. It concerned him sufficiently that he ignored the trickle of blood from his temple that was gradually soaking his collar and reached for the 1MC. "All hands, this is the captain. We've just collided with a Russian sub and are taking on water in the engine room. We've lost our main engines and have conducted an emergency blow. We're at four hundred feet and headed for the surface. Everything's going to be fine. I want all stations to report any injuries and stow your spaces. We're in for a bumpy ride." Richter clicked off the microphone and contemplated his most recent masterpiece of understatement. With no forward momentum, it was going to be impossible to control the attitude of the boat as it rose through the water. Almost seven thousand tons of fast-attack submarine was about to behave like a bubble in a whiskey and soda.

1400A, RFS *Gepard*

The control room of the Akula was unusually quiet. Commander Borzhov glanced at the officer of the deck, who was standing beside him, clinging to the plotting table. The color had drained from the younger man's face at the moment of impact and he looked as if he was about to faint. "You'd better sit down before you fall down, Meltzer." A flicker of a smile rippled across the face of the young lieutenant as he cast around for something to sit on. The *Gepard* would never have collided with the 688 had the target just held its course. Borzhov cursed beneath his breath. He had arrived in the control room too late to alter the course of events. Meltzer had taken it upon himself to charge at the *Tulsa*. He would deal with the young man later.

Borzhov concentrated on the immediate problems that presented themselves. "Damage reports please, gentlemen." He commonly resorted to politeness when he wanted to appear unruffled which, surprisingly, he felt. The collision had been violent, but he had hit Mother Earth much harder than that before, and lived to tell the tale. The boat felt good despite a slight list to starboard.

The planesman had given up wrestling with the wheel in front of him and was protesting:

"Sir, I repeat, the starboard forward plane is jammed."

Borzhov would have been surprised if he had escaped from a collision like that without a scratch, but a jammed plane was going to be a problem.

"What position is it jammed in?"

"Five degrees down, sir," replied the planesman.

"What's our speed?"

"Eighteen knots, sir." Borzhov thought for a moment—it didn't make sense.

"Ahead one-third. Take us up to periscope depth, Mr. Meltzer." As Borzhov finished the order, the control room was filled with the sound of the *Tulsa's* emergency blow. He blurted, "Sonar, Conn!"

"Sonar!"

"What's your status?"

"Sir, I think the forward sonar dome is damaged."

"Have you heard anything from the 688?"

"Before the emergency blow, the target had shut down her propulsion. It was making a dreadful noise. I think we must have hit her screw."

"Is she surfacing?"

"Hard to tell . . . but I don't think so, sir."

Borzhov did not want a diplomatic incident to develop over this. Times had changed, and the pressure was really on to improve relations with the West despite NATO's expansion to the east and its antics in Yugoslavia. If the 688 was seriously damaged, it would do his career no good. God forbid she should sink. The sound of the 688's emergency blow was waning as the ballast blow in the *Gepard* began. "Sonar, what's the target doing now?"

"I think she's on her way up, sir, but very slowly." Thank God for that, thought Borzhov. The 688 would accelerate to the surface as the air in her ballast tanks expanded on the way up.

"Periscope depth, sir," announced Meltzer. Borzhov flicked a switch and the search periscope moved noiselessly above the waves. Positioned adjacent to it, he squinted into the binocular eyepiece and scanned the horizon.

"Raise the radar mast. Surface search radar on."

"Aye, aye, sir."

A couple of screens in the control room blinked as a rotating amber phosphorescent glow appeared. Two more screens lit up as Borzhov switched on the periscope video. Meltzer alternated his attention between the two.

"Pray God that submarine surfaces," he whispered to himself. A petty officer handed him a piece of paper.

"Damage report, sir."

"OK, what have we got?" asked Borzhov, still peering into the periscope.

"The outer doors of tubes 1, 3, and 5 all jammed. Tubes 1 and 3 are flooded, forward sonar dome is unserviceable. Pressure hull intact, no flooding, minor injuries only."

"Thank you Mr. Meltzer," replied Borzhov. If the 688 was in serious trouble, the *Gepard* could render assistance if he surfaced. Furthermore, the divers would need to take a look at the bow and the starboard plane soon anyway. In the absence of any surface contacts he delayed no longer. "Surface!"

As soon as the *Gepard* was stable on the surface, Borzhov sprinted up the ladder to the sail. He undogged both hatches on the way up and leapt onto the bridge, Meltzer close on his heels. They were met by an icy blast of Arctic air and immediately regretted not putting on something warm. Borzhov scanned the horizon with his prized pair of Zeiss binoculars, a personal gift from Admiral Konstantin, who was an old, and now powerful, friend. The heavy cloud cover threatened rain—or snow, more likely. He checked his watch. If it were visible, the sun would be low on the southwest horizon and just about to set. There would be twilight for about another hour. He was startled by what sounded like a small explosion to his right. Both officers snapped their heads round and stared in disbelief. Just three hundred yards away, the elongated bow of the *Tulsa* had surfaced at an extraordinary angle, a mixture of water and compressed air spewing out of the open flooding holes in the underside of her forward main ballast tanks. Her upward momentum kept her moving until the sail was almost clear of the water. The 688 had a pronounced list to port.

"She can't stay like that for long," said Borzhov, casting a glance toward Meltzer, whose eyes were riveted to the stricken boat. "She's losing too much air from those ballast tanks." As if in agreement, the angle of the bow decreased, and the *Tulsa* began to settle back into the water. Meltzer noticed that, aft of the sail, the sea continued to boil. He looked at Borzhov, pointing at the turbulent water.

"What's that, sir?" Borzhov briefly looked towards the stern of the 688.

"The question you should have asked is: where is that coming from?" Borzhov then focused on the torn superstructure around his bow. It looked as if someone had attacked it with a vast can opener. He couldn't see the damaged plane, but could imagine what it looked like. "The answer to that question is the after ballast tanks. At least, their port-side compartments—probably all three of them. I'll wager a month's salary on it." It sounded more of a bet than it was. Like the rest of the ship's company, he had not been paid for the past three months. "That explains the list and why she's down by the stern. She may be flooding aft as well." Borzhov glanced in the direction of the junior officer. His face was paler than ever, and his forehead was wrinkled by a frown of concern. "I'll also wager," continued Borzhov, "that the divers will find very little of our starboard plane. The remainder of it is buried in the stern of that 688."

1402A, USS *Tulsa*

Richter's relief that the *Tulsa* was surfacing was short-lived. As she gathered speed, the attitude of the boat was increasingly down by the stern and, for some reason, listing farther to port. He knew there was nothing that he could do about it. What he could do was minimize the effect on his men. He reached for the 1MC: "All hands, this is the captain. We have no control over the trim of the boat right now. Take cover and brace yourselves. I'll speak to you again as soon as we are topside." Richter switched off the microphone and was immediately aware of the hush that had overtaken the control room. "The same applies in here. Take cover everybody."

The events of the next few minutes came fast and furious as the *Tulsa* took on a life of her own. For some reason the stern started to oscillate up and down, like the tail of a dolphin. At first, the movement was imperceptible, moving through four or five degrees. But as the submarine gathered momentum the movement became more violent. It soon became apparent that the galley had not been secured properly. The contents of the deep-fat fryer were tossed over the adjacent deck, working surfaces, and eventually a hot plate. The galley caught fire. Within moments, choking black smoke was billowing out into the crew's mess room and along the passageway at the center of the middle level. The hull started to pop as the surrounding pressure decreased and, all of a sudden, the violent pitching stopped. Like a swing that has reached the top of its arc, the *Tulsa* slowed her ascent, stopped, and started to sink back into the water. Despite Richter's instructions, people had been thrown around like balls in a lottery machine and had come to rest against just about every bulkhead. This didn't stop those who could from breaking out into a spontaneous round of cheering once the boat was on the surface.

Richter, who had jammed himself under his chair and hung on for grim life, was less jubilant. He knew that the *Tulsa* was going to sink. Air was escaping from the ballast tanks and was being replaced by water. Already she had settled and was starting back down. As she did so, she began to lose her bow-up trim. The angle of the deck decreased from almost forty degrees to thirty, and then twenty. In a moment he might risk trying to move. Richter's mind was racing. He had to get a mayday off. He tried to remember the last bottom depth he'd seen—was it five hundred feet? Close to that. Well above hull-crush depth in any case, so they weren't going to die—at least not immediately. They could be rescued, but only if he could get an alert off. Without one it could be days before they were missed and SUBLANT raised the alarm. On covert missions check reports were not expected. What was he to tell the crew? And what was happening aft? He needed to hear again from John.

"What's your depth?" Richter inquired.

"Forty-five feet, sir," replied Chief Hicks.

"Shit!" Richter hissed under his breath. They were already submerged and would be below periscope depth in a few moments. There was no more cheering in the control room. The trim of the *Tulsa* was now at a manageable fifteen degrees bow-up so Richter moved from underneath his chair to sitting on it. He glanced over his shoulder at Schwartz, who had apparently regained control of his faculties. "Schwartz, get a mayday off right away."

"Aye, sir," he replied, as Richter reached again for the growler and spun the handle.

"Engineer," was the welcome response.

"What's happening at your end, John?"

"Not good news, I'm afraid." Richter could detect the strain in the normally imperturbable twang of his best buddy. "Can't control the flooding from the stern seal, and I've lost three men—they were thrown into the floodwater and haven't surfaced. There's a lot of injuries back here. Chief Armstrong has busted a bunch of ribs. He can barely breathe and looks pretty bad. A couple of others have broken arms . . . it got kinda rough on the way up. . . ."

"OK, John, do what you can for them. What's your estimate of the extent of the flooding?"

"No more than 15 percent at the moment."

Richter thought for a moment. He wanted to retain the output of the reactor if at all possible. Hopefully it hadn't shut down automatically, given the extraordinary maneuvers the *Tulsa* had just completed. With power, survival on the bottom was going to be possible for a long time, and they could even be comfortable. He'd leave the engineers where they were for the moment and reassess the situation once they had bottomed. Bottoming a nuke was not a standard procedure—there were the cooling water intakes to think of. . . .

His thoughts were interrupted by the fire alarm as

Schwartz appeared beside him looking crestfallen. "We're too deep to transmit, sir."

"This is not my day," muttered Richter. "OK, Harvey, once we've bottomed I'll ask Chief Czapek to launch a SLOT buoy." This was an unsatisfactory second best. The output of the buoy had a very limited range, just ten miles for a surface interception, although aircraft could pick it up at a range of almost one hundred miles. The trouble was that there were few commercial airline routes that overflew this position and, seeing as there were no surface contacts, it would be a fluke if the SOS message it would transmit for the next eighteen hours was received. Richter switched to the next problem. "Where's the fire?"

"In the galley, sir," replied Schwartz. "The forward firefighting party is tackling it."

"I want it out as soon as possible, and I don't want to go onto EABs unless we absolutely have to."

"I'll pass that along, sir."

This is turning into a nightmare, thought Richter. The last thing he wanted was to try and survive in an atmosphere poisoned by the fire. Although the emergency air breathing apparatus could provide the entire crew with fresh air for many hours, it was at the expense of raising the pressure in the boat. That wouldn't matter immediately, but it could be a real problem when it came time to leave. They would become like deep-sea divers who have to decompress at the end of their dive to avoid getting the bends. Another concern was that there was a high possibility that he was going to lose power once on the bottom, which meant that his capacity to scrub the atmosphere of toxic contaminants was likely to disappear. If they were forced onto breathing apparatus, the chances were that they would not be able to come off them and that would mean exiting through the escape trunk. He didn't want to contemplate that. Even if they made it to the surface, the water temperature was almost freezing and none of the crew would survive for more than an hour.

The *Tulsa* was "flying" backwards and accelerating. As she got deeper, the pressure increased and the air in her ballast tanks was compressed into a smaller and smaller volume. Water rushed in to take its place and the boat became heavier and heavier. The early part of the descent was slightly smoother than the ascent had been. That changed as her speed increased. The damage to the after planes, stabilizers, and rudder, which had presumably caused the violent pitching on the way up, was beginning to have the same effect on the way back down. Richter reached for the 1MC again. "All hands, this is the captain again. I had hoped to speak to you once we were on the surface, but as things turned out, I didn't have time. We're sinking and will shortly hit the bottom. Judging by our trim, we'll hit stern first. Take cover, just as you did before, and brace yourselves. We may touch down pretty hard. I want everyone to stay calm. Just because we've sunk doesn't mean it's the end of us. Far from it! Thanksgiving is only four weeks away, and I fully intend to celebrate it at home. Carry on."

Richter retreated to the haven beneath his chair and braced himself for the grounding. He didn't have long to wait. The *Tulsa* hit the rocky bottom stern first with a crunching impact. A moment later the bow hit the bottom with a clang that sounded like a poorly struck gong. In the control room, a coffee mug, its handle already broken, rolled unevenly across the deck and fetched up against the helmsman's foot. Then there was silence.

Richter crawled from under his chair, stood up, and promptly collapsed back onto it. His headache was growing worse. He probed the left side of his head with a finger. It felt sticky and was obviously still oozing blood. Although the edges of the cut felt numb, it hurt if he pressed on it. He dabbed the wound again with his handkerchief but knew it was a pointless gesture. It was already soaking wet. The good news was that the *Tulsa* had settled on an almost even keel. He tried to think of any more good news, but couldn't. His mind raced to deal with the priorities that faced him: the fire must be extinguished, and he needed to find out what was happening back aft. "Officer of the deck." Lieutenant Schwartz leapt to his feet.

"Sir."

"I want you to relieve the XO, take charge of the firefighting party, and report back to me when it's out. Oh, and kindly ask Mr. Mitchell to come to the control room."

"Aye, aye, sir." Richter reached for the growler. As soon as it was answered Richter recognized Dowling's voice.

"John, what's new?"

"There's uncontrollable flooding back here. We're taking on water real fast. There's so much of it I can't tell where it's coming from, but I'll bet it's the stern seal. That grounding felt mighty hard from here."

"What's the extent of the flooding?"

"Just covered the lower level, I guess that's about 25 percent. Won't be long before we lose the generators. The inverters and motor generators will be next, GB." Richter smiled briefly. John had always struggled to call him "sir," but equally felt that he couldn't use his first name, Geoff, in anything other than social settings. His compromise of using his first two initials was fine by Richter so long as no tight-assed senior officers were within earshot.

"OK, John. You know I can't afford to pressurize the whole boat by bringing your guys forward. I want you to shut down the reactor and start escaping through the trunk. How many have you got back there?"

"Total, or those who might be able to use the trunk?"

"Both."

"I think there's seventeen of us left alive here, eight of us might make it out."

"OK. Get the fit ones out first, including yourself. The others can take their chance after that. Wrap up warm, the water's damned near freezing."

"I know, GB, I'm soaked in it."

It wasn't long before the lights went out and the hum of the fans that cooled the impressive array of electronics deployed around the control room died along with their masters. In the eerie glow of the emergency lighting, the full impact of the *Tulsa*'s predicament was suddenly apparent. "You wanted me, sir?" Richter looked up to see Lieutenant Commander Curtis Mitchell, his executive officer, standing beside him. His right arm was in an improvised sling made from what had once been a pillowcase and was now stained with blood. Mitchell looked pale, and his eyes expressed the pain that he was clearly fighting to keep from showing in the rest of his face.

"That looks pretty bad, Curtis."

"No worse than your head, sir. I'll live."

"What happened?"

"I was turned in and got thrown out of my bunk during the emergency blow. I landed awkwardly and broke my arm. I've twisted my ankle as well, but it's not too bad. I can still walk on it."

Richter looked a little more closely at what he could see of Mitchell's arm. The break was obvious—his forearm looked like it had grown a second elbow that flexed at an angle of almost ninety degrees to the one he was born with. It looked grotesque. Mitchell coughed twice, but could not suppress the grimace that creased his face. He swallowed hard and tried to smile. His teeth were covered in a thin film of bright red blood. "Oh, and I think I might have cracked a few ribs." He coughed again. "But that's nothing much—I used to do that a fair bit playing football." He tried to smile again, but his face twisted in obvious pain.

"Petty Officer Chavez, take the XO to the sick bay and ask Doc Richards to fix him up."

"Yes, sir."

"Alright everyone, there's not much point in staying here, I need to speak to the crew and get a few things organized. I want everyone who can be moved to gather in the crew's mess. I'll be along in a moment."

The control room emptied and Richter was left in his seat. He lowered his head and rested it between his hands. He desperately wanted to sleep. It was the only way he was going to shake off the splitting head-ache that was threatening to cause his head to erupt like a volcano. He reached for the growler again, but didn't recognize the voice that replied. "Is Lieutenant Commander Dowling there? This is the captain."

"Yes, sir, please hold. . . ."

"Yes, GB?"

"How's it going, John?"

"We've just about got the trunk prepped and we're testing the Steinke Hoods. I guess you were joking about wrapping up, as we've only got what we're al-ready wearing back here. Never mind, a brisk swim will give us an appetite for dinner. The reactor's shut down, by the way, but there's no sign that the flood is slackening."

"I don't really know what to say, John."

"There's not much more to say, GB. . . . Sir. It's been a privilege to know you and serve with you."

"Hey, don't give up. I expect that Russkie's still topside. He couldn't have gotten off scot-free from an impact like that, and must be nursing a pretty mangled bow. I expect that's where you'll be dining tonight. Hell, we're going to have to make do with something out of a can and even that'll be stone-cold."

"I haven't given up, but I'm having some difficulty convincing anybody else back here that the trunk will work and they'll be alive when they reach the sur-face," replied Dowling.

"Well if anyone can, you can. After all, you per-suaded me to buy that pile-of-junk Monte Carlo off you."

Richter smiled, it was almost thirteen years ago that he had bought that jalopy off John. The only thing keeping it from being a true lemon was that it was metallic brown in color and not bright yellow. In the eighteen months he'd owned it he had driven it only six thousand miles. It seemed like the rest of the time it had been in the shop for one reason or another. It had been an absolute rip-off, and it still surprised him that they had remained friends afterward. Although he didn't want to, Richter realized that he had to bring this conversation to an end and get below to the crew's mess. "John, I've got to get off and sort the mess out at this end. I'll get back to you as soon as I can."

"Sure, GB, but don't leave it too long. We're going to be either dead or out of here in under an hour." Richter had no intention of leaving it that long. If somebody could make it to the surface and get aboard that Russian submarine, assuming it was still there, the chances that everybody up front would be rescued increased from none too good to better than evens.

"Roger that, John."

Richter returned the receiver to its cradle and thought for a moment. What he had asked John to do was not going to be easy. As far as he knew, no American escape trunk had been used in a real emergency in recent years. It was simple enough in theory. Two people, each wearing an inflatable Steinke Hood over his head, would climb up into the trunk. Once the lower hatch was closed, the trunk would be flooded with seawater. As soon as it was just about up to the escapers' necks, called "the bubble line," the flood would be halted and compressed air bled into the trunk to raise the pressure until it equaled that of the seawater outside the boat. The upper hatch would then open and the two escapers would float to the surface and wait to be recovered. The upper hatch would then be pumped shut hydraulically, the water drained into the bilges, and two more people would get ready to make their escape. If used efficiently, six people could get out in an hour. That was the theory. What he didn't know was whether the trunk would work at a depth of five hundred feet, and whether the escapers would be alive when they reached the surface. After all, they were going to be compressed to more than sixteen times atmospheric pressure and back to normal again in a very short period. There were a lot of things that could go wrong. He realized that the engineers had little choice, but it was still going to take a lot of guts to attempt an escape. Richter rose to go down to the crew's mess and had to reach out to grab hold of an armrest to stop himself from falling. His head was swimming and he still felt unsteady on his feet. He blinked, took a deep breath and straightened himself. His balance restored, he carefully made his way out of the control room and down to the middle level. The smell of smoke was still strong, and the air was hazy. He coughed, and his eyes started to smart.

"The fire's out, sir," said Schwartz, who had materialized by his side.

"Good. Anybody hurt?"

"Sir, there are a lot of injured people, but the fire claimed only one."

"Who's that?"

"Mess Specialist Taylor, sir. He was badly burned and died in the fire."

"So what's the total casualty figures?"

Schwartz glanced down at a dog-eared piece of paper that he held in his right hand. "We haven't accounted for everybody yet, but it looks like twenty-two personnel are aft. Of the 106 forward, eight are dead, sixteen have major injuries: broken bones, head injuries, and the like, and thirty-nine have cuts and bruises."

"Which group have you put me in?" inquired Richter.

"Sorry, sir, forty have cuts and bruises." Schwartz tried to smile but there was no joy in it.

"Doc Richards is going to earn his pay."

"I regret not, sir. He is among the dead." Richter was stunned. The one time he could really use a corpsman . . .

"Jesus, what happened to him?"

"He was thrown out of his bunk. He's a big guy, and I'm told he landed on his head and broke his neck."

Richter paused and thought for a moment. "What are we going to do with all these injured men? What about the XO—that arm needs professional attention," he asked.

"First aid, sir. That's all we can offer them."

"This really is not my day," he replied, then braced himself and turned to face his men.

The babble of conversation, which had been muted at best, died away. Richter started right in. "We've sunk, the after compartment is flooding, we have no power apart from the ship's main batteries and no means of getting this boat to the surface. How we got into this predicament is not important. How we get out of it is. The first point I want to make is that the situation isn't hopeless. Unless the Russian who hit us has also sunk, which I doubt, there's every chance that he's topside right now. The engineers are going to start escaping shortly." As if on cue, the muffled roar of the aft escape trunk being pressurized was distinctly audible. "There go the first two. I expect them to raise the alarm. To help them along, we'll launch a red smoke and a SLOT buoy right away." Richter looked around the room and spotted Chief Czapek. "See to that, will you, Chief?"

"Aye, aye, sir."

"Given our position, it's going to be a while before our rescue vehicle, the DSRV, can get to us. As most of you know, it's kept in San Diego, and it'll take them a few hours to load it onto a C5 and fly it across the pond. I expect it'll come into Reykjavik or Stavanger—could even be Glasgow. They'll then piggyback it to a mother submarine—that could be one of ours, or a Brit-

ish or French boat, and then it'll make a surface passage
out to us. My best guess at the moment is that the
whole process will take something like five or six days.
Alternatively, both the Swedes and the Brits have rescue
vehicles that might get to us before then. The whole
world will be looking for us, and I intend to make it very
easy for them to find us. In the meantime, we're going to
have to make ourselves as comfortable as possible."

Richter paused and gently dabbed the side of his
head. "Our first priority will be to get an atmosphere-
control system working. The carbon dioxide we breathe
out is going to build up quickly and make even the fittest
of us feel pretty lousy unless we scrub it. So we need
to find the hoppers and all the lithium hydroxide canisters we can." He paused for a moment and looked
round the room at his audience. Despite the silence, the
long, serious faces spoke volumes. "Who can tell me
what the lithium hydroxide is for?" The silence was un-
broken. "Don't all speak at once." He noticed a flicker
of a smile cross Sonarman Evans's face. "Evans?"

"It reacts with carbon dioxide to form lithium car-
bonate. It takes the stuff out of the air."

"Very good. And what do the hoppers do?"

"They blow air through the canisters."

"Why is it, Evans, that I've never appreciated your
genius before? Don't answer that." Richter smiled.
"Well done, Evans. The point is that it's really important we find every canister of lithium on board. I want
each and every space searched thoroughly." Richter
coughed again. The smoky atmosphere was irritating
his throat. "We'll eventually need the oxygen furnace
and candles as well. This is a good central location,
so we'll run the atmosphere control from here. I want
all the portable monitoring equipment and any spare
batteries found and stored here as well."

Richter's head was throbbing, and he felt obliged to
pause again. "Now, it is going to get cold over the next
day or two. Very cold," he continued, "so I want all the
warm clothing, blankets, and sleeping bags inventoried.

At the moment, I am happy for people to make do with their own clothes and bedding. If anyone doesn't have enough to keep warm, there'll be plenty spare to go around. Just in case things don't go according to plan, we'll rig the forward trunk for escape; however, I don't anticipate having to use that at the moment.

"Now about food. We're not going to enjoy the level of cuisine we normally do. I've no idea what we can eat at the moment, I just know that we can't cook anything." Richter looked around and saw the supply officer propped up against the after bulkhead. He looked awful. Lieutenant Gallagher's normally rugged, handsome features were so distorted that Richter barely recognized him. The left side of his face was horribly puffy and blue, and his eye was swollen shut. "Tim, do you feel up to sorting out the food?" Gallagher made to speak, but only the right side of his face moved properly. Richter could barely hear or understand Gallagher's mumbled reply, but took it to be in the affirmative. "OK, use anyone you need to help out with an inventory of what's fit to eat."

Richter transferred his gaze to the center of his audience. "We've got very limited sources of power. The emergency lighting should last quite a while, but just in case it doesn't, I want any unnecessary bulbs removed from the emergency lighting circuit and all the battle lanterns, flashlights, and spare batteries you can find collected and brought here. We should be OK for drinking water. The freshwater tank is pressurized from the ship's service air bank, so all the faucets should work. But we mustn't waste it—so there's no hope of showers, not even cold ones. However, I do want everybody to attend to their personal hygiene. If you use the head, wash your hands, please. Whoever prepares the food, make sure to do the same. The last thing I want is for us to get sick." He paused again, trying to stem the throbbing in his head.

"I've been in the submarine service for seventeen

years," Richter pressed on. "One or two of you have a little more experience." Richter looked around and saw Master Chief Steadman, the Chief of the Boat, with a weary grin across his face. "None of us has had to deal with a situation like this before, so I'll deem any suggestions you may have equally worthy of consideration. The last thing I have to say will sound a little odd, especially since there's a lot to do right now. The fact is that the harder you work, the more carbon dioxide you'll produce and the more lithium hydroxide we'll use up. Take it easy—we're not going anywhere soon. If you don't have a task allocated to you, turn in and get some rest. I am well aware that one or two of you will need no encouragement to do so. We all know who you are." There was a ripple of laughter. "Follow their example. I will inaugurate and personally award the Sonarman Evans Golden Dreams award to the man who sleeps the longest." There was more laughter, and Evans blushed a bright red, which all could see—even in the reduced lighting. His reputation for sleeping was such that some of his colleagues had nicknamed him "Rip." "I have some things to attend to right now. With Lieutenant Commander Mitchell being injured, the navigator will be in charge down here." He looked over to Lieutenant Enzo Raschello. "OK, Enzo?"

"Yes, sir."

"Do your best, everybody." With that, Richter turned and headed back to the control room. He hadn't expected a round of applause, but the silence that attended his departure worried him a little. He would have to keep these people motivated; otherwise, the outcome could be grim indeed.

1420A, RFS *Gepard*

It had just started to snow. Borzhov shivered and slapped his arms against his chest, hugging himself to keep warm. With the 688 gone, there was no point in freezing to death. Having asked the XO to relieve him on the bridge, he nodded to Meltzer, and they headed back down into the warmth of the *Gepard*. "What are we going to do, sir?" asked Meltzer.

"We're going to my stateroom and I don't want to hear another squeak out of you until we get there," replied Borzhov, whose mind was racing more rapidly than usual. He had made a mental list of his problems and wanted to tackle them in order of priority. Reporting the accident was on that list, but not at the top, yet he found it hard to suppress the urge to address it first. What on earth was going to happen? Although he had been raised to believe that honesty was the best policy, he'd also learned in the school of hard knocks that expediency was an even better one. An unavoidable fact was that the truth would be discovered—sooner or later. The *Uriy Dolgorukiy* must have heard what had happened and developed a pretty good idea of the consequences. With the *Gepard* unable to contribute to her trials program, she would probably return to port early and submit a report. Furthermore, pieces of the 688 would inevitably be found under the twisted superstructure of his boat as soon as she was in dry dock for repairs. He could try to cover it up, but without distributing a lot of money he couldn't be certain of keeping it quiet for long and, in any case, he didn't have access to that kind of money. So the issue was quite simple: he would have to inform Fleet HQ eventually. Under the international law of the sea, he was obliged to raise the alarm as soon as possible and under normal conditions that is what he would do. But these were not normal conditions. The worthy people who drafted that law would not have had covert submarine operations in mind, for a start. In addition there was the political angle to consider. Regardless of Meltzer's intentions, what he had just done could be interpreted as the deliberate sinking of a vessel belonging to another nation. Had there been a period of tension, it could even be construed as an act of war. The management of this situation now represented a task that was well above his pay grade. It would have to be handled by Fleet HQ at least and more likely in Moscow. Broadcasting a general mayday now would compromise that process, because it would deprive the command of the time they would need to respond appropriately. He would have to give them that time.

Another aspect of the problem was troubling him as well. What if there were survivors in the 688? Judging from what he had seen, the crew must have been pretty severely shaken up, but some were likely to have made it. She would have used just about all her compressed air for her emergency blow and without her main engine she was never going to come up again under her own power. Borzhov's thought process stalled. The Americans would surely salvage their boat, if only to protect the codes and ciphers she carried. And the environmentalists would demand that the reactor was recovered. . . . Yes, she would be salvaged. And guess what they would find in her after ballast tanks in all probability? Most of his starboard forward plane. Any doubts he had regarding the accuracy of his report to Fleet HQ were removed. He would have to let them know exactly what had happened and do so soon.

Borzhov's mind was racing flat out as he made his way forward to his stateroom. The political situation was going to be rather more involved than just finding a suitable way to say sorry. Russia had spent the past six months pleading with the IMF and the World Bank for yet another rescheduling of her outstanding loans—a process that had become excruciatingly difficult and protracted since the economic debacle of the late nineties. Since the USA dominated these organizations and probably always would, it would be all too easy for them to respond to an incident like this by saying no. Any further delay could be critical. Although he'd played no part in it, he had heard rumors that colleagues of his were organizing a military coup. The failure of capitalism to work in Russia was at the root of it. Would the consequence of his sinking the 688 be to trigger a deepening of the economic depression and an armed insurrection? The mere thought of it horrified him.

They arrived at Borzhov's stateroom. The captain ushered Meltzer in, shut the door behind him, and sat down at his desk. After a few moments of silence Borzhov waved his hand indicating that Meltzer should be seated. Borzhov raised his eyebrows. "Congratulations—your first confirmed kill." His voice was thick with sarcasm. "Call me a traditionalist," he continued, "but I prefer to use torpedoes or missiles to take out targets. Oh, and it's generally considered conventional to limit one's aggression to attacking hostiles. Are you aware of any hostilities between Russia and America . . . before this diplomatic coup of yours?"

"No, sir." Meltzer had anticipated a dressing down. After all, he'd had control of the boat immediately before the impact and was expecting Borzhov to ride him hard. He was used to it. It would be bearable, he thought, if only the captain displayed the anger he so obviously felt and just shouted at him. But that wasn't his style. Meltzer had never heard him even raise his voice.

"No, sir, indeed. As a matter of interest, had it occurred to you, as you launched my submarine at that Yankee, that it could have been us that sank?" Meltzer had been expecting this question and had outlined an answer.

"Yes, sir. However, these boats are incredibly strong. We're also quite a bit bigger than the target and I reckoned that the chances of us sinking were remote. It is not like hitting rock. . . ." Meltzer's voice faded away as it dawned on him that he could have phrased his response somewhat better.

"Are you telling me that you intended to ram the 688?"

"No, sir, not at all. But I had to consider the consequences if we did, and I thought we'd be OK."

"You thought, eh? Did it hurt?" Meltzer shifted in his seat, but could not get comfortable. This verbal assault was going to be worse than normal and, to rub it in, Borzhov looked like he was beginning to enjoy himself. "You'll forgive me if I don't appear relieved by the knowledge that you considered that my submarine and my men were not going to be harmed by what was, by any standards, a completely reckless maneuver."

Meltzer treated the comment as rhetorical and cast his mind back to the minutes before he had decided to go for the 688. The reason he had been left in charge was because the captain was in the head. He often was. Borzhov had apparently caught a dose of amebic dysentery, or something similar, in Vladivostok a few years previously and had never managed to shake it off completely. The control-room crew and officers of the deck all knew about it.

"What's my standing order when I have to leave the control room at short notice?" continued Borzhov.

"Well, sir, usually it's to maintain course, speed and depth, but on this occasion the target passed right over us and you had made your intentions perfectly plain."

"I'll repeat, what's my standing order when I have to leave the control room suddenly?"

"I've just told you, sir."

"And what did you do on this occasion?"

"Sir, our orders were to—"

"Don't tell me what my orders were, Mr. Meltzer," Borzhov interrupted. Incredibly, his voice was slightly raised. "As a matter of fact, I don't want to hear another word from you." Borzhov paused again. The veins in his neck were bulging, and his face was pink with rage. It was something that both amazed and frightened Meltzer. "You knew my plan perfectly well. At no time did I indicate that we would close the *Tulsa* at 28 knots . . . did I?" He lowered his voice and appeared to compose himself. "Don't answer that." Meltzer watched as Borzhov slowly rubbed his face with both hands. "Have you any idea what you'll do as a civilian?"

So that was it, thought Meltzer. He had suspected for some time that submarines, and even the navy at large, were unlikely to be a career for life, and Borzhov had just confirmed that. He knew that this was no empty threat.

"Now go and get me the most recent weather forecast, relieve the XO on the bridge, and ask him to come and see me. Your watch is not yet over." Almost as an afterthought, Borzhov added, "One final thing. You will inform me if the CPA of any vessel is within five miles. Do you remember how to calculate the closest point of approach of an oncoming vessel?"

"Yes, sir."

"Good. I don't want to hit anything else today."

"No, sir." Meltzer rose and turned to leave. "Please accept my apologies for . . ." The captain was clearly not paying the slightest attention to what he was saying and had started to busy himself with the paperwork that was neatly piled in trays on his desk.

Borzhov looked up after Meltzer had left and steered his mind back to his list of priorities. The XO should be able to confirm the extent of the damage by now but, given what he knew already, it was clear that they were going to have to return to base. Before then, he would send the divers down to inspect the bow. It would be dark soon, but since they would need lights anyway that was not an issue. The timing really depended on the weather. His train of thought was interrupted by a knock at the door. "Come in." Borzhov turned and saw the XO, Lieutenant Commander Vladimir Zerchev, enter. "And close the door behind you."

"I have the weather forecast, sir." Zerchev handed over the piece of paper he was clutching.

"I suppose Meltzer hasn't the balls to give it to me personally. I am heartily sick of that little dickhead." Zerchev was surprised by the vehemence of Borzhov's remark.

"You realize, sir, that the collision wasn't really his fault, I'm told that the 688 turned into our track."

"I know it, but he should never have been making turns for 28 knots in the first place. In fact, he shouldn't have done a damned thing until I returned to the control room. This is just the latest and most spectacular of a long series of screw-ups. The man's a menace. He's the first person I've ever met who's made a science out of incompetence and yet remains an arrogant little shit for no obvious reason. For somebody with such limited abilities one might imagine that a little humility would be in order. But I can't detect even a suggestion of it in Meltzer. If that man is representative of what's passing out of sub school these days, our great nation had better get used to the idea that before long we'll not have an effective submarine force, regardless of the state of the hardware. Anyway, enough of that. What have you got for me?"

"The initial damage reports are confirmed, and there are two minor casualties. We're in no danger of sinking, but the starboard plane is jammed solid, and the boat's going to be difficult to control dived."

"Maybe. I want the divers to survey the bow." Borzhov looked up from the weather report. "It's looking good—no more than sea-state three, and its going to snow all night."

"I'll get the divers in the water right away, sir."

"Good. We can decide what's to be done once we know the extent of the damage."

"One more thing, sir." Zerchev looked a little pensive.

"Yes?"

"The 688 has just launched a red smoke and a SLOT buoy."

Borzhov frowned. "So there are survivors." He paused and wrinkled his brow. "I don't want the world alerted until Fleet HQ has had a chance to think about this. The divers had better recover the buoy. They can leave the smoke to burn itself out—there's nobody else around to see it. Please draft a message for me to Fleet HQ as soon as we can report on the extent of the damage."

"Yes sir."

"Thank you, Vladimir, and keep an eye on Meltzer."

"I will, sir."

1430A, USS *Tulsa*

"Thanks for getting back to me, GB." Dowling's voice sounded rather nasal and flat beyond the normal distortion imposed by sound-powered telephony.

"What's up, John?"

"You don't want to know."

"Yes I do."

"I've lost two more men." Dowling's voice was not just flat now. He sounded utterly dejected.

"Go on . . ."

"The first pair, Domico and Shapiro, got into the trunk just fine, although it was a bit of a squeeze—there's not a lot of headroom in there. Maybe I shouldn't have picked Shapiro seeing as he's nearly six-foot-three. Anyway, the problems began when they started to flood the trunk. They stopped when the water reached their bellies because it was so cold. I could hear their teeth chattering over the 31MC. I tried to persuade them to keep going, but they refused, so I turned the flood valve from the access compartment. They turned it off at the bubble line and we ventilated the bubble for a bit. When it came time to pressurize the trunk, they were so cold they couldn't turn the blow valve. So I did it for them. I shut it off when the trunk and sea pressure read the same and told them to get out."

Dowling paused as Richter laid his head in his hands. He didn't need to hear any more to know this had turned into a disaster. "I couldn't really hear what they were saying," Dowling continued. "They were breathing so fast—gasping more like. It seems like the hatch only half opened. . . . The gap wasn't wide enough for them to get out. . . ." Richter could hear Dowling swallow, his voice was suddenly thick with emotion. It sounded like he'd started to cry. "They were too cold to do anything about it. . . . Shapiro's a strong man but he couldn't . . ." Richter could hear Dowling blow his nose and sniff. "I didn't know what to do. In the end, I decided I'd better drain the trunk and get them out. I asked Petty Officer Willmot to hand-pump the upper hatch closed. It was only when I heard Shapiro screaming over the 31MC that I realized that Domico must be stuck in the hatch. . . ." Dowling broke down in hopeless sobbing.

Richter was seriously worried by what he had just heard. "John?"

"Yes, GB," Dowling replied, having composed himself.

"I need to know the status of your trunk," he demanded abruptly, though it wasn't easy to be so direct at such a moment.

"Unserviceable, sir. It contains a lot of water, two dead men, and the upper hatch is jammed open by one of them. Willmot's pumped the hydraulics to 3500 psi, in the hope that whatever was jammed in the hatch would be crushed and allow it to seat, but without success. That is as high as I dare go."

"Have you tried opening the hydraulic relief valve to see if whatever is in the way will float free?"

"No, but I will. I guess that's just about the only thing left to do." John sniffed again and changed the subject. "Does my voice sound odd to you, 'cause it sure sounds odd to me."

"What's the extent of the flooding back there now?" Richter asked.

"It's up to my knees."

"That means the pressure must be getting up around two and a half atmospheres. That's enough to make your voice sound a bit odd." Richter had found that his experience as a diver was useful in the most extraordinary circumstances. Another couple of atmospheres and narcosis, described so eloquently by the late Jacques Cousteau as "rapture of the deep," would be a blessed relief for John. Having experienced narcosis, he was quite confident that was not a bad way to go—like an overdose of sleeping tablets. Unfortunately, it was likely that hypothermia would claim him well before then. That terrified him, he hated the cold. God, he felt sorry for John. Knowing his fear of water, this was the last thing he would have wished on him. If the escape trunk remained unserviceable there was no way that John was going to get out of this situation. Bringing the engineers forward was not an option. That would jeopardize the whole crew. What on earth was he going to say to Marie?

Richter had reserved a soft spot for John's wife for many years. They'd enjoyed a dalliance of several months' duration before he'd called it off. It was only then that John had moved in and eventually popped the question. Marie had wanted to get married so badly, but he'd not been ready for it then—he still wasn't. Yet, when she'd told him about her engagement to John, he'd felt more than a pang of envy. It was completely irrational. After all, he'd turned her down. It was definitely envy and not anger, so he'd not refused John's request for him to be his best man at the wedding. One day he would sit down and fully analyze the reason for his envy. After all, Marie was the sort of woman who looked like the girl next door, nothing special. It had nothing to do with her looks, nor that she was a kind and considerate woman, qualities which, if anything, had grown over the years. It was that she exuded a powerful sexuality. Just being in the same room as she was enough to arouse him.

Richter had not felt that way with anyone else either before or since. One of life's little curiosities, he thought.

"Let's face it, I'm not going to get out of here, GB." John sounded calmer, although the warble in his voice betrayed the fact that he was now shivering. There was no point in bullshitting him, thought Richter.

"No, I don't think you are, John. If it's of any comfort to you, I don't rate my own chances a whole heap higher unless we can tell the world where we are."

"What about the Russian boat? Where's that?"

"I've no idea. We've launched a smoke and a SLOT buoy. If he's topside, he'll know we're here and that somebody's left alive in this can." Richter was mad. In an era of satellite communication that even coastal yachtsmen had access to, he was unable to tell COM-SUBLANT in Norfolk that he was in trouble. It wasn't as if the technology was unavailable—it was. There were a number of buoys with satellite communication capability, but their supply was limited, and he didn't need to carry them on this mission.

"What if he's submerged?"

"What about it?"

"Have you thought of using sonar?" Richter thought for a moment. He couldn't "ping" the Russian because there was no power for the main sonar, but the sonar beacon sets ran off batteries.

"Thanks, John, I'll flash up the forward BNQ-13. You've got one aft, the switch should be right by your escape trunk. No harm in setting it off as well. They kick out eighty decibels or thereabouts, the Russkies would have to be stone-deaf or miles away to miss it." Richter felt a bit more cheerful.

"Back to what I was saying, GB, it doesn't look as if I'm going to make it out of here. Your chances are looking somewhat better, so will you do me a favor?"

"All you have to do is ask, buddy." Richter was

aware of movement beside him and turned to see that Enzo Raschello had entered the control room. "Just a moment, John. Yes, Enzo?"

"We've got a major problem, sir, the hoppers are unserviceable."

"What?"

"The hoppers run AC and we're fresh out of it."

"For God's sake. . . . who the hell designed them? Any damned fool should know AC is unlikely to be available when we need it." He tried to organize his thoughts, but ended up just expressing his frustration. "There's enough juice in the main batteries to drive the *Tulsa* through the water at a respectable speed for God knows how many miles, and you're telling me that we can't use it to run the damned hoppers? Terrific." Richter regretted his outburst immediately. It wasn't going to help Enzo. "What are the options?"

"Well, sir, according to the manual, we're meant to open the canisters of lithium hydroxide and pour the stuff over the deck."

"I guess that is what we'd better do then." He thought for a moment. "No. Wait below, I'll be right down." Richter paused and looked back at Raschello. "How much do you know of what's going on back aft?"

"I've heard enough to know it's bad news, sir."

"OK. Keep it to yourself. Oh, and energize the BNQ-13."

"Yes, sir."

Enzo left, and Richter returned to the growler. "What can I do for you, John?"

"Look after Marie and the kids for me. You're like a second father in the family anyway, and it would mean a whole lot to me." Richter couldn't refuse. He would do his best for Marie and the two boys . . . if he could get out of this elaborate coffin.

"Sure, John, I would consider it an honor—if Marie will let me."

"She will. We've discussed this possibility before. You know, she always wanted you—but you ran away." Richter could hardly hear John through the noise of his chattering teeth.

"Look, John, I'm going to have to get back to the crew's mess. You won't believe it, but the hoppers need AC."

"Yeah! Life's a bitch . . . until it's almost over. Shit, I'm cold, I can't feel my feet at all. Don't be gone long, GB."

"I'll be right back. Oh, and John, they can hear your trunk being pressurized forward. Run it through a few more cycles while you can. It'll do morale no harm. Just don't use too much air—we may need it."

"OK, GB." As John signed off, the BNQ-13 began to squawk a sharp pulse every five seconds. For one accustomed to silence, this racket was going to take some getting used to, Richter thought. He wiped his eyes, rose gingerly to his feet, and headed to the crew's mess.

As Richter entered, he saw a group of men armed with wrenches and screwdrivers gathered round a table upon which there was a large, gray cylindrical machine that was half-dismantled. Enzo appeared at his shoulder. "Sparks reckons he might be able to make the hopper work."

"Great, would you get me one of those canisters of lithium please?" Enzo walked over to another table, picked up a gray tin, and returned.

"There you are, sir. Six and a half pounds of lithium hydroxide."

"What's your chemistry like?"

"I can remember some of it."

"Correct me if I'm wrong, but this stuff is a strong alkali, isn't it?"

"Sure is. It's as nasty as caustic soda. Actually, more so." Richter shook the canister, hearing the granules shifting around inside it. He inspected the can; it was manufactured in 1989. This stuff has been sitting around for over ten years, he thought.

"OK, let's open it." Enzo went over to the hopper wrecking crew and returned with a large screwdriver, which he dug under the silicone-sealed lip of the lid and twisted. Eventually the lid lifted off and they looked inside. There was a metallic grille and, beneath it, what looked like a piece of filter paper. Richter grabbed the can, inverted it, and gave it a hard shake. A fine dusting of white powder fell from the open end of the can onto the deck. He stooped and sniffed the dust, recoiling as he started to gag. Immediately his head began to throb, and he became dizzy and fell to his hands and knees—which only served to give him a closer whiff of lithium hydroxide. He started to crawl away from it, coughing, his eyes smarting with pain. "Fuck me!" he exclaimed, reaching for his handkerchief that had now solidified into a blood-caked ball. The mess deck fell silent. "Get me a tissue or towel or something I can wipe my eyes with, for God's sake." Enzo passed him a paper towel and Richter wiped his streaming eyes. "There's one decision that's been made for us already." Richter slowly got to his feet. "I would rather eat that shit than empty it over the deck. I'd love to meet the asshole who dreamed up that dumb idea. Gentlemen, we're going to have to find an alternative way of using these canisters, and that means it is really up to you, Sparks."

"It may take some time, sir. A lot of the tools I'd like to use are back aft."

"Just do your best. I can't ask for more."

"May I have permission to use the battery-well fan?"

Richter thought for a moment. "Well, we're not going to be charging the batteries for a while—sure, go ahead."

Richter was painfully aware that John probably only had a matter of minutes to live but felt compelled to get the rest of atmosphere control under way and gain some idea of how long they were likely to maintain a breathable atmosphere. He was reassured that someone was still alive back aft by more roaring from the trunk. Two small mountains of canisters had been stacked in the forward end of the mess deck—one group containing the nasty lithium hydroxide and the other cakes of potassium chlorate, which can be "burned" in a furnace to make oxygen. The array of equipment that was arranged on top of an adjacent table was growing as more was located by the crew. Richter glanced round and spotted Lieutenant Schwartz, who was crouched next to the XO. He caught his eye and beckoned him over.

"OK, Harvey, I want you to take charge of the atmosphere monitoring and control. You need to grab ahold of the atmosphere-control manual. I think you'll find there's a hard copy in the wardroom, unless Enzo has already removed it. You need to read up on how we are meant to use all this stuff." He glanced over to the growing mound of equipment. "You'll need some help because this is going to be a twenty-four-hour-a-day commitment. Let me know when you've worked out a plan of how you're going to do this. One more thing—check to see if there's a diver's depth gauge on the table over there. If not, get one from the dive locker."

"Yes, sir." Richter looked around the mess room once more and summoned the navigator.

"Enzo, I don't see any first aid being given to the injured."

"I've not given it much of a priority, sir. I've been collecting everything we're going to need, and . . ." He paused. "Well, sir, I don't think anybody's been trained—at least, not recently."

"That can't be right. Get the COB onto it right away. You've seen his service record, and I don't think there is a single course the navy offers that the Master Chief hasn't done at least once. Furthermore, he'll know if anybody else has any medical skills. I seem to remember we've got at least four men who've received EMT training."

"Aye, aye, sir." Enzo turned to go and find Master Chief Steadman.

"One more thing, Enzo." The navigator stopped and looked over his shoulder at Richter. "Get Steadman to organize the casualties. The sick bay is far too small to deal with them all. Clear the deck in the wardroom and put some mattresses down. I want all the seriously injured men in there. The walking wounded can rest in the berthing spaces. We can get by for the moment with using just the fit men to sort out this mess. Oh, and better get all the medical books you can find—we've got some reading to do."

Richter had not heard a sham trunk run from back aft for some time and was left with no further excuse to delay his return to the control room. He paused only because he feared he would get no response or, worse, he'd have to suffer hearing John's last words. Would John benefit from that? Richter tried to put himself in his position. John had already said the most important thing, about Marie and the children. He wasn't too sure exactly what John had meant by "look after," but he could sort that out later. Could there be anything else? Of course there might. He threaded his way through the hive of industry that the mess deck had become and headed back up to the control room. He spun the handle on the growler and listened. There was no reply. Was he too late? Then Richter heard John's slow breathing.

"Maneuvering." His voice sounded labored, as if John had vocalized it during a long sigh. At least he didn't sound as if he was freezing. The chattering of teeth that had so distorted his voice the last time they'd spoken was gone. Richter was suddenly lost for words.

"You wanted me to get back to you, so here I am, John." Another pause.

"I just wanted you to know . . . there's some money. . . ." This is agonizing, thought Richter, his old friend clearly struggling to get something out.

"What money, John?"

"It's for Marie and the kids . . . and, of course, you now." Richter was confused, John had no money. He must be hallucinating. "I have an account with Schwab—I put the money you gave me for that Monte Carlo in it. I've never touched it. . . . It's almost funny, I felt bad about taking it from you in the first place, and now it's yours again." Richter thought for a moment. He couldn't remember exactly how much he'd paid for that useless vehicle but it was something like $7000. If he'd put it in even an average stock fund, it must have increased at least tenfold. That would take a fair load off the kids' college fees. "Marie knows about it."

There was a long pause. Richter became anxious "Are you still there, John?" Immediately he realized what a stupid thing he'd said—after all, John wasn't going anywhere.

"I'm tired, GB." Another pause. "I'm going to take a brief nap. Don't bother to wake me." Before Richter could say anything he heard a large splash and then there was silence. Alone in the control room, he started to weep.

1900A, USS *Tulsa*

Richter had become obsessed with the idea of sleep. Almost everything else was of a lower priority—except for the atmosphere control. There was a knock at his stateroom door and Lieutenant Schwartz half opened it. "You wanted to know when I had sorted out the atmosphere control, sir."

"Sure, come in, Harvey." Schwartz was carrying a bundle of books and a sheaf of papers that were covered in a rather untidy scrawl. Richter beckoned for him to place them on his desk. "Show me what you've got."

"As far as the atmosphere control's concerned, carbon dioxide is easily going to be our biggest problem." Schwartz shuffled through his papers and retrieved a page covered in equations. "First of all, if Sparks can fix it, we'll have only one working hopper and 155 canisters of lithium hydroxide. According to the manual that should give us a maximum stay-time of just about four days."

"Have you checked those calculations?"

"Both Enzo and I have, sir. Oxygen isn't a problem, between the oxygen banks and the candles, there's enough for over two weeks. Pressure should not be a problem for the moment either, so long as the bulkhead holds. There's just two feet of seawater by diver's depth gauge at the moment, and it's holding more or less steady. We've found no major leaks of water or HP air. If we need to escape, though, there will be trouble. We're deeper than the nominal limit for the Steinke Hood, and the pressure increase that will occur each time we use the trunk means that the later escapers will probably get the bends." In one sense Richter felt a sense of relief. His decision to use the aft escape trunk was a desperation measure in the absence of an alternative and it would appear that the engineers would have had little hope regardless of whether the trunk had worked properly or not. It was just a pity he hadn't spared John the misery of trying to send the first two up. On the other hand, it made his situation all the more difficult. Escape was, at best, a marginal option. He would think about this a bit more once he'd had a chance to rest his exhausted mind and body.

"How many of the injured are likely to make it?"

"I really can't tell, sir, the COB's still sorting them out. Two of them look really bad—they're unconscious. But even if they died, it wouldn't make a big difference to the stay-time."

"I've been doing a few calculations as well." Richter opened a drawer and brought out a chart. "We're here," he said, stabbing a finger at a point to the west of Bear Island. "Not to put too fine a point on it, we're a long way from anywhere useful. From the point of view of rescue we're about 1400 miles from Glasgow, 780 miles from Trondheim, and even farther from Stavanger. I can't remember if the airport at Trondheim can take a C5."

"Probably not, sir. I think Bergen and Stavanger are the designated airports in Norway."

"If push comes to shove, they might bend the rules." Richter paused. "I want Enzo to hear this. Would you fetch him please?"

Schwartz returned with the navigator, and Richter resumed after a brief recapitulation for Enzo's benefit. "It's going to take 60 hours to transport the DSRV to any of these ports. Let's just say that we, or the Brits, could get a MOSUB to Trondheim in that time. Add, say, another 12 hours to unload and prepare the system—optimistically. With a surface speed of 10 knots we're looking at a total of 150 hours. That's 6 days and 6 hours."

"After they've worked out that we're missing," noted Enzo.

"That's right."

Schwartz looked up from the chart and stared at Richter. "Sir, have you any idea when that's likely to be?"

"No. It depends on the Russians. They could have issued an alert already—it's not as if that Akula doesn't know what is going on. Just in case they haven't, the SLOT buoy may have been picked up at one of the weather stations on Bear Island, but since they are more than thirty miles away, that's a long shot—literally. It's more likely, it'll be detected by an aircraft. The flights to Spitzbergen must just about overfly us, and there has to be several of those each day. So I don't suppose it'll be long. Nonetheless, the conclusion's unavoidable that we're going to have to survive for rather longer than your calculations suggest we can. We'll have to cut down our carbon-dioxide production as far as possible. Any ideas?"

"I wish we had Doc with us—if anyone would know, he would," Harvey thought aloud.

"Enzo, is there anything about this in those medical books I asked you to look at?"

"Not that I've found yet, sir."

"There is a small section in the atmosphere-control manual, but it's not very helpful," responded Schwartz. "It seems that people make least carbon dioxide when they're asleep."

"All we can do, then, is make sure that everybody sleeps most of the time. Are there any sleeping medications in the sick bay?" asked Richter.

"I expect so. I'll check it out, sir," replied Enzo.

"Good. Keep this to yourselves, please. Morale is not exactly sky-high right now—even with everybody busy. Once they've settled down it could become a real issue. The situation looks bad, but it isn't hopeless. We haven't explored the possibility of the other available rescue vehicles getting here sooner. The Swedish one—I think they call it the Urf—should be real close. So there's light at the end of the tunnel." Richter tried to smile, but it was obviously forced and served only to launch another trickle of blood down the left side of his face, which he wiped away with his hand. "I'm going to wash and get some rest now. I suggest you do the same."

"Aye, aye, sir," the lieutenants chirped in unison. "Good night."

"I nearly forgot," continued Richter. "Did Sparks get the hopper going, Harvey?"

"He was still assembling it when I left, but he reckons it should work, sir."

"What did he want with the battery-well fan?"

"It's got a DC motor. The only other ones up front are in the torpedoes, and we thought you wouldn't want them dismantled."

"Too damned right. I know we're going to have to do whatever is needed, but I'm glad it didn't come to that." Harvey glanced at his watch and then at Richter. He was obviously fighting to keep his eyes open.

"Sparks should have finished by now. I'll report back only if he hasn't been successful."

"Thank you, Harvey, and say 'well-done' to Sparks for me. He deserves a medal for this. Good night, gentlemen."

1910A, RFS *Gepard*

"Come in." Lieutenant Commander Zerchev entered Borzhov's stateroom carrying a message pad.

"The draft message for Fleet HQ, sir."

"Good, take a seat." Borzhov read through the message, making small alterations in red ink. "So, there's more damage than we thought?"

"That's the way it looks, sir, but it's confined to the superstructure at the moment. The pressure hull is fine."

"I see you recommend a top speed of ten knots."

"That's because of the starboard tubes, sir. If we lose much more of the superstructure, we could compromise one of them."

"Are the divers out of the water?" asked Borzhov.

"Yes, sir. They've completed the survey and recovered and disabled that buoy."

"Good, that should buy us some time before the Americans work out what's happened."

"We can get under way whenever you wish, sir."

"I want this sent with an immediate priority," said Borzhov, handing the message back to Zerchev. "There's not a lot more we can do here, so let's head for home at ten knots. I'll relieve you at 2000 hours."

"Yes, sir!" Borzhov could not ignore the beaming grin on Zerchev's face.

"Glad to be going home?"

"Well, I suppose the circumstances could be better but, as you know, I have a four-week-old son that I want to get to know, and I expect Natasha will welcome another pair of hands in the house."

"I expect she will."

CHAPTER

2

Friday, 29 October

0600A, USS *Tulsa*

Richter turned over and slowly opened his eyes. His head felt thick, and he still had the splitting headache that had dogged him since the sinking. But at least he didn't feel quite so tired. In the dim light that spilled in from the passageway, he saw the silhouette of Lieutenant Schwartz, who had entered the stateroom. "Good morning, Harvey. I didn't hear you knock."

"I'm sorry, sir, I knocked repeatedly and then decided to look in to see if you're all right."

"I'm OK." He sat up and immediately regretted it, his head pounding even more. "At least I think I am. Harvey, get me a couple of aspirin, please."

"Yes, sir." Schwartz spun on his heel and made for the sick bay. He returned in a few moments, poured a glass of water from the faucet in the adjacent head, and handed it to the captain. "Here you are, sir."

"Thanks." Richter swallowed the tablets and took a sip of water. "How's it going?" He noticed that Schwartz was looking at his pillow and turned round to see what he was staring at. The cut on Richter's head had obviously oozed overnight and it looked as if somebody had beheaded a chicken on his rack. He decided to ignore the mess and returned his attention to Schwartz.

"I've got a watch system established, and we're running the atmosphere control according to chapter thirteen of the manual. However, it leaves a lot of questions unanswered, and I thought I'd ask your opinion on two issues. But if you like, sir, I'll come back once you're up and about."

"OK, Harvey. Give me ten minutes."

Richter rose from his bunk and had to grasp hold of its cold, steel edge to retain his balance. His head was swimming. "Shit! This is all I need," he muttered to himself, and resolved to take things a little easier than usual. He got dressed and took a look in the mirror. The blurred image that greeted him was a source of worry for two reasons. First, he had never needed glasses, and, secondly, he looked worse than he felt. Richter blinked and rubbed his eyes. He was relieved to see that the image was a little less fuzzy. He thought about shaving and decided against it. There was no power for his shaver and a wet shave would waste precious water. In any case, he had to set an example. He resigned himself to sporting the designer stubble that he so despised in modern youth. However, he would try to wash off the blood that caked the left side of his face, if only for vanity's sake.

No sooner had he sat down at his desk than Schwartz returned, clutching his copy of the atmosphere-control manual.

"The problem, sir, is that there's no advice about how frequently to monitor the carbon dioxide level and how often to change the lithium canisters."

"How have you managed overnight?"

"Well, guesswork really, sir."

"You're using Draeger tubes to measure the carbon-dioxide level?"

"Yes, sir. That's all we've got."

"How many tubes have you got left?"

"Unless Doc has some hidden away someplace, only thirty-eight, sir," replied Schwartz, amazed that the captain had hit upon the cause of the problem immediately. Each tube could only be used once, which meant that he was going to have to ration carefully how frequently readings were taken.

"Now that much of the activity has died down and the boat's getting cooler, the rate of production of CO_2 should stabilize," mused Richter. "Once we get into a stable routine, I figure we can just about stick to it. So, what we need to do is establish what that routine should be." Richter paused. "When did you last change the canisters in the hopper?" Schwartz looked down at a piece of paper that was tucked into the cover of the manual. It was an unnecessary gesture.

"Well, I haven't, sir."

"You've been running the hopper all night with the same canisters?"

"Yes, sir."

"What's the CO_2 level now?"

Schwartz glanced at his piece of paper again.

"About 2.5 percent, sir."

"What was it when we started?"

"About 0.5 percent."

"What level does the manual recommend we try to maintain?"

"Well, we've got to keep it below 6 percent because that's when it recommends we should escape." He flicked through a few pages and looked up. "There's this chart which lists the symptoms of carbon-dioxide toxicity. Looking at it, I think we should try to stay below about 3 percent," replied Schwartz, beginning to feel a little more confident. "Much more than that and we'll start to feel nauseated and unable to work."

"OK. Three percent it is." Richter paused for a moment before continuing, "If you think about it, we've only got a fixed capacity to scrub CO_2, and that's whatever the capacity of 155 canisters of lithium hydroxide is. Have you worked out how much that is?"

"Yes, sir. A canister of lithium hydroxide should absorb about forty cubic feet of CO_2. According to the manual, the crew's producing it at a rate of roughly eighty cubic feet per hour. So that's about two canisters worth per hour."

"OK, so it doesn't take a genius to work out that in about eighty hours we'll have run out of lithium. God! That's even less than you calculated yesterday."

"There will be a bit longer until the level reaches 6 percent."

"How much longer?" Schwartz looked at his piece of paper.

"I've calculated it at another thirty-four hours, sir, but that assumes we can keep the level down to 0.5 percent."

"Well, we are not going to be able to do that for sure. What if we try to keep it at about 3 percent?"

Schwartz produced a calculator from his breast pocket and tapped a few keys. "Say nineteen hours, sir."

"Fine, that still means that we'll have to be out of here by Tuesday morning. There's no way a rescue can be mounted in that time. That means we're going to have to escape unless we can keep the rate of production of CO_2 down somehow. Didn't we discuss using sleeping medication to do that last night?"

"It was an idea that was kicked around a bit, sir. I think Enzo was going to look into it."

"OK, the sooner we tackle that the better."

Richter was aware that he was breathing rather faster than usual and, despite it being decidedly cool, he felt slightly sweaty. "Do you feel a bit odd, Harvey?"

"Yes, sir, kinda short of breath and a bit thick-headed." Richter smiled to himself and resisted the impulse to pursue that line. Harvey Schwartz was a nice guy, but by no means an intellectual. Sharp remarks impugning his intelligence were not going to help matters right now. However, the thought that Harvey wasn't feeling one hundred percent had the perverse effect of making him feel a little better. He remembered that he'd felt rather like this years ago when diving the old Mk5 set, the one with the copper helmet and leaden boots. One of its design flaws had been a buildup of CO_2 in the helmet, and it had produced symptoms rather like this. So maybe his problem was just carbon-dioxide poisoning and his head injury wasn't serious. He prayed so.

"I expect everybody will be feeling the same," replied Richter, "although I seem to remember that some people are remarkably tolerant of carbon dioxide. Anyway, I think you've just answered your first question. We need to run the hopper at a rate of two canisters per hour, initially at least. With five canisters per load, that means changing them every two and a half hours. If you monitor the CO_2 every six hours, we should get a good idea of what's going on. What was the other issue?"

"Oxygen, sir. I have no idea how fast to bleed oxygen from the O_2 bank."

"How much have we got?"

"There's 2700 psi in bank number one and we have 190 chlorate candles. Unfortunately, access to the number two bank was lost when the bulkhead was isolated."

"What's the oxygen reading?"

Harvey looked down at the scrawl on his piece of paper. "Right now, sir, it's 17 percent."

"We don't need to keep it that low. We've got more than enough. What bleed rate have you set?"

"Well, I haven't set one, sir."

"OK. If I recall there is a value for oxygen consumption in the manual. It should be a simple matter just to multiply for the number of survivors and set the bleed rate appropriately. That one did not make my headache worse." Schwartz was embarrassed. Un-

like the captain, he had not slept overnight and had
just gotten more and more confused by the cryptic
advice in the manual. He frowned.

"Sorry, sir."

Richter noticed the dark rings under Schwartz's
eyes and his heavy eyelids. He rose to his feet and
patted the young man on the back. "Go and get some
sleep, Harvey."

"Yes, sir." Schwartz paused for a moment before
continuing. "There's just one more thing, sir."

"What's that?"

"Yesterday I thought the pressure in the boat was
just about constant, and we found no leaks of water
or HP air."

"I remember."

"Well, there are still no leaks, but the pressure's
rising—although only slowly."

"What's it now?"

Schwartz glanced down at his untidy scrawl once
more and found the number he was looking for. "It's
just over three feet of seawater, sir."

"Hmmm. Curious. You're sure the pressure is
steady in all the HP air banks?"

"Yes, sir."

"Well, just keep an eye on it. It'll have to rise a lot
more than that to cause a problem. Now go and get
some rest. You're doing a great job, Harvey, but everyone needs sleep occasionally." Almost as an afterthought, he concluded with: "Oh, and ask Lieutenant
Raschello and the COB to come and see me."

"Yes, sir." As Harvey turned to leave, Richter shivered. It was getting distinctly cold. The boat was cooling
rather more quickly than he had expected. He reached
into a drawer, pulled out a sweater, and put it on.

Enzo Raschello and the COB stood at the stateroom door, and Enzo knocked. Harvey had told them
that Richter wasn't in particularly good shape and neither of them was looking forward to finding out what
he meant.

"Come in." Enzo put his head round the door.

"You wanted to see me, sir?"

"Yes, thank you, Enzo. Have a seat. You too, Master Chief." He beckoned them to the two spare seats by his desk. "How are the injured?"

It was the Master Chief who replied. "I'm concerned about the XO's arm, sir. Without going into too many details, he can't feel anything below the fracture site. It's stone-cold and, well, it looks almost blue. The good news is that it's stopped bleeding—not that it ever bled a lot anyway."

"Have you had a chance to do any reading up on it?"

"A little, sir. Oddly enough, the first-aid manual was the most useful. Basically it said that if there was numbness and I couldn't feel a pulse, which I can't, it was an emergency, and he should get to a hospital right away."

"Call that helpful?" replied Richter sarcastically. Everyone smiled, but it was no laughing matter. "Without a pulse his arm is going to die, right?"

"I think it already has, sir. The broken part, anyway."

"Doesn't that mean one of us will have to amputate it? He's headed for gangrene otherwise, isn't he?"

The Master Chief looked at Enzo, who looked at Richter. It didn't look like the Master Chief wanted to say anything, nor did Enzo, so they both treated the questions as rhetorical. There was a pause before Richter continued. "It's no good denying that the problem exists. It just won't go away by hoping. Who's going to do it?"

Enzo realized that Harvey had been right about the captain—he looked awful. It was obviously unfair of him, and the XO for that matter, to leave it to Richter. There was no reason for the Master Chief to do it— heck, he was so clumsy it was all he could do to just sharpen a pencil. What concerned Enzo was that he had absolutely no idea what to do. Although he had worked in a civilian hospital briefly as a trainee operating-room technician before joining the navy, and had even toyed with the idea of going to medical school, he had received no formal training. To make matters worse, he had found no "arm amputation made simple" textbook in the sick bay.

"I'll do it, sir," replied Enzo. "I'll need to read everything we've got on amputations and check out what there is in the sick bay in terms of instruments, anesthetic, and the like."

"What's the situation with EMTs on board?" asked Richter. This time Steadman didn't hesitate before answering.

"Not good news, sir. Two of the men who were trained as emergency med techs were back aft, and the others were Richards and Mess Specialist Taylor." He paused uneasily. "And me. But I'm not up-to-date—the last course I took was over ten years ago."

Richter released a long, slow sigh and rested his head on his hands. "I don't believe this. I just don't believe it. If I were a betting man, the odds I would have placed on us losing just about all our medical expertise in a single accident would be over a thousand to one. Yet here we are. What have I done to deserve this?" Enzo glanced at Steadman, who just looked down at the deck. Neither replied. "Well, there's nothing else for it, Enzo, the job's yours. There's no point in rushing things. Let me know when you feel ready. I'll give you any assistance I can. What about the other casualties?"

The Master Chief felt it was his turn to respond. Thinking the captain would want to hear about the officers first, he began with the supply officer. "Lieutenant Gallagher has broken his cheekbone. The books call it a depressed fracture of the zygoma. Anyway, it looks like it's messed up some of the nerves in his face. Chief Maddison and Petty Officer Sanchez are still deeply unconscious. I am rather concerned about them because they'll need fluids and catheters, and the last time I put up an IV or placed a catheter, Reagan was president."

Steadman looked at the navigator. "Don't look at me like that, Master Chief," responded Enzo before Richter interrupted.

"Enzo, if you're going to read up on basic surgery, you might as well read up on the rest of it."

The navigator looked somewhat dubious, as if he was weighing up what was ahead. "I don't suppose my appointment as the ship's doctor attracts medical specialty pay does it, sir?" Richter and Steadman both smiled.

"Sure it does, Enzo, and if it doesn't, I'll see if I can persuade the president to give you one of those rare bronze medals with a pretty light blue ribbon with white stars on it," said Richter, referring to the Medal of Honor.

"And if you fail there, sir, an autographed tape of *ER* will do."

"OK, Enzo, you're on. Any other major problems, Master Chief?"

"Just one, sir. Yesterday, Sonarman Washington was thrown across the mess and smacked up against the leg of one of the tables. He was complaining of some pain in his lower chest last night, and I was sure that he'd broken one or two ribs on the left side. Apart from that he was OK, if a bit quiet, so I let him sleep in his own bunk. But this morning I can't wake him up, although he moves around if I shake him."

Richter was unprepared to deal with all this and felt thoroughly exasperated. For God's sake, he thought, why did Richards have to die? Isn't this a bad enough situation without all this medical hassle?

"Any idea what might be wrong with him?"

"No, sir."

"Well, what's under the ribs on the left side of his chest?" asked Richter, almost in desperation.

"The lung, I guess. But he's breathing OK, he's not

coughing up blood or anything. What else could it be? Well, there's some guts, at the back there's a kidney, and at the front there's the spleen. . . ." That triggered a thought in Richter's mind. In car accidents if the spleen got ruptured it sometimes had to be taken out. It had happened to a friend of his at college.

"Do you think he might have ruptured his spleen?" There was a long pause while Master Chief Steadman flicked through the first-aid manual that he'd brought with him.

"Oh shit! Pardon the expression, sir."

"What is it, Master Chief?"

"Please excuse me one minute, I'm just going to take another look at Washington." He got up and left the stateroom. He was gone for five minutes and returned, rather more breathless than when he left. "I'm afraid you might be right, sir. His belly's all bloated, his skin's clammy, and I can barely feel his pulse. He's in shock."

Richter glanced at Enzo, who just stared down at the deck. While it might be reasonable to ask him to take off an arm, or part of one, messing around inside the belly was quite another matter. The mere thought of it filled Richter with anxiety. God only knew how Enzo felt about it. Could he really ask him to tackle this? It sounded like Washington was in pretty poor shape, but he really didn't want to put Enzo in the position of providing the coup de grace. It would be better if he were to die peacefully, leaving Enzo with some confidence to tackle the XO's arm.

"Apart from removing his spleen, is there anything else we could do for him?" The Master Chief looked up from his first-aid book.

"We could give him some fluids, sir," he continued. "Seeing as he's unconscious, they'd have to be given by IV." It would give Enzo a little practice, thought Richter.

"How about it, Enzo?"

"OK, sir, I'll do my best."

"Just one other thing—you were going to look into sleeping medications. Have we got anything?"

"I'm really sorry, sir, I clean forgot. I'll get back to you right away."

"Thank you, I'll be down later to see how you're getting on. Can you ask Lieutenant Gallagher to come up? I haven't had my breakfast yet!" Enzo and Steadman both smiled and left. Nobody had had any breakfast.

0830C, Northern Fleet HQ, Severomorsk

Admiral Konstantin looked up from the papers that he was speed-reading, beside himself with rage. "This is an immediate message," he thundered. "Why wasn't I informed as soon as it was received last night? You can tell the duty officer that I wish to see him in my office at . . ." he paused, "thirteen hundred."

"Yes, sir," replied his secretary, as he reached for the telephone. Konstantin had calculated that the appointment should deprive the man of a day's sleep. The idiot deserved it. His eyes returned to the five-page message at the top of the pile. This was terrible news. The only positive aspect of Borzhov's report was that both boats had not sunk. The question that needed an answer today—no, this very morning—was who should be told what? He considered the matter. American intelligence was going to pick up the *Gepard* via satellite sooner or later—if they hadn't done so already. However, the chances of that right now were small, given the combination of darkness, heavy cloud, and snow over the area. He wandered across his office to the notice board by the door and read the latest weather report. It looked like tomorrow morning was the most likely time that they would find her. It was going to stop snowing after dark this evening, but the thick cloud cover wouldn't disperse until daybreak. The wind was also forecast to pick up if this report was to be believed. However, by this time tomorrow the *Gepard* would be well into the Barents Sea.

He could imagine what she might look like from space—yes, they might well notice the irregularity of the bow and wash around it and zoom to her damaged superstructure. What would they conclude? It would not be immediately obvious that she had sunk a 688 only two days before. Nor would there be any indication as to where the accident had happened. It might provoke a reconnaissance flight, either from the UK or Iceland—probably the latter. Konstantin's gaze turned to the large chart of the Arctic Ocean on the wall. A reconnaissance flight from Keflavik might possibly overfly the 688 but, unless there was a decent quantity of flotsam or oil, it would be difficult to conclude that the submarine was in trouble. With pollution being as prevalent as it was these days, even that might be an insufficient signal, particularly if the weather should deteriorate as forecast. Borzhov had used his initiative and recovered the emergency transmitter, so that wasn't going to give the game away. So what was the chance of the boat being found? The probability of the weather clearing sufficiently for detection of the *Gepard* multiplied by the probability that the damage would be noticed multiplied by . . . Konstantin worked through the sequence of events that would be required for the 688 to be detected and concluded that there was a one-in-fifty chance. Pretty good odds against. If it wasn't found within about ten days, the occupants of the American submarine and the little distress sonar their boats carried would be dead. It would be much more difficult to locate without anybody on board to respond to a search.

The 688 was on a secret mission, so there would be no check reports. COMSUBLANT would therefore not miss his submarine and initiate a search—at least, not right away. When would she have been due to be relieved, in time for Thanksgiving? Konstantin knew he'd been tailing the *Uriy Dolgorukiy* for five weeks.

Say it had taken her a week to cross the Atlantic and would take another week to return. It was now four weeks to Thanksgiving—yes, that would be about right, and by then they would be getting low on food. She would be reported missing just before Thanksgiving. That would give him a month to hide it. Making it invisible to sonar should be quite simple, even side-scan sonar—several thousand tons of dredged silt would see to that. But avoiding magnetic-anomaly detection would be more difficult, unless they sank something else nearby. Even so, a fresh wreck might provoke a more detailed investigation of the area, he thought. The chances of success? No more than even, he considered.

Konstantin returned to his desk and sat down on the green leather chair behind his desk. His finger reached for the intercom. "I'll have my coffee now."

"Yes, Admiral," replied his secretary, and within moments she entered the room and set a large mug of steaming black coffee down on a silver coaster that she used to protect the tooled leather set into the admiral's heavy oak desk. She glanced at Konstantin and saw that he was deep in thought. The brief nod that he aimed in her direction was her cue to leave. He reached for the coffee and took a noisy slurp of the pungent, black liquid. It was time to look at the problem from the opposite direction. It might be possible to keep quiet about the sinking and get away with it. The benefit would be to avoid a nasty diplomatic situation with potentially unfortunate political and economic repercussions. The risk was that the Americans would find their boat and salvage it. If Borzhov's description of the accident was accurate, and his starboard plane really was lodged inside, or lay near the wreck, it was not going to take a rocket scientist to put two and two together when they found it. It would also be very obvious that Russia had tried to cover up the incident. A nasty diplomatic incident would become a disaster. So was there an alternative?

What if Russia admitted the sinking, told the Americans where the wreck was, and offered to help get the survivors out? The American DSRV was a rather aging piece of technology and they had reduced their submarine fleet to such an extent that they had very few mother submarines available that were equipped to support a rescue operation. They could use a British boat, of course—all the Vanguards were equipped to support the DSRV, as were the French missile boats. Then there was the British rescue vehicle, the LR5 and the Swedish one. He paused, wondering whether the Russian DSRV, Project 1837, was still operational. He had heard nothing about it for months, despite it being part of his command. Konstantin lifted the telephone and hit the auto-dialer.

The news was predictably depressing. Konstantin was all too keenly aware that the current financial constraints made it difficult enough to keep the regular submarine fleet operational. The Belomorskaya and Zvezdochka shipyards in Severodvinsk were replete with laid-up boats awaiting decommissioning. Not all of them were there because they had reached the end of their operational lives. So he was not surprised to learn that both of the Russian DSRVs were nonoperational: one because the mating skirt had been damaged in a crane accident, and the other because it had been cannibalized for years to keep its sister operational. Not only that, but the India class submarine from which they operate was in Sevmorput awaiting repairs to her hull and could not put to sea. This meant that offers of assistance to recover the survivors in the 688 were going to ring somewhat hollow, but the offer could be made nonetheless, and they could certainly provide support in other ways. After all, accidents happen, it was a fact of life. He'd lost count of the number of times that Russian submarines had collided not just with NATO boats, but with each other. It was not that many years ago that a British Sovereign class boat had nearly been sunk in very similar circumstances. It was all part of the game, and the players knew the risks. He took another slurp of coffee and tapped a key on the intercom. "Miss Petrova, please make an appointment for me to see Admiral Gromyko this morning. It's very urgent."

"Yes, sir."

0700A, USS *Tulsa*

Lieutenant Gallagher knocked lightly on the captain's door, hoping he wouldn't hear, but he did. "Come in." As Gallagher opened the door, Richter looked up from his desk. Gallagher had obviously been to see the first-aid team. Much of his face was covered with a generous bandage. "Ah, Tim, how are you feeling?"

"I'm OK, sir. I expect you want to know about the food situation." Richter had more luck interpreting Gallagher's speech than yesterday afternoon, although he was still mumbling most of his words.

"Hole in one, Tim."

"Well, we have two kinds of food we can eat without risk, sir. The canned and the dehydrated foods. If you want a little more hazard, we could add in the 'fresh' food—salad and vegetables that are not so fresh now, but they should still be OK. There's still a fair bit of fruit left, too. With the chillers down, I would suggest we attack them soon."

"The whole boat's going to be like a reefer by tomorrow, don't worry about that," interjected Richter.

"In the freezers we have the meat, fish, and other goodies. They're still frozen—I've not allowed anyone in there."

"OK, Tim, let's say that we can survive in the *Tulsa* for ten days. Give me the gourmet menus."

"I haven't exactly developed any menus, sir." Richter looked at him in disbelief. He was furious.

"For fuck's sake, why not?"

"I've been in the hands of the Master Chief, I had to sleep, and—"

"I asked you yesterday if you would sort out the food. What did you say? Don't answer that. Have you inventoried what's fit to eat?"

"In outline, sir."

"What does that mean? Either you have or you haven't."

"I maintain an inventory, sir. There's no need to sort through everything."

"Is that a fact? Has it occurred to you that our dive yesterday was rated, in terms of difficulty, just below a backward double somersault with a full twist, piked? How much of your food will have survived that unscathed?" Richter paused for a moment, seeing the pained expression on the young officer's face. Was he riding Gallagher too hard? "Look, I know your head hurts. If it's any consolation, so does mine. I'll ask you one more time—are you up to looking after the catering?" Gallagher looked disconsolate.

"Yes, sir."

"Well, please go and do as I asked. I want some menus by midday and a meal shortly after that." Gallagher avoided Richter's gaze as he got up and made to leave. "One more thing before you go. I want everybody issued with a pint of water, bug juice, fruit juice, or whatever's available right away. In the future, I want this done twice a day, and you are personally to make sure that it's consumed. Is that clear?"

"Yes, sir." Gallagher replied, as he turned and left the stateroom.

Enzo looked up from the nursing textbook that was open on his desk, sat back, and rested his head on his hands. The enormity of what he had committed himself to was hitting home with each paragraph he read. Why on earth had he volunteered to serve as the ship's doctor? After a moment's reflection the answer was fairly obvious: there was nobody else. He hadn't formally consulted the crew, or even the wardroom, but he was pretty certain there would have been no takers even if he had. So he was stuck with it. It had been the same for much of his childhood. As the only son of six children, tasks had fallen to him ever since he could remember. His family had been poor, as were so many in the small fishing community of Swampscott, Massachusetts. As soon as he had learned how to use a paintbrush he'd helped his father overhaul the boat each spring. Later he regularly accompanied him on fishing runs and eventually learned how to mend the nets. He'd helped his mother grow vegetables in their small garden plot. It was he who chopped the wood and he who used to run errands to the stores. By the age of ten he had become perfectly capable of independent living.

But, with his knowledge and experience had also come an awareness of the financial stresses in the family. His five sisters had insatiable appetites for new clothes, and the boat's engine constantly needed maintenance. One by one, the older girls had found fiancés and then there were the weddings to pay for. His father had insufficient means to meet these demands. The result was furious arguments, which Enzo hated. He could remember lying awake in bed at night listening to his parents scream at each other. There were many times when their fighting reduced him to tears, and he cried himself to sleep.

One Christmas, when Enzo was twelve, Grandfather Raschello had come to stay. Enzo had asked him why he had brought the family over to the States from Calabria when he did, just after the war. He was curious because it had never made much sense to him. Ever since he was small, his mother had told him stories while she did the ironing. Many of them were about the glories of southern Italy. She had only moved to the States in 1962 to get married, and her memories of her home town, Scilla, were still vivid. She had recounted its rich history, stretching way back to classical times. He'd learned about the sense of community the people felt, the extended families, the relaxed way of life, and, above all, the wonderful weather. The way she had told her stories, the place sounded idyllic, and it had puzzled him why anybody would choose to leave. Grandfather had explained how the war had devastated not just the physical structure, but the whole economy of the region. "You have no idea what poverty is," he'd said in his heavily accented English. "Look, you have a car, a television, a refrigerator. . . . We had none of that after the war. We had few clothes and barely enough to eat. We were not alone. There were many thousands of us who decided that America was a land of opportunity, a land of the future and the place to go. And that is what it has proved to be. You should remember that."

It was only the following March that he was forced to do exactly that. The fighting between his parents had become continuous, and his mother had grown to hate the long New England winters. After one blazing row, involving the whole family, she announced that she was going to return to Italy. His two remaining sisters had always sided with their mother, and they agreed to leave with her. Enzo had been faced with a stark choice, and he'd taken some time to think about it. It had been an impossible decision to make. In the end, he'd felt sorry for his father and couldn't bear to leave him all alone. On top of that he had remembered Grandfather's words about the land of opportunity, and decided to stay.

Enzo snapped out of his meditation of the past and focused once more on the matter at hand. He was going to have to establish an IV on Washington and introduce a catheter. He had read the appropriate sections of the book twice, and he understood what he was going to have to do. Next he would have to memorize the procedures, so he settled down to read them over again. There was no time to lose.

1130C, Northern Fleet HQ, Severomorsk

"Come in, Peter, it's good to see you. Can I offer you a drink?" Konstantin studied the ruddy, pockmarked complexion of his immediate superior, Admiral Gromyko. Judging by the pink tinge to his eyes, Konstantin doubted that this would be his first drink of the morning.

"I won't, thank you, sir."

"Very well, tell me what's so urgent." Konstantin handed Gromyko a copy of Borzhov's message and took five minutes to summarize the events of the previous day in as much detail as he could. He then outlined the two options that he had formulated earlier in the morning. The commander of the Northern Fleet sat and listened without interrupting. As soon as Konstantin had finished he broke his silence. "How could this happen?" It was obvious that the man was furious. "What were Borzhov's orders? Surely he wasn't authorized to sink the American?"

"No he was not, sir. You will see from his message that this was an accident. The collision and sinking were unintentional."

"Come on, you can't persuade me that an officer as experienced as Borzhov just let this happen. It's not like tripping on a staircase."

"Sir, it may have been the XO or even a junior officer who caused the collision. In fact, for all we know, it may have been the American's fault. The message doesn't apportion any blame, and I don't think there's much point in us trying to do so now in the absence of more information."

"Maybe, but somebody screwed up, and he—or they—will be identified and blamed. The Kremlin will want that, and so will I for that matter."

"Yes, sir, I appreciate that, but the pressing issue right now is what's to be done?"

Gromyko was looking a little less apoplectic. "So you're telling me that the choice is between telling the Americans everything and guaranteeing to incur their displeasure, not to put too fine a point on it, or attempting to cover up the incident and run the risk of making them really mad. Do you really consider the probability of success with the latter approach at only 50 percent?"

"It might be a little bit better than that, but not much. I'm convinced the Yanks would keep surveying the Norwegian and Barents Seas until they found their boat. I really don't think they would have any alternative course open to them. They'll have the security aspect to consider and relentless pressure to find out what happened from the crew's relatives, the press, and, of course, Congress. Look how they're still investigating the MIAs in Vietnam, and that was all over more than a quarter of a century ago. I dread to think what the consequences would be if they were eventually to find the 688 under our attempt to bury it. They may even have a clue where to start looking if they've spotted the *Gepard* already."

"Any chance that they'll have heard what happened on their hydrophone network? What's it called . . . SOSUS?"

"I don't think so. At least, if they did hear something they won't have a good fix on where it happened. We did a pretty thorough sweep of the local area immediately before the *Uriy Dolgorukiy*'s sea trials. Even if they did hear something, they'd be hard-pressed to locate it with any precision."

"Could we not salvage the 688?"

"I am not a salvage specialist, sir," replied Konstantin. "If she's lying in water only 150 meters deep, I would imagine there's every chance that we could—but not covertly. Even if we had a *Glomar Explorer* they would see what we were up to in a heartbeat. The area would be filled with a flotilla of manned and unmanned submersibles in no time."

"She's only just over the continental shelf, isn't she?"

"If you call seventeen nautical miles 'just'—yes, sir."

"Could we not use divers to attach a line and tow the 688 into deeper water? If it sank below crush depth, it would be virtually impossible to tell what had happened, wouldn't it?"

"It would make the whole episode considerably more deniable. However, I have my doubts as to the practicality of that suggestion. I don't think it could be done without a surface vessel."

"My instinct tells me that this episode should be covered up. You know as well as I do how delicately balanced the IMF talks are. Where's the *Gepard* now?" Konstantin moved over to a large chart showing the Barents and Norwegian Seas and stabbed a finger at a point about halfway between Bear Island and Nordkapp, the Norwegian North Cape.

"She is making a surface passage back to Gadzhievo. She should be about here."

"Divert her to Severomorsk and get her into a roofed dry dock, as soon as possible. If we're to cover this up successfully, the *Gepard* must raise no suspicions." The admiral looked out of his aboveground office window at the panoramic view of the Murmansk fjord and the harbor, blanketed in a pristine white sheet of freshly fallen snow from an early storm. "When's this due to blow over?"

"Not until after dark, sir."

"I need to speak to my diving and salvage officers. I'll set that up for early this afternoon. I'd like you to sit in on the discussion, too. Bring anybody you need with you as I want to explore the possibility of using a Typhoon to move that 688. I'll let you know when the meeting will be." Konstantin stopped himself from querying Gromyko's sanity. He had accepted ever since his appointment that working with a superior who had never served in submarines was occasionally going to be a testing experience and decided to change the subject.

"Sir, there's one aspect of this situation we've not discussed."

"What's that?"

"There are survivors in that boat. If they're to have

any chance of staying alive, a rescue mission must be launched very soon. If we're going to tell the Americans and derive any benefit from doing so, it will have to be in the next twelve hours or so."

"Thank you, Peter. This decision's going to have to be a political one. I don't want to go to Moscow without an analysis of all the possible options. We'll have an outline answer to a covert salvage/disposal operation this afternoon. I'll arrange a meeting with the commander in chief and the minister of defense for this evening. You will, of course, come with me. Are you certain I can't offer you a vodka?"

"No thank you, sir. I must speak urgently with my engineering staff." Konstantin turned to leave.

"Look, I don't want you to worry too much about this. I'll cover your ass from here." Konstantin smiled as he left Gromyko's office. He couldn't help liking his boss despite his decadent lifestyle and occasionally flighty ideas. He was very much one of the "old school," hard as nails and just as sharp, so long as you caught him before lunch. He just prayed that his boss would moderate his intake of vodka over the next twelve hours. Otherwise, despite Gromyko's good intentions, his ass was going to be very exposed indeed.

1200A, USS *Tulsa*

Richter had decided that a tour of the boat was required. Although he would rather stay in his stateroom and nurse his thumping head, he knew he should see what was going on and get a feel for how the men were making out. The first place to visit was the wardroom. The table had been removed, and the room was now filled with the more severely injured, who were lying on mattresses arranged in two rows over the deck. He stood at the door and looked in.

"How's it going, Master Chief?" Richter studied the face of a man whom he'd known for years but whose expression he didn't recognize. Yes, he was exhausted, but there was something else. He looked worried.

Steadman got to his feet and made his way over to the door, threading his way between the mattresses. "We've brought Washington in here, sir. He's just over there," he said, pointing at the far corner. "Lieutenant Raschello's about to try and establish an IV line. He's been doing a lot of reading." As if on cue, Enzo appeared at the far door, carrying a bundle of medical equipment with him.

"Come to see the ship's doctor at work, sir?" he inquired breezily.

"Amongst other things. Do you need a hand, Enzo?"

"That's very kind, sir, but the COB and I should be able to manage. By all means stay and watch."

"I'll stay for a few minutes. I'm on a mission to find lunch." Both Steadman and Enzo smiled. Nobody had eaten a thing since the sinking, and even the thought of food was thoroughly appealing.

"You know I like my steak rare, don't you, sir?" continued Enzo.

"I'm afraid tartare is the only way it's being served at Chez Gallagher this afternoon. Joking aside, though, you two deserve a good meal. I'll see what can be done. You should both get some rest, too." Enzo knelt down next to Washington and unwrapped the bundle he had brought. He spread out a sheet of green paper and put on a pair of rubber gloves. Next, he slipped an elastic tourniquet around Washington's left upper arm and tightened it. He rummaged among the pieces of equipment on the paper and found a ball of cotton wool. He poured some antiseptic onto it and rubbed it over the inside of Washington's elbow.

"Since I'm rather new to this, I think I'm going to go for the largest vein that I can. It's not going to be very convenient for Washington, but I figure that doesn't matter much right now. There should be one right here." Enzo stopped talking for a moment and removed the cannula from its plastic container. "Master Chief, can you fill up the IV line, please?"

"Certainly, sir, if you remind me what needs doing." Enzo showed him, and within moments they were ready.

"The moment of truth." Enzo smiled and felt around again for a vein. "This isn't easy," he admitted. "If Washington were white, I might be able to see where the vein is. As it is I can only go by feel, and I don't want to stick this thing into a tendon." Beads of sweat were forming on his brow. Richter moved closer, knelt beside Enzo, and wiped his forehead with his handkerchief that, thankfully for Enzo, was clean.

"Look, Enzo. You can only do your best. Do you need any more light?"

"That might help, sir." Richter got up and headed forward to the crew's mess, picked up a battle lantern, and returned to the wardroom. By the time he had arrived back, Enzo was grinning from ear to ear. The reason for his pleasure was evident. The green paper contained a needle sitting in a small puddle of blood that had just been removed from the plastic cannula that Enzo was now taping to Washington's arm. The IV line had been connected and the only slight blemish on an otherwise exemplary procedure was the column of blood that was slowly rising up the tubing. Enzo finished taping the arm and spotted the problem. "Oops, better remove the tourniquet," he muttered, and busied himself with cleaning up.

The next task was the catheter. Buoyed by his success with the IV, Enzo was almost looking forward to it. He picked up the bundle of used equipment and left for the sick bay. He was back in moments with a fresh bundle and knelt beside Washington, who was, by now, deeply unconscious. "Sir, could you lend me a hand? We need to remove his pants."

"Sure." Richter knelt, and Enzo noticed that the captain looked pale and was swallowing hard. He rested for a moment on all fours before returning to a kneeling position.

"Are you alright, sir?" Enzo inquired, anxiety replacing his cheerful smile.

"I'm fine. It's just that I've occasionally been getting a little light-headed since the sinking. It'll go away." They removed Washington's pants and briefs. Enzo hesitated wondering what it would be like to handle another man's organ. He couldn't help feeling a little uncomfortable about it but drew his eyes away and busied himself with unwrapping the equipment that he'd just brought over from the sick bay. He put on a fresh pair of gloves and checked that everything was ready. His gaze alternated between the catheter and Washington's penis. Was that little rubber tube going to be long enough? Well, he thought, only one way to find out, and with that he grasped the organ. Having washed it with antiseptic, he squeezed a generous measure of anesthetic gel into the opening at the end and started to thread in the tube. His concern was unjustified. As he massaged the tubing into place a jet of urine hit him full in the chest. Unprepared for this eventuality, he dropped Washington's penis and reached for the catheter bag. "Watch it," exclaimed Richter, who found himself next on the receiving end of the stream. "Isn't there a cork or something you can stick in that?"

"I'm sorry, sir," replied Enzo, trying not to snigger. "I'll put this on the end." With the bag attached, they both stood up. Enzo's chest was soaked, as was Richter's left leg. They stared at each other and simultaneously broke out in a bout of helpless laughter.

1230A, USS *Tulsa*

After a quick change, Richter went down to the dry-food store, where he found Gallagher. "I've given some thought to the menus, sir."

"I'm glad to hear it. What are you proposing?"

"I'd like to suggest two meals per day. You said that people shouldn't eat too much."

"That's right, but they need to keep warm."

"I've designed the menus on the basis that we'll have no power. However, things could be made immeasurably better if I could just heat water. There's plenty of canned and packet soups along with crackers and cookies to provide one good meal per day, but it would be so much more palatable if it was hot."

"I agree. Let's see what Sparks can conjure up. What about the other meal?"

"There's enough canned meat, baked beans, and vegetables to make a kind of stew that shouldn't be too repulsive. Again, if we could heat it up and add in some ground beef, we could make it really tasty. There's enough fruit juice for one pint each per day. Their other pint will have to be water or bug juice. If we could heat the water, of course, there could be coffee."

"Thank you, Tim. You've made your point. I agree with two meals per day, no point in getting everybody up three times a day. I want people to eat something as soon as you can get it prepared. You can then swing into a catering routine. Meal times will be 0800 and 1800. I'll go and see Sparks. I don't see why one hot plate couldn't be made to work on DC power. After all, it's just a big resistor."

1530C, Northern Fleet HQ, Severomorsk

It had been a short, stormy meeting, although the outcome was satisfactory from Konstantin's point of view. The covert salvage idea had been consigned to history, but Gromyko had accepted this conclusion with ill grace. They sat together in the rear of the Kamov V62 helicopter as it lifted off and clattered off toward the military airport outside Murmansk, where an aging Antonov AN-32, converted for use by senior military and government officers, was waiting to take them to Moscow. The noise of the helicopter precluded normal conversation, and Konstantin was spared the need to talk to Gromyko, who sat beside him, sucking noisily on a mint, wearing a thunderous expression. Perhaps it was the lack of anything else to do that made Konstantin aware of his olfactory sense. Whatever the reason, he could no longer overlook the peppermint-flavored, alcoholic fumes emanating from his neighbor. His worst fears were slowly being realized. The bar on the Antonov would doubtless be well stocked, and Konstantin started to explore strategies whereby he could prevent Gromyko from getting completely paralytic in the aircraft. He was not optimistic. He'd been down this track before and had reluctantly concluded that there was little he could do except make a point of not joining him.

1400A, USS *Tulsa*

Richter had made his way forward as far as the sick bay, which was little more than an oversize cupboard. With most of the stores and all of the casualties in the wardroom, it was deserted except for Chief Czapek. He was carrying out some routine preventive maintenance on the three-inch launcher that was located in the overhead. "There's nothing wrong with it, Chief, is there?"

"No, sir, it's just fine."

"Good. It's just about the only means we have of telling the world where we are. How many smokes have we got?"

"Any particular color, sir, or total?"

"Total."

"I'll have to check the pyro locker, but I think we have more than thirty. We also have two SLOT buoys left."

"Good. That should be plenty. How are you feeling, Chief?"

"I'd be lying if I said better than ever, but I'm fine.

How about you, sir? That cut on your head looks pretty bad."

"Looks worse than it is. When you're through there, you'll get some rest, won't you?"

"Will do, sir. What's that prize you're going to give out—the Golden Dreams Award? I intend to shoot for it myself."

"Good for you."

Richter thought about carrying on forward but, with most of the space devoted to berthing, he decided against it. He didn't want to wake anyone. He decided to take one more look in the crew's mess room before climbing up one level and returning to his stateroom. As he looked in it appeared that the room was deserted. The atmosphere-control crew must be out taking readings, he thought. Then he noticed that a solitary figure with red hair was sitting at a table in the corner. "Sonarman Evans, good afternoon. What's kept you up? Can't you sleep?" As Richter approached the table, he could see that Evans was writing a letter. "Who's that to?"

"It's to Kate, my girlfriend, sir. I don't suppose she'll ever get to read it, but I thought I'd write anyway. Makes me feel a li'l better in a funny kinda way."

"How long have you known her?"

"Oh, forever. Thing is, being based in Groton, I don't get to see her that much. So we write to each other a lot."

"Where does she live?"

"Just outside Pineville, Kentucky."

"Appalachian country. That's where you're from, isn't it? I'm told it's very beautiful there."

"Yes, sir. It is. Kate and I have been neighbors since I can recall."

"Have you had other girlfriends?"

"No, sir, not much point. One good one should be enough for any man."

"That's true. The trouble is most people aren't as lucky as you and get it right the first time. Are you planning on getting married?"

"Yes, sir, in the spring. Saturday, April 16."

"Are you looking forward to it?"

"I was, sir, and I'd give you your invitation right now if I thought for one moment that either of us could be there. But I don't think we will. That's what I'm telling Kate in this here letter, that I'm sorry to have let her down. She was real excited 'bout it all."

"That's taking things a bit far isn't it? We've got every chance of getting out of here. The search will be under way already, and we will be out of here within the week. See if I'm not right."

"That's one way of look'n at it, sir, and I sure hope you're right. Myself, I ain't so certain, so I thought I'd write and let Kate know 'bout how I'm feelin'."

"Well, that's fine, Evans. You'll get some rest when you're through, won't you?"

"Sure will, sir."

1830A, USS *Tulsa*

Richter lay on his bunk almost oblivious to the headache that had been his persistent companion for the last twenty-eight hours. A full stomach was a wonderful thing, he thought. Things were definitely looking up. Even the crew briefing before the meal had gone better than expected. Having heard how Sonarman Evans felt about the situation, earlier in the afternoon, he had been concerned that everybody else was feeling the same way. That didn't seem to be the case, although there were clearly two camps of thought: the optimists and the pessimists. But on a show of hands, it seemed that the former group was clearly the larger. But, unless there was some evidence quite soon that the *Tulsa* had been found, things could and probably would deteriorate. Nonetheless, compared with his worst fears shortly after the sinking, and the tragic loss of John and the other men back aft, Richter felt satisfied that morale was holding up OK.

Still, there was one man who had worried him—

Chief Santana. He had always struck Richter as something of a loner, a taciturn and rather reserved character. Santana had asked if he could have a word after the briefing, and it was clear from his comments that he was far from optimistic about the situation. He'd have to keep an eye on him, Richter thought to himself. The chiefs were going to be key players in keeping the crew together, and if Santana should infect some of the others with his negativity, it could bring down the morale of the whole crew.

There was a knock at his stateroom door. "Come in." It was Master Chief Steadman who poked his head into the room.

"I'm very sorry to trouble you, sir." Richter sat up slowly, but the precaution failed to prevent him from wincing at the recurrence of the kettledrum solo in his head.

"Not at all, have a seat. What is it?"

"I think Washington's died, sir." Although Richter was half-expecting this sooner or later, he couldn't control a sinking feeling in the pit of his stomach.

"Has Lieutenant Raschello taken a look at him?"

"No, sir. He's in his stateroom. I think he's resting."

"Fine, let him rest. OK, I'd better come and see." They descended to the second level and headed aft to the wardroom. It was very quiet, and the only lights that were energized were around Washington's mattress. Richter knelt down beside him and felt his wrist for a pulse, without success. The skin was cool to the touch. He racked his brain. How do you tell if somebody's truly dead? He leaned over, put his ear next to Washington's nose, and waited for a full minute. He could neither hear nor feel any evidence of breathing. Then it dawned on him, he'd seen it on TV endless times—the pupils normally react to light. "Master Chief, can you pass me a flashlight, please?" The instrument was passed and he opened one of Washington's eyes. The pupil was dilated so wide that he could barely see the familiar, brown iris that normally surrounded it. It didn't look good. Nothing had happened when he had opened the eye. He flicked on the flashlight and shined it directly at the pupil. Nothing. He checked the other eye. It was the same. Richter slowly got to his feet, weaved his way out of the wardroom, and turned to Steadman, who had followed him. "I think you're right. He's dead," he whispered. "Where are you stowing the deceased?"

"In the torpedo room, sir."

"Well, Washington had better join them. Don't feel bad, Master Chief, you did all you could, and more. I thought that both you and Lieutenant Raschello did an incredible job and when we get out of here, I will make damned sure that a lot of people get to know that."

As Richter returned to his stateroom, Schwartz appeared at his side. "Something rather odd's happening, sir."

"What's up?"

"Right after we talked this morning, I opened up the oxygen bleed valve and set the rate to the one suggested in the manual—one cubic foot per hour per man. The strange thing is that the level's rising. I'd expected it to stay more or less the same."

"What's it now?" Harvey looked at yet another piece of paper that was sticking out of the manual.

"Eighteen point four percent, sir. It's increased from 18.0 in just eleven hours. That's nearly a full percentage point per day."

"That is odd. I guess there are four possibilities. Either the oxygen meter, the bleed rate or the manual is wrong, or there's a problem with mixing. What's happening with the CO_2?"

"I've used fifteen canisters of lithium and the CO_2 reading is now 2.8 percent."

"I thought you were going to change the canisters every two and a half hours?" Richter paused for a moment to check his watch and do a quick calculation. "You should've used twenty-five by now." They paused outside Richter's stateroom door.

"I know it, but Sparks had some trouble with the hopper. He put it together in a bit of a hurry yesterday and spent four hours fixing it this afternoon."

"But this is great news. It would seem that we're using less oxygen and producing less CO_2 than we, or the manual, predicted. Quite a bit less—about 70 percent less if my math is correct." He thought for a moment. "That means we might have an extra two days. Oh, this is great news." Richter slapped Schwartz on the back as they entered his stateroom. "What about the pressure?"

"It's still rising slowly—just about four feet of seawater now."

"And still no sign of leaks?"

"No, sir."

"Have you checked the bilges?"

"Yes, sir. We're not taking on water."

"Well, there has to be a leak somewhere. Keep looking. Have you got all the atmosphere readings with you?"

"Yes, sir."

"Right. Let's go through them in detail."

2000A, USS *Tulsa*

Enzo stopped reading and rubbed his aching eyes. He had decided to stop not because he was exhausted, although he was, but because he was becoming overwhelmed with detail. If the XO was going to survive this operation, he would have to keep things simple. One principle that he had absorbed from the books he'd been studying was that the main objective in war surgery is to remove all the dead tissue from the wound. One could debate whether or not the situation could be construed as being appropriate for war surgery, thought Enzo, but regardless, the principle should hold true. That boiled down to trimming away tissue until it bled. He reckoned that he could do that. It should be no more difficult than carving a shoulder of lamb. He wasn't going to worry about what the wound looked like—it was going to look messy no matter what. His second decision was that he wasn't going to stitch it up. It was apparently better to leave the wound open. That way it was less likely to get infected. Thirdly, he was going to ignore the anatomy of the arm. It was far too complicated and, in the final analysis, it didn't seem to matter much if all he was going to do was trim away dead tissue. He would hack and hope. If something bled, he would clip the bleeding point and tie it off.

What had concerned him most was the prospect of giving the XO an anesthetic. Whatever he did, there was no way that he was going to use a ventilator. How those things worked was a mystery, and, as a matter of fact, he had little choice because there wasn't one on board. So the anesthetic would have to be local, and he could give him a shot of morphine as well for good luck. Having decided not to bother with the anatomy of the arm, he was not going to try to numb individual nerves. He would just inject a lot of the stuff into the living bit of his forearm and hope that did the trick. He had toyed with the idea of using a tourniquet to keep down the blood loss but rejected it because it would prevent him from determining which tissues were alive and which were not. The XO would bleed, and so he would have to set up yet another IV to replace the lost fluid. This no longer fazed him, as it would be his fourth and, so far, he had a perfect score—so long as he didn't count the three attempts it took to get one into Chief Maddison. He'd had it easy so far, though. All of his patients had been deeply unconscious. If he was clumsy with the XO, he might move around, and that could make things a whole lot more difficult. But it was all just details, Enzo thought. His introduction to the practice of medicine had gone remarkably smoothly. He was on a roll. Perhaps he should have gone to med school after all.

Enzo was as prepared as he was going to be. He

rose from his desk and headed for the wardroom. He was met at the door by the COB.

"I've some bad news, sir. Sonarman Washington died earlier this evening."

"Why didn't anybody tell me?" Enzo's normal composure had left him, and he was shouting. "Am I the ship's doctor or what?"

"The captain wanted you to rest. He dealt with it personally. He wants to see you before the XO's operation anyway." Enzo's short-lived elation had evaporated. He reached into his pocket, withdrew a handkerchief, and discharged a long blow into it. He then screwed it into a ball and dabbed both eyes. His distress was not just for Washington. He barely knew the man. It had suddenly dawned on him that there was more to this medicine business than had so far met his eye, and the thought of attacking the XO with a knife now filled him with fresh horrors. He sniffed, blew his nose again, and turned to make his way up to the captain's stateroom.

"I'm sorry, Master Chief."

"What for, sir?"

"Well, for raising my voice and . . ."

"That's alright, sir. I'm just as stressed out as you are."

There was no reply when Enzo knocked on Richter's stateroom door. Rather than chase him around the boat, he decided to peek inside to see if the captain was there. Richter had drifted into a deep sleep, so Enzo entered and coughed loudly. "You wanted to see me, sir?" Richter stirred and slowly woke, blinked, and rubbed his eyes. "There's no need to get up, sir."

"Thanks, Enzo. Look, I'm sorry about Washington. We knew his chances were somewhere between not a lot and none at all. You did your best, and more. I've told the Master Chief, and I might as well tell you, that if—no, *when* we get out of here—I am going to make it widely known that the two of you have done the most remarkable job. What's more, it would seem that our chances of getting out alive are getting better. Harvey reckons that we're producing CO_2 at a slower rate than expected, so we might now have enough lithium to last a whole week."

"That's great news, sir. I've found a load of tranquilizers in the sick bay—Valium and the like. I don't see any harm in handing those out. They might slow people down even more."

"Sure, but I don't want any key players on that stuff. When we're rescued, I want to have a good team ready to receive the vehicle. But that's not the reason I wanted to see you. Have you had a word with the XO?"

"About the operation?"

"No, about herding cattle. What do you think?"

"No, sir. But you're right, one of us should. I can hardly walk up to him with a knife and tell him that its time to prune his right arm."

"Exactly. When do you reckon you'll be ready to do it?"

"I'm ready right now. But we'll have to find somewhere to do it—there's not enough space in the wardroom."

"We'll use the chief's lounge. I'll get Steadman to set it up. In the meantime, you and I had better step next door and speak with the Exec." As Richter stood up he winced, held his head, and wobbled on his feet. Enzo grabbed him and held him until he was steady. "Don't ask—I'm fine," exclaimed Richter. "After this is over, though, I'm going to lie down for a good long while."

The response to Richter's knock at the XO's door was barely audible, but they both entered regardless. Mitchell was lying on his bunk propped up by pillows. Despite the cold, his forehead was covered in a patina of sweat that trickled down the side of his face forming a little rivulet at the base of his neck. His hair was soaking wet, and it looked like steam was rising from it. He was short of breath. His discarded sling lay on the deck beside his bunk and he held his right arm awkwardly across his belly. The exposed skin of his fingers and hand was a dull blue-gray. The rest of his forearm was swathed in one of Master Chief Steadman's expansive, white bandages, the center of which was disfigured by a large, dark maroon stain surrounded by a lighter, straw-colored halo. Both of the newcomers were struck by the musty smell.

"You're looking a little better than the last time I saw you, Curtis," lied Richter.

"So do you, sir." The Exec tried to smile.

"How's that arm of yours?" Richter asked, as he sat down on the edge of Mitchell's bunk.

"Oh, it's just fine. I think I'm getting a little feeling back into it. It doesn't hurt as much as it did." Richter noticed the empty bottle of Tylenol beside the bed.

"Can you move your hand?"

"No, sir. I expect it'll be a while before I get the use of it back. I'm rather thirsty, Enzo. Would you pour me some water, please?"

"Sure."

Enzo walked into the head, filled a glass, then returned and placed it beside the XO's bunk. Richter continued: "Curtis. You know I don't believe in beating about the bush, so I'll come straight to the point. It's quite obvious that part of your right arm is dead and, in order to save your life, it will need to be removed. . . ."

"No!" protested Mitchell. Richter ignored the interruption and continued:

"Otherwise, gangrene will set in." He wrinkled his nose. "If it hasn't already." He reached over and felt Mitchell's forehead. It was very warm, he obviously had a fever. Mitchell instinctively knew that Richter was probably right, but he just didn't want to accept it.

"We don't have a doctor. Who's going to do the operation?" Mitchell asked.

"I am," interjected Enzo. "I've spent much of today reading up on what to do. It really isn't that difficult."

"But I write with that hand. . . . I'll be unfit to stay

in the navy if I lose it," he pleaded, stammering for another reason not to proceed with the operation. "With the best will in the world, Enzo, you're not a doctor. How do you know it won't get better?" There was an awkward silence that Richter eventually broke.

"Curtis, he doesn't need to be a doctor. My nose tells me that your arm is just not going to recover. Do you really want it to claim the rest of you? If you don't believe me, take a look yourself. That dressing needs changing anyway." Richter got up to make way for the navigator to take his place. Enzo gently unraveled Steadman's handiwork until Mitchell's arm was uncovered except for a patch of gauze that was stubbornly stuck to the wound. Nobody could avoid noticing that it was a purulent green, or ignore the offensive smell.

"You see, it's not so bad," started Mitchell. "It's stopped bleeding. Why can't you just leave it a while? I'm sure it will keep healing." Mitchell had convinced nobody, least of all himself. Everyone just stared at the wound.

Enzo felt it was his turn to say something if only to break the uneasy silence. "Sir, I can't do anything about this without your permission. Will you let me deal with it?"

"What about an anesthetic?" replied Mitchell. "There's nobody to give an anesthetic. Do you know I once read that anesthesiologists kill more patients than surgeons?"

"Who worked that one out, I wonder?" replied Enzo. "Surely any operating-room death is a team effort." No sooner had he said it than Enzo realized the unfortunate interpretation that could be placed on his remark. "In any case, I'm not going to use a general anesthetic. I'll do it with local and a shot of morphine."

"You mean I'll be awake during this?"

"Yes, sir."

"You can have a slug of medicinal brandy as well," said Richter in an obvious effort to encourage a conclusion to the discussion. "If we have any on board," he added. Mitchell looked to Enzo as if he were about to cry.

"Please—give me a few minutes to think about this," he almost pleaded as a rattle that started deep in his chest grew until he coughed and spat a large, blood-flecked ball of yellow phlegm into a tissue, wincing with pain as he did so.

"OK, Curtis, take it easy. There's no hurry," soothed Richter. "You don't have to make your mind up right away. A few minutes one way or the other won't make any difference. We'll leave you in peace to think it over." Richter nodded to Enzo, and the two of them left the room. They paused once outside the door. "He's a sick man, Enzo," whispered Richter. "Do you really want to go ahead? It strikes me that if his arm doesn't claim him, that chest of his surely will."

"I hadn't realized his lungs were so bad, sir. He didn't want to come down to the wardroom. I haven't seen him all day. He's going to need some antibiotics, and I'm going to have to do some more reading to figure out what to give him." Enzo paused. The captain was right. Mitchell might not recover. But without getting rid of that arm, he stood no chance at all. "Look, sir. I'm no expert—none of us are. The XO might not make it. Come to think about it, none of us might. His only chance is if somebody removes that dead tissue, and seeing as you asked me to do it and there isn't a long line of volunteers for the task, I might as well go ahead and get it done."

"You missed my point, Enzo. I'm no longer asking you to do it."

"Thank you, sir. I'll do it anyway, if that's alright with you and the XO."

"OK, good luck. I'll get the COB to fix up an operating room for you."

2100C, The Kremlin, Moscow

The welcoming handshakes, hugs, and backslaps complete, the small group filed into the minister of defense's conference room, where they were beckoned to take their seats at the large table that dominated the room. It was a high-powered group. In addition to the minister, Gromyko, and the commander in chief, Konstantin noted that there were senior representatives from the army, the air force, and spokesmen from the president's political office and the foreign ministry. After formally greeting the participants and apologizing for the late hour, the defense minister invited Konstantin to outline the problem. This he did in as great a detail as he had facts to support. A number of irritating questions followed: "Is it normal for submarines to try to ram each other?" was the first offering from the army representative.

"Why can't the Americans survive for the normal length of a patrol?" was another little jewel thrown in by the president's man. Konstantin carefully responded to each one, desperately trying not to display the irritation he felt. Next the minister nodded to Gromyko and asked him to lay out the available options. It was the moment Konstantin had been dreading.

He was soon gratified that his concern had been misplaced. Nobody rises to be an admiral in the Russian Navy if they can't gather their wits when it matters, regardless of their intake of vodka. Konstantin marveled as Gromyko delivered a faultless analysis and cogent discussion of the two viable options that presented themselves, despite having emptied an entire bottle of Stolichnaya down his throat during the flight. They could confess and offer assistance in recovering any survivors, or attempt to cover up the episode and conceal the wreck. To his credit, he did not express his personal opinion or offer up the third option that had been scuttled that afternoon. There were more questions and comments. This time they focused on the technical problems of trying to conceal the wreck, how magnetic-anomaly detectors worked, whether it might be possible to confuse the return from a submarine with other signals, such as another wreck or a load of scrap metal—all issues that had already been thrashed out earlier in the day. Finally, when there were no more questions, the minister summed up, thanked everyone for attending at such short notice, and ushered the visitors out of his office. It was time for him to see the president.

In accordance with the defense minister's request, Gromyko and Konstantin were to remain in Moscow overnight, just in case there were any further developments. Gromyko's secretary had booked them into the Metropol, which offered a generous discount to senior military officers. An elderly, black Zil limousine drove them the quarter mile between the Kremlin and the hotel, and no sooner had Gromyko entered the building than he grasped Konstantin's elbow in a viselike grip and headed straight for the bar. Konstantin had little option but to follow. There was no way that he was going to escape from this situation without a drink, and he resigned himself to putting a brave face on what was a *fait accompli*. He would survive if he stuck to beer . . . he hoped.

2300A, USS *Tulsa*

It had been almost an hour since Enzo persuaded Mitchell to swallow thirty milligrams of Valium. The effect could not have been better from Enzo's point of view. The XO was snoring like an adenoidal child and had not noticed his two attempts to establish an IV. It was time to start. Enzo, who had donned a green gown, drew up six vials of Lidocaine into a twenty-milliliter syringe and injected it through a series of sites around the forearm, just below the elbow. He just hoped that he had used enough and chosen the right spots. He waited for fifteen minutes to let the stuff work and decided to test the efficacy of his administrations by removing the stubborn gauze dressing from the wound. His previous attempts had resulted in Mitchell crying with pain. Not this time. With the dressing off, Enzo, Steadman, and the captain all

surveyed the injury. It was not a pretty sight. A pale,
straw-colored fluid slowly oozed from the gashes in
the skin through which the two broken bones had
forced themselves. Their shattered ends were moist
with a greenish tinge. Enzo reached over and picked
up a fresh gauze pad, soaked it with Betadine, and
started to clean up the skin. He did a thorough job
and, surprisingly, failed to wake the XO in the process.
He then put on a pair of gloves. Steadman, who was
similarly attired, stood opposite him. He lifted the injured arm, allowing Enzo to lay a waterproof, paper
towel over the Exec's torso. This he covered with a
large, green towel that finished just short of his head.
Enzo wrapped another sterile towel round Mitchell's
upper arm and secured it with a pair of forceps.

It was time to do some cutting. Enzo picked up a
scalpel from the tray beside him and, in a series of
rapid strokes, removed the forearm below the frac-
tures. Because Enzo hadn't asked anyone to hold the
injured limb, it rolled off the XO and onto the deck,
landing with a thud. Richter winced. The exercise was
assuming a ghoulish complexion that was beginning to
turn his stomach.

"Don't worry about that, sir," said Steadman, who
was acutely aware that the atmosphere had become
chilly. "I'll take it to the torpedo room once you're
through."

"Thank you, Master Chief." Enzo paused to survey
the wound. "That was the easy bit. What I'm going
to do now is keep trimming away tissue until it bleeds.
Please keep a weather eye open. If I cut a vessel, I'd
appreciate it if you would put a clip on it right away."

"I'll do my best, sir."

"OK, here we go."

Enzo made to start cutting, but stopped and looked
up at Richter. "Sir, can you shine some light directly
on the arm please?" Richter adjusted two of the lights
that Sparks had rigged overhead.

"How's that?"

"Right on the money, sir." With that, Richter watched with amazement as Enzo started to remove tissue in deft slices from around the bones. There was very little bleeding. It soon became obvious that there was a lot more dead muscle and skin than anybody had expected. Suddenly a pulsing jet of blood sprang from the arm as Enzo sliced through the radial artery. It hit Richter full in the face. He recoiled instinctively, his head swimming, the world starting to revolve and grow dark.

Steadman spun round in time to see the captain collapse to the deck. Enzo, who hadn't seen what had happened, just thought he'd fainted.

"Master Chief, the captain can't fall down any farther. We have to clip this artery."

"I'm not sure he just fainted, sir. He's been unsteady on his feet all day."

"I know, but if we don't stop this bleeding, we're going to lose the XO. We'll deal with the captain in a minute." The two of them aimed forceps at the source of the red fountain, and soon the bleeding was under control. "Better tie it off while we can," Enzo continued as he selected a length of black thread from the tray beside him and somewhat clumsily tied off the vessel.

Steadman finished dabbing at the wound with a swab and looked over his shoulder as Richter started to stir. "I think the captain's going to be OK, sir. What do you want me to do next?" he asked, the corners of his mouth turned up in the merest suggestion of a smile.

"Can you get a saw ready? I'm going to have to trim these bones. By the way, is the cauldron of pitch boiling yet?" It took Steadman a moment to realize that the navigator was referring to navy practice of two hundred years ago, when an amputation took just a few seconds and the bleeding was staunched by dipping the stump in boiling tar.

"Aye, aye, sir. Me parrot's giving it a stir!" he replied in an approximation of an English West Country accent. They both laughed.

It took another twenty minutes to complete the task. The only time that the XO had stirred was while Enzo was actually sawing. Both men stood back to admire the navigator's handiwork. Despite the size and irregularity of the wound, most of the tissue now looked pink rather than dusky blue. Enzo left Steadman to apply one of his voluminous dressings, removed his gloves and gown, and went over to take a look at Richter, who was sitting cross-legged on the deck holding his head in his hands.

"Are you all right, sir?"

"I'll be OK, Enzo. I think I must have a concussion from when I hit my head during the collision yesterday. I just need some rest."

"It's been a long day, sir. Do you need any help getting to your stateroom?"

"No thanks, Enzo. When you've finished up here, be sure to get some sleep yourself. A lot of people here need you to be in good shape—and I'll include myself on that list." Enzo was touched by Richter's obvious trust in him. There was nothing more to be said. Richter took himself off to bed, and thirty minutes later Enzo was fast asleep for the first time in two days.

CHAPTER
3

Saturday, 30 October

0200C, US Embassy, Moscow

Having been woken by a firm nudge in the ribs from
his wife's elbow, the ambassador rolled over and lifted
the receiver to quell the incessant ringing. His hangover this morning was courtesy of the French, who
always put on an embassy cocktail party sans pareil.
He checked the bedside clock and swore under his
breath. It was only two in the morning, and he had
been in bed for all of forty-five minutes. Who on earth
could be calling at this wretched time of night?

"Ambassador?" It was the switchboard, through
which all his calls out of office hours were routed.
"Sir, I have the Russian foreign minister on the line."
That was odd, the ambassador thought, the minister
invariably received an invitation to the embassy func-
tions and usually attended the larger ones, but he had
been notably absent at last night's extravaganza.
Something must be up, he thought.

"Put him on."

"I am sorry to trouble you at this time of night,
Your Excellency," the Russian apologized.

"No problem, Yuri, what can I do for you?" The ambassador was noted for his studied informality.

"I have a rather delicate naval issue that I need to discuss with you as a matter of some urgency. Can you come to my office in, say, an hour?"

It must be really urgent, thought the ambassador. "Of course. I'll bring my naval attaché with me."

"That would be most helpful."

"I'll see you in an hour, Yuri."

After making calls to the attaché and his chauffeur, the ambassador got up and went to the bathroom. With two Alka-Seltzer and some coffee he would surely be able to face the world. He'd have to make his own coffee though, he remembered. There were no kitchen staff available at this time on weekends, thanks to the bean counters.

0340C, Outside the Kremlin, Moscow

"What did you make of that?" The ambassador had turned to the attaché, Captain Daniel Fairchild, who sat beside him in the leather-lined luxury of a black, bulletproof Cadillac as it sped them back to the embassy.

"Incredible, but not impossible. I'll get straight on to COMSUBLANT and see what he has to say."

"Be sure to use the secure line. If it is true, we'll need to keep this quiet for as long as possible, or the press will make our lives a misery," remarked the ambassador wearily, determined to avoid any more disturbances tonight if at all possible.

"I will, sir."

"Brief me in the morning. I'll need to tell the State Department, who'll want to pass it on to the White House and the Pentagon. I would appreciate it if COMSUBLANT could keep it to himself until it's been through the channels."

"Sir, with respect, if there is a possibility that this is true, COMSUBLANT will need to act fast or we'll be dealing with a salvage rather than a rescue—if you can appreciate the distinction."

"So what are you telling me?"

"Quite simply, sir, that I will know in twenty minutes whether there is any chance that the Russian story is true, and if it is, we'll need to get those channels moving PDQ." The ambassador groaned at the prospect of no further sleep. He had accepted this job as a reward for substantial contributions to the Republican party in the belief that it would be fun and he could enjoy significant status and a generous lifestyle at the taxpayer's expense. Unfortunately, he had discovered that there were times when the wretched job really got to him, and this was one of them.

"Very well, you can use my office while I put some fresh coffee on."

The Cadillac swept into the embassy compound past a smart salute from the Marine guard on the gate. Fairchild leapt out of his side of the car and walked briskly through the main door and on to his office to pick up his personal phone book, before making his way to the ambassador's office. Once there he lifted the receiver of the secure phone and checked his watch. It would be 8 P.M. in Norfolk—he'd try COM-SUBLANT's home number. He flicked through the pages, dialed a long number, and waited with the fingers of his empty hand beating the rhythm of a cantering horse on the mahogany desk. "Admiral Talisker? USNA Moscow, sir. I apologize for having to trouble you at home."

"Is that you, Danny?" Fairchild was astonished that the admiral could recognize his voice, let alone remember his first name. After all, they'd only served together once before, and that was in the *Grayback* eighteen years earlier.

"Yes, sir. I'll get straight to the point. I've just returned from a meeting with the Russian foreign minister, the minister of defense and the chief of the armed forces." There was a brief pause.

"At that time of the morning? What's up?"

"They are claiming to have sunk one of our submarines, sir."

"What, deliberately?"

"No, sir, they claim it was an accident, a collision. Do we have a 688 operating in the Norwegian Sea?"

"Whereabouts?"

"74° 27' North, 17° 20' East."

"As a matter of fact we do. The *Tulsa*. I can't tell you what she's doing."

"No need for that, sir. Have you had any check reports from her?"

"Look, you've caught me cold on this one, I'll get right back to you. What number are you on?" Fairchild gave him the number.

"The sooner you can let me know, the better, sir. It looks like the ambassador may have to wake up Washington."

"I'll get right back to you as soon as I can, Danny."

"Appreciate it, sir."

He returned the receiver to its cradle as the ambassador entered the room carrying a silver tray adorned with a carton of milk and two rather full, colored mugs surrounded by small puddles of coffee. "You don't take sugar do you?"

"No, sir."

"I thought not, but I couldn't remember if you take milk."

"Not at this time of night, sir."

"Well, take your pick." Fairchild had difficulty keeping a straight face. One mug was decorated with an image of Sylvester the cat wearing a chef's hat, standing in front of a smoking barbecue saying "Suffering Sausages!" The other was a cartoon of Inspector Clouseau about to tread in some dog litter with the caption "SHIT HAPPENS!" This cast a new light on the ambassador which the attaché had not seen before. The man, or whoever bought his crockery, clearly had a sense of humor.

"COMSUBLANT's going to call right back."

"Good. What did he say?"

"Just that there is a possibility that the Russians are right. He's looking into it." The ambassador took a long pull on his coffee. Quite how he could swallow the scalding liquid was a mystery to Captain Fairchild. He watched the ambassador move over to a magnificent glass-fronted bureau that contained four rows of crystal glasses on its upper shelves and a large humidor below them.

"Care for a cigar? I have a selection of Havanas courtesy of Yuri."

"No, thank you, sir."

"You don't mind if I do?"

"Not at all," replied Danny, suspecting that it would have made little difference had he objected. The ambassador selected a half corona, clipped the end in a well-practiced maneuver, and lit up. In moments his head was obscured by a cloud of pale blue smoke.

"That was quite a party the French put on last night," started the ambassador.

"It was, although I had to leave early. You know we've got Lucy's rather frail parents staying."

"I know what you mean. When they get on in age you almost need a baby-sitter for them. I was spared all that because mine were killed in a road accident while they still had all their faculties."

"I'm sorry, sir. I didn't know."

"Don't be. It was some years ago now and it did my bank balance no harm. I expect my father would still be running the company if he hadn't met a premature end." Fairchild had no difficulty recalling that the ambassador's wealth was based on his ownership of a substantial share of what had become a well-known computer software company. He wanted to change the subject. The man became insufferable once he got into the groove of reviewing his success as a corporate executive. But Fairchild didn't have to. The phone rang. The ambassador waved toward the phone, indicating that Danny should pick it up while he took another long drag on his cigar.

"USNA Moscow, how can I help you?"

"Danny. I'm going to initiate a SUBLOOK and see if she responds. It's a bit tricky, given the *Tulsa*'s mission, but better safe than sorry. It's not as if the Russians are unaware of her activities, and the *Tulsa* should respond if she's OK. Thanks for the heads-up."

"Thank you, sir. We'll inform State." Fairchild replaced the receiver and looked up at the ambassador, who was little more than a shadow behind the pall of smoke that now surrounded the red leather sofa on which he was now seated.

"Well, sir, COMSUBLANT's going to try and find the *Tulsa*."

"I guessed as much. I'd better make a few calls now. Thanks for your help this evening, Danny. You'd better get off back to bed."

"Thank you, sir. I hope you'll be able to get some rest. It was a very good party the French put on."

The ambassador smiled. "I'll survive," he replied. "Now go on, and get home!"

2130R, 29 October, Atlantic Fleet HQ, Norfolk, Virginia

"We're agreed then," said Vice Admiral Talisker, looking around the table at which his staff officers were gathered. "We'll need the assistance of the Norwegians with the search and, possibly, a rescue operation—which will presumably be coordinated from Bodø. We'll also need the use of their airport at Hammerfest. I'll get onto CNO to initiate that request. I'll also request an air search from Keflavik by CTF-84. Ops, you'll inform the Navy Department duty captain and COMSUBPAC. Given the distances involved and the fact that the boat may well have been down for thirty-eight hours already, we should recommend the DSRV and Submarine Rescue Chamber be made ready to move right away. Communications officer, alert the comms stations to look out for transmissions from the *Tulsa*. Get Group 2 to commence calling the *Tulsa* every ten minutes on their assigned circuit and ask the other groups to keep a listening watch. If the *Tulsa*'s where the Russians report it is, a P3 should find her pretty quickly, and I'll escalate to SUBSUNK right away. If she's not found or doesn't respond . . ." he glanced at his watch, ". . . in twenty hours from now, I'll call SUBMISS." There were nods of agreement.

The admiral continued: "Public affairs. Since we are currently at SUBLOOK, we're under no obligation to inform the public. If I have to go to SUBMISS, or worse, we will be. PAO, I needn't tell you of the interest that will be stirred up as soon as this hits the streets. There will be mayhem. The regulations require that, initially at least, the announcement is made by the assistant secretary of defense, public affairs. I would be delighted if the entire operation were handled from his office, should it come to that. However, I want you to prepare a brief for CINCLANT, CNO, and CHINFO, and be ready to handle the press that will inevitably beat the door down once this gets out. You don't need me to tell you what will be required—the names of those on board, their hometown, bios of the senior officers and the COB and so on. Liaise with the PAO in Groton, who's also liable to be under siege—you two need to sing the same tune. However, I don't want any personal details released to the media until the next of kin have been informed. Is that clear?"

"Yes, sir."

"Gentlemen, I reiterate my apologies for dragging you in on a Friday night. I hope as much as you all do that we'll all enjoy a quiet weekend. We'll know before long. Now, I want the operations, material, rescue and diving, deep submergence systems, and medical officers to remain behind, and I'll wish the rest of you a good night." The usual banter that attended the

termination of staff meetings was notably absent, and
the long faces on those who filed out of the conference
room told a bitter story. Many of them knew Geoff
Richter. Even those who didn't could imagine his
likely predicament. All the submariners among them
were chastened by the thought that *"There, but for
the grace of God, go I."*

The smaller group gathered at the admiral's end of
the table. "I've asked you to remain behind because
we're likely to need a rescue plan very shortly, and
this situation hasn't been addressed by the planners—
at least, not recently. The fact is that the nearest available MOSUB is in Groton and the nearest designated
MOSUB port to the *Tulsa* is Stavanger. The delay in
getting a boat from Groton to Stavanger is unacceptable, particularly as we're looking at something like a
four-day transit from there to the DISSUB." The admiral turned to Commander Mike Selby, his staff medical officer. "How long can they be expected to last,
Mike?"

"A very difficult question, sir. There are so many
variables."

"Just give me an idea."

"Can you give me a few moments, sir? I need to
do some calculations."

"OK, I want a realistic estimate, and your best guess
as to the longest time we might have to recover anybody alive."

"Yes, sir." Selby got to his feet and left the room.
He broke into a trot and headed for his office. How
on earth was he going to answer this question? He
had only a sketchy idea of what had happened, no
idea of how many people were left alive after the sinking, how much lithium hydroxide the *Tulsa* carried or,
more importantly, where it was stowed. He needed to
know how much of the boat was flooded, what the
internal pressure was, if there was any power . . . the
list went on and on. He arrived at his desk and
scanned the bookshelf beside it for an atmosphere-

control manual. His heart missed a beat as his first pass failed to locate it. "Shit," he exclaimed, "where is the goddamned thing?" He repeated his search more slowly and finally located the volume in a blue binder that enveloped his copy. He turned to Chapter 13 and started to jot down some figures.

It was reasonable to assume that carbon dioxide would be the limiting factor—it was for most credible scenarios. How many people would there be? If the forward compartment had been flooded and only those in the after compartment were left alive we would probably be dealing with a small number, say twenty. How many canisters of lithium would there be stored there? God only knew. As a pure guess he put down thirty. He did the calculation and worked out that their stay-time for carbon dioxide would be 262 hours. Wow, he thought, that's almost eleven days. Selby worked through a series of other parameters. With reasonable guesses the oxygen stay-time would be longer and, assuming the compartment wasn't leaking and there had been no fire, there should be no problem with pressure. Radiation leak? That was a crap shoot, and, seeing as he was compiling an optimistic calculation, Selby decided to ignore that possibility for now. Where's the problem? he thought. Water shouldn't be an issue, as they could use the deionized water for the reactor. Temperature—they were going to get cold. Back aft they had no access to additional clothing and, although there was a lot of hot machinery, that would take a few days to cool down. Once it did, they were going to get cold. To make matters worse, they wouldn't have any food. What had been looking like a rather promising scenario was now not so promising. They would never survive eleven days in freezing cold without additional clothing or food.

What about the front end? He embarked on a series of calculations and eventually arrived at the two scenarios the admiral required. A realistic estimate of three days and a really optimistic one of twelve. Selby checked his watch. He would dearly have loved an opportunity to check his figures with somebody else, but it was already nearly ten and even DEVRON FIVE in San Diego would have gone home for the weekend. He decided that he'd try anyway. He spun his Rolodex in search of Lieutenant Commander Pat Kellman's home number. His luck was holding—it was there, and there was an answer. He ran the situation by his colleague. Apart from agreeing that this event was going to ruin their weekends, Pat concurred with the estimates. Feeling a little more confident, Selby returned to the conference room. "What have you got, Doc?" asked Talisker, and Selby reported the results of his calculations. "Damn! We really don't have much time at all then. Perhaps I should just fill you in on our discussion while you were away," he continued. "We've decided to activate the DSRV but really don't expect to be able to use it unless the Brits can provide a MOSUB in Stavanger in sixty hours' time. If they have a boat they can spare, it might just be possible, and I'll talk informally with Rear Admiral Patterson, the British FOSM, right away and get the ball rolling with a formal request through CNO."

"What's a FOSM?" whispered the material officer to the deep submergence officer who was sitting next to him.

"Flag Officer Submarines," he hissed curtly and returned his attention to the admiral, who had barely noticed the interruption.

"The fallback position is to use another rescue vehicle, and I'll again ask the Brits to help out informally. I've not met the Swedish admiral, so that request will have to go through channels. Any questions?"

"Yes, sir." It was the rescue and diving officer, Commander Sangster. "Can the doc tell us the basis for his estimate of three days? We don't have a hope in hell of getting them out in that time scale. I assume you mean seventy-two hours?"

"Yes—slightly less actually," replied Selby.

"But that's in just thirty-three hours' time."

"Doc?" The admiral looked at Selby.

"I've assumed that most of the men in the forward compartment survived. For argument's sake, that's roughly 115 men. I've also assumed that there will be no power to run the CO_2 scrubbers, which effectively cuts the capacity of their lithium hydroxide by about half. They may have as much as 150 canisters of that, which translates into roughly forty hours of CO_2 production. Give them another thirty hours or so to breathe the atmosphere up to 6 percent, which is about all they'll be able to tolerate before they must get out, and you get a rather depressing total of seventy hours. In fact, it's going to be worse than that. If they follow the advice in the atmosphere-control manual, they'll start escaping well before the CO_2 level reaches 6 percent."

There was a stunned silence around the table. It was the admiral who broke it. "Is there any possibility that these numbers are too pessimistic?"

"Yes, sir. There may be fewer survivors and they may generate less CO_2 than the model predicts if they really cut back on the amount of work that they do—like if they sleep the whole time. The only problem there is that most of the bunk spaces are likely to be covered in lithium hydroxide which is horribly caustic and really not the kind of stuff you would like to go to sleep on."

"But say they can sleep—might that buy them an extra day?"

"That would be pushing a realistic estimate toward an optimistic one, but I guess so."

"Then how did you come up with twelve days?" asked Commander Sangster.

"I reiterate, that is a very optimistic figure, and I based it on only fifty survivors in the forward compartment, with working hoppers, and they sleep continuously."

"What happened to the other men? These boats normally have a complement of 130 or more."

"I reckoned that whatever caused the boat to sink must have been very violent, and a lot of them were killed."

"And this is the optimistic scenario?" continued the RDO.

"From a survival perspective, yes," replied Selby.

"Wouldn't a really rosy scenario include an operational power plant?" pitched in the material officer.

"It would," replied Selby, "but that would presume that neither end of the boat was flooded. It is difficult to construct a scenario where a submarine would have sunk under such conditions."

"Then why assume that the hoppers are working when there is little chance that they will be?" The killer remark, thought Selby.

"They could jury-rig something. Anyway, I told you it was an optimistic scenario."

"It's not optimistic, it's impossible," persisted the material officer. "The only way you could get a prolonged survival is if a few men were trapped aft."

"I've discounted that—they would quickly freeze without additional clothing or food."

"We'll use Doc's figures for planning purposes, recognizing that the longer period is indeed optimistic," concluded the admiral. "I think we've covered all the bases for now. I've got some phone calls to make, and then I'll have to brief the commander in chief."

0300Z, Northwood, Middlesex, United Kingdom

Rear Admiral Patterson blinked, glanced at the dull red glow from the clock on his radio alarm, then rolled over and answered the phone. It was unusual for him to be called at home at this time of night, as his staff normally handled everything out of office hours. As he lifted his head, he regretted staying at the mess Halloween party for quite as long as he had. The beginnings of a headache greeted him, and his mouth was horribly dry. "FOSM," he rasped.

"Duty officer, sir."

"What's up, Carl?"

"COMSUBLANT wants to have a word. I thought I'd check if you were at home and it was OK for me to give him your number."

"No problem, I've known him for years."

"Thank you, sir. I expect he'll call back within a few minutes."

"Good night, Carl, and thank you." Patterson got up, donned his bathrobe, and went downstairs. There was no point in irritating his wife more than absolutely necessary. He went straight to the refrigerator and poured a glass of 7UP, took a substantial gulp, and headed for his study. No sooner had he arrived, turned on the lights, and closed the curtains, than the phone rang. "FOSM."

"Henry? It's Gerry." Patterson recognized the voice immediately. He'd gotten to know COMSUBLANT during his tour with the British Navy Staff in Washington in the early 1980s and they had become good friends. "I'm really sorry to call you at such an hour. This is a secure line, isn't it?"

"It is. What can I do for you?"

"A bunch of things will happen through the proper channels very shortly, but I wanted to get some feedback from you on a couple of matters." Talisker went on to explain the situation and outlined his request for help with the search and rescue operation.

"Strictly between you and me," started Patterson, "I can't see too many problems. HMS *Vindictive* is in Faslane. She's currently in a self-maintenance period, but can be made ready for sea very quickly. No problem with the LR5—I can get SM 514 onto that right away. I'll need to speak to my boss about a first-reaction ship. We might even be able to supply two. I can get the submarine escape and rescue advisory team activated, but I expect quite a few will need to be recalled because they will have gone home for the weekend. What's the probability that any of this will be needed?"

"Rather high, I fear, and the really bad news is that the *Tulsa* may have been down for nearly two days already."

"Shit! How come?"

"The Russians took their time letting us know. She was on a 'sneakie,' as you call them."

"Well, I can get my troops ready to roll by the time the balloon officially goes up. But I could get my ass chewed pretty hard if this turns into a busted flush, as you guys say."

"You'll survive. As I recall, it's rather well covered."

"How did we ever become friends? OK, Gerry. You'll owe me one."

"Call it pay-back time for the Falklands."

"God above. What does it take to make an American grateful?"

"Much the same as a Brit. Thanks a lot, Henry."

"Keep in touch, Gerry."

"Sure. So long now."

0330Z, Royal Hospital, Haslar, United Kingdom

Surgeon Lieutenant Commander David Sheppard completed his notes and handed the chart to the army nurse beside him. "D5 ward?"

"Yes, sir."

"Well, thanks for your help, I'm off to bed now. He should be OK," he said, casting a glance at the young man on the gurney beside him. "Hourly observations will do. I've jotted down my cell-phone number at the end of the notes just in case you need me, although the houseman should be able to take care of any problems. As carbon-monoxide poisonings go, he got off pretty lightly. I'll visit him tomorrow morning and see if I can interest the shrinks in yet another suicidal teenager."

"Good night, sir."

"Good night." With that, David Sheppard left the hyperbaric unit and jumped into his car. He didn't really need to drive to the hospital. He only lived two miles from Haslar. He used the car on these occasions because he loved it and he hated cycling in the rain. Even the threat of rain was a sufficient stimulus for him to unlock the garage and jump into his Porsche. He turned the key in the ignition and rejoiced as the 2.5-liter, six-cylinder engine spun effortlessly to 3000 rpms and started to howl. Better keep the noise down a bit, he thought. He'd already been on the end of a verbal rebuke from the master-at-arms and received a snotty letter from the medical officer in command complaining about the way he drove on hospital grounds. One more error and he would lose his car pass, and that would force him to cycle to the hyper-baric unit. The hospital had gone to buggery since it had been taken over by the United Nations, he thought—-an irreverent reference to the triservice manning of what had been a naval hospital until 1996. Small wonder, he thought, it had been decided that it should close.

Sheppard left the main gate, turned left, and floored the pedal. The silver Boxster leapt out of the starting blocks and sprinted to seventy miles per hour before he stamped on the brakes for a sharp left at the "T" junction at the end of the road. He'd once managed to reach almost eighty along the quarter-mile straight but the shuddering protest from the car's ABS when he'd tried to slow down for the corner had unnerved him a little, and he was not prepared to push it that hard again. He took the bend at thirty miles per hour with the rear tires chirruping and the tail wagging like a happy puppy's. He selected third gear, floored the gas pedal again, and scorched down Fort Road. By God, he loved this car. In no time he was back up to sixty and flashed past the Institute of Naval Medicine on his right, where he worked for most of the week, and the old physiology labs on his left. He would have gone quicker but a thirty-mile-per-hour limit was posted, and the road was a little narrow and twisted.

At the traffic circle he flicked down to second gear and treated it as a chicane, wiggling past it and carrying on down another brief straight before slowing for a sharp right turn. It was only at this time of night that he could really drive his car the way it was meant to be driven, unless he got right out into the countryside. The tires screeched in protest as he executed a well-controlled four-wheel drift through the corner and then anchored out for the next turn to the right. Better take it easy now, Sheppard thought. I don't want too many complaints from the neighbors. And there would be hell to pay if he woke the wife.

He pulled up in front of his terraced house, a monstrosity of ill-considered design dating back to the 1960s. Only the Ministry of Defense or an utterly corrupt town hall could possibly have commissioned such an ugly and poorly constructed estate. He killed the engine and decided to leave the car outside as the clear, starry sky no longer threatened rain. No sooner had he closed the front door and slipped off his shoes to avoid making too much noise, than he was startled by the shrill twittering of his cell phone. "Oh fuck it!" he muttered under his breath as he fished around in his jacket pocket for the infernal machine that seemed to run his life when he was on call. "Duty diving medical officer," he said in a loud whisper as he went into the kitchen.

"David?"

" 'Tis I, who's this?"

"Richard Tremble from the Tank."

"Hi, Richard, what the fuck do you want? Have you seen the time? I thought submarine escape trainers went home at three, were pissed by nine, and tucked up in bed by ten o'clock."

"Very funny. This is a heads-up. FOSM's called a SUBLOOK."

"Shit, one of ours?"

"No, it's a Yank."

"Oh Lord, what happened?"

"The details are sketchy, but it sounds like a 688 might have gone down in the North Sea. The crabs have scrambled a couple of Nimrods to go and find it, and the Yanks and Norwegians are looking as well." Despite being so tired, David couldn't help smiling at Richard's use of the term "crabs." With interservice rivalry being what it was, Richard, like so many of his colleagues, couldn't resist referring to RAF personnel as "crabs" and soldiers as "pongos." He had no idea how either name originated or how the other services referred to sailors. He focused once again on the monologue he was receiving from Tremble. . . . "The SMERAT have been told to stand by, and we are at one hour's notice. I just thought you might like to know, seeing as how you docs are meant to play in this game."

"Do you want us to come in now?"

"No, stay where you are, you guys need your beauty sleep. I'll give you another call if we have to move out."

"OK, thanks for the call, Richard. And by the way, I'm about to go to bed now. I've been up all bloody night with a patient. One of these days even submarine escape trainers might have to work for a living. Call me when you need us."

Sleep, eh? Sheppard thought to himself, Wouldn't I be the lucky bastard? He wondered what to do. It would take him about half an hour to call his colleagues in. Thankfully, they all lived nearby so they could be at the submarine escape training tank at Fort Blockhouse within an hour. He'd let them sleep. If this boat really had gone down, sleep would become a precious commodity. He decided not to go upstairs to bed but get some rest on the settee in the lounge instead. But before he could sleep he had some studying to do. He went into his little office and dug around in the desk before he pulled out a dog-eared, pale-covered document from the drawer. He sat down and started to read.

The British Royal Navy maintains a Submarine Escape and Rescue Advisory Team, known as SMERAT. It consists of a group of twelve submariners who are expert in submarine escape and rescue, and a small contingent of doctors and other medical staff from the Institute of Naval Medicine and Fort Blockhouse, who are trained in the esoteric area of diving and submarine medicine. In the event of a submarine sinking, the SMERAT takes the quickest available route to the port where a warship that has been designated as the first-reaction vessel is docked. She takes on a load of special stores, including a compression chamber, and heads out to the site of the sinking at her best speed. Another group called the Submarine Parachute Assistance Group, or SPAG, are trained parachutists and can be dropped over a sunken submarine to assist any survivors who escape to the surface. To help them do this, they are equipped with twenty-five-man life rafts, some medical supplies, and two inflatable boats with outboard motors.

David had been at the INM for nearly two years, but had not been involved in the last exercise where this procedure (known as SMASHEX) is practiced because he had been in hospital with appendicitis. He read through the instructions, but it was all rather above his head. His boss, Surgeon Commander Eric Freeman, was going to have to carry the weight on this one. David yawned, glanced at his watch, wondered once more whether he should give him a call, and decided against it. He was a cantankerous bastard at the best of times and 4 A.M. on Saturday morning was not the best of times. He would have a nap instead. He turned off the light, crept upstairs to the lounge, and collapsed on the settee. He was asleep immediately.

0530A, USS *Tulsa*

Richter woke with a start because he was being shaken violently. His head felt thick and ached, made worse each time his shoulder was given a firm jolt by his assailant. It took a couple of seconds before he was fully conscious. ". . . Sir. Please wake up and listen." It was dark, but he recognized Enzo's voice.

"OK, Enzo, enough of that. What's up?" There was no need for a reply because an explosion was clearly audible. An initial muffled report was followed by a series of diminishing echoes as the sound waves bounced between the water's surface and the rocky seafloor. What a blessed relief, thought Richter. It could mean only one thing. They'd been found, and whoever had found them was signaling the fact with explosive charges. Were they being released by an aircraft or a ship? he wondered. "How many have there been?"

"That's number seven, sir." They both waited expectantly for a couple of minutes, but no more came.

"That must be it. Seven charges means 'we are looking for you.' We should respond. What did they sound like, Enzo? Were they all the same?"

"No, sir. The first one was quite faint—actually I wasn't sure what it was until the second and third ones. They were louder, so I came to wake you so you could listen."

"If they were released from a ship, they would have sounded just about the same. I think an aircraft must have released them as it overflew us. I expect it'll turn around and fly back. If it is an aircraft, I expect it's a P3 or a Nimrod, and it will have dropped a sonobuoy or two along the way. They should be able to pick up our distress pinger, but we'll make life easy for them. Send up another SLOT buoy." He glanced automatically at the electric clock by his bunk, but it wasn't working. "What's the time?"

"Five-thirty, sir."

"Hmmm. It'll be dark. I don't suppose a smoke would be seen from an aircraft. Just send up the SLOT buoy. They should be able to get a good fix on that."

"Aye, aye, sir, I'll see to it right away." Enzo made for the door and paused before leaving. "I'm sorry about waking you like that, sir, but I thought you'd want to hear the charges."

"I did. Thank you." As Enzo closed the door behind him Richter realized that he felt nauseated to the point that he knew he was about to vomit. His head was still throbbing and, as usual, he felt dizzy as he climbed off his bunk and made his way to the head between his and the XO's stateroom. He sank to his knees and heaved repeatedly into the bowl, but little came up. He staggered to his feet, energized a battle lantern, and splashed some cold water over his face. He felt a little better. It must have been something I ate, he thought, and immediately became concerned that his men might be similarly afflicted. He shivered, returned to his bunk, and covered himself once again with the mountain of blankets that was piled on top of it. It had become very cold during the night, and bouts of shivering had woken him repeatedly. Despite feeling unwell, he was now a lot happier than he had been ever since the sinking. It would be six days, at most, before they would be out of here. The omens from the atmosphere control were encouraging—there was even a remote possibility that they might survive that long in the boat, although it would be a close shave.

Richter started to think beyond the immediate crisis that had consumed him for the past three days. Life was never going to be the same because of the promise he had made to John. He wanted to kick himself for having made the commitment, but couldn't. He'd really had no choice but to agree to look after Marie and the two boys, Jamie and Geoff. Of course, he was the only witness to that undertaking and could recant. Marie would be none the wiser, nor would anyone else be—except himself. But could he live with that? Did he even want to find out if he could? No, of course not. There was a practical question as well. How was he going to look after a family? What did it mean? Was "looking after" a financial thing or was it rather more? He was already young Geoffrey's godfather with its quasi-moral responsibilities. What more was going to be asked of him? The more he thought about it, the more difficult the question became. The frustrating part was that it didn't really matter how he resolved the matter in his own mind. He was going to have to discuss it with Marie, and she would be the final arbiter.

There was a knock at the door. "Come in." It was Enzo again.

"I've been taking a look at the XO and couldn't help overhearing you in the head, sir. Are you alright?"

"Sure, Enzo. I was probably just reacting to Tim Gallagher's gastronomic horror of last night. How could anybody combine New England clam chowder with canned corn and baked beans? That it was stone-cold didn't improve it, and it was only a liberal splash of Tabasco sauce that allowed me to attempt it at all. I don't suppose I'm the only one with problems this morning."

"I'm not aware of anybody else being sick, sir."

"Well, I must just have a delicate stomach. How's the XO?"

"He's awake, sir. His fever's down a bit, but I don't like the sound of his chest. I've been trying to listen to it with these things," he replied, brandishing a stethoscope. "Not knowing what I'm listening for makes it rather difficult to say what's wrong, but the XO seemed impressed that I should even try."

"So am I."

Enzo decided to change the subject. "It's great news that we've been found. The mood has lightened up down below. A clear majority think we're going to survive now."

"I'm glad to hear it, although don't build their hopes up too high. There are too many unforeseen things that could go wrong before we get out of here. Is Harvey around?"

"Yes, sir, I believe he's on his way up to see you, but he wanted to be sure you were awake."

"OK. Well, tell him I am. Has Sparks fixed the hot plate? I really can't face another meal like last night's."

"Yes, sir. He had to run a new line from the forward DC panel and hook it up to a rheostat, but we have one working hot plate, and the coffee is on."

"That, Enzo, is music to my ears."

0200R, Norfolk, Virginia

Admiral Talisker had been in bed for only an hour when he was awoken by the phone. Instantly alert, he grabbed the receiver. "Talisker."

"CDO, sir. A P3 out of Keflavik has picked up a BNQ-13 at the position provided by the Russians but can't confirm it's the *Tulsa* by underwater telephone."

"Any more details available?"

"Yes, sir. They responded to the charges the P3 dropped by launching a SLOT buoy."

"Well, that can't have come from anyone else. Go to SUBSUNK right away. I'm coming in."

0715Z, Fort Blockhouse, Gosport, United Kingdom

Richard Tremble's eyes lit up as he received the news from FOSM's HQ. At long last there was a real live SUBSUNK. After all the years of training, all the battles he'd fought to keep his little unit alive despite tremendous pressure to close them down, they were needed at last. Right now the endless justification of their existence to bean counters, skeptical submariners and medics alike, all seemed worthwhile. "Jock!"

"Yes, sir?" replied Warrant Officer Sharples.

"Get the troops in, we're going to rescue some submariners."

"Shall I wake up the doctors?"

"No. I'll do that, you get the lads in." Tremble left the recreation room and took the elevator to his office. There was an unmistakable spring in his step. He'd rarely felt such excitement before. As he sat at his desk, with its panoramic view over a town that was just waking to a new day, he punched a number into the phone and waited for a reply. "Answer the bloody phone, David," he muttered under his breath as he waited for the DDMO to reply.

David Sheppard awoke with a start. It took a moment for him to orient himself. He was on the settee, it was light, and the irritating twittering of the cell phone reminded him that he was on call. He groped for it, swinging his legs round and sitting up.

"Duty diving medical officer."

"Good morning, David, it's Richard."

"What could possibly be good about it?" Sheppard growled.

"It's official—we're off to find some submariners."

"Oh God, that's all I need." Sheppard rubbed his bleary eyes. "What's the game plan?"

"I'll sort out the travel as soon as I'm told which ship we'll be joining and where. Can you get your colleagues into the SETT? I expect I'll have it fixed by the time you arrive."

"Sure. See you shortly." David looked up at the clock on the mantel and realized that he'd had barely three hours' sleep. Seeing as it was Saturday, it was even a bit early to make his wife a cup of tea. He would, however, make himself some strong coffee. The only bright spot was that he had to give his boss a wake-up call. Freeman was not going to enjoy that.

"Good morning, gentlemen." Tremble looked around the crowded classroom located on the ground floor of the tower that housed the escape training tank. All but three of the SMERAT were present. "The situation is that an American submarine has

sunk north of Norway, to the west of Bear Island.
The early reports that she was in the North Sea were
incorrect, although I expect the crabs are still looking
there." There was a titter of laughter. "She's a 688
class hunter-killer, the USS *Tulsa*." Tremble checked
his watch. "The information I have is that she sank at
1300 Zulu on Thursday, which is just short of three
days ago. If it was one of ours, we could be confident
that any survivors would be in good shape. Seeing as
it is a Yank, I can only guess at the situation on board,
but I wouldn't be surprised if they are wandering
around up to their ankles in lithium hydroxide, very
thirsty, cold, and hungry. Isn't that right, Lieutenant
Commander Stemple?" He addressed the only American in the audience, a diving medical officer who was
on exchange with the Royal Navy. Although ostensi-
bly submarine qualified, he had not served in an
American boat and only spent his limited time at sea
in British submarines during his tour in the UK.

"I guess so," he replied.

"Anyway, C in C Fleet has designated HMS
Wellington, a Type 23, as the first-reaction vessel.
She's alongside in Faslane and the SMERAT will be
leaving very shortly to join her. A Sea King will pick
us up from here and take us to Lyneham where, a
Hercules will take us on to Glasgow. The ship's helicopter will then come and pick us up from the airport.
The SPAG will come with us as far as Lyneham, then
they'll take another plane to Hammerfest in Norway.
You're going to be guests of the Vikings. Any
questions?"

"Where's the search and rescue being coordinated
from?" The question came from Surgeon Commander
Freeman.

"Interesting question, sir. The short answer is, I've
got no idea. But it seems that the Americans and Norwegians are all involved as well. If common sense pre-
vails, it should be directed from COMJTFNON HQ,
a NATO headquarters in Bodø, northern Norway."

"The reason I ask is that there needs to be a medical specialist there to advise the command. Has this been dealt with?"

"I can't tell you, sir."

"OK, leave it with me. I'll get onto FOSM and see what's happening."

"Do we know the depth of the boat, or how many survivors there are, whether there's flooding . . . ?" David Sheppard was groping for more ideas. "I mean, do we have any idea what's happening in the boat?"

" 'Fraid not. I expect we'll find out once we reach the *Wellington*." There was a pause before the next question.

"Sir, is beer really £3 a bottle in Norway?" Leading Seaman Percival's quip was accompanied by another round of laughter. Being a member of SPAG, he was contemplating how he was going to spend the long nights in Hammerfest.

Tremble didn't dignify the comment with a response. "Well, if that's all, we'd better get out to the field. The chopper should be here any minute."

"Right. I want all the medical personnel to stay here. I have one or two more things to discuss," announced Freeman. David Sheppard began to wonder what the mighty Freeman was going to contribute. It was pretty obvious that he didn't want to join in the action. All he wanted was to have his men fly off to Norway while he played the expert in front of the nearest flag officer he could find with time to listen. He'd seen it all too often before. In fact, Freeman really did know a fair bit about submarine rescue, and his knowledge would have the greatest practical impact in the *Wellington*. A group of seven doctors and five medical assistants encircled the surgeon commander. "We're going to need as many of you as possible for this operation; that includes you, David. Give the duty to Michael. As a civvy he'll stay and cover the hyperbaric unit. Peter, what'll happen to the sick bay here?" he asked, looking at Surgeon Lieutenant

Commander Sweeny, the Principal Medical Officer of Fort Blockhouse.

"Simple. I'll close it. If anybody needs medical care, they can go to *Collingwood* or *Sultan*. I'll get the duty officer to sort it out."

"Great. Do we have everything we need? Books, signal pads, cell phone?" He looked around the group, who were all nodding. "Are we taking any medical gear with us?" Freeman's mouth was in auto. He regretted the comment immediately.

"Shouldn't be any need to," replied Sweeny. "*Wellington* will have the first-reaction stores on board—there are several tons of them." David wanted to laugh but restrained himself. Like Sweeny, he had always believed that he was a doctor first and a naval officer second. He also considered that his colleagues should feel the same way. His problem with Freeman was that though the man wore the red, distinguishing cloth between his gold stripes to indicate that he was a doctor, he did not display any of the compassionate qualities one normally associated with a physician. He was a bombastic, intolerant prig with no reason to sport the arrogance he so frequently displayed. In other words, Freeman was the ideal target for barbed comments and both he and Peter Sweeny derived great pleasure from aiming them at him at every opportunity.

"Who's got the cell phone?" inquired Freeman.

"Here, sir," responded Petty Officer Blackman.

"Get FOSM for me please, I want to speak to the duty officer." But the call was never made as the sound of a large helicopter setting down on Dolphin Field drowned out the interchange. It was time to leave.

0600R, The Pentagon, Arlington, Virginia

Under the bright television lights that illuminated the pressroom, the assistant secretary of defense, public affairs received the signal that the feeds for all the major networks were now live. He cleared his throat: "Good morning, ladies and gentlemen. I have a statement to make, and then I'll take a few questions. At two o'clock this morning, I was notified that an American submarine of the Los Angeles class, the USS *Tulsa*, was involved in an unfortunate accident. . . ." It took him just two minutes to complete the statement, and then the questions began:

"How many people are on board?"

"The boat normally carries a crew of 130. I don't know how many were injured or killed in the sinking, as we have yet to make contact with the survivors. Once I get further details, you will be informed just as soon as the families concerned have been contacted."

"So, Mr. Secretary, there are survivors on board?"

"Yes, Sam, we know that there are survivors on board, but we don't yet know how many." He pointed at another reporter.

"Mr. Secretary, when did the submarine sink?"

"We're not certain, but the indications are that she sank three days ago."

"How long can the survivors remain alive?"

"Why has it taken three days for the sinking to be acknowledged?"

"How do you know if anyone is alive on board?" The questions came thick and fast. Many were ducked, and only the most simple were responded to accurately.

0615R, Groton, Connecticut

Marie Dowling was used to being woken by the boys or the radio alarm, but not by the telephone— at least, not when John was at sea. She rolled over and picked up the receiver. "Hello?"

"Marie, it's Jean." Jean Houghton was a fellow member of the spouses association, married to a colleague of John's who was currently in a shore-based job with Submarine Group 2. "Have you seen the news?"

"No, you've just woken me up."

"Turn it on. The *Tulsa* has some problems."

"What do you mean, problems?" Marie reached for the remote and a small Panasonic on top of the chest of drawers at the end of her bed blinked into life. She selected CNN, but it could have been any of the networks. The story was the same. The *Tulsa* had sunk, but there were survivors in the boat. She didn't quite know whether to cry or rejoice. "Jean, what's going on?" Jean summarized what she'd seen.

"Do you want me to come round? You know I'd be pleased to be with you." Marie was transfixed by the screen.

"No. . . . I've got to get the boys ready for school." Realizing it was Saturday, she changed her mind. "Yes. Yes please, Jean. Give me half an hour." Marie replaced the receiver, not taking her eyes off the television. The format of the news report was familiar enough. She'd seen it before with the Challenger, Lockerbie, and TWA 800 disasters and the deaths of Princess Diana and JFK Jr., to mention just a few examples. It was news without content. The anchor introduced video clips of submarines, then a retired admiral sitting next to him tried to explain how a submarine could sink and how the survivors could remain alive. Then there was a chart of northern Norway showing where the wreck was thought to be. A meteorologist was next up with a weather forecast for the Barents Sea, then it was back to the admiral who had just acquired a model of a submarine. This he was repeatedly diving and surfacing in a glass-sided water tank. Then it was:

"We'll be right back after this." Cut to a sincere but healthy-looking woman of indeterminate age:

"Do you have a problem with dryness?" That was Marie's cue to get out of bed. She had no need for vaginal lubricants this morning and would take a quick

shower before the "news" returned. The shower woke
her up but did nothing to clear her mind. She was well
aware of John's fatalistic approach to the possibility of
a submarine sinking. They had discussed it in the early
years of their relationship, but not since then. Was his
fatalism misplaced? There were survivors. . . . Would
he be among them? How could she find out? Who
would know? If anyone should, it would be the squadron, she reasoned. She toweled off, returned to the
phone, scanned the short list of numbers that John
kept on the nightstand, and dialed.

1215A, USS *Tulsa*

Richter had decided to overrule his throbbing head,
which kept pleading for him to take a nap, and go
down to the crew's mess to see what was going on. It
was a tougher mission than he had intended. As he
left his stateroom and made his way down to the middle level he realized that he was much more unsteady
on his feet than the day before, and his double vision
was worse than ever. As he entered the crew's mess
he saw someone bent over the hopper, but was unsure
who it was. "Problems?" inquired Richter.

"Oh, hello, sir. I'm in the impossible position of
trying to make a silk purse out of a sow's ear. This
pile of shit should have been condemned to history in
the sixties. I'm not sure that it should ever have been
accepted into service—it was designed by a fucking
moron." He paused for a moment. "Sorry, sir, excuse
the language."

"Do you need some more light? It's pretty dark
in here."

"The light's OK, sir. It's this damned thing that's
the problem," he said, poking a screwdriver at the
large gray cylinder in front of him.

"Petty Officer . . . umm . . ."

"Cotton, sir."

"Of course." Richter quickly remembered his nickname and continued: "Sorry, Sparks, I'm not feeling quite myself today." Richter was angry with himself. He should have recognized Sparks's voice, even if he couldn't see that well. Then again, Sparks very rarely resorted to foul language, so maybe his lapse was forgivable.

"You see this?" Sparks pointed to the electric motor and squirrel-cage fan beneath it. Richter mumbled in the affirmative. "That, sir, is a quarter-horsepower motor. If it were connected to a modern blower, it should be able to drive three or four times the amount of air through this contraption than it actually does. Why can't it? I'll tell you. . . . crap design."

"I thought the hopper had an AC motor that was useless in this situation anyway."

"It has. Unfortunately, it and this useless, fucking blower are stuck in the middle of the air channel I'm trying to establish with the battery-well fan. So I've decided to remove them. It'll greatly improve the efficiency of the unit."

"Keep up the good work, Sparks, and try to keep your cool." Richter patted him on the shoulder. "Remember, this thing will only have to work for another week or so at the most. So don't lose too much sleep over it." He turned to move away and bumped into a table with a pile of canisters on top of it. Two of them fell to the ground and started to roll across the deck.

"Don't worry about those, sir. They've been used," said Harvey Schwartz, who had suddenly materialized at his side. "Do you have a moment, sir?"

"Sure."

"I've been going over the atmosphere-control data, and the news couldn't be better. I figure the crew's breathing almost half as much oxygen and producing about half as much carbon dioxide as we initially calculated. This means we might be able to stay in the boat until Thursday."

"That's great news." Richter wobbled on his feet,

and Schwartz reached up and grabbed him by the upper arm.

"Sir, are you sure you are alright?"

"No, I'm not. . . ." Richter wanted to use a name. He was pretty sure it was Harvey, but he hesitated.

"What's the problem, sir?" Yes, it was definitely Harvey.

"I'm sorry, Harvey, I can't see too well." He screwed his hands into his eyes and blinked a couple of times. "That's a bit better," he announced. "I think I'd better be getting back to my stateroom."

"Sure, let me give you a hand."

"Thanks, Harvey. I'm sure all I need is a rest."

In the chiefs' mess, a game of cards was about to resume. It had started the night before and had kept going until the early hours. It had started because the cold and boredom had driven Bill Hicks and Larry Czapek out of their bunks, and they'd been joined by Carl Lehner and Mitch Santana. An earlier game of spades had been abandoned in favor of hearts once they had decided to liven things up and play for money. "Where's Mitch?" asked Chief Lehner.

"I wouldn't be surprised if he's still racked out," replied Bill Hicks. "How much did he lose last night?"

"Couple of hundred," mumbled Chief Czapek. "Let's get on with it."

"We need a fourth player," responded Hicks, as the door opened and the missing chief made his way to the table.

"Sorry I'm late. The head's not flushing properly."

"The dealer's dealing," announced Lehner as he finished shuffling the pack. "Hell, these cards are falling apart, look at them." They all stared at the cards. The damp had caused them to delaminate and the edges and corners were splayed open and frayed. "Has anybody got some new ones?"

"Yep, I've got some that claim to be plastic. I'll be back with them in a moment." Santana got up and left the room, returning immediately.

Lehner finished shuffling the new deck and dealt.

"How 'bout we up the stakes to five bucks a point?" he suggested.

"Fine by me," replied Hicks. "Larry?"

"Sure." Everybody turned and looked at Santana.

"My luck's bound to change sooner or later. . . ." He paused. "Oh fuck it, what do I need money for anyway, right?"

"It would seem the penny has dropped." Hicks grinned. "Well done, my friend, you've seen the light. There's no need for money in the next world, as the Good Lord will provide."

"Leave God out of this if you don't mind," snapped Lehner. "We're passing to the left. Have fun with these, Larry," he said, smiling as he slid three cards, facedown, to his left.

"Hmmm," responded Czapek as he and the others picked up and looked at their new cards. Chief Czapek was a master at "shooting the moon" in which—unlike normal play, when you avoid winning tricks that contain a heart or the queen of spades—you try to win them all. He studied his hand. He had kept the ace and king of spades rather than pass them on, but was still missing the queen. More importantly though, he didn't have the king of hearts or a winner in diamonds. Was it worth the risk? The downside of missing even a single heart would be substantial—he would be penalized one point for each heart and thirteen for the queen of spades. On the other hand, if he succeeded, each of his opponents would get twenty-six points while his score would be zero. That was a juicy prospect. He decided to play out the early tricks before making up his mind how to play the rest of the hand.

1200Z, Glasgow, Scotland

The journey in the Hercules was both uncomfortable and deafening. The C130 was never designed as a luxury mode of transport, and the combination of vibration and the cacophonous din that the four turboprop engines generated frustrated any attempts at communication. Freeman considered the idea of calling FOSM from the flight deck but decided to wait until their arrival in Scotland.

As the SMERAT filed out of the rear of the aircraft, they were greeted by characteristic Glaswegian weather. The pelting rain was being driven almost horizontally across the taxiway by a twenty-five-knot wind from the west. Freeman immediately reached for the cell phone but, as he did so, he noticed that the *Wellington*'s Merlin was waiting on the tarmac right beside the Hercules and was ready to take off. There was only time to climb into an immersion suit and don a "bone dome," as the flying helmets were affectionately termed, and then board the aircraft. His chance of making an impact on the medical management of the operation having disappeared, presumably in favor of a Norwegian or even an American, Freeman was resigned to being stuck with the "grunts." It irked him because opportunities to impress senior officers were few and far between in the somewhat sleepy hollow of INM. With promotion prospects severely reduced from what they had been before the last round of manpower cuts, it was an event like this that could really make a difference. Bodø was a NATO HQ to boot. He thrust the cell phone deep into a pocket and reluctantly took his seat in the helicopter. No sooner was he aboard than it lifted off and climbed into the leaden sky.

Twenty minutes later they were out over the western end of the Firth of Clyde, approaching the Isle of Arran. Beneath the helicopter, among the whitecaps of breaking waves, Freeman could just discern the outline of a warship at the head of a long, white wake that scarred the gray water. As the helicopter descended, the ship slowed and altered course into the wind. Within moments they had landed on the pitching flight deck and were headed to the cavernous hangar to remove their immersion suits. Freeman

beckoned to Tremble and, having identified themselves to the master-at-arms, they headed off to the
bridge to see the captain. Experience with previous
SMASHEXs had dulled Eric's enthusiasm for introducing himself to his host. All too often the visitors
were seen as an unnecessary intrusion. Without the
medical input, a SMASHEX was a fairly basic exercise. On this occasion, since it was the real thing, perhaps his reception would be a little warmer.

Commander Muggeridge could not have been more
welcoming. In essence he was prepared to offer every
facility within his ship to prosecute the mission. His
orders were to make his best speed for the datum
which, in the prevailing conditions, would mean no
more than twenty-five knots and maybe somewhat
less. On that basis it was going to take until midnight
on Monday to get there—at the earliest. That should
allow plenty of time to unpack and organize the first-
reaction stores and undertake any training of his men
and the ship's company that might be needed. The
good news was that they had the squadron medical
officer on board, plus two more from Faslane. In addition, a medical services officer, trained in administra-
tion, and four more medical assistants were also on
board. These were manpower riches beyond Freeman's wildest dreams. However, if the conditions in
the *Tulsa* deteriorated to the point where they had to
initiate an escape, he would need every one of them.
Tremble requested an opportunity to brief the ship's
company, and it was agreed that this would take place
in the junior rates' dining hall at 1600Z, by which time
the picture of the conditions in the DISSUB might be
somewhat clearer. The bad news was that there was
little spare accommodation on board. Sufficient room
had been made for Freeman and Tremble to share a
cabin in the wardroom flat, but most of the remainder
of SMERAT would have to bunk down in the hangar.

Once out of the lee of the Isle of Arran, the sea
became considerably more choppy and, with the *Wel-*

lington charging through it at speed, the ride became very uncomfortable indeed. Despite his best intentions to get the escape gear in the hangar sorted out, Freeman began to feel distinctly unwell from seasickness and took to his bunk.

0730R, Groton, Connecticut

After a brief period of confused emotions, Marie had become really worried. She'd received no positive news from the squadron. Although they had called her with an update on the situation, all they could provide was a repetition of what she'd seen on TV. Whenever she had tried to call them for more details, all she ever got was a busy tone. She had flicked repeatedly through every television channel in an attempt to find more information and was frustrated by her lack of success. She'd done the same with the radio. She was tempted to give up, but couldn't. The media had their hooks into her. . . . And what about the kids? Aged just six and four, what would Jamie and Geoff make of this? They had a TV in their room, what would they be watching? She switched over to the Cartoon Network and was relieved to see that it was still delivering its usual fare. If Jamie had any choice in the matter, and he usually did, that's what they would be watching. She thought for a moment. What if they weren't? There were normally cartoon shows on most of the networks at this time of day, but today was different. What on earth were they watching? She got dressed rapidly and went into the boys' room demanding, to their delight, that they could watch cartoons but nothing else.

1400A, USS *Tulsa*

Richter was already feeling exhausted despite having been awake for only six hours. He lay on his bunk and contemplated what Gallagher had passed off as breakfast that morning. Despite it being the first hot meal he'd been presented with in three days, Richter had left most of it in the bowl. Not because the cream of tomato soup was bad—although an unorthodox recipe for the start of the day—it had been something of a triumph by recent culinary standards. The problem was that he hadn't felt particularly hungry. And the bitter flavor of bile that he could sense at the back of his throat was a warning that he would surely throw up again soon. He took a sip of water, but it did nothing to freshen his palate. He was concerned that his headache was, if anything, worse than before, and his double vision was now seemingly permanent. It prevented him from reading, and he still cringed with embarrassment at failing to recognize Sparks. He didn't want his men to see him in this state again.

Since returning to his stateroom he'd not been bored. He had received two visitors. Enzo had reported on the condition of the two head-injury cases, but it was a particularly unencouraging report. The COB had brought even less joyous news. The sanitary tanks were now full and, because there was no power to pump out their contents, new arrangements had to be made for the disposal of human waste. Steadman had presented the captain with a black, plastic trash bag for solid waste. The liquid variety was to be discharged into the bilges. Richter had yet to test the practicality of either technique. Given his difficulty with walking, the latter task sounded like a virtual impossibility.

What had been playing on his mind, and was surely behind his worsening headache, was the prospect, however remote, of getting together with Marie again. The brutal truth was that he didn't think a long-term relationship was possible. He'd never managed to live with anyone continuously for more than a year without a crisis. Years ago he had reached the conclusion that men and women were not designed to live with one another. Or at least, he had yet to find a woman who could put up with him. He had convinced himself that the only reason cohabitation was ever attempted was to satiate an irritating yet powerful instinct to reproduce—one which still afflicted him occasionally, not least because of the incessant nagging from his father. It was an attitude with which he had little sympathy. It was none of his father's business and, in any case, weren't there enough Richters in the phone book already? Family life, he considered, was only perpetuated to raise the offspring of a union, and, with the stresses of modern life, only a minority of his acquaintances could manage even that. On the other hand, he was not entirely immune to social pressure to find a wife—or at least a steady girlfriend. He found it incomprehensible that, despite the wreckage of broken marriages that littered the society he kept, he was expected to travel the same disastrous route. The pressure was very subtle, but undeniable. The confounding factor was that, more often than not, he had really enjoyed the companionship of his girlfriends before things had inevitably turned sour.

As he thought about it he realized that, in the past, he had been content neither with a woman in his life nor without one. He had chosen the latter option for the past few years for the pragmatic reason that it was emotionally less traumatic than repeatedly going through the cycle of courtship, cohabitation, conflict, and separation. It was also a lot less expensive. He began to wonder why he had been such a failure at maintaining relationships. There was no obvious pattern to the ones he could remember. The frequent separations caused by his being at sea had served as a catalyst for many of the breakups, but that hadn't really been the root cause. One of his big problems had been the demands that girlfriends made on his time. He had little enough of it to himself and objected to its theft for utterly frivolous pastimes such as shopping. Conversation was another problem. All the women he'd known loved to talk. It didn't appear to matter what the subject matter was, and more often than not there was no obvious point to the dialogue at all. It was apparently the process that mattered. He, on the other hand, only said anything if it needed to be said and rapidly grew weary of pointless inter-course. That attitude had sparked more than its fair share of arguments. So there it was. If his relationship with Marie was ever to develop beyond the current one of family friend, he would have to loosen up and devote time to it. That would be easier said than done. Richter realized that his head was about to explode, and it was time to see if two aspirin and some sleep might ameliorate it. He swallowed the former, switched off his battle lantern, rolled onto his stomach, and closed his eyes.

0800R, Atlantic Fleet HQ, Norfolk, Virginia

Talisker looked around the table. There were a lot of tired men in the room and he counted himself among them. The meeting had already lasted an hour. He looked at Commander Sangster and then at the deep submergence systems officer. "So what you're telling me is that the DSRV is going to take another three days just to get as far as Stavanger?" They glanced at each other and returned their gaze to the admiral.

"Yes, sir." The exasperation that COMSUBLANT felt showed in his face. When it had been finalized some years earlier, everybody had accepted that the decision to have only one DSRV operational after the *Avalon* was decommissioned had a measure of risk attached to it. That there had been no fatal submarine accidents for over thirty years had lured too many into the trap of believing that there would be no more in the future. He forced himself to focus on the matter at hand—there would be time for recrimination later.

"And the transit from Stavanger will take at least another, what, four days?"

"Nearer to five, sir."

"That's not good enough. Are you sure that Hammerfest isn't an option?"

"Yes, sir. The runway there is too short for a C5, and the harbor has no Z berth for nuclear-powered vessels."

"OK, Ops, what about the Brits and the Swedes?"

"Better news from the British, sir. The LR5 is operational and will be loaded onto one of their SAL class ships in Aberdeen within the hour. I'm told it will depart immediately for the datum. Those ships have a top speed of fifteen knots, and she should arrive by early morning, local, on Wednesday the third. Weather permitting, of course. Unfortunately, the Swedish rescue vehicle is in refit and is not available. You're aware, sir, that the Russians have offered to assist?"

"Yes, but what can they provide? I seem to recall that their DSRV system hasn't been supported by an operational MOSUB for many months."

"Murmansk. If we could load the DSRV onto a MOSUB in Murmansk, we could cut the surface transit time down to just under forty hours and save three days." The admiral's eyebrows lifted, and he almost smiled.

"Right, that looks like the best shot we've got. Ops, you'd better get on to San Diego and advise them that there may be a change of plan. I'll speak to CNO and get a request for the use of Murmansk rolling. We've agreed that the only available MOSUB will be a British Vanguard class boat. I'd better sound out FOSM and see if he'd be willing to use Murmansk. There'll be some sucking on teeth and hand-wringing, I expect, but given the circumstances, I can't imagine they'll refuse."

The admiral turned to his medical officer. "Doc, can you give us any idea what the conditions in the boat will be like right now?" Selby looked somewhat nonplussed. He'd not been expecting this.

"All I can offer, sir, is an educated guess."

"Sure. None of us has ever been in this situation before, we can only guess."

"Well, I think I've covered the atmosphere-control problem as far as I can. I expect the carbon-dioxide level is already rising uncontrollably. At about 4 percent they'll start to feel nauseated and short of breath. At 5 percent they'll likely start feeling dizzy, they'll have tremors, and be capable of almost no work. At 6 percent, well, they should be out of there by then. Their eyes'll be stinging, they'll have quite severe air hunger even lying down. . . . Do I need to go on?"

"No, Doc, I think we've got the picture. Can you tell us any more?" Selby thought for a few moments before replying.

"It'll be darned cold in the boat, almost icy. As the atmosphere cools, the air will contain less water vapor and, like warm, moist air that's forced to rise over a mountain range, the water will condense out."

"You mean like clouds?" asked the material officer.

"Exactly. I'm not sure if the atmosphere will actually become hazy, but even if it does, they won't have much light to judge it by. The point is, though, that it'll get damp—an effect that'll be compounded by the moisture the survivors breathe out and all the water that's produced by the reaction between lithium hydroxide and carbon dioxide—so everything will get wet: bulkheads, clothing, bedding, everything." Selby paused for a moment. "Did any of you ever see that film *Das Boot*, about the World War II German boat that had to stay submerged for ages to escape from the British? Do you remember just how wet everything got in the boat?"

"Sure," replied the salvage officer, "but that boat was holed as well."

"Even where there was no seawater, everything was wet. That's the way it'll be in the *Tulsa*. Another thing—they're going to feel isolated. Even if they can hear the rescue forces that arrive, which I doubt unless they release more explosive charges—they'll be unable to respond. They will literally be deaf and dumb because they'll have no means of communication. Can you imagine how frustrating that'll be? Add to that the stress of being poisoned by the air they breathe, no cooked food or coffee, and the feeling of confinement that only a coffin could provide better, and I expect that some of them could well go mad." Selby paused as he contemplated the horrific situation that Richter and his crew were facing.

"Nothing like that happened in the *Squalus*," said the chief of staff, referring to the submarine that sank off New England during sea trials in 1939.

"No, but they were only down for thirty-six hours or so." Selby stopped because he didn't want to pursue this line. "I think that's about all I have to say, sir. I can't see any further into my crystal ball." There was silence around the table. The long faces said it all—*Thank God it isn't me.* Eventually, Talisker broke the gloomy silence. "Thank you, Doc. Given the very limited time we may have before Richter's forced to start escaping, I'm going to request that the British SPAG team be deployed sooner rather than later. Ops, can you see if we can't help them with a SEAL team?"

"I'll look into that, sir."

The admiral didn't respond immediately, taking his time to look around the room. "I don't like to say this, but I don't have any choice. Regardless of whether or not we can save Richter and his men, we'll have to recover and investigate the wreck. Ops, get on to the supervisor of salvage at NAVSEA. He's going to have to get the *Grapple* or *Grasp* or both ships out to the Norwegian Sea if we're to retrieve the *Tulsa*. Better get a dry dock from Groton out there, too." Talisker returned his gaze to the briefing notes in front of him and mentally checked that each point had been covered before looking up again. "Well, gentlemen, this is the last full meeting we'll have here on the *Tulsa* rescue—which is now officially Operation Deep Hope,

by the way. Many of you are off to the NATO HQ
in Bodø to assist with coordinating the rescue. Good
luck to you. Let's bring Geoff Richter and his men
home alive."

1000R, Groton, Connecticut

Marie was still glued to the TV and clearly wasn't
in the mood for conversation. It made Jean feel awkward. She had spent much of her time with the boys
but, having left their room and come down to the
sitting room, she really wanted to have a conversation.
Marie had been trying to avoid this for two reasons:
Jean was incapable of keeping a secret. Anything and
everything she told her would be common knowledge
within moments of her leaving the house. The second
reason was that Marie actually wanted to be left alone
to think through the issues before discussing them
with anybody. But that was difficult when she had so
little idea of what was going on. What she really
wanted was some positive news. She tried SNN. The
anchor had paused to listen to something in his earpiece. "There's an unconfirmed report on the wire that
there are ninety-one survivors on board the USS
Tulsa. What does this tell you, Jim?" The anchor
turned to a screen to his right where yet another retired submariner—Captain Jim McPherson, according
to the caption—was about to pontificate.

"Well, Dan, it tells me a lot. It tells me that the
survivors are almost certainly in the forward part of
the boat. It's really unlikely that so many men would
be aft." The camera zoomed out to include a cutaway
diagram of a 688 class submarine. "They would most
likely be in this area here"—he used a pointer to outline the forward compartment of the boat—"between
the bow and the watertight bulkhead of the reactor
compartment."

"Is it possible that some survivors might be trapped
in the rear of the submarine?"

"It's possible, but I doubt it. The most likely way for one of these submarines to sink is if there is a substantial amount of flooding. The crew spend most of their time in the forward compartment. That's where they sleep and eat. There's only one small passageway back to the engineering spaces and, after a collision in which the watertight bulkhead will have been isolated, I can't imagine many people getting into the aft compartment. So, with ninety-one survivors the flooding is almost certainly in the aft compartment, back here." He tapped the pointer on the rear of the submarine.

"Why is that, Jim?"

The pointer moved again. "Without getting too technical, the ship's main batteries are located here, in the bottom of the forward compartment. If there was a substantial amount of flooding in this compartment, then either the battery itself or one of the electrical panels that control the flow of current out of it would eventually come into contact with seawater. This will result in a process called electrolysis, which I expect you remember from school. In addition to hydrogen and oxygen, chlorine gas is released. This is highly toxic and would force any survivors in the forward compartment to escape in order to survive."

"Is there no breathing apparatus that the men could wear?"

"Yes, there is. However, with this many men alive I would expect the air bank that supplies the breathing apparatus to have been exhausted by now."

"Could the men who usually work in the back of the boat have escaped from the flooding by moving toward the front?"

"It really depends on what happened, and we haven't been told yet. It's possible, but if they had, I would have expected more men to have survived."

"Thank you, Jim." The anchor turned to speak to the camera. "Jim McPherson is a retired captain in the US Navy and has commanded a 688 fast-attack submarine similar to the *Tulsa*." He reached under the desk and produced a telephone. "On the line, now, I have Dr. Bernard Salinger who was, until last year, a design engineer with the Electric Boat Division of General Dynamics. Dr. Salinger, you were involved in designing the 688 class submarine back in the 1970s. What could have caused the *Tulsa* to sink?"

"Any number of things. I presume that we are dealing with accidental circumstances?"

"Yes, we have no indication of any act of war."

"Well, the most likely cause is a collision, with either a surface vessel, another submarine, or with the bottom."

"I understand. We heard the same thing from Jim McPherson a few moments ago. What I was really after was what could impact the buoyancy of a submarine sufficiently to cause it to sink?"

"Submarines are designed to sink. Because of that, and unlike surface vessels, they have limited reserves of buoyancy. Take out the ballast tanks or add weight—in the form of water, for example—and they will sink. Another factor is that, unlike older designs, submarines have become much larger, and the number of watertight compartments has gradually been reduced."

"How does that make submarines more likely to sink?"

"If there is uncontrollable flooding in a small compartment, it can be sealed off and the submarine may remain capable of reaching the surface. If the same thing happens in a large compartment, this is much less likely to—"

"Why are there fewer of these watertight compartments, Dr. Salinger?" interrupted the anchor.

"To save weight and space. As I was saying, the number of compartments has been reduced so that a submarine like the 688, for example, has just two in addition to the reactor compartment. If there is an uncontrollable flood in either of them, it is more than enough to sink the boat. Another way a submarine can sink is if some of its ballast tanks are punctured. I would need to check my calculations, but I think I'm right in saying that more than one ballast tank would need to be punctured to sink a 688. In any case, loss of ballast alone is insufficient to sink most boats, because if they have forward propulsion, they can drive themselves to the surface using the upward force generated by the planes."

"In other words, and if I understand you correctly, Doctor, if there was an accident that caused a ballast tank to be holed, the submarine would also have to lose power or a plane or two for it to sink?"

"That's correct."

"Thank you, Dr. Salinger. Please stay on the line, I know that our producer wishes to speak with you." The anchor returned the handset to its receiver under the desk, then looked up. To his right and behind him a superimposed image of an auburn-haired woman in her mid-thirties wearing a beige raincoat appeared. She was staring at the camera, holding a microphone in one hand, while the other was deployed in a losing battle to control her hair in the gusting wind. The anchor's voice was a little quieter than before. "The sinking of the *Tulsa* has come as a shock to the town of Groton, Connecticut, where the submarine was based. Our reporter Mary Ellis is outside a supermarket there. Mary, what's the reaction of the people of Groton to the news of the *Tulsa*?"

"Well, Dan, I think shocked is about right. With me I have Nancy Richards." The camera zoomed out to show the two women. Nancy Richards was wearing jeans and a brightly colored ski jacket. She only looked to be in her mid-twenties and her face was still blemished by acne. "Nancy, your husband is on board the *Tulsa*?"

"Yes, he's the corpsman."

"The doctor on board?"

"That's right."

"How do you feel about what's happened?"

"I don't really know what's happened."

"Well, we know that the *Tulsa* has sunk and that there are ninety-one survivors on board."

"Yeah. I just hope that my Denzel is one of them. . . ."

Marie couldn't bear it anymore and reluctantly switched the TV off and started to cry. Jean leapt up from her chair and put an arm around her. "Here, use this," she said as she thrust a tissue into Marie's hand.

"Thank you." Marie paused, trying not to sniffle. "Jean you've been so kind to come."

"I'll stay for as long as you want, Marie. I know you'd do the same for me."

"I just need some time to myself, Jean . . . a little time to think."

"Marie, honey. This is no time to be alone. Can I make you some fresh coffee?" Marie would have loved some more coffee but to accept it would mean that Jean would hang around for at least another half hour. She'd been so useful occupying the kids, but now it seemed she wanted to talk. If she only had some time to sit and think things through. Although John was the engineer in the *Tulsa,* he didn't spend all of his time in the back end of the boat. His stateroom was in the front end; John had showed it to her. It was hardly luxurious, but it was a lot more than a hammock slung between steam pipes in the engine room that she had imagined when he'd first told her about the cramped conditions in fast-attack boats. Furthermore, he stood only occasional watches in the engine room, so he could have been asleep or in the wardroom when the accident happened. Just because SNN was reporting that the back end of the *Tulsa* was flooded didn't mean that John was dead. How did they know when neither the squadron nor Group 2 seemed to? She'd give them another call.

"No thank you," she replied. "I'm going to try the squadron again." With that she got up, dabbed her eyes, and made for the phone.

It took forever, but eventually the endless drone of

busy signals was broken by somebody who answered. Jean Houghton looked over her shoulder and raised her eyebrows, anxious to learn what was going on.

"Yes, this is Marie Dowling. . . . No, my husband's the engineer. . . . That's right. Well, I've just been watching SNN and heard that there are ninety-one survivors. . . . What . . . ? Then how can they report that . . . ? Can't you tell them . . . ? Well, if you can't, who will?" Jean could see that Marie's attitude had changed. Gone was the lost girl and here was the self-reliant Marie she knew and respected.

"OK, so if it's a load of bullshit, when will you know . . . ? That's just not good enough. . . . No, I'm not interested in excuses. My husband's down there, and I want to know whether he's alive or not, and I also want to know what you're going to do to bring him home. I'm not the only one either. There are a 130 families who feel the same way. . . . Well, when you do, will you let us all know . . . ?" There was a longer pause, and then Marie said firmly: "Perhaps that's something I can do for you then."

She replaced the receiver and turned to Jean. "Would you believe it? They still don't know how many people are alive in the boat, they don't know when they will know, and, to top it off, when they do know they don't even have the phone numbers of all the families to let them know." Marie paused to let some of her exasperation blow off. "Well," she continued, "that's something we can sort out. Did you have anything else planned for today?" Jean didn't have time to reply. The phone rang. "I'll get it," said Marie. "Hello?"

"My name is Marcia Jones, and I work for SNN. I understand that your husband is the engineering officer on board the *Tulsa*."

"That's right."

"I'm in Groton this morning—may I come and see you?"

"What do you want?"

"Well, both my colleague, John Scott, and I would like to interview you. Nothing intrusive, we'd just like to get a feel for how you are feeling, get a little background on John. His name is John, isn't it?"

"How do you know?"

"I've been making some inquiries on the base. He's a very popular man. A bit of a rebel, they say, but good at his job. Very good." Marie didn't know what to say. She sounded nice enough. "The thing is," Marcia continued, "there are a lot of people around here who are concerned about what's happened to the *Tulsa*, and I thought you might be able to vocalize those feelings for them for a national audience." Marie thought for a moment. She'd received several calls from members of the spouses' association, and it was obvious that the squadron wasn't in a position to help any of them. It might be a good idea to use television to communicate with everybody and perhaps move the navy into some kind of action.

She thought about it some more. Satellite Network News was a commercial organization, and they weren't known for their subtlety. What else would they want? "I assure you, all we want to do is talk to you about your feelings," continued Marcia Jones. "We know you must be under terrible pressure right now, as are so many other families. Do you think you might be able to be like a representative for them, Mrs. Dowling?" Marie paused before replying. Geoff wasn't married, nor was Curtis Mitchell. She was therefore the most senior wife, if one could think of it that way. She hated wearing her husband's rank, but on this occasion it seemed that she would have to. Would doing an interview damage his career? Why should it? She wore no uniform, although too often it felt like she did. Her ingrained mistrust of the press was melting in favor of telling the world the way she felt. Yes, she would do it. "Will you film it?"

"This'll be for television, so it'll be on camera and live. One other thing—this must be exclusive. You must agree not to talk to any other news organization—even the local paper, whatever it's called."

"*The Day.*"

"That's right." That put a rather different complexion on it, Marie thought. She had never appeared on television before, let alone live. But if it moved things along, it was worth doing live.

"OK, when do you want to do it?"

"It'll take us about an hour to set up. Shall we say one o'clock?"

"One o'clock will be fine."

1645C, Naval Shipyard, Severomorsk

The approach to the dock was quite straightforward, but Borzhov was unfamiliar with it. In accordance with standing orders, he had accepted a pilot on board for the final few miles of the journey. Borzhov had watched him like an eagle for the past twenty minutes as he threaded an intricate path up the fjord and into the military dockyard, past the submarine berths, to a secluded, covered dry dock that lay ahead of them. Borzhov had to concede that the man knew both his job and the vast harbor well. The bright lights of the dock beckoned, and the prospect of getting under cover was more than enticing. Although the snow had diminished to no more than flurries, the bitter cold and gusting wind had completely defeated the insulation afforded by his greatcoat. Borzhov was doing his best not to shiver.

"Right twenty degrees rudder, slow ahead," announced the pilot into the microphone that he held tightly in his heavily gloved right hand.

"Twenty right wheel on," squawked a speaker to his left.

"All ahead slow," squawked another.

"Midships," ordered the pilot crisply.

"Wheel's amidships," echoed back from the speaker. The *Gepard* was perfectly lined up to enter the dock. As the crumpled bow eased past the caisson, the pilot barked again.

"All stop!" He waited until the sail was level with the caisson before adding, "Astern one-third." The *Gepard* vibrated a little as the screw began to turn in the opposite direction slowing the damaged submarine to a halt just as the rudder passed into the dock. He issued his last orders into the microphone and handed it back to Borzhov. "You have the ship, sir."

"Thank you, pilot. A nice piece of parking. Can I offer you a libation?"

"No thank you, Captain, I must get home. My wife gets angry if I drive after drinking. If it were just ten years ago, I'd have accepted your kind offer and, in all probability, not have bothered to go home at all. Modern times."

"Indeed. Nonetheless, you will allow me to escort you to the brow."

"Of course." They left the bridge, descended one level, and exited through the sail hatch. The brow was just about lashed in place.

"Thank you again." Borzhov saluted as the pilot left the boat and noticed that a smartly dressed lieutenant was elbowing his way through the milling crowd of dockyard workers that had gathered to start work on the *Gepard*.

"Permission to come aboard, sir?"

"Yes please, Lieutenant, what can I do for you?" The officer walked briskly over the brow, saluted, and reached into his breast pocket for a pale blue envelope that he passed to Borzhov.

"Sir, this is very urgent." Borzhov opened the envelope immediately and read the brief note that was handwritten on Admiral Konstantin's letterhead.

"Thank you, Lieutenant. Where is the nearest phone?"

"In the dock manager's office, sir. It's just over there," he replied, indicating a glass-fronted office beyond the *Gepard*'s bow. Borzhov leapt over the brow and made for the office. The door was open, and he picked up the phone and dialed the number that Konstantin had written in the note. It was his home number. A woman answered the phone.

"Mrs. Konstantin?"

"Yes, who is this?"

"My name is Borzhov. Is your husband at home?"

"Yes he is, just one moment." There was a pause before Konstantin picked up.

"Borzhov, you're back. I must speak to you as soon as possible. There's to be an urgent court of inquiry about the collision. It'll be highly political, regrettably, so we must sort a few things out beforehand." Konstantin gave Borzhov his address and invited him to dinner that evening.

1100R, SNN Headquarters, New York

There were only three people sitting at the table, the producer, the news editor, and the military correspondent. The other participants in the conference were displayed on a series of screens set into the wall facing them. The producer was talking: "We've had a request to travel with the DSRV turned down on the grounds that there's no space available, but we do have a crew ready to cover its preparation and departure, so we can file two or three stories from San Diego. The Norwegians won't allow us into their HQ in Bodø, but they are setting up a press center, and we have a crew to cover that. The Brits won't let us into their base at Faslane, and in any case, there is nothing to see now, as the ships have all sailed. There's no point in overflying the site of the sinking—it's expensive, and there's nothing to see yet. We have a crew on its way to Hammerfest—it's where they will fly from when there's something to film, and I heard that the Brits may have some specially trained men already there. We'll find out what that's all about."

"Where's the DSRV flying to, Fergus?" asked the editor.

"I don't know," replied the military correspondent, "but I'll find out."

"Good," continued the producer. "As soon as you do, we'll send a crew there. We've got the Pentagon and White House covered, but don't expect any fireworks from there. I want some human interest. Any ideas anyone?" He turned to the screen where John Scott's face appeared. "OK, John, I remember you've got Marie . . . what's her name?"

"Dowling, Marie Dowling. We've locked up an exclusive."

"Great. And we're nearly certain that her husband's dead?" There were nods at the table and from three of the screens. "OK, John, I can rely on you to do your best there. I'm interested in the safety angle— are submarines safe? Use this interview to get the ball rolling." He turned to the military correspondent. "Fergus, you've got an engineer lined up to follow?"

"Sure."

A young-looking female on another screen started to speak: "What about previous submarine sinkings— there were two in the sixties, I think. How about talking to the families of people who died in those?"

"That's great, well done, Karen. Do it."

"There must be a memorial someplace—do the interview from there," another person piped in.

"Good, we're thinking now," responded the producer. "Anybody got anything else?" He looked at John Scott's screen.

"I've been doing some background at the base. You wouldn't believe what some of the 'spouses,' be it a formal or informal arrangement, seem to get up to while their men are away. If it ends up with nobody getting out of the *Tulsa* alive, its going to uncomplicate a lot of lives in New London."

The editor jumped in. "OK, John, but I think we could lose an audience with that angle. We need to tug at heartstrings not make the damned thing beat quicker."

Next the producer spoke up. "I agree, John, nice thinking though. What else do we have?" There was nothing. "Come on people, I want imagination! This is the biggest news story since Oklahoma or the TWA thing. No it's bigger—a lot of these people are still alive. How can we get to them?"

"Why don't we get a small submarine and go look for the *Tulsa*?" Karen offered. The producer turned to look at the military correspondent.

"What do you think, Fergus?"

"No reason why not, except it won't be cheap. We're looking at chartering a specialist ship with a minisub for two weeks. That'll run to at least a hundred thousand bucks . . . per day. And we're likely to have to pay for the fuel and supplies as well."

"Sure, but we could have two crews on board—one to film the activity on the surface and one in the minisub to get the actual rescue. Could we make contact with the survivors?"

"They'll have an underwater telephone on board. The quality of the sound may not be fantastic, as these things are notorious for distortion—especially if the sound has to travel any distance through the water."

"But we'll have our sub right next to it. That would be incredible!"

"The military won't like it."

"Too bad. If the position we have is half-correct, the *Tulsa* is lying in international waters. There's nothing they can do about it."

"I thought that territorial waters extended to two hundred miles these days," interrupted John Scott. "That would give control to the Norwegians. They could stop us."

"I'll get the legal boys to check this, but I think the two-hundred-mile limit is for economic purposes only—you know, fishing, oil rights, pollution control. We can charter a ship and park it there for as long as we like. OK," the producer continued, "I want Simon and Mick to get onto this one. It'll be some days before we can air the footage, so I want more ideas for today and tomorrow. Come on people, you're supposed to be the most imaginative in the business. I want some free association. . . ."

1600Z, HMS *Wellington*

It was only because Commander Muggeridge's orders were to make his best speed to the datum that he was driving his ship quite so hard. Having been shoreside in Faslane for almost three weeks, too many of his men had lost their sea legs and had succumbed to the violent motion of *The Boot,* as his ship was affectionately known. For those who had the stomach for it, the view from the bridge was fantastic even though it was getting quite dark. As she crested each wave, the *Wellington*'s bow angled down, and she charged into the following trough. With a knee-buckling crash, she buried her bow in it, generating an explosion of spray. She seemed to wait there while the vibration from the impact shook its way down the length of the ship, like a dog drying off after a swim. After a few seconds the fo'c'sle, covered in dark gray ocean, started to rise. It broke up into a cloud of creamy spray as it was taken by the wind and tossed, first against the 4.5-inch gun, then the Seawolf missile silo, before finally smashing into the superstructure. As the bow rose the free water on the fo'c'sle scurried along the deck, forming little white plumes at each obstruction in its path before flowing over the side. At the crest of the wave, a slight roll preceded the ship's plunging down into the next trough.

A fantastic sight it might have been for those on the bridge, but in the heat of the junior rates' dining hall, the smell of the evening meal wafting out of the galley, the ship's violent motion made many feel somewhat queasy. With the ship's company assembled, excluding the watch keepers, Richard Tremble began. "Well, good evening, ladies and gentlemen. I know the buzz around the ship is that we are off to rescue some American submariners and it is my task, as well as my colleague Surgeon Commander Freeman's, to tell you how we intend to do it. I would like to be able to tell you precisely what we want to do. Unfortunately, we don't have enough information on the conditions in the DISSUB to be certain what will be required. However, I can tell you that these men are depending on you for help." There was a muted rumble from the unusually attentive audience. Tremble turned to a chart that had been crudely taped to the bulkhead behind him. "The submarine, which is called the *Tulsa*, by the way, is just here." He pointed to a spot just to the west of Bear Island. "There are two ways that the survivors can get out. If they're lucky, they'll be able to wait until they are rescued. As I speak, two rescue craft are on their way—ours, the LR5, will probably get there first, and the American DSRV should arrive later in the week. They are both capable of carrying the survivors from the *Tulsa* either to another submarine or to the surface. We're hopeful that, in either case, the crew will only require conventional medical attention. If for any reason they are forced to escape from their boat, and they're deep, at about 155 meters, they're quite likely to get the bends and require treating in a compression chamber. Commander Freeman will tell you about that in a minute. In this situation, we'll need your help to get these people out of the water immediately. I don't have to remind you that the sea is bloody cold up there, so it'll be up to you to fish them out as fast as you can and then get them into the hangar where the medical station will be set up."

At that point Freeman, who had been sweating profusely, succumbed to the urge to vomit. He attempted to make a dash for the door but, as the ship pitched, he was knocked off course, bounced off a table, and

lost his footing. As he fell to the deck he launched
the contents of his stomach into the air in a series of
uncontrolled retches. The best of these reached a
range of almost three feet before splattering over a
group of petty officers that sat at a table nearby. After
a few moments of stunned silence the reaction was
riotous. The hoots and guffaws from the junior rates
filled the mess deck, and even the captain and officers
had difficulty keeping straight faces.

1800A, USS *Tulsa*

"The captain wanted to be here this evening to tell
you what's happening, but he's still suffering from the
head injury he sustained in the collision. He's asked
me to apologize on his behalf, that he can't be here
right now. He needs to rest." Enzo looked up at the
crowd that was gathered in the crew's mess for their
second meal of the day. The smell of hot food was
overpowering. "Now I know you want to eat, and so
I'll be brief. You all heard those charges from the P3
this morning. Yes, they were from an aircraft. Nothing
else could have found us this quickly. I know that a
lot of you started to feel real good about the situation,
like we'll be out by tomorrow. But I have to tell you
that we won't be. Now, I'm not here to throw cold
water over you—you're all cold enough already."
There were a few smiles, but that was all. His message
was obviously working rather too well. He'd lighten
up a bit. "I just want to tell you that it could be a
few more days before we can get out of here. So the
same rules will apply as the captain laid out just after
the sinking. Sleep, sleep, sleep. You've all been fantastic and deserve a lot of praise. Most of you have
stayed in your bunks and crashed out the whole time.
Since when in your careers in the navy has anybody
praised you for doing that?" There was a little more
laughter now, and it almost drowned out the gurgling
of expectant stomachs. "I've just about said what I

have to say. We've been found. We have enough life-support stores to keep us going for at least another four days, possibly longer. Sparks, do we have enough juice to have hot food for that long?''

"Yes, sir, we do.'' There was a greater roar of enthusiasm.

"Right. So eat well and rest well, men. I'll keep you informed as to what the hell is going on topside as best I can. I'll talk to you again at the same time tomorrow.'' Enzo nodded and made his way to the door. He was almost deafened by the roars of approval from his audience and nearly trampled in the rush for food.

1300R, Groton, Connecticut

Marie got up to answer the door with some apprehension. Ever since agreeing to the interview she'd been regretting her decision. If John was alive, it might well have an adverse effect on his career and she was only too well aware of how important it was that his next appointment was as an XO. Jean had talked about little else and, between them, they'd reached the conclusion that it was too late to back out, but Marie would say as little as possible. All she could do was be positive for the benefit of other families and set the record straight about the number of survivors.

The woman at the door was thin, fair-haired, and young. She was wearing a radiant smile that was framed by generously full lips freshly covered in a light pink lipstick. Her blue eyes were looking directly into Marie's. "Mrs. Dowling?''

"That's right. You must be Marcia Jones.''

"I am, how nice to meet you. Can I introduce my colleague, John Scott?'' Marie looked to her left and noticed a slim, young, dark-haired man standing just behind Marcia. He was clean-shaven, and the first thing that struck Marie as he smiled warmly were his perfect teeth. He took a step forward and extended his hand.

"Good afternoon, Mrs. Dowling. It's so good of you to let us come and see you at such short notice. May we come in?"

"Of course, I was forgetting myself. Can I offer you anything? Tea? Coffee?"

"Yes, tea would be fine," replied Scott.

"I prefer coffee if you have any brewed; otherwise, just water would be fine," added Marcia.

"Did you bring anybody else with you?"

"Yes, there are four of us—the other two are unloading some gear from the van. Did you have any preference as to where we should set up?" Marie had given no thought as to where the interview was to take place. She had spent the brief interludes in conversation with Jean deciding what to wear and had chosen an off-white silk blouse and a floral skirt.

"How about the yard?" she replied.

"I'd prefer somewhere where there are photographs of the family," replied Scott. "How about the living room?"

"OK, most of the family photos are down in the den, but I can set up the ones you'd like in the living room."

"That would be great."

It took just over an hour for all the TV equipment to be unloaded and set up. Marie was sitting in an easy chair with John Scott in a similar chair beside her. They were both illuminated by bright, hooded lights, and both wore small microphones on their lapels. One camera was set up on a tripod, while the cameraman held another, rehearsing a number of different angles. The soundman was finally happy with the levels. Marcia had busied herself jotting things down on a clipboard. The floor was littered with wires and cables that snaked their way out through the front door and down to the van, the roof of which was adorned with a satellite uplink.

"You understand that once we start, everything will be beamed to the studio and the producer will decide what goes out and when? I'll have no say over that," said Scott, somewhat defensively, but in as reassuring a manner as he could manage.

"Yes, I understand," replied Marie.

"Also, it'll be recorded, and we may use it again."

"That's fine."

"Would anybody like some more tea or coffee?" asked Jean, who was feeling rather left out of things.

"Jean, that would be most welcome once the interview is completed," replied the reporter.

"Yes, I'd like one then as well, Jean," replied Marie, who paused momentarily before continuing. "Look, could you just check on the boys right now? I've not heard a squeak out of them recently, and that normally means trouble."

Jean beamed. "Of course, honey, just leave them to me."

"OK, Mrs. Dowling—or may I call you Marie?"

"Marie's fine."

"OK, Marie. Are you ready?" John Scott looked up at Marcia, who was chattering into a cell phone and nodded back to him.

"As ready as I'll ever be," she replied, and with that, John Scott began his interview. They started with a few questions about how Marie had met John, then moved on to his career in submarines, the children, and her part-time job as a nursing auxiliary in the local hospital. It was all intended to make her feel at ease, and it worked well. She was on familiar territory, and she felt comfortable and began to relax.

"Has John's job working in submarines ever been a source of worry to you?"

"To begin with it took a bit of getting used to, but I got over that years ago. Submarines are as safe as airplanes—safer probably."

"Until something goes wrong."

"Sure, but look at the safety record. The US Navy

hasn't had an accident involving the loss of a boat in over twenty years . . . over thirty, actually."

"Until last Thursday. Are you aware that in the design of recent submarines, safety has been sacrificed in favor of performance? How do you feel about that, Mrs. Dowling?"

"Well, I can't comment on the design of submarines. I don't know anything about it. I do feel that if we're to ask our men to go to sea in warships, they should be designed both for safety and for performance. After all, they're meant to fight, and so the boats should be designed to win. There's not much point otherwise, is there?"

John Scott changed the subject. "Marie, have you heard that there are ninety-one survivors in the *Tulsa*?"

"Well, actually I've been checking up on that, and as far as the squadron here at the base is concerned, they can't confirm that." Scott looked a little taken aback.

"Let's say that number's correct. Do you think your husband is one of the survivors?"

"I obviously hope so," Marie replied, becoming concerned at the direction the conversation was going. Of course she was hoping that John was alright, she had to believe he was.

"But he's an engineer, and the best available analysis indicates that it's those in the engineering spaces who are most likely to have died." Marie was shocked. She had taken this John Scott to be a nice guy. Why should he do this? Wasn't it bad enough not knowing? Why make things worse? Tears began to well up in her eyes, she couldn't prevent them. She reached for a tissue and blew her nose.

"Excuse me," she sniffed.

"I am sorry to press you, Mrs. Dowling, but surely you realize that John may not have made it?" He paused. The cameraman was squatting at her feet and filled the frame with a close-up of Marie obviously in great distress. "Don't you think that submarines should be designed to the highest safety standards?" Marie was fighting to control herself. She was on the verge of uncontrollable anger or despair, but wasn't sure which. She reminded herself that the interview was probably live on television, and her objective had always been to get out of it as soon as possible and that had now become an imperative. This Scott fellow clearly wasn't going to give up until he got what he wanted. Her reply was therefore obvious.

"Yes, of course they should be safe. In war, that means being faster and quieter than the enemy. All of these things should be designed into our submarines. I must tell you however, that your best analysis sucks. . . ." The monitor in front of the reporter blinked back to an image of the studio. On TV screens around the world it was Fergus Daugherty's face that greeted the viewers.

"To discuss the issue of submarine safety I have with me . . ."

2000Z, Aberdeen, Scotland

Nobody could accuse the MV *Salminster* of being an imposing or elegant vessel. Built in 1986 for the British Ministry of Defense, she was operated by the Royal Maritime Auxiliary Service and crewed by civilians. To prove the point she was painted in the dirty yellow-and-black livery of the organization. Weighing in at just twenty-two hundred tons, she was not large, and, powered by two Ruston diesels generating just four thousand horsepower between them, she was not particularly fast. In the prevailing weather conditions of a brisk northwesterly, she might manage a most uncomfortable twelve knots. The *Salminster* rolled like a pig in anything but a flat calm.

A feature that distinguished her from other ships was the two horns that protruded from her bow and the large crane that dominated her fo'c'sle. It was the latter that allowed her to operate the LR5 rescue vehicle that was now secured to the deck beneath it. Once out of the lee of the harbor, she steadied on a northeasterly course with the weather almost on her beam. In the officers' mess, a group of men had gathered around a table to plan the rescue. Only two of them wore naval uniforms. The remainder were civilians—mainly the cable and wireless personnel who operate the LR5. None of them had undertaken a real rescue before, although they had all participated in exercises. An aura of gloom hovered above the group much like the slate gray clouds choking the sky. Unless the weather moderated by the time they reached the datum, they were not going to be able to get anybody out of the *Tulsa*. The *Salminster* could only operate the LR5 in sea-state three or less. With the ship presently rolling through an arc of almost forty degrees, they were painfully aware that the sea-state was considerably more than that.

2350A, USS *Tulsa*

"Look, I don't know about the rest of you guys, but I'm pooped. Definitely time for some shut-eye." Chief Lehner threw his cards facedown on the table and rubbed his eyes.

"Yeah, I'll go along with that," concurred Larry Czapek.

"Me too," joined in Bill Hicks.

"Come on, guys," began Santana. "Do you think for one minute that we'll be able to sleep if we turn in right now? Remember what happened the last time we tried?"

"Mitch, by all means sit here and play solitaire all night," Hicks answered wearily. "You're a whole heap better at it than hearts in any case. Me, I could sleep facedown in a bucket of shit right now." With that he rose from the table.

"The way that bunk of yours stinks, you're going to have to," retorted Santana.

"Cool it, kids," interrupted Lehner. "We're all tired. There's no point in fighting. How about we start again after breakfast tomorrow?"

"Sounds good to me," replied Hicks. Czapek grunted with approval and rose to leave the room. Hicks and Lehner followed. Santana gathered up the cards, shuffled the deck, and dealt himself a hand of solitaire.

Enzo gritted his teeth to stop them from chattering and rolled over in his bunk. His eyes were still burning with fatigue, but sleep eluded him. He was just too cold and damp to nod off. His mind drifted back to his life in Massachusetts nearly sixteen years earlier. Running the house had not been easy after his mother and sisters had left. His father had gradually slid into a deep depression that he appeared powerless to shake off. His fishing runs had become sporadic, as had his attempts to maintain the boat. It was in the early fall that the crisis had hit. One day Enzo had returned from school to find that his father was not home. He'd waited and waited for him to return, but by eight o'clock was driven by pangs of hunger to heat up some cold fish pie. Having eaten, Enzo had walked down to the dock to find the boat out of the water, with the engine on blocks beside it. His father was standing a little unsteadily beside the engine, drinking from a bottle concealed in a brown paper bag.

"So, Enzo," he belched. "You come to see the great fisherman?"

"Hello, Papa. What's wrong with the boat?"

"Nothing is wrong with the boat, it is a wonderful boat." He was gesticulating wildly and tottering as he did so. "Have you ever seen a more beautiful boat?"

"No, Papa. You must be hungry, there's some fish pie. Why not come home and eat some?" As he was speaking, Enzo had walked up to his father, grabbed him by the elbow, and started to lead him home. On the way, his father had dropped his bottle, fallen over trying to retrieve it and then insisted on relieving himself in the street in full view of anybody who happened to be looking in his direction. Enzo had never felt more embarrassed. Once home, Enzo had heated up the pie again, but his father never ate it. He had collapsed into an armchair in front of the television and had stayed there, snoring loudly, until the following morning.

Over the next two days the extent of the crisis had become apparent. The boat needed a new engine, but there was no money to pay for it. The house was mortgaged to the hilt, and the bank would extend no further lines of credit. Father had explained that he had been sending much more money back to Scilla than he could afford in the hope that it might induce his wife and daughters to return. It hadn't, and he was effectively bankrupt. He couldn't even sell the boat. The days of fruitful inshore fishing were over. If he wanted to carry on, he would need to get a bigger boat. All that was left for him was the uncertain and harsh life of crewing. That was a daunting prospect for a man who would be fifty next birthday.

Salvation had arrived in the form of a letter with a New York postmark. Enzo had only met his Uncle Alberto once, many years previously. His lasting memories of him were from photographs of his family standing in front of a lavishly decorated tree, which arrived in a Christmas card each year. Uncle Alberto had left Massachusetts after graduating high school, and having drifted for a while, eventually started a laundry business in Brooklyn. Based on the evidence in those photographs, it was a successful enterprise. The letter contained an invitation for the two of them to go to Brooklyn and for his father, the offer of a job. It was too good an offer to refuse.

Although Enzo had quite enjoyed life in a big city, his love of the sea had never left him. It was for that reason, and because the streets of New York, or

Brooklyn at least, had not proved to be paved with gold that he jumped at an offer of a place at the Naval Academy. Having contemplated the past, Enzo realized that his upbringing had not prepared him for the task that faced him now. Perhaps no upbringing could, so maybe that wasn't the point. All he could do was his best. He drifted off to sleep praying to God that it would be good enough.

CHAPTER

4

Sunday, 31 October

0400A, Hammerfest Airport

Although it would be another three hours before any commercial flights would arrive or depart, there was an unusual amount of activity in the airport. In the terminal bar, three tables had been pulled together and around them sat the SPAG, dressed in black jumpsuits and dark blue, naval berets. The group was led by Richard Tremble's deputy, Lieutenant Steve Marchant. Warrant Officer Sharples was next to him, delivering the jump brief. In a few minutes they would board the Royal Air Force C130 that was just visible on the taxiway through the large plate-glass windows that overlooked the airfield. Sharples cut an impressive figure. Of a slim, but muscular, build, he stood over six feet four inches tall, and his short, gray hair and ruddy complexion made him appear somewhat more mature than his thirty-four years. He was speaking slowly in a broad Lancashire accent. The bar was otherwise empty apart from two middle-aged ladies who wielded large machines with rotating brushes that hummed in unison as they cleaned the floor. Suddenly the doors swung open and three men entered the room. One of them had a camera mounted on his right shoulder with a bright light just above it, while another was carrying a large microphone on a boom. The third, clutching a clipboard, led the group directly toward the small contingent of British sailors.

"Lieutenant Marchant, I'm Donald Forman of SNN, can you tell me when you and your men are going to rescue the men in the *Tulsa*?"

"No, I can't. Look, we are in the middle of a briefing, would you please leave us in peace?"

"We all have our jobs to do, Lieutenant. Mine is to inform our viewers of the measures that are being taken to rescue the men in the *Tulsa*." The TV crew had reached the tables, and Donald Forman was standing immediately adjacent to Marchant. The bright light above the camera caused him to squint and look away from it.

"I'll ask you politely once more to leave us alone. Your presence here is serving only to postpone the rescue that you're apparently so keen to report. Mr. Sharples, is there another room we can use?"

"Not that I am aware of, sir. Most of the airport's shut at this time of day. I can escort these gentlemen from the room if you wish." Marchant looked at Forman.

"Is that going to be necessary, or will you do as I ask?"

"That's up to you. This isn't a restricted area; we're as free to use it as you are."

"I don't intend to conduct this briefing in front of television cameras. Please leave now."

By raising his voice, Marchant had indicated to Sharples that it was time to remove the reporters. Without prompting, the SPAG team rose to their feet, surrounded the TV crew, and began to herd them toward the door. It was at this point that the sound-man did something stupid. He brought the boom of his microphone down on the head of Leading Seaman

Percival, who spun on his heel, grabbed it, ripped its lead from the camera, and hurled it across the room. A moment later he brought his knee up sharply and drove it into the groin of the unfortunate soundman, who let out a shriek as he doubled up in pain. A second later the cameraman was relieved of his load and it followed the microphone's aerial journey across the canteen, breaking into several large pieces as it clattered to the floor. With no reason to remain in the bar, Donald Forman and the cameraman grabbed their winded colleague and retreated. The SPAG reassembled at their table and Sharples concluded the briefing before they filed out to the C130 that was shortly to fly them out over the Arctic Ocean.

0500A, USS *Tulsa*

Wrapped in a blanket and sitting in a chair, from which he could observe his patients, Master Chief Steadman had finally managed to ignore his freezing feet and drifted into a light sleep. Soon enough, he woke with a start. As he gathered his wits he realized one of the men was anxiously calling him. "It's all right, Jacko, what do you want?"

"Master Chief, I think Sanchez has stopped breathing." Steadman stood up and sidestepped his way around the mattresses on the deck until he reached the one on which Petty Officer Sanchez had been lying motionless ever since the sinking. Through the hazy light he looked quickly at the IV, which was still dripping into his right arm, then knelt to examine him. He removed the woolen socks that were serving as improvised mittens and repeated the examination that the captain had performed two days before on Washington. He could detect no sign of life. He thought briefly about starting CPR, but decided not to. Lieutenant Raschello and the captain had discussed Sanchez and Chief Maddison just yesterday, and it was agreed that they were likely to die. CPR might serve to postpone the inevitable but at the cost of a lot of hard work, which meant blowing a lot more carbon dioxide into the atmosphere. Steadman turned off the IV and removed the cannula from Sanchez's arm. The air had thickened over the past few hours, but through the haze Sanchez looked much the same as he always had. With the wardroom close to freezing, he wouldn't start to smell in the next three hours. Steadman would get a couple of men to take the body to the torpedo room after breakfast.

0545A, Above the USS *Tulsa*

Warrant Officer Sharples felt a shake at his shoulder and was instantly awake. As a result of many years operating in the most unusual places, he could sleep almost anywhere. This morning he had made a point of falling asleep almost as soon as the aircraft had taken off—many of the SPAG team were anxious about this jump, and Sharples reckoned that a display of sangfroid would do no harm. He'd been woken by the load master, who indicated that they had reached the drop zone. He looked toward the rear of the aircraft just as the large tailgate slowly began to open. Marchant was sitting closest to it, and the LMA was next to him. There was no conversation—the deafening noise from the engines precluded that. Like the rest of the team, they were staring into the black abyss beyond the aircraft. In the center of the fuselage were two large pallets packed with their equipment. Very shortly they would be rolled toward the tailgate and out into the darkness. The SPAG would follow.

Despite his years of experience, Sharples always felt a hollow sensation in the pit of his stomach just before a jump, but this morning it was more noticeable than usual. Their training jumps were usually into the relatively warm waters of the English Channel or the Mediterranean, and these were invariably conducted in daylight and in fair weather. Splashing down in a heavy sea being driven by winds that were gusting over thirty knots, in the dead of night with the threat of snow, was going to be a novel and daunting experience. Although the SPAG would be protected from the elements by their dry suits, they faced the hazard of being scattered over the ocean and unable to find either each other or their equipment. His concern was that the rescuers were running the risk of becoming the next group of casualties.

The jump had only been undertaken because the crew of the *Tulsa* was expected to start escaping very shortly. Since they would be dressed only in what clothing they could wear, their survival time in the water could be measured in minutes rather than hours. If the SPAG could get them out of the water and into the protection afforded by their four twenty-five-man life rafts, they would at least avoid certain death from hypothermia, drowning, or both. Any injured personnel would also face a brighter future. With the SPAG having among its members both a doctor and a medical assistant, emergency care would also be available— although exactly what could be achieved with the limited equipment they carried, and in these conditions, had never been carefully assessed. The other purpose of the jump was to make contact with the submarine and get a better picture of the conditions on board. That wasn't going to be easy either. The P3 had apparently failed to get through, and there seemed to be mixed messages as to whether the underwater telephone in the *Tulsa* was operational. The only bright spot on an otherwise bleak horizon was that the Norwegian Coast Guard ship *Nordvik* was due in the area within a few hours, and would recover the SPAG and any escapees from the stormy sea.

It was dark and bitterly cold, and the wind blew in icy gusts across the turbulent sea, driving flurries of snow before it. The C130 had circled the drop zone once already and at the start of its second circuit, three large white parachutes blossomed beneath and astern of it, then three more, followed by a series of smaller chutes. Warrant Officer Sharples hit the water and gasped as the freezing, salty water washed over his face. Somewhere not too far from him was an inflatable boat with an outboard motor. All he had to do was find it. He groped for the powerful flashlight that was hanging from a lanyard around his waist. He gripped it tightly in his right hand, already becoming numb with cold, fumbled with the switch, and shined it in an arc around him. It was only as he crested each wave that he could see any distance, and nowhere could he spot any of the white reflective strips that adorned all the containers that had been dropped from the aircraft. Sharples refused to panic. He waited until he reached the crest of another wave and screamed at the top of his voice in an effort to make contact with his colleagues. There was no reply. As he floated down the lee side of the wave he had just crested, it broke over his head and he was left gasping for air. He was determined not to panic.

0600A, USS *Tulsa*

"Larry, are you awake?" hissed Chief Lehner to the man in the bunk below him.

"No."

"Have you seen Mitch?" he continued. "Did he turn in, or is he still in the mess?"

"Why didn't you ask me directly, Carl? I'm right here," replied Santana. "God knows I wish I wasn't, though."

"And so say all of us," interrupted Czapek. "Now shut the fuck up, I'm trying to sleep."

"I've given up trying," continued Santana through chattering teeth. "It's too fucking cold. I've been shivering so much I ache all over. I think even my toes are shivering."

"I know my toes are shivering. So's my dick for that matter," exclaimed Czapek.

"That explains a lot," interjected Santana.

"Hilarious, Mitch, but that's not the point. I can live with the cold, but I can't sleep with you bleating like a lost sheep."

"Well, with such control over that sad excuse of a body of yours, you should be able to shut your god-damned ears," replied Santana, pausing before continuing in subdued tones. "I'm not so lucky. I've hardly slept at all. There's not much point when you think about it. Why spend your last few hours asleep? Might as well spend them awake, even if I have to spend them with an asshole like you, Larry." Chief Hicks stirred beneath the pile of bedclothes on his bunk, swung his legs round, and sat up.

"For Christ's sake, Mitch, stow that gloom and doom shit! Think positive, we're going to get out of here."

"Yeah, cheer up, Mitch," rejoined Lehner. "We'll get out alive, just wait and see."

"Wanna bet?" replied Mitch. "I can feel it in my bones."

"Lucky you. I can't feel shit in my bones, or my feet for that matter," complained Hicks.

"Why are you so negative, Mitch?" inquired Lehner. "You've got a wife and kid. That's more than I have to live for."

"He's not my kid, he's Paula's. The father was apparently some basketball scholar she met at school." Santana paused reflectively. "You know, if I had to draw up a ledger of my life right now, I'd be hard-pressed to decide if they should be entered under assets or liabilities."

"How come? Is something wrong?"

"You could say that, but I don't want to talk about it right now."

"It must be just about the only fucking thing you don't want to talk about," complained Czapek in exasperated tones. "Oh, fuck it! I'm wide-awake now. Thanks, everybody, for such a gripping conversation."

With that he swung around in his bunk and thudded to the deck. "You know the worst thing about being so fucking cold? It's making me have to piss like a horse," he exclaimed. With steam rising from the exposed skin on his head, he pulled on a green quilted jacket. "I'm going to top up the bilges, and then I'm off to the mess. If anybody wants to join me in some cards, don't hesitate to follow."

0630A, Radisson SAS Hotel, Bodø

Commander Selby awoke with a start in response to his alarm call, mumbled something into the telephone, and checked his watch. Although it was 0630 it felt like the middle of the night. The reason was obvious when he thought about it. It was still dark outside and, back in Norfolk, it was the middle of the night. Nonetheless, he leapt out of bed and headed for the shower, switching on the electric kettle by the television as he passed it. It was going to be a long day and a rather caffeine-intensive one, judging by the way he felt. He showered, dressed rapidly, and just had time to down the barely drinkable instant coffee he had made before it was time to assemble at the front of the building for transport to the HQ.

It was a dull, overcast day with a bitter wind that blew in gusts. As the group gradually grew in numbers there were sporadic attempts at conversation, but it was muted. None of the American contingent really wanted to be awake, let alone sociable. The sullen atmosphere persisted on the bus, and it was only toward the end of the twenty-minute drive, through increasingly mountainous terrain, that the sky began to brighten and, with it, their spirits. As they rounded an almost sheer granite cliff and entered a large compound, the extraordinary location of the HQ became apparent. All that could be seen of it was a path snaking toward a stack of sandbags that sheltered a hole in the side of the huge mountain dominating the skyline ahead. The group advanced up the path and into the entrance. There were no guards. Selby noticed the vast steel blast doors recessed into the walls of the tunnel, which was lit by a solitary string of lightbulbs suspended from the center of the ceiling. The path inclined uphill and curved to the right and, at last, a checkpoint came into view. The group was met by a young US Marine lieutenant serving on the NATO staff, who introduced himself as Ferdinand Sherman. The Marine proceeded to shepherd each of them through the elaborate security check, which culminated in the issuance of a temporary pass.

It took another six minutes of walking through tunnels, past another set of blast doors, and a brief elevator ride before their surroundings became less overtly subterranean, the only clue to their location being an eerie silence and the absence of any source of natural light. They were shown into a large office which, judging by the variety of posters of armored vehicles, guns, and missile launchers that decorated the walls, looked like it had recently been vacated by a multinational group of army officers. They were each allocated a desk and a telephone. "And this, sirs, will be your home for the next few days," announced Sherman. "The briefing this morning will be at 0830, and I will return in ten minutes to escort you to it. If you need anything, I'll be at extension 3349. Any questions?" There were many of them, thought Selby, but they could wait.

0130R, Groton, Connecticut

Marie woke with a start and sat up. She felt a chill run down her back and realized that the oversize shirt that she wore in bed was damp with sweat. Her pulse was racing. She reached over and switched on the bedside lamp. The house was silent apart from the muted groans and clicks of the radiators. The dream had been so real that she still couldn't believe she was at home in bed. It had been the volley of gunfire that had woken her. Gunfire from the honor guard that just a moment ago had been standing smartly at attention opposite her on the other side of the grave in Arlington Cemetery. She looked down at her hands and noticed with relief that she was not holding the flag that had been draped over John's coffin, the one that had been neatly folded into a dark blue triangle adorned with white, five-pointed stars and presented to her. She took a deep breath and exhaled loudly. It had been so very real.

Realizing that she was thirsty, Marie got out of bed, tiptoed past the boys' room, and went downstairs to the kitchen. She felt that she could use a belt of whiskey but settled instead for orange juice. When John was away she drank very little. When he was at home, it was a different story. They almost always had wine with their evening meal. Her mind had started to wander. Would he be coming home again? Would they cuddle up together on the settee after the kids were in bed and finish the wine while watching TV? Would he ever carry her to bed again and leave her breathless with excitement and overwhelmed with affection for the man who had claimed her just twelve short years ago? The corners of her mouth started to twitch, and she fought back the tears that were welling up in her eyes and threatening to spill out. She wasn't sure that she could deal with the loss of her husband. It would be a terrible blow, not just for her, but for the boys, too. Just not knowing whether he was alive or not was bad enough. Even though she took her dream to be evidence that she might be preparing herself, albeit subconsciously, for the worst, there was still a good chance that he was alive—despite all the prognostications of the TV pundits. So there was little point in crying about it. She dried her eyes and bullied herself into a positive attitude. It was a dream, just a bad dream. John was alive, she knew it. Of course he was. She picked up the glass of juice and returned to bed.

It had been three hours since she had fallen asleep, and she thought there might be more news. She reached for the remote and switched on the TV. The late-night news anchor was talking: "Members of the British Navy attacked an SNN camera crew in Hammerfest, Norway, this morning." There were pictures of men dressed in black jumpsuits in what looked like a diner, involved in some kind of scuffle. "The British were gathering before flying out over the Arctic Ocean to take part in the rescue of the crew of the USS *Tulsa*. No reason has been given for the attack. A spokesperson at the British Embassy in Oslo would only say that there would be an inquiry in the morning." The anchor, an attractive woman in her mid-thirties, continued. "We'll be right back with more headlines after this." Good for them, thought Marie. More people should attack aggressive reporters. The image cut to a commercial featuring two women chatting on the telephone, arranging to meet up.

"I'll even buy you an ice cream," said one of them.

"Make it a soda, you know dairy does a number on my stomach."

"You mean cramps, bloating, and gas?"

"Yeah, how did you know that?"

"I used to have that problem until my doctor recommended Lactozyme. It's the natural way to tackle lactose intolerance. Now I can eat what I like." Marie grabbed the remote and selected CNN. It was something that she'd not really noticed before, or perhaps she had become immune to it, but the number of ads for health-care products was truly staggering. Anybody would think that America was overwhelmed with disease, she thought. Could the nation's capital be compared with Calcutta, Manhattan with Manila, or Boston with Bangkok? Of course not. Were her compatriots all hypochondriacs? Maybe that was closer to the mark. To think that each day our mighty news organizations report real disasters from all over the world. People surviving floods and earthquakes, experiencing genuine loss and grief. Yet in the same broadcast, the viewer is routinely bombarded with the idea that everyday inconveniences such as diarrhea and menopausal hot flashes represent crises that demand an instant remedy. Who could expect her to be interested in lactose intolerance when John might be dead? The very idea was ridiculous. Marie realized that inadvertently she had slipped into a negative thinking pattern. She would have to be more positive. John was not dead. She had to believe that. She turned off the TV and the bedside lamp and settled back onto her pillow. Lactose intolerance? Oh God, who gives a damn about that, she thought.

0800Z, HMS *Wellington*

Freeman rolled over to the extent that his narrow cot would permit and instinctively stuck his index finger into the cup of tea that the steward had delivered some time ago. The tea was stone-cold, which indicated that it must be well after 0730, and he groped around beside the cup for his watch. It wasn't there. He groaned and reluctantly opened an eye. From the light in the passageway that spilled under his cabin door he saw that it had fallen to the deck and was too far away to reach. Richard Tremble had already gotten up and left for breakfast so, if he was to know the time, he would have to pick the damned thing up. Getting out of bed was the last thing Freeman wanted to do. Just moving his head was a sufficient stimulus to induce waves of nausea. There was no way he was going to eat breakfast, so he might as well stay put.

Freeman had served his sea time in ballistic-missile submarines and had never been interested in sailing. So, despite his twice-daily commute across Portsmouth Harbor on the Gosport ferry, he had never really had an opportunity to gain his sea legs. He'd slept only fitfully during the night between visits to the sink to bring up small volumes of bile-stained stomach contents. His throat was raw from the effort, and the ache in his upper abdomen told him that his diaphragm had received a workout that was unprecedented in recent years. The last time he'd tried to vomit quite so much was after an all-night drinking contest back when he was in medical school. He knew that he was exhausted and unwell, and wanted nothing more than to rest. He would advise any patient in his predicament to do the same. But he was cursed with a sense of duty and realized that he had to make some attempt to salvage his dignity in this miserable vessel. Although every fiber in his body urged him to stay where he was, he felt compelled to get up and sort out the first-reaction stores, which still occupied much of the hangar. The only good thing about this morning, he considered as he attempted to balance on one leg to get into his pants, was that the movement of *The Boot* was, if anything, a little less violent than yesterday.

0830A, COMJTFNON HQ, Bodø

An unusually large number of people were gathered in the briefing room. It was an unprecedented crowd for a Sunday. The regular NATO staff had been augmented by the large American contingent, a smaller one from the UK, and delegations from a number of other nations. Rear Admiral Risberg, a Norwegian, called the gathering to order in English, speaking with only a trace of an accent: "I would like to thank everybody for taking the trouble to give up their weekend to get here. I think we are all aware of why we are gathered. This meeting will deal only with the rescue of the crew of the USS *Tulsa*," he announced. "In order for this to be performed efficiently, it will be necessary for those around this table to get to know each other. And so I ask you each to introduce yourself, starting with Captain Eistvig of the Norwegian Coast Guard on my left."

It was a remarkably diverse group, including members of the Norwegian army, air force, and navy—one of them a meteorologist. There were two representatives from the Norwegian rescue coordination center, NATO staff officers from most of the northern European nations, two police officers, and two senior civil servants from the Norwegian departments of defense and health. To the admiral's right was an officer in his mid-forties with piercing blue eyes and dark hair that was graying at the temples. He was resplendent in the uniform of a captain in the Russian Navy. As it became his turn to introduce himself, Admiral Risberg interrupted him. "Thank you, ladies and gentlemen. To my right, I am delighted to introduce Captain Viktor Smetena, who is the head of logistics on the staff of Admiral Konstantin, deputy commander of the Russian Northern Fleet. He is with us to offer whatever assistance we require from the Russian Navy." He paused as a young lieutenant entered the room, whispered something in the admiral's ear, then left.

"Before I proceed, a little bit of etiquette needs to be addressed. We have, of course, simultaneous translation available, but I think I am right in saying that everyone present speaks English. Are there any objections to conducting the meeting in English?" The admiral eyed the two French officers halfway down the table to his left. There was no dissent. "Thank you," he continued. "I have not published a formal agenda for this meeting, although you should all have received by now a copy of the briefing notes that my staff prepared last night. What I would like to do first is to review the situation and the measures that have been taken already, then discuss the adequacy of these and identify if more needs to be done. From there, we will agree on a program of events that those around this table will arrange to be actioned. I am delighted to say that my government has given me the authority to deploy any and every asset available in Norway to achieve this rescue, and I am aware that many other nations are willing to make whatever contribution they can to ensure a satisfactory conclusion." There were nods around the table. "Good. You are all aware of the circumstances of the sinking—at least, what we know about the event. Is there anything more that the Russian Navy can tell us?" He looked at Captain Smetena, who paused before replying in flawless English.

"The investigation has only just commenced, but I do know that the USS *Tulsa* was involved in a collision last Thursday at about 1400 local time with the *Gepard*, or 'Cheetah' in English, which is an Akula II class submarine. It appears likely that the after main ballast tanks of the *Tulsa,* at least those on her port side, and her screw were damaged, and she may also have been holed. That is all I know. I understand that no direct contact has been made with the survivors, who are almost certainly in the forward compartment."

"Thank you, Captain," replied Admiral Risberg. "Ladies and gentlemen, if you now turn to page two of the briefing notes, I will quickly review the measures that I am aware have been taken already. First, the British SPAG team parachuted over the datum earlier this morning. Their mission is to recover survivors, should an early escape be necessary. They are also equipped to communicate with the submarine and, with any luck, we will soon know more about the conditions in the DISSUB."

"Excuse me, sir," interrupted Commander Sangster. "I think it's most unlikely that it will be possible for the SPAG to make contact with the *Tulsa*—at least, not by UWT. The system in 688s requires AC power. If what Captain Smetena said is correct, and the after compartment of the *Tulsa* is flooded, this will not be available." There was a stunned silence around the table. A bearded British lieutenant commander raised his hand.

"Lieutenant Commander Murphy?"

"Can I ask Commander Sangster how a rescue is

going to be mounted without UWT communications? To my knowledge this has never been attempted, certainly not on the exercises in which I have taken part."

"There are hull tap codes for all the important maneuvers. I don't think that will be a problem."

0915A, MV *Nordvik*

What remained of the SPAG team had been recovered by the *Nordvik*, and they now sat, dejected, in front of a meal for which they had little appetite. Warrant Officer Sharples, with his head heavily bandaged, was relating what had happened after he had splashed down into the sea. "I don't have to tell you what the water was like. Christ it was cold! The only way I could catch my breath was by treading water and facing downwind. Facing that way also meant that I could see something as I crested each wave without being blinded by spray . . . and what did I see? Fuck all. I didn't see a damned thing for twenty minutes. Then with my hands and just about everything else numb with cold, the outboard of one of the Gemin's hit me on the head. It didn't hurt at the time—" He smiled ruefully and rubbed the bandage. "—but it's pretty bloody sore now."

"Don't worry about that, Mr. Sharples, the *Nordvik*'s LMA will sew it up shortly. I'd do it myself, but I'm still feeling queasy and my hands are still quite numb," responded Surgeon Lieutenant Ward. "Anyway, don't let me interrupt, please carry on."

"Well, I got into the boat and eventually managed to start the engine and then began driving in wider and wider circles until I found the three of you."

"And weren't we glad to see you?" interjected Leading Seaman Percival. "I must say I was beginning to wonder if we were any better off than those poor sods in the *Tulsa*."

"Another hour in the water and I wouldn't have put money on it. . . ." The other three looked at

Surgeon Lieutenant Ward with some anxiety. Four of their colleagues were still missing and could be in exactly that situation. Ward looked directly at Warrant Officer Sharples and decided to change the subject. "Anyway, as soon as we had deployed the life rafts and you left, Percival called up the OSC, the pilot of the P3, who told him that the *Nordvik* should arrive at first light. He then got the underwater telephone ready while Martins and I prepared to receive escapers."

Leading Seaman Percival couldn't resist smiling at his recollection of the events that followed. "As soon as I had checked out the UWT I called the doctor over to talk to the *Tulsa*. You know, sir, even by flashlight you looked green." He started to chuckle. "I'm sure you won't mind if I tell everyone what happened next." Not waiting for a reply, he continued. "The boss came over from the next raft and no sooner had he grabbed hold of the handset than he threw up into it." Percival lost all control of his mirth and started to emit loud guffaws. The others, including Ward, joined in. "Now that's what I call a spew," he stammered as he started to turn bright red. "I've never seen such a fucking mess." They were all shrieking with laughter. "It must have taken us a good fifteen minutes to dismantle the mouthpiece and clean it out before we could use it again." He was beginning to control himself, as were his colleagues, but the effect of the laughter had been cathartic and they were noticeably more relaxed about the situation. Percival wiped his eyes and continued in more sober tones. "I don't know why we bothered. Even when we got the bloody thing working, there was no reply."

"It's all very well for you to make fun of me, leader, but I was not well. I really wasn't," pleaded Ward. "We were being tossed around like peas on a drum in those wretched rafts. It's convinced me of one thing—we're going to have to rethink how we do our business. I can tell you now, any idea that we could do anything more than haul survivors out of the water in weather like that is just fanciful."

"I think you're right, sir. We also need to take a look at how we can keep position over the DISSUB. After screaming into the UWT for fifteen minutes, I checked our position with the P3 and we were three miles downwind of the *Tulsa*. The sea anchors on those rafts are about as much use as a duck's left tit. No wonder we couldn't hear anything. I don't suppose they did in the *Tulsa* either."

"Except the doctor losing his breakfast."

"Very funny, Mr. Sharples," responded Ward. "Can't we drop that one now? Anyway, it's time to fix the gash on your head. I'll just wrap up by saying that we may want to look at equipping the Geminis with bigger engines. Forty horsepower was not enough to tow even two rafts in those conditions."

"I'll go along with that," replied Sharples. "Do you want me to make some notes about the problems we had, sir?"

"Yes, please, and the sooner the better. There's bound to be an inquiry when we get back."

0930A, COMJTFNON HQ, Bodø

Admiral Risberg continued by reviewing the dispatch and the estimated times of arrival of the MV *Salminster* and HMS *Wellington* at the datum and summarized their capabilities. He moved on to the departure of HMS *Vindictive* for Murmansk and the arrangements for flying the DSRV to its new destination. "That, ladies and gentlemen, is what we have so far. The question is, is it sufficient?" There was silence around the table. "Perhaps we should begin by building likely scenarios based on what we know, and seeing whether we can deal adequately with them," he continued. He looked at the American contingent, which was sitting immediately to the right of the Russian. "Do we have any idea how long the survivors will be able to remain in the boat?" Mike Selby glanced at his colleagues and realized that they expected him to respond.

"Well, sir, I performed some calculations before departing from Norfolk and nothing I have heard leads me to believe that they need to be modified. The precise timing depends on a number of factors but I estimate that they could start escaping anytime now."

"My staff have reached a similar estimate," replied Admiral Risberg, "which is why the SPAG was deployed early this morning. With the *Nordvik* now on task, I think we should be able to deal with the immediate consequences of an early escape."

"With respect, sir," Mike Selby interrupted. "I disagree. All we'll be able to do is retrieve the survivors from the water. I think I'm correct in saying that they will be making their escapes from a depth close to five hundred feet. The deepest that the Steinke Hood has been successfully tested is 450 feet, and that was many years ago and in an experimental rather than an operational setting. We're in uncharted water here, so to speak. The problem with deep escapes is that the brain absorbs a large amount of nitrogen while the escape trunk is being compressed, and during the early stages of an ascent through the water. So much, in fact, that there is not enough time for the bloodstream to clear it before reaching the surface. The result? Bubbles of gas form in the brain."

"You mean that they get the bends?" replied Admiral Risberg.

"That's right, sir."

"Surely escapes have been made successfully from deeper than five hundred feet?" It was Lieutenant Commander Murphy who was speaking. "I recall that in 1987 we made a series of escapes from a submarine, coincidentally in Norwegian waters, from something like six hundred feet."

"Yes you did," replied Selby. "However, there are substantial differences in the design and operation of our escape trunks and yours—as you know. Although it grieves me to say so, your design is superior to ours, and that is why we are currently refitting our boats with a similar system. Unfortunately, the *Tulsa* has not yet been modified and so we are stuck with a situation where we really don't know if an escape from five hundred feet can be made safely. I suppose my point is that we can't assume that there won't be problems, serious ones, and we need to plan for them."

"What do you have in mind?" asked the admiral.

"Well, sir, the fact is that we'll require the capability to treat the escapees in a compression chamber. We would need that anyway in this situation because the brain can be injured in other ways during submarine escapes."

"How?"

"At its most simple, the air in the lungs expands as the escapee rises through the water, through a physical principle known as Boyle's Law. This means that the submariner has to breathe out all the way to the surface. If he doesn't, the lungs become overexpanded and, basically, explode." There was a hushed silence around the room.

"That sounds pretty lethal to me," replied the admiral. "More a job for a body bag than a chamber, surely."

"It can be fatal, but not usually. The biggest problem arises if the air that escapes from the lungs gets into the bloodstream. If it does, it is quickly transported to the brain by the circulation and blocks its oxygen supply. The brain doesn't like that."

"OK, Doc, I think I understand. The HMS *Wellington* will be on task within two days or so, and she is carrying a chamber and a full medical team to deal with these cases. I suppose the question we have to deal with is what to do if an escape occurs in the meantime?"

"Not quite, sir. I think I am right in saying that the

chamber on the *Wellington* is one of the transportable ones known as a Type B." There were nods from the British group. Selby continued. "It's a great chamber, don't get me wrong. However, realistically it only has sufficient capacity for three seriously ill patients and one inside tender. If an escape from five hundred feet is as dangerous as I fear, then we will need considerably greater capacity than that."

"Thank you, Commander. Ladies and gentlemen, I'll throw the discussion open now. Has anyone any ideas as to how we can get additional chambers to the datum?"

The discussion lasted for more than thirty minutes. There were two possible solutions. The first was to get a North Sea oil-platform support ship, equipped with a saturation diving system, up to the Arctic Ocean. The Department of Defense would look into chartering one of them and the Norwegian Navy would supply the medical support. The other solution was to fly the casualties ashore to one of the many clinical hyperbaric complexes in Norway. Some additional airlift capability was going to be required to achieve that. Although the flight deck of the *Wellington* could accept helicopters as large as the triple-engined Merlin, it was the only one that could in the currently planned flotilla. The *Nordvik* could only handle smaller aircraft and the *Salminster* had no flight deck at all. Given that it was a 520-nautical-mile round-trip from Hammerfest to the datum, another, preferably larger, flight deck would be highly desirable. In addition, more substantial hospital facilities would be well worth having—the facilities in the *Wellington* were, after all, designed to provide little more than first aid. The British and French agreed to look into getting an aircraft carrier on task. Captain Smetana also offered to assist in this respect, although he was uncertain of the time frame in which a ship might be made ready. In fact, he knew perfectly well that there was no chance of getting a Russian helicopter carrier operational in the time available. Nonetheless, the gesture was warmly received.

0930A, MV *Nordvik*

With daylight, the view over the stormy sea became both beautiful and fearsome. The deep blue-gray of the water was speckled with white as the wind blew the tops off the waves and deposited them in white streaks down their lee sides. Although the air temperature was just above freezing, the wind made it feel much colder, and no member of the ship's company stayed on the upper deck for a moment longer than he had to. The same rules did not apply to the three members of the SPAG who were huddled together on the flight deck, anxious to catch the first glimpse of the helicopter as it returned. The good news was that two of their colleagues had been found. As the Lynx landed, their exuberance overwhelmed them, and they began their dash toward the helicopter. Reeling like drunkards, they raced across the pitching deck, anxious to greet their long-lost colleagues. Although barely conscious, both Marchant and the leading medical assistant were pale and shaking with cold to the point that they were barely able to walk. As they were escorted into the hangar and down to the sick bay, Lieutenant Marchant began to assimilate the news of the rest of his group. He realized that the chances of his two missing colleagues being recovered alive were receding as each minute passed. All they had to do was lose consciousness in the water, just briefly, and they would surely drown in these conditions. Indeed, it was probably too late already.

Such thoughts were not uppermost in the minds of the other members of the SPAG. Even Warrant Officer Sharples, who had remained in the sick bay to have his scalp wound sutured, was keen to hear what had happened to the new arrivals. As they stripped and sat down in the shower to warm up,

Marchant and the LMA took turns recounting their
story through chattering teeth. They had been the
first two to jump and, upon landing in the water,
had no difficulty in finding one of the inflatables.
They had both climbed into it and tried to get the
engine started. They had been rewarded with a stubborn refusal. Try as they might, the damned thing
wouldn't start. It wasn't the only thing that didn't
work. Despite having been checked only the previous day, the battery in their radio appeared to be
dead. Realizing that they were rapidly drifting away
from the drop zone, they eventually gave up trying
to start the engine, lay exhausted on the plywood
deck of the Gemini, and waited for daylight. During
the following half hour they had been repeatedly
swamped by breaking waves and, while they were
bailing out, a particularly large wave capsized the
boat, throwing them both into the water. Although
they had managed to swim back to it, they could
not right it. Each time they scrambled onto the up-
turned hull they were either thrown or washed off
it, and they eventually realized that their only hope
was to hang on for as long as they could—which is
what they did until they were found. They had neither seen nor heard anything of the rest of the
group.

1000A, COMJTFNON HQ, Bodø

The meeting had already lasted for ninety minutes,
and those around the table had begun to realize that
they had only scratched the surface of the many issues that
presented themselves. It was decided that, rather than
meet as a group, they would break up into smaller,
specialized working parties. "Before we break up,
there is one issue which will impact us all that we
have not discussed yet, and that is a weather forecast
at the datum," announced the admiral. He turned to
his left and caught the eye of his meteorological offi-

cer. "If you please, Commander." Commander Lars-son rose to his feet.

"Rather than bore you with lengthy explanations, I will quickly summarize. A slow-moving cold front has just passed over the area, and it has brought with it some precipitation, mainly snow, and winds gusting to Force 7, that's about thirty knots. I expect this will have blown over by this evening, when an area of high pressure will bring with it a window of calmer seas, but it will be much colder. So I'm forecasting diminish-ing winds, down to Force 3, accompanied by a sea-state of two to three by midday tomorrow. The daily high temperature will be no more than zero Celsius, falling to minus fifteen overnight. There is another depression with two frontal systems following on, but I am not expecting that to materialize until Wednes-day evening."

"Thank you, Commander Larsson. Any questions?"

"Yes, sir." It was Lieutenant Commander Murphy. "How confident is the commander of this forecast? The only reason I ask is because our rescue capability is highly dependent on the weather."

"Commander?" inquired the admiral.

"Forecasting the weather in this part of the world is, as yet, a rather imprecise science. It is not like San Diego!" There were chuckles around the table. "My confidence decreases with time. I am 90 percent con-fident of tomorrow's forecast, for Tuesday it would fall to, say, 70 percent, and after that no more than 50 percent. I should say that I am quite confident about what is going to happen—it's the timing that presents the problem."

"Just one more thing," continued the British officer. "Do you expect the next depression to be as bad as the last one?"

"Hard to say. At the moment it is reading 970 milli-bars and falling. If this keeps up, it will be at least as bad as the last one."

"Well, if there are no more questions, I will ask the

working parties to leave, and we will reconvene at 1300." With that, the admiral turned to Captain Smetana and escorted him out of the room.

1100A, USS *Tulsa*

Enzo was frustrated. As time went by, it was increasingly likely that a ship would arrive topside but, unless they carried explosive charges, they would be none the wiser. It was part of a bigger problem. The *Tulsa* could receive a small number of specific messages via these charges, but there was no way for them to reply other than to indicate their position with smokes or their one remaining SLOT buoy. If they were to get any other information out of the boat, a new approach would be needed. Everybody on board had family and loved ones back in the States and desperately wanted to let them know that they were still alive. He had to find a way of doing this.

He was also painfully aware that it had been two days since he had last moved his bowels. He had been postponing it because the prospect of using a plastic bag lacked appeal, particularly as he was unlikely to be the first to use it. He was not even convinced of the practicality of the idea. There had been a conspiracy of silence over the issue amongst his colleagues, and he felt sufficiently embarrassed about it that he was reluctant to discuss the finer points of technique with anyone who might have been successful. However, the cramping sensations in his belly made the urgency of the situation undeniable, and he therefore decided to bite the bullet. He normally enjoyed some of his more lucid moments in the confines of the head and it might be that this would be a good opportunity to ponder the signaling problem before discussing it with the captain. He was aware that Richter did not wish to be disturbed this morning, and so he would only bother him once he had a fully formed proposal.

Just as he had predicted, Enzo found squatting over a plastic bag impossibly difficult. He quickly lost his balance and stepped in the mess that he had hoped to avoid. Having cleaned up, he realized that the solution was to place the bag in the commode, which he did. Comfortable at last, he considered the morning's problem anew and within moments it became obvious what he should do.

1120A, USS *Tulsa*

"Come in." Richter sounded tired, but Enzo had no option but to disturb him.

"I'm sorry to bother you, sir." Richter slowly turned onto his side and used a pillow to prop up his head. He then reached for the battle lantern and switched it on. Enzo studied his captain, at least, the small bit that he could see. All but his head was covered by layers of blankets that seemingly were doing little to keep him warm. He was obviously shivering and looked dreadful. Even the stubble that covered most of his face and the deep shadows cast by the lantern couldn't disguise the fact that he was horribly pale. The dark bags under his eyes indicated that he was tired and, as well as being cold, he was obviously in considerable pain. Even his cheeks looked thin and hollow. If anything, Richter's stateroom felt colder than the rest of the boat—even Enzo had to suppress a shiver.

"Oh, it's you, Enzo. Take a seat. What's up?"

"How are you feeling, sir?"

"Between you and me, not too good. Don't ask me to read anything. I'm seeing double. It's not so bad with you in the room. If it was Gallagher, I might not like it so much!" He half smiled. "How about you?"

"Oh, I'm fine. I got almost eight hours sleep last night and feel better for it, but I'm sorry to report that Petty Officer Sanchez died earlier this morning. I don't think that there was much more we could have done."

"No indeed. You're not too cut up about it, are you? I know you were upset about Washington."

"No, sir, I think we all expected it. I'm afraid it looks like Chief Maddison is going the same way. His breathing is very irregular this morning." Enzo noticed that Richter was fighting to suppress a shiver and was gritting his teeth.

"How are the rest of the men?"

"I don't really know, sir. The high spirits that followed the P3 contact has largely evaporated. The atmosphere's almost sullen. Nobody's saying much, not even at breakfast. It's quiet. I expect the Valium has something to do with it. Nobody's gone crazy or anything like that. I suppose that's good news."

"Do you think we're going to get out?"

Enzo paused and rubbed his chin before replying. He had found that the early stages of growing a beard were uncomfortably itchy. "Sir, I really don't know what to think. Sometimes I can convince myself that we will, other times I'm not so sure."

"You know why I asked, don't you?" Enzo didn't reply immediately because the captain was suddenly convulsed with shivering. As soon as he stopped shaking Richter drew the blankets over his shoulders and continued. "You see, if you're not certain yourself that we're going to be rescued, you're never going to persuade anybody else. You have many good points, Enzo, but acting isn't one of them."

"You mean that unless I am convinced, nobody else will be?"

"More or less."

"I'll work on it, sir." Enzo paused again, unsure if he should trouble Richter with his problems now or wait until he was looking a bit better. Since he didn't know when that would be he went ahead. "It would help if we could communicate with topside, assuming anyone is there. At the moment we can't. That's actually why I disturbed you this morning. Sure we can tell people where we are, but that's about it. There's another problem, if there is anyone topside, the chances are they won't be American—there's not been enough time for one of our ships to get here. In all probability it'll be Norwegian or Russian. I've looked and we don't carry the NATO underwater charge codes. So understanding the Norwegians is going to be tough, and I have absolutely no idea what codes the Russians might use. So I can see a crazy situation in which all we will be able to do is say to each other 'I'm here.' "

"Oh God," Richter replied and closed his eyes. "I should have thought of that. Give me a few moments to think about it and see if there isn't a way around it."

"I've actually had an idea, sir. We could put a message in a container, secure it to a smoke, and send it up through the signal ejector." Richter thought for a moment.

"Nice idea, Enzo, but there are some problems you'll have to overcome first. What are you going to use as a container? It must be flexible, otherwise it'll be crushed by the water pressure as soon as it leaves the boat."

"Yes, it also has to be waterproof. So how about using one Zip-loc bag inside another? That would probably do the trick. You see, they're also light, and so they shouldn't interfere too much with the buoyancy of the smoke."

"Sure, but they're plastic, and the smoke will get darned hot once it ignites. How are you going to secure the bag to it? Duct tape won't do."

"No it won't. I thought of using torpedo guidance wire. It is very fine and strong, and should be ideal."

"You might just be right, Enzo. Give it a try. Are you planning on sending a message right now?"

"I don't see why not, sir. It's not as if we're short of smokes."

"True. Let me see it before you send it."

"I'll get right to it, sir."

0720R, Groton, Connecticut

Marie reluctantly acknowledged that she was unlikely to go back to sleep. Despite going to bed late, she had been half-awake ever since the latest nightmare and was exhausted. The house was silent apart from the clicking of the heating system, so the boys were obviously still asleep. As it was Sunday, she would let them wake up in their own time. She considered the matter and decided to give church a miss. There was no way she could handle the sympathy. Yesterday had been bad enough with all the phone calls. It had seemed that just about everybody she had ever known had called. It had been kind of them, and she was sure that most of the calls were well intentioned, unlike the prying ones from the press. She'd reached the point of not answering the phone unless she recognized the number on the caller ID and was seriously considering getting the Southern New England Telephone Company to change her number to an unlisted one. There was another reason for missing church. Yesterday, as soon as it became clear that the squadron was having trouble contacting all the families, Marie and Jean had managed to reach all but five of them. This morning she wanted to make it a clean sweep. They knew their names, but it was going to take some detective work to locate them. The phone rang abruptly. "Hello?"

"Marie, honey, it's Jean."

The introduction had been unnecessary. Marie had recognized her voice immediately. Unlike the day before, she was actually quite glad to hear from her. With her own phone being so busy, it had actually been Jean who had run the battery flat on her mobile as she compiled the families' phone list. She'd even managed to do so while keeping an eye on the boys. Maybe she had been a little hasty in her judgment of Jean. One thing was sure, Marie could no longer doubt her good intentions. "I've not woken you, have I?"

"No. I didn't sleep too well."

"I can understand that. Look, I thought I'd call to let you know that I've found the Simpsons and the Gallaghers." There was a distinct tone of triumph in her voice.

"That's fantastic! I'm afraid I've made no more progress. The phone just kept ringing after you went home. I even had a call from Commodore Phillips."

"What did he want?"

"Well, he said that he wanted to thank us for helping to find the families, but then went on to talk about the interview."

"Oh. What did he say?"

"He was quite nice about it, but it was obvious he wasn't too pleased."

"You were afraid of that, weren't you?"

"Well, I was able to convince him that I wouldn't do it again, even though SNN offered me $10,000 for another interview."

"They did what?"

"They offered me 10K for another interview." There was a pause, and Marie heard a sharp intake of breath from Jean. "Golly, and you turned them down?"

"Look, Jean, they're just manipulative bastards. It takes quite a bit to reduce me to tears, but they managed it in short order yesterday. That's all they wanted—pictures of a weeping widow, and I'm not even a widow. No, I turned them down flat. I think that convinced the commodore that he wouldn't be seeing me on the tube again."

"Hell, I would think that would convince anybody."

"There's something else. I had a call from the chaplain service. They're offering the families accommodation on the base. You might want to mention that if you manage to get in touch with the last three."

"Is that to keep the press away?"

"I don't think so. They were talking about counseling."

"Are you going to take them up on the offer?"

"Are you kidding? I can only imagine what it would be like locked up in the Susse Chalet with wall-to-wall

clerics, welfare officers, and shrinks. Not my scene,
I think."

Jean didn't reply immediately. It sounded like Marie
was holding up remarkably well, given the circumstances. "I can understand your feelings about that,
especially after working in a hospital. Look, do you
want me to come over? You know it's no trouble."

"Thanks, Jean. But I think I'll spend a little time
with the boys this morning. I'm going to have to talk
to them some more about what's happened. Is it OK
if I call you later?"

"Of course it is. And let me know if you find any
of the missing three."

"I will. You do the same. Bye for now."

"Bye, honey."

Marie replaced the receiver and contemplated her
decision not to move onto the base. There was more
to it than the prospect of cloying sympathy. She was
proud of the fact with John being away so much of
the time, she'd always managed pretty well by herself
and would ride this storm out in her own way. It was
not that she was fiercely independent—she wasn't. It
was just that she had grown into a life that she had
largely shaped, and she wasn't prepared to yield it at
the first sign of trouble. One positive move she would
make, however, would be to visit the ambulatory care
center on the base and get something to help her
sleep. Another night like last night was more than she
could handle. If anything would drive her into the
Susse Chalet, it would be a combination of exhaustion
and nightmares. She had suffered terribly from them
as a child, and it was only when her doctor had pre-
scribed a strong sedative that she eventually managed
to sleep through the night. She would try them again.

Marie rolled over, stretched out her hand, turned on
the television, and automatically began to click through
the news channels. The news was that there was no
more news on the *Tulsa*. Instead there was saturation
punditry, with each channel offering a similar diet. The

graphic artists had sufficient time to churn out endless images of what the forward compartment of the *Tulsa* might look like. On one channel, a dietician was expounding on what the survivors might be eating and drinking. On another, an air-conditioning engineer, a retired submariner and a physiologist from Duke University were discussing the difficulties that the survivors faced in maintaining a breathable atmosphere. On yet another there was an animation of how the DSRV works, illustrated further with clips from *The Hunt for Red October*. Her sense of compulsion to watch eventually overwhelmed her instinct to try to go back to sleep, so she fluffed up her pillow and stared at the screen.

She was roused from her trancelike state by an image of her own home. In what looked like a live broadcast, that bastard John Scott was standing in front of a camera right in front of her house. Suddenly consumed with curiosity, she went to the window, separated the curtains slightly, and peered out. She couldn't believe her eyes. There were no fewer than three TV vans with people milling around them, a couple of still photographers, and, in a gaggle of their own, what Marie took to be a group of journalists. Standing in front of the SNN van, illuminated by arc lights, stood John Scott. She closed her curtains and went back to bed. On the TV now was a rerun of the interview she'd given yesterday. She'd not seen it before. God I look pale, she thought. Marie watched, mesmerized, up to the point when she'd started to cry. Despite her determination to keep a positive attitude, tears welled up in her eyes as she turned off the TV.

1300A, USS *Tulsa*

Enzo put the finishing touches to his SITREP and took it to the captain. Richter desperately wanted to read it and found that by closing one eye, his double vision ameliorated to the point where he could just do so if he didn't shiver. Squinting through his right eye, he read the following:

USS TULSA

DTG OF SINKING	281400 OCT
DTG OF SITREP	311220 OCT
SENIOR SURVIVOR	Commander G B Richter, USN
AVAILABLE COMPARTMENTS	FWD only
ESTIMATED EXTENT OF FLOODING	2% fwd, 100% aft, reactor compartment unknown
STATUS OF REACTOR	Shut Down
ESCAPE DEPTH	473 fsw
TRIM	3° bow up
LIST	8° to starboard
NUMBER OF SURVIVORS	97
INTERNAL PRESSURE	7 fsw rising at 2 fsw per day
LAST O_2 READING	19.6 % (SE) TIME TAKEN 1200A
LAST CO_2 READING (Draeger)	2.9 % (SE) TIME TAKEN 1200A
OXYGEN BANK PRESSURE	Bank 1 2069 psi TIME TAKEN 1210A Bank 2 unavailable
# CHLORATE CANDLES UNUSED	172
CO_2 SCRUBBING METHOD	Modified Hopper (employing battery-well fan)
# LiOH CANISTERS UNUSED	105

DAMAGE TO SUBMARINE: After ballast tanks holed, stern seal and propeller damaged in collision with an Akula class submarine. After compartment flooded, watertight bulkhead holding. After escape trunk jammed OPEN and unserviceable. Forward trunk checked and serviceable. No escapes through it attempted to date.

INJURED PERSONNEL	DECEASED PERSONNEL		
CDR Geoff Richter	LCDR John Dowling	MM3(SS) Gresham Moden	
*LCDR Curtis Mitchell	ENS Craig Wagner	EM2(SS) Jerry Cramer	
LT Tim Gallagher	MMC(SS) Felix Armstrong	EM2(SS) Bill Crang	
*ETC(SS) Richard Maddison	EMC(SS) Noel Adams	EM3(SS) Robb Wong	
MSC(SS) Adam Percival	ETC(SS) Brian Keeling	EM3(SS) Euian Forte	
ET1(SS) Claude Toynbee	FTC(SS) Joseph Grimaldi	ET3(SS) Earl Courtney	
STS1(SS) Jason Simpson	MM1(SS) Pete Shapiro	ET3(SS) William Schriver	
STS2(SS) Carl Hyldegaard	MM1(SS) Eugene Smith	ET3(SS) Proctor Emmanuel	
*STS2(SS) Kevin Goring	ET1(SS) Samuel Pierce	YN3(SS) Pedro Sanchez	
STS2(SS) Mario Lombardi	HM1(SS) Denzel Richards	FT3(SU) Darrell Boyd	
ET2(SS) Floyd Grumann	MM2(SS) Gene Willmot	SK3(SS) Nathan Shafer	
MM2(SS) Tor Schiffer	ET2(SS) Terry Prosser	STSSN(SS) Jacob Washington	
ET2(SS) Jacko Sherman	MM2(SS) Michael Yokumkus	STSSR(SS) Kennedy Belford	
ET2(SS) Ben Crawford	MS2(SS) Robert Taylor	MMFN(SU) Salvatore Deniro	
FT2(SS) Joel Goldblatt	MM2(SS) Conran Domico	ETSA(SU) Shaun Tuttle	
SN(SS) Uri Formann	MM2(SS) Tony Edge	ETSA(SU) Dominic Lewis	
MSSN(SU) Greg Chapman	MM2(SU) Solomon Webb		
(*seriously injured)			

ISSUES: UWT not operational. If NATO charge codes are being used, these are not understood. Request that USN codes be employed from now on. Also request estimated time of rescue.

Richter frowned. "The pressure's up to seven feet of seawater now is it? What the hell's going on? Have you done a radiation survey?"

"Not since the sinking. As you know, we were clean then."

"Do another one. I'm just wondering if anything is coming over from the reactor compartment."

"Even if it is, sir, it doesn't have to be radioactive."

"I know that, Enzo. The point is that it could be if the reactor was damaged in the collision. If it wasn't, that's fine, we can forget about the pressure for the moment, as the leak must be very small."

"What if we do detect radiation?"

"We'll cross that bridge when we get to it. You know as well as I do that if the dose rate is high enough, we'll have a choice of either sitting here and cooking or making an escape to the surface. I don't want to contemplate either unless I must." Richter screwed up one eye again and returned his gaze to the SITREP. "I guess you've covered the bases. This should give the folks topside, if there are any, something to sink their teeth into. I don't suppose they need persuading that the sooner they come and get us, the better?"

"I doubt it, sir."

"OK, Enzo, send it up. If there is anything we've missed, we can always send another."

"Aye, aye, sir." Enzo spun on his heel and left Richter's stateroom to find Chief Czapek.

1310A, MV *Nordvik*

Commander Jan Jonsson sat in his chair on the starboard side of the bridge staring at the sea. He loved rough weather, despite the additional wear and tear it imposed on his ship. There were few sights to match the wild beauty of an angry ocean. Today's weather could hardly be put into that category, as there were now breaks in the cloud, and it was obvious that the storm was blowing itself out. Nonetheless, he was mes-

merized by the power of the elements and, from the
vantage point of his warm, dry bridge, there were few
better places to view it. The downside to today's
weather was that it seriously degraded the performance of his Simrad sonar. Being a Coast Guard vessel, the *Nordvik* was not equipped to hunt submarines.
The Simrad was mainly used to detect ice. Nonetheless, Jonsson had hoped that it might be able to locate
the *Tulsa* and had been more than a little disappointed
that, so far, his hopes were being dashed.

His attention dwelled for a moment on a black-
backed gull that was gliding on the prevailing wind
with effortless skill, just above the starboard bridge
wing. Its head bobbed from side to side as it surveyed
the scene below it, almost as if it was trying to make
up its mind whether to land or not. It decided not to
and, with a squawk, banked to its right and dived
down toward the water. It must have spotted some
food, Jonsson thought. As he followed the bird down
he noticed a slight discoloration of the water about
three miles off the starboard beam. He reached down
to a pocket just below the right armrest on his chair
and retrieved his binoculars. It took a few moments
for him to train them on the spot he'd noticed, but
once he had done so, there was no mistaking it.

"Officer of the watch!"

The young, blond lieutenant who had been peering
out of the port-side bridge windows, snapped his head
round and looked at the captain. "Yes, sir?"

"Take a look at this. What do you see?" He pointed
to the area of discoloration. "Here, use these." He
handed the lieutenant his glasses. The young man
stared through the binoculars for a full minute before
replying. "Red smoke, sir."

"Meaning?"

"It can only be the *Tulsa*, sir."

"I agree. Let's go and tell her we're here."

1330A, USS *Tulsa*

Everybody on board heard them: six small explosions, one after the other, and then silence. Enzo was delighted. Either this was an incredible coincidence, or there was a surface craft up there that had spotted his smoke signal. He had no idea what six charges meant, but then again, it really didn't matter right now. The fact that contact had been made was the overwhelming priority. Once they had read the SITREP, they would presumably use codes that did make some sense. He was torn between giving the captain the good news about the radiation survey and gauging the reaction of the crew to the explosive charges. He chose the latter and headed into the crew's mess. The place was transformed. The small group running the atmosphere control were grinning like Cheshire cats, slapping each other on the back. Others were arriving from the bunk spaces and joining in the celebration. Enzo could hear cheering coming from those who had yet to leave their bunks. The sense of relief was palpable. Enzo wondered if he should dampen the enthusiasm with a brief dose of reality—the plain fact was that they were still a long way from being rescued. But he decided against it. He'd let the men enjoy themselves for now and would address them over the evening meal.

Just about the only place that had not been transformed was the chiefs' mess. The four men who sat around the table just carried on playing cards. The stakes had reached $25 a point, and Mitch Santana was extremely tired. Larry Czapek was on a roll. His last trick, led with the ten of clubs, had drawn the ace of hearts, and he had just shot the moon. "So what's the score?" he asked triumphantly. Chief Hicks looked down at the piece of paper in front of him and jotted down a series of numbers.

"OK, Larry won that game. It cost the rest of us $650 each. Adding that to the previous totals. . . ."

Chief Hicks picked up his calculator and punched in
a series of numbers. . . . "Carl, you're winning, you're
up $8,250; Larry's next with $3,017; I'm down $1,164
and Mitch, guess what? This is a zero sum game, so
I'm proud to announce that you've lost an impressive $10,103."

Despite not joining the celebrations, the significance
of the explosive charges had not been lost on those
around the table. Mitch Santana's conviction that he
was going to die meant that playing for high stakes
and losing was not a problem. It would, however, become one for his wife if the winners ever claimed their
money, an outcome that had just become a little more
likely. However, there would almost be a poetic justice
to that, he considered. The last time he'd been home
he had become suspicious of her infidelity. He'd answered too many phone calls at home where the caller
had presumably dialed the wrong number, but never
said anything. Paula had not changed jobs, but she
was now apparently required to attend unscheduled
meetings late into the evening. Worse, on three occasions when he'd called to ask what time she'd be
home, she was not even in the office. Then there were
the innuendo-laden e-mails from an "Alex Hoffman,"
apparently a female friend but one with the writing
style of a horny, adolescent male. Even the quality of
their sex life had taken a nose dive. Whenever she
wasn't too tired, she was uncharacteristically cold and
distant. It had taken Santana a month to work out
what was going on, but that had left him with no time
to confront her with any prospect of a satisfactory
resolution before sailing for this deployment. One
thing he never wanted to do was sail in the middle of
a big fight. He had therefore decided to postpone any
argument until his return. This would allow him an
opportunity to see if anything had changed before he
challenged her, and, in the meantime, he had resolved
to set the matter to one side.

Unfortunately, in the nearly seven weeks since

leaving Groton, he had been able to think of little else, and his meticulous recollection of events and analysis of the evidence had increasingly absorbed him with each passing day. His reluctance to discuss the matter with anybody, however, resulted in the process being less than evenhanded to the point that he had now convinced himself of her guilt. Ever since the sinking, his overwhelming feelings of betrayal and bitterness toward his wife had led him to accept that dying in the *Tulsa* might not be too bad an outcome. The high probability of such an eventuality had served as a fertilizer for the thought and the idea of dying and leaving Paula with an enormous debt to settle had provided warmth and sunlight for the seedling plan that was now growing precociously in his mind.

Uncharacteristically, it was Larry Czapek who broke the silence. "No comment, Mitch?" Santana snapped his thoughts back to the game.

"I suppose I've had worse days," he replied phlegmatically. The raised eyebrows encouraged him to continue. "I've just had a run of bad luck. Things will turn around, just you wait and see."

"I suppose," started Hicks. "If God had wanted you to be rich, he would never have given you a wife." He grinned from ear to ear. Perhaps because he was so tired, Santana took the remark seriously and bit back.

"For an intelligent man, Bill, you occasionally say some incredibly stupid things. For one thing, my wife's worth more than I am and, for another, what the hell has God got to do with it? He had absolutely nothing to do with my getting married. I don't know how you get off on this crap. What about the Hicks's breeding program? Has that been organized by God, or have you had something to do with it? How many kids do you have now anyway? Six is it?"

"Five."

"And you'll be in hock to each of them emotionally

and financially until either you or they drop dead. Call that a gift from God?"

"I believe God played an important part in their creation, just like he did with everything else."

"I'd forgotten, you've been brainwashed."

Santana had become really angry with Bill Hicks, whose piety and self-satisfaction had always grated on him. And the combination of fatigue, foul air, and the cold had eroded his self-control to the point that he decided to take another shot at him. "Tell me, Bill, what's with all this God shit? I mean, it's the biggest con going. Forget tech stocks or casinos, even the drug gangs. They all deliver products of a kind. What does the church offer?" Before Bill had a chance to reply, Mitch continued. "No idea? Then I'll tell you. Holy water, funny smells, and hot air by the balloonful. Oh, and a book that gets revised every three hundred years or so, whether it needs it or not. What a scam."

"Look, we agreed to leave religion out of this," insisted Chief Lehner. "Stow it, Mitch."

"Bill started it, and anyway, I've got just one more thing to say." He looked around the group in an almost conspiratorial manner, lowering his voice. "Do you know the real genius of the church is its marketing plan?" Once again Santana didn't wait for a reaction. "It's clever because it's almost effortless. All they have to do is encourage their sheep—sorry, flock—to breed like flies, reckoning, rightly, that the parents will brainwash the next generation of suckers for them. The clergy then just hold out their hands and expect these patsies to cough up their hard-earned dough each week to provide the hierarchy with housing, food, and fancy clothes. All the church has to do is to persuade them that birth control is evil and the cycle is repeated. It has to be the ultimate parasite's charter and, incredibly, it's perfectly legal. Now, I wouldn't mind if they just kept to themselves, but they don't. The rational folk who refuse to be conned haven't just been called nasty names and burned at the stake over the years. Oh no. Like it or not, they've been dragged into one war after another that has, as its root cause, intolerant religious bigotry. And in periods of peace, everyone suffers the inevitable consequences of un-controlled breeding—urban sprawl, pollution, deforestation, and overfishing that will eventually ruin the planet. That's God's church for you and, as far as I am concerned, you can shove it up your ass."

"Is that it? Are you through now? Do you feel better?" asked Hicks. "Because I'm not going to respond to that sacrilegious crap. Everybody around the table can judge who the intolerant bigot in here is."

"Look, break it up, guys," interrupted Lehner. "Let's play cards."

"OK, Carl, but Bill, just leave God out of this if you don't want another broadside."

They all looked around as the door opened and Master Chief Steadman walked in. He didn't look to be in a particularly good mood. "What's going on in here?" he demanded.

"A game of hearts. Do you have a problem with that?"

"How come just about everyone else is doing their damnedest to sleep and keep their carbon-dioxide production down, and the four of you feel entitled to play cards, huh?"

Larry Czapek felt that he could speak for them all. "Have you tried to sleep recently?"

"It may have escaped your notice, but I have been busy with the injured. I'd give my grandmother away to get some sleep right now."

"Well, don't bother, it's not possible. I tell you, I never thought I'd see the day when I didn't want to lie in bed, but that day has arrived. It has for all of us."

"I was going crazy in my bunk," said Mitch. "There's not enough light to read by and, in any case, I couldn't concentrate. We've run out of jokes, and so we thought we'd try cards. Do you have a problem with that?"

"You're all chiefs. You're supposed to set an example. Don't you think that everybody else feels the same way? What would happen if they all followed your example and got up? I'll tell you, it would probably cut a whole day off the time we can survive down here."

"Look, we've not broadcast this, nobody else knows we're here. Let it drop. Do you need a hand in the wardroom?"

"When was the last time you took a first-aid course Mitch?"

"Sometime in the last century."

"Yeah, so thanks but no thanks." Steadman thought for a few moments. "OK, I'll let you stay in here and, so long as nobody else starts a card school, I'll turn a blind eye."

"Thanks, Stan."

"Yeah, thanks, Stan," chimed in the other three. As the COB turned and made to leave, it was Carl Lehner who spoke next.

"Dealer's dealing, we'll be passing across the table, it's still $25 a point. . . ."

1500A, COMJTFNON HQ, Bodø

"That's incredible," exclaimed Mike Selby as he re-read the message from the *Nordvik* that had just been passed to him. "Quite incredible."

"What is?" inquired Surgeon Commander Engelsen, who was sitting next to him and was chairing the medical working party.

"I'll need to check with my spreadsheet, but those guys in the *Tulsa* are generating about half as much CO_2 as I was expecting. They've even managed to jury-rig a hopper to work on DC power. Whoever did that has saved a lot of lives."

"Show me."

Selby handed the message to Engelsen, then reached under the table to retrieve his notebook computer. He waited for the few moments it took to boot up before opening the spreadsheet file that he had received that morning by e-mail from the Naval Submarine Medical Research Laboratory in Groton. It contained a reasonably sophisticated mathematical model of the forward compartment of a 688, and Selby started to load in the information that had been sent up from the *Tulsa*. He tilted the screen toward Engelsen and moved the pointer over the cell containing the CO_2 production rate.

"You see? As I thought. Those guys must all be fast asleep. It's the only way I can begin to explain these numbers. You realize this takes a lot of heat off us. If you look at the prediction now," he said, pointing at another cell, "we've got another four days or so before the atmosphere down there becomes unbreathable. I guess we'd better tell the admiral."

"Sure. You'd better come with me. And bring that little box of tricks. I expect he'd like to see that spreadsheet."

0900R, Groton, Connecticut

Marie didn't normally smack the boys, but this morning they were driving her inexorably toward a policy reversal. Geoff had just knocked the side of a bowl with his elbow and catapulted its contents over the table. A large puddle of milk was rapidly soaking into the tablecloth now decorated with Coco Pops. Jamie was laughing uncontrollably as he picked more sodden Coco Pops out of his hair. His shrieks served only to worsen Marie's headache, which had started shortly after she got up. Geoff was also consumed with riotous giggling. "Shut up, the pair of you!" she exclaimed. "Do you hear me?" They didn't. There were more gales of laughter. "If you don't be quiet right now, it'll be time out in your room." To reinforce the message she slammed her right hand, palm down, onto

the table. The noise startled the boys, but the effect
was short-lived, and the laughter erupted once more.

Marie recognized that she was running on a very
short fuse and was convinced that the cause was her
lack of sleep the previous night. She had wanted to
wait until the boys had eaten before discussing the
Tulsa, but she was rapidly losing control of the situation as Jamie and Geoff began flicking soggy cereal at
each other. "OK, that's it! You've had your chance
and blown it. Off to your room, the two of you, right
now!" The laughter stopped, the boys looked at each
other and got down from the table and left the room.
"And no television," she added as they climbed the
stairs. As Marie started to mop up the mess, it dawned
on her that the boys' room looked out over the yard
at the rear of the house, where they wouldn't notice
the press. That meant she could postpone discussing
the situation with them. Instead, she would tidy up, take
a look at the newspaper, and collect her thoughts before talking to them.

The telephone rang, and Marie answered it. A Commander Thompson announced that he was on the staff
of Group 2 at the base, and wanted to know if it
would be convenient to visit her in about an hour. She
replied that it would. But before she had a chance to
ask if there was any news, he hung up. Her initial
sense of puzzlement slowly dissipated as she thought
about the phone call. A dreadful hollowness was growing in the pit of her stomach and her pulse had started
to race. It could only be bad news, she thought, if
Thompson wanted to see her in person. She stopped
clearing the table and sat down heavily on one of the
wooden chairs. She placed her elbows on the table,
cupped her head in her hands, and started to cry. The
sense of fatigue and despair that had been growing
over the past two days was now compounded by a
deep, gut-wrenching sense of loss.

1430Z, HMS *Wellington*

At long last the ship had altered course and was heading northeast. The beam sea had been replaced by a following one and the ship's violent pitching and rolling had moderated to an almost languid motion that was considerably more comfortable. To complete the good news, it looked like the weather was improving as well. Surgeon Commander Freeman was feeling better and had even managed to retain a morsel of lunch. The course alteration had also made the problem of organizing the first-reaction stores more manageable because heavy items, like cylinders of oxygen, could be relocated without the risk of injury to those who were moving them.

The hangar was swarming with people who were gradually eroding the mountain of supplies that, only a few hours ago, had still been wrapped up in the cargo netting in which it had been craned onto the ship. Just to the port side of the hangar door stood the compression chamber, a large gray cylinder decorated on its outside by yards of bronze-colored piping and a console of dials and valves. Forward of that an area had been cleared that now contained a series of large, colored, plastic boxes in which the medical supplies were located. Forward of that, the primary treatment area was being prepared. Two rows of mattresses were being arranged with an IV set, a cylinder of oxygen, and a mask beside each one. On the starboard side of the hangar Freeman was having a heated discussion with Sheppard and Sweeny. The problem concerned the decontamination of the survivors. Although the message from the *Nordvik* had stated that the reactor was shut down, there was no indication as to whether there had been any release of radioactive material. If there had been, each survivor would have to be decontaminated before entering the triage area. Sweeny was clearly getting frustrated: "For God's sake, how contaminated can they possibly be? When they reach the surface they will have traveled up through five hundred feet of water, wearing next to bugger all. Even if they were glowing in the dark in the DISSUB, they would be clean by the time they reached us."

"There's no need for bad language," retorted Freeman. "Their heads and necks could remain contaminated under the hood and, in any case, we may be looking at a rescue rather than an escape."

"Forgive me, I've been wasting everybody's time," replied Sweeny in his most sarcastic tone. "I thought we were preparing to receive potential casualties from an escape which could occur at any moment."

"The indications from the *Nordvik* message are that an escape will not be necessary for three or four days."

"Flooding or a fire could drive them out well before then," interrupted Sweeny. "That's what we're here for isn't it?" David Sheppard could see that the debate was going nowhere and decided it was time to settle the matter.

"It'll be quite a while before a rescue can be mounted. When it happens, we'll know about it well in advance. In the event of a rescue, we'll not need most of this stuff." He gestured to the chamber and the primary treatment area. "In any case, they'll be recovered onto the *Salminster*. It looks like she's going to beat the *Vindictive* to the datum quite comfortably. So I'm going to suggest that we establish a decontamination station there. In the meantime, we should signal the *Nordvik* and ask them to find out if there is a contamination problem in the DISSUB. If there's nothing more to discuss, I'll set up my triage area here." The other two looked at him for a moment.

"Sounds good to me," responded Sweeny. "What do you think, Boss?"

"OK, we'll play it that way. The advantage, as I see it, is that we will have rather more room in here to deal with the sick ones. Well done, David." Sheppard was astonished. Not only had Freeman just agreed with him, but he'd thanked him as well. He'd have to make a note of it in his diary.

1530A, COMJTFNON HQ, Bodø

"I understand about the carbon dioxide," repeated Admiral Risberg a little testily. "What about the pressure in the boat? What's that going to do to the survivors?" Commander Selby looked at Surgeon Commander Engelsen, who nodded to indicate that he should answer the question.

"Well, sir, it depends—"

"It always does with you doctors, doesn't it?" interrupted the admiral.

"It really does, sir. It depends on what the cause of the increasing pressure is, and there's no indication of that in the message. If the increase in pressure is caused by flooding, then it'll compress the atmosphere in the *Tulsa* and increase the concentration of all the gases."

"So it will raise the concentration of carbon dioxide?"

"Yes, sir, it will—until it's scrubbed."

"But doesn't that mean that the lithium hydroxide won't last as long as you've calculated?"

Selby thought for a moment. Admiral Risberg was clearly no fool. "I'll need to do some more math, sir, but I don't think the effect will be great and, as I say, it only applies if the pressure rise is due to flooding. If it's because of a compressed-air leak, there won't be a problem. There should be very little carbon dioxide in that."

"OK, what about the effects of the pressure increase on the men. Will it affect their ability to breathe?"

"It shouldn't, sir. According to the message, the pressure is only seven feet of seawater now. That's less than a quarter of an atmosphere. I don't expect that to have any effect at all."

"Good. Just one more question, Commander. I seem to remember you talking about the bends this morning. If the pressure goes up in the boat, will the survivors get the bends when we try to get them out?"

"The pressure will have to increase quite a bit more than it has so far. People can be decompressed from a pressure of about seven-tenths of an atmosphere directly to the surface. That's the equivalent of about twenty-three feet of seawater. If the rate of increase stays roughly the same as it is now—just two feet per day—the pressure shouldn't become a problem for another eight days. We should have them out by then."

"Thank you, Commander Selby, I'm most grateful to you. I'll ask you to repeat this at the next plenary session so that everyone can understand the problem."

"I'd be pleased to, sir."

1600A, USS *Tulsa*

Although he'd tried to get some sleep, Richter had just been lying on his bunk with his eyes closed, thinking—and shivering. Despite being curled up under a pile of half a dozen blankets, he was still cold to the core. Over the past twenty-four hours he'd been unable to retain any food, and all he could keep down was an occasional sip of water. He knew he was seriously ill, and his attempts to blame his condition on the composition of the atmosphere or Gallagher's food were no longer persuasive, even to himself. It wasn't just a concussion. His splitting headache betrayed the fact that something serious was wrong inside his head. Since nothing could be done about it at the moment, he had merely troubled Enzo to provide him with a substantial stock of painkillers.

He'd tried to read a little about head injuries, but had given up. Even squinting through one eye, he couldn't focus properly on the fine print, and attempting to do so merely served to make his headache worse. Having realized that the situation in the boat was stable, and would benefit little from further interventions by him until the rescue began, he had drifted away from his present predicament and was twenty-five again. It was summer and he was on leave, having just left the USS *Groton*. For the first time since college he had some spare time and, unlike his college days, he had some spare money. For three whole weeks he was free to do as he wished. He'd played with the idea of buying a new car, a convertible, and just taking off. No matter what, he had to escape from the Bachelor Officers' Quarters, and a tour of the Great Lakes, or as much as he could manage in the time available, was one ambition that he was seriously considering.

He wanted somebody to go with him, a girl ideally. Despite his throbbing head, Richter's memory was crystal clear. Over the years, advancing maturity, an escalating naval rank, and his status as a submarine captain had served virtually to eliminate the cowering shyness that had so afflicted him in his youth. It had permeated just about everything he did. At school it had inhibited him from answering questions in class, even though he knew the answers. It had reduced his early, stuttering attempts at small talk with even his male friends to a complete farce. He'd rarely even contemplated starting a conversation with a girl until he was almost twenty. Even now, his shyness still troubled him occasionally at large social gatherings, but these were mercifully rare at the operational end of the modern navy. Fourteen years ago, however, it was a different story. Even the simplest of social interactions still caused him concern, particularly if they involved women.

That summer John Dowling was still in sub school and his girlfriend at the time, Phoebe, had been invited to a party that Marie, a friend of hers, was throwing on the beach. Phoebe was under orders to bring some men with her, so Richter had tagged along. He had discovered that his hostess was a few years

younger than he, having only just graduated from
Choate Rosemary Hall, an exclusive private school in
Connecticut. She normally lived with her parents
somewhere in New Jersey, but had moved into her
father's vacation home on the beach at Groton Long
Point for the summer.

He'd joined in a game of Frisbee and had watched
her playing volleyball and splash around in the water.
He couldn't understand his reaction to her. It was
quite unlike anything he had experienced before. The
beach was littered with girls who, by any standard,
looked better than she did. Marie's hair was short,
straight, and mousy. She didn't have much of a tan,
nor was she particularly well endowed. She was actually rather on the skinny side. However, she moved
beautifully, with the grace of a natural athlete. Her
every gesture was elegant. Her voice was low-pitched
and gentle. She didn't shriek like so many of the others on the beach that day. He'd thought that his
shades would disguise the fact that he was staring at
her, but he began to wonder if they did, because she
started to cast glances at him with increasing frequency. It was a hot July day, and the beer flowed
freely. Gradually, he began to relax. He fell into conversation with Phoebe and learned more about Marie.

She was an only child. Her father was a successful
attorney who enjoyed nothing more than indulging his
daughter. Recently divorced from Marie's mother and
unhappily remarried, his daughter was everything to
him. He remembered being staggered when Phoebe
had told him that for graduating her father had given
her a Mercedes 500 SL. Not only had his jaw dropped
but, in realizing the extent of her father's indulgence,
alarm bells had begun to ring in his head. He'd seen
a similar pattern before. Her father would have ambi-
tions for Marie that were unlikely to include a son-in-
law who served in submarines. In fact, it was unlikely
that anybody who strayed too far from Wall Street or
the Capitol Building in Washington was going to be

received into the family with good grace. Antipathy or even outright animosity was probably nearer the mark.

He realized that this analysis represented the result of years of reflection. At the time he had become intrigued with her even before they were introduced—which occurred after the beach party, when a selected minority of those who had spent the afternoon on the sand were invited back for a more intimate evening. He had been astonished to receive an invitation. It could only be, he remembered concluding, that Marie's furtive glances in his direction must have represented more than mere curiosity or a reaction to being stared at.

A knock at his door broke Richter's train of thought. "Come in." Enzo entered gingerly.

"Do you have a moment, sir?"

"Of course, Enzo, I wasn't asleep."

"I'm sorry to disturb you, but I thought you ought to know that Chief Maddison has just died."

"Oh, I'm sorry," replied Richter earnestly. "He was one hell of a guy. You know, this was the third boat we served in together." He reached under his pillow, rummaged around for a handkerchief, and blew his nose. "I think you and I both knew this was going to be the outcome, didn't we?"

"Yes, sir. I just feel bad that there was nothing more we could do."

"If it's any consolation, Enzo, I don't think even Doc Richards could have saved him. Hell, he might have struggled for survival in intensive care. Who's to tell?"

"What about you, sir?"

"What do you mean?"

"May I be direct with you?"

Richter paused a moment before replying. "OK. Only it's between you and me, though. I don't want this spread around the boat."

"Of course. I am your medical officer, am I not?"

"Sure. What do you want to know?"

"How bad is your head?" Richter told Enzo the whole truth.

1010R, Groton, Connecticut

Marie had stopped crying and had dried her eyes, although they were still a little pink. She had gone upstairs and applied some makeup and fresh lipstick and felt ready to face the world. She had decided to ignore the bedlam that echoed from the boys' room. In the event of bad news from the commander, she could always excuse herself to go and sort it out. Nonetheless, she was determined not to lose her composure in front of him. There were two reasons for this, she thought. The first was her own pride. She had always felt that female histrionics in response to bad news, as portrayed by TV and the movies, were grossly overplayed. The second was that, if it was bad news, John wasn't the only one who had died. Commander Thompson was going to have a bad enough day without her giving him a hard time.

She looked out of the living-room window and saw a white military sedan draw up behind the SNN van. A naval officer emerged wearing a service dress blue uniform bearing commander's stripes on his sleeve with dolphins above the three rows of medal ribbons that decorated the left breast of his jacket. He was also carrying a briefcase. He threaded his way through the mob of reporters, waving his hand to indicate that he had nothing to say as he sidestepped a reporter who had thrust a microphone in front of his face. Marie couldn't hear what was being said and thought of turning on the TV, as it would surely be reported live. The gaggle of press followed him to the front door. It was a dull, overcast morning, and the scene was illuminated by camera lights, the highest shadows being cast by microphones on booms that were deployed above the huddle.

The doorbell rang. Marie realized that she would

have to let the commander in alone. But what if she couldn't? Should she call the police? It had never occurred to her. It was too late now anyway. She left the window and went to the front door. She opened it a crack to the glare of television lights augmented by the flashes from the bulbs of the still photographers. The naval officer eased himself through the partially opened door and immediately closed it behind him. He reached inside his jacket and produced his ID card. "Mrs. Dowling? I am Commander Thompson, we talked on the phone about an hour ago. Has the press been out there all night?"

"I think so. Can you do anything about it?"

"You know you can move onto the base if you want, don't you?"

"Yes, maybe I'll think about that again."

"Good. Is there anyplace we can sit down?"

"Sure, we'll go down to the den. Let's hope the piranhas outside won't find us there. Would you like a cup of coffee?"

"Thank you," replied Commander Thompson, "I'd love one." He followed Marie into the kitchen, and she busied herself setting up the coffeemaker and ladled three generous scoops of dark-roasted Sumatran beans into the grinder.

"John loves this stuff, you know. At first I found it rather strong, but I'm so used to it now I buy it even when he's away." She poured the ground beans into the coffeemaker and set it to percolate.

Commander Thompson changed the subject. "I recognize you from somewhere, don't I?"

"Very likely. I've been on TV recently."

"No, it's not that. You don't bowl do you?"

"Well, I used to. . . ." She paused. "I remember now, your wife's Julia, isn't she?"

"That's right."

"Yes, a few years ago we used to be in the same league."

"What a memory you have," remarked Commander

Thompson. "But shortly after we moved to Norfolk she injured her hand in a car accident, and she's not been able to bowl since."

"I'm sorry about the accident. I didn't know."

"Thankfully, it was nothing much, and she's fit and well now. Totaled our truck though."

Marie set two coffee cups on a tray along with some milk and sugar as the coffeemaker started to hiss and splutter. She poured a good measure of coffee into each cup and lifted the tray. "It's probably best if we go downstairs."

"Who's making the noise upstairs?"

"Oh, that's the boys. If you've got bad news, I'd rather leave them there," replied Marie over her shoulder as she led the way down to the den. Commander Thompson waited until they were seated before continuing:

"I do have some news of the *Tulsa*."

"At long last. I've tried to get some news out of the squadron, but they've not been able to say much. What have you been up to? Why couldn't you let me know what was going on earlier?"

"Look, I am here to apologize for that. You don't want to know what kind of a mess has been stirred up by this. The fact is that we've been told not to release information until we're sure of its source, and yet the phone has been ringing off the hook with people wanting to know what's going on. It's been a nightmare. It's only this morning that we've gotten any real news. We told you all we could, but that was no more than was given to the press. Anyway, why on earth are they camped outside your house?"

"You know I was interviewed by SNN yesterday."

"Yes."

"They seem to think that my husband died in the accident. He has, hasn't he?"

"Mrs. Dowling . . . Marie. You're not making this easy for me. I had something prepared to say and, well, I guess you got there before me."

Marie studied the young man in front of her. He

looked young—not much older than her thirty-two years, anyway. He had blue eyes and short, blond hair. His expression was one of sheer desperation. This was obviously not a task that he was used to or for which he had probably received much training. He looked just about how she felt. Despite her intention to stay calm, despite the outbreak of World War III in the boys' room upstairs, her eyes began to fill again. As if in sympathy, the good commander's looked like they were doing so as well. He had kind features that could not conceal the grief that he was obviously feeling. "I know Geoff Richter well, and through him I got to know John. Not well, of course, not like you did. . . . But he was a great guy . . . the best." Marie couldn't bear it anymore. She left her seat and reached out for him, and he rose to embrace her. The two of them cried together. Through the partially open curtains, camera bulbs flashed like strobe lights.

1700A, USS *Tulsa*

The full impact of what Richter had told him was dawning on Enzo. He'd been doing the reading that Richter had requested and decided to look in on the XO before discussing the matter again over dinner, which he would take with the captain in his stateroom. He prayed that Gallagher would serve up something half-edible that could tempt the captain out of his anorexia. Enzo knocked gently on the XO's door. There was no reply, but he entered anyway. The room was dark. The battery in the battle lantern beside the bunk was capable of generating little more than a dull glimmer. Mitchell was lying on his back, his face turned slightly away from the door. He didn't move. Enzo was immediately struck by the return of the musty smell that had been dispelled, albeit briefly, by the surgery. He walked over to the bunk and gently shook Mitchell by the shoulder. There was no response. The XO was breathing, but his chest was clearly bad as it emitted a rattling sound each time he exhaled. Enzo reached for Mitchell's remaining wrist to feel for a pulse. His skin was cold and clammy, and his pulse was so rapid that Enzo could barely count it. If he was going to do much more, he'd have to get some better light. He left the stateroom and went down to the crew's mess room to find a fresh battle lantern.

On returning he noticed that the XO had not moved. He shined the light at his face. His eyes were closed, a patina of sweat covered his forehead and his short, dark hair glistened with it. Enzo shook him again. "Sir, I need to talk to you." He shook him once more. "Please, sir, say something." Mitchell stirred, but the effort of doing so merely provoked a rumbling in his chest that ended with a series of rasping coughs that left him breathless. Enzo reached for a tissue and wiped away the blood-flecked green mucus that had appeared at his mouth. Mitchell opened his eyes and started to speak, although all he could generate was a whisper.

"Hello, Enzo. Could you get me some water? I'm really thirsty." There was another rumble in his chest and a fresh outbreak of coughing that left him gasping for air. Enzo noticed that the IV had ceased dripping despite there being plenty of saline in the bag. He shook the tubing and squeezed the bag, but without success. He was unsure what to do. He had wanted to talk about the captain's head injury and what they should do if he was to get any worse. However, there didn't seem to be much point. The XO was obviously desperately ill himself.

Enzo went into the head and poured a glass of water. He returned and helped Mitchell into a sitting position while he drank it. As he settled him back onto his sweat-soaked pillow, Enzo couldn't help noticing that the musty smell was coming from the dressing on his right arm. Even without removing it, he knew more surgery was going to be required, but that begged the question as to whether the XO was up to it. And was *he* up to it, for that matter? One conclusion that could be drawn from Enzo's first foray into surgery was that his efforts had been inadequate. Why else hadn't the XO made a straightforward recovery? His mind drifted on. So what had gone wrong? Having thought about it for a moment he concluded that either he had failed to remove all the dead tissue or somehow he had managed to introduce a new infection. As he looked at the sorry state of the XO and pondered the seemingly inexorable decline of the captain, it was becoming clear that, without divine intervention, it wouldn't be long before he was going to have to assume command. Not only that, but do so in circumstances that would test even the most experienced of submariners. It was a scary thought, far too frightening to contemplate for long. Enzo looked at his watch and realized that it was time to wash and address the crew before dining with the captain. He'd tell the XO that Master Chief Steadman would be up shortly to change the dressing.

1200R, The Pentagon, Arlington, Virginia

Talisker was ushered into the richly wood-paneled office of the Chief of Naval Operations. A group of senior naval officers consisting of CINCLANT, COMSUBPAC, N87, and COMSUBDEVRON FIVE were already there. The CNO rose to greet him with an outstretched hand, which Talisker shook firmly.

"Good to see you, Gerry, have a seat." The CNO beckoned to one of the two empty red leather chairs.

"Thank you, sir. I apologize for being late. I had a couple of things to attend to in Norfolk."

"No problem. Norman and Scott have briefed me and I now have the full picture. Gentlemen, we all know that JAG will be obliged to hold a court of inquiry into the sinking of the *Tulsa*. No real threat from that quarter. However, I've asked you here because you may not be aware of recent political developments that will surely affect the situation. Although the president and the secretaries of defense and the navy are completely behind us, some unpleasant noises are beginning to filter through from Congress. News of those who have lost their lives is out and every congressman and senator with a dead constituent looks like they are going to try to raise some political capital with it. We can expect some unpleasant questions even if we get the rest of the crew out alive. If we fail, I don't want to even think about what'll happen. At the very least there will be a cull of senior officers and, the way I see it, the six of us are ripe for plucking."

He paused to look round the room at the grim faces that stared back at him. "You have the reins," he continued, "and I don't intend to micromanage this operation. I'll therefore limit myself to asking if there's anything more that I can do for you?"

CINCLANT responded. "I don't think so at the moment, Bill. We have Murmansk, which is the main thing, and the Brits have agreed to dispatch the *Centaur*. She's a helicopter carrier, and her medical department will be augmented with a field ambulance, or whatever they call their second-echelon medical units. She'll also provide an adequate helicopter support capability. The *Centaur* should leave Portsmouth, UK, tomorrow morning and be on station sometime early Wednesday. The Norwegians are bending over backwards to help. I really can't think of anything else that is needed at present. Can you, Gerry—apart from more time?" He looked at Talisker, who creased his grim expression with a brief attempt at a smile.

"I received a message from my medical officer very early this morning asking about the casualty evacuation route. Has anything been sorted out there? I understand that there are some very sick men on board and, of course, there may be more if they have to escape."

"I believe the air force is gearing up to handle that," replied the CNO, "but I'll check. The usual evacuation route out of Europe is via Ramstein Air Base and Landstühe Military Hospital in Germany, I can't see much point in changing it. Anything else?" There was not. "I don't have to tell you how serious the situation is. The press have a stranglehold on this story and are not going to let go of it and, as I said, I fear Congress is getting testy. I'll do all that I can to keep them off your backs and let you get on with the task at hand. What I am not going to be able to do is defend screw-ups. So there won't be any. Do I make myself clear?" The CNO paused for impact and looked at each of the men in front of him. "I don't need to remind you, gentlemen, that the selection process for the next Chairman of the Joint Chiefs is under way. I am well in the running, and it is in all of our interests that it goes to a Navy man. Get the crew out of the *Tulsa*, and I believe we can all look to better times ahead. Should we fail, we may need to find something to do in retirement somewhat sooner than any of us has planned."

1800A, MV *Nordvik*

With the end of twilight, the search for the remaining members of the SPAG had been called off for the night, although everyone knew that meant indefinitely. Even with dry suits on, their chances of survival until daybreak were zero. The conditions in the water were far too severe. Surgeon Lieutenant Ward had persuaded Marchant that the SPAG should eat together and had reserved a corner of the junior rates' dining hall for that purpose. It was his objective to get everyone to talk about the events of the day in the hope that people would feel a little bit better about the way things had turned out. Unfortunately, it was going horribly wrong. Ward had tried to lead the discussion, but it had gone nowhere. Each attempt had petered out into an uneasy silence. Some made the pretense of picking at the pickled fish in front of them, but most couldn't be bothered. The pall of gloom that had descended over the group was almost palpable.

Marchant was regretting his decision not to dine in the wardroom. Although he had tried to cheer the men up and persuade them that none of this was their fault, it had merely served to bring home to him that any fault was his own. Ultimately, it had been his decision to jump, and it was one that he would surely be required to defend at the board of inquiry that inevitably followed a death on active duty. Already he could see himself in front of the board trying to explain why the SPAG had entered the water when the weather conditions had been so adverse. The short answer was that they had been ordered to jump, but that was by no means the whole answer. He could quite simply have called the jump off, or postponed it until the weather had improved or, at least, until daylight. Why had he not done so? It was weighing heavily on Steve Marchant's mind.

Warrant Officer Sharples could see that it was eating him up. "You know, sir, we were all behind you when you made the decision to go. Every one of us, Sean and Eddie included, God bless 'em. What's more, given the same conditions, we'd all do it again." There was a muttering of encouragement from the other SPAG members gathered round the table.

"Thank you for that, Mr. Sharples, and, indeed, all of you. I don't mean to be rude when I say that I think it may be a little bit early for us to go over what has happened. I certainly feel that it's all a bit fresh, and I need some time to get my thoughts in order. I think I'll take my duff in the wardroom. I'll just close by saying that I am proud of you, each and every one of you. What we did today took a lot of courage, and not one of you bottled out. No man could ask for a better team." As he rose to leave, Surgeon Lieutenant

Ward joined him, and together they left for the wardroom.

1800A, USS *Tulsa*

"Quiet, everybody." Enzo waited while the crew settled down. It was extraordinary how the atmosphere had changed. The muted conversation and long faces that had recently attended mealtimes had been replaced by lively banter and smiles. "Look, I've got a few things to say, and I'm not going to shout." Enzo waved his hands up and down to encourage the men to settle down. "Now, I know we've been found. . . ." Wolf whistles pierced the air above the whoops of joy that filled the mess room. Enzo waved his hands again. He was beginning to feel a bit like a politician at a campaign rally delivering a series of shallow one-liners designed solely to whip up the crowd. "But we have a long way to go yet. I don't want you to get your hopes up too high and then feel disappointed when nothing seems to be happening like the last time we heard charges." The buzz died down to a rumble. "We all know that the first charges we heard almost certainly came from an aircraft, and this time they probably came from a ship. And don't get me wrong, it is good news. Not least because if we do have to escape, there will be someone topside to haul us out of the water. So at least we won't freeze to death. However, I expect there will be some delay before we're rescued, because if that ship above us is equipped to mount a rescue, we would have heard a lot more from her by now." The room was completely silent. "It may take another day or two before we're out of here, and I want you all to realize that. We're on the home stretch, but we haven't yet crossed the finishing line. Now, because of this, we must get back into the routine of resting as much as we can and I want you all to take your Valium after you've eaten and get back to sleep right away."

Enzo looked around the room and saw that he'd made his point. Had he done so too abruptly? he wondered. Either way, the point had to be made. He paused for a moment before carrying on. "I expect you're wondering why the captain isn't here to talk to you this evening. I am sorry to say that he's unwell. As we all know he sustained a nasty cut on his head in the collision. It seems that he's been suffering from concussion, and it's getting worse. I don't expect him to leave his stateroom much more, even though I know he wants to. He needs to rest." This was not a startling revelation to the crew. The stories of Richter stumbling over things in the crew's mess and forgetting names had spread quickly, and just about everybody had guessed that something was wrong. "I'm sorry to report that the XO is also seriously ill. As well as his bad arm, he has a chest infection, and I've reached the point that I can do little more than pray for him. If you feel like doing the same, go ahead." Enzo looked down briefly and then back up at the crew. He had done an amazing job of defusing their exuberance. "Any questions?"

"Sir." It was Sonarman Evans.

"Yes."

"Can the captain and XO get off first as soon as we are rescued?" There were nods and grunts of approval around the room.

"Well, Evans, we'll tackle that when it becomes an issue. I just want to assure you all that everything we can do for both of them will be done. Anything else?" There were no more questions, and so Enzo made his way to the galley, collected his and the captain's meals, and made his way up to Richter's stateroom.

Balancing the tray on one hand, he knocked at the door and entered. Richter had made the effort to get up and had cleared his desk to make room for the food that Enzo placed upon it. Richter glanced at the steaming plates. "What have we got here, Enzo?"

"You'll not believe this, sir, but under all that steam we have pasta."

"What's in the sauce?"

"I've no idea. I thought it best not to ask, although it looks like there's some salami and a lot of chopped tomato." He gave his plate a sniff. "And even a little garlic. A feast indeed. Doubtless this will feature on the cover of Tim's forthcoming best-seller, *The Deep-sea Diet.*" Richter couldn't help chuckling, despite it initiating a more severe pounding in his head. "I hope it tickles your palate, sir, because you are never going to feel better unless you eat something."

"Enzo, you sound like my old mom."

"Well, if she were here, I'm sure she'd say the same thing."

With that Enzo picked up a fork, plunged it into the pasta, and mixed it with the sauce. In his left hand he held a spoon and before long he had wrapped a tidy-looking collection of pasta around his fork, which he placed in his mouth and started to chew. "Whew, that is good. Possibly a little generous with the cayenne pepper, but this matches anything we've had to date. No, it far exceeds it. That it's basically an Italian dish has not, of course, clouded my judgment. You really must try it, sir." Enzo looked up from his plate and saw Richter wait until he had stopped shivering before he coaxed a little pasta onto his fork and launched it toward his mouth. His lack of skill resulted in much of it falling back onto his plate, but he munched mechanically on what had made it.

"I must concede that this is good. Well done, Tim."

"And don't forget Sparks, sir. Without him, this would just be a dream."

"Or a rather cold and crunchy reality," riposted Richter. Enzo chuckled while Richter tried not to laugh. Enzo recognized that his good humor was amplified by relief that the captain appeared to be in such good form. "I heard you visit the XO a little earlier. It was you wasn't it?"

"Yes, sir, it was."

"How is he?" Enzo paused before replying, concerned that the whole truth might put Richter off his food. He was already well into his third mouthful which, to his surprise, had survived its journey from his plate almost intact.

"Not too good, sir. His chest is getting worse."

"So's his arm. I can smell it in the head."

"I thought you might have. What do you suggest we do, sir?"

Richter thought for a moment and sighed. He'd become resigned to the endless stream of bad news on the medical front. "I really don't think that there is much we can do. Is he in pain?"

"I don't think so—except when he coughs. That also makes him breathless, which obviously distresses him. He's barely able to remain conscious, I think he's in shock and he must be dehydrated. God knows what happened to his IV. It looks like some sort of infection has a hold on his arm, and the antibiotics I gave him don't seem to be working. . . ." Without saying as much, Richter realized that Enzo had given up hope for the XO. And from what he was saying, he could understand why. The decision he faced boiled down to more surgery or letting the man die.

"Enzo, before we discuss what to do about the XO, what have you read about head injuries? I mean, what do you think is wrong with me?"

"Sir, I really don't know. It takes doctors years to become skilled neurologists, and they have access to scanners and God knows what else." He paused. "I'm not being a very good ship's doctor, am I?" Richter took the question to be rhetorical. Enzo obviously did have something to say, but was having difficulty knowing how to do so. Finally he continued, "I think you might have what's known as a subdural hemorrhage.

It's basically a slow bleed in your head which causes gradually increasing pressure.''

"What does that do?"

"It fits pretty well with what you've got—headache, dizziness, double vision. . . .''

"Sorry, Enzo, that's not quite what I meant. What will it do? What'll happen next?"

"Well, sir, I might as well tell you that it can be fatal if nobody relieves the pressure. You'll lose consciousness and eventually stop breathing.''

"Jesus, I didn't think it was that bad. I just thought it was a concussion," he lied for Enzo's benefit. "Any idea when that'll happen?"

"Sir, I'm only guessing at what's wrong. It could be a simple concussion. However, if it's not, and your problem really is a subdural, I can't say how long it will take. The books are evasive on the subject, which leads me to think that it must be rather variable. I guess it depends on the speed of the bleed, so to speak. I mean, you've lasted well for, what, over eighty hours now. Who's to say that you won't last another eighty? Heck, we should be out of here by then.'' Richter had stopped eating. Not only had his appetite evaporated, but he was feeling nauseated.

"I don't think we can count on that—I mean my lasting another four days. It's getting worse, and we both know it. It looks like the XO is on his way out as well, which means that you'll probably have to take charge here. Your first command—a fast-attack, and you're only a lieutenant. Congratulations!"

Despite the captain's kind words, Enzo felt no elation. He'd received no training for this. "Well, sir, the *Tulsa*'s not particularly fast at the moment, and I don't think we can attack anything, so it's not going to be too demanding from an operational point of view. In any case, we're being a little premature, aren't we?"

"Sure, Enzo, I'm not letting go just yet, merely pre-

paring you for what's ahead. I'll tell the rest of the
wardroom and the COB, so it won't come as a surprise
to them if I should have to hand over to you." Richter
paused, got up from his chair, staggered into the head,
and closed the door. Enzo couldn't bring himself to
leave the remainder of his meal and attacked it with
gusto despite the muted retching from next door. If
he was going to be the CO, he'd have to eat properly
and keep his strength up.

1230R, Groton, Connecticut

Marie had cried for almost a full hour after Commander Thompson had left. She couldn't help it. The
good commander had been unable to tell her how he
had died, but she could imagine it. Poor John must
have drowned as the engine room flooded. What a horrible way for him to go, hating water as much as he did.
As if losing a husband she had loved so completely
wasn't bad enough, she was reduced to being a virtual
prisoner in her own home by the camera-toting bastards outside. Perhaps it was time to ask the police
for help, or move onto the base. She hesitated only
because she was going to have to tell the boys now
and had not worked out whether she should do it
before they saw anything about it on TV, or a bit later
when she had worked out what to say. The telephone
interrupted her thoughts on the matter. She answered
it without thinking and forgot to check the caller ID.
"Hello?"

"Hello, Marie." Her surprise at hearing the familiar,
deep, gravelly voice was so complete, she almost
dropped the receiver.

"Hello, Father. . . ." She was lost for words. "What
prompted you to call?"

"I'm just back from a trip to Ireland, I've had
some business to attend to over there. I heard about
the *Tulsa*, of course. I guess it's playing worldwide,

but I only heard about John this morning. Look, I'm really very sorry. I can't tell you how sorry I am."

"I'll get over it someday. It's all a bit fresh at the moment." She couldn't help sniffing.

"I saw you on SNN this morning. Are the press giving you a hard time?"

"Oh, that. No, they persuaded me to do that voluntarily, although I'll not do it again even if they do offer me a ridiculous amount of money. It's what's happening around here right now . . ." She started to cry, but fought hard to control herself.

"What's that?"

"Oh, they've surrounded the house," she exaggerated.

"Look, do you want to come to Cherry Hill? Bring the boys. If the press follow you here onto my land, I'll sue them until they squeak." Marie thought about it for a few moments. Quite deliberately, it had been years since she had been home, but this was too good an offer to turn down. "I've had a better idea," continued Father. "I'll come and fetch you. It's only two hundred miles. I'll have you out of there before dark." That clinched it.

"OK, Father. Thanks. I'll see you at four or so. It'll give me time to pack."

"I might make it a little sooner—it'll depend on the traffic in New York. Bye for now."

"Bye." She replaced the receiver and sighed. It was nearly fourteen years since she had last gone home. She had taken an instant dislike to Christine, her stepmother. It was a dislike that had grown to a hatred that extended from the tip of her coiffured head down to the soles of her Gucci-clad feet. She despised Christine's affected New England accent and the way that, no sooner had she got a ring on her finger, than she had insisted on remodeling her family home in dubious taste and at outrageous expense. The icing on the cake, as far as Marie was concerned, had been Christine's refusal to sign a prenuptial agreement. There had been furious rows about it. Incredibly, Christine had eventually managed to persuade her father that it was unnecessary, an achievement that must have taken every ounce of her guile. Marie had merely wondered what pressure the cow had brought to bear on her father to achieve it.

Although Marie had sided with him over his separation from her mother, within weeks of the divorce, her father had set a stubbornly unswerving course toward another marriage, one which Marie knew would never work. It was, perhaps, the origin of the breakdown of their relationship. It took only a few months after the wedding for her worst fears to be confirmed. The friction between Christine and Marie spread to involve her father. His loyalties were divided, and eventually he chose to side with his new bride. To escape from the fallout, Marie had moved into the summer home in Groton as soon as she could. It was a move she had never regretted. It had come as no surprise to hear that, although they were not formally separated, Christine now spent much of the year away from Cherry Hill. With any luck she might be vacationing right now in the new condo that father had apparently bought for her on Maui.

Marie focused back on the present. If she and the boys were going to New Jersey, she would have to give Jean a call. She lifted the receiver again and dialed. "Jean?"

"Hi, honey. How's things?"

"Not too good, I'm afraid. Group two sent a commander to the house to tell me that John was dead." Her nose had started to run again and she sniffed.

"Oh, that's terrible news. . . . What can I say? Oh God, I'm so sorry, honey. Do you want me to come over?"

"That's kind, Jean, but I've got to pack. You're not going to believe this, but my father called a few moments ago, and he's coming over to take us down to

Cherry Hill. Is that going to be OK for you? Have you managed to get all the phone numbers?"

"Don't worry about that, there's just one missing. I've got a number, but I never get an answer. Just leave that with me. Will you be gone long? Would you like me to come around and water the house plants occasionally?"

"Thanks, that would be very kind. The goldfish will need some food as well. . . ." Marie was beginning to cry again.

"Look, honey, let me come over and give you a hand packing."

"No, really, I'd rather do it myself, and I'm going to have to talk to the boys. God knows what I'll tell them. . . ." Marie broke down sobbing quietly into the phone. "This is no good," she said with a sniff, pulling herself together. "I must get going. I'll give you a call from New Jersey."

"All right honey, but if you need anything, and I mean *anything*, just let me know. Have a good trip."

"Thanks, Jean. Bye."

2000A, MV *Nordvik*

Steve Marchant had decided to turn in. As he lay in his bunk, he reflected on the evening. He was right to leave the junior rates' mess. That had gone badly wrong. Once back in the wardroom, he had declined Simon's kind invitation to drink on his mess number, despite his desire to get utterly wrecked. Apart from anything else, he was the leader of his team, and they were in a foreign ship. Regardless of the circumstances, it would not look good if he had to be carried to his cabin. But it wasn't just Simon—the Norwegians had been incredibly kind and supportive. They, too, had appreciated his desperation and offered to provide him with copious quantities of liquor. They would surely have been forgiving if he had overimbibed, but it didn't matter if they were. He could not bring himself to get drunk. Apart from anything else, he felt too depressed. It wouldn't be fun. He would almost certainly end up crying on somebody's shoulder, and that wouldn't do. He was better off in bed.

As he lay there a question required an answer. Why had he chosen to jump? It was blatantly obvious that it was fraught with danger. Who would support him when it came to the inquiry? Yes, he had received the order to go. Yes, not only had the weather forecast been wrong, but badly wrong. Yes, the captain of the C130 had advised him not to jump. Yes, he'd had reservations about it, but those Yanks could have needed the SPAG. Why had he done it?

His mind wandered on. Basically, it boiled down to the fact that this is what they had been trained for. It was as simple as that. That it had turned into a disaster was not his fault. After all, this was their mission. That it had proved over the years to be an elusive one had merely served to reduce the extent and realism of the training they had received. That was one defense, he thought: inadequate training—or at least, inadequately realistic training. It might explain why things had gone so horribly wrong once they had left the aircraft, but it still begged the question as to why he had chosen to jump in the first place. If he had delayed, of course, there would have been no point, as the *Nordvik* would have been on station. That was the crux of it. His choice had boiled down to going right away or not going at all. The latter choice would have meant that the SPAG failed to meet its *raison d'être*. That was not uppermost in his mind at the time, but it was probably not far beneath the surface. His justification at the time, which still held water, was that he thought the crew of the *Tulsa* was going to have to escape. They could have already been in the water. The SPAG could have saved lives.

Exhaustion was preventing Marchant from making further headway. His eyes were already closed, he was warm and dry. The nightmare that had been substituted for his day was over, and he drifted into a deep sleep.

1600R, Groton, Connecticut

Jamie and Geoff had enjoyed packing. They had taken turns bringing armfuls of toys into their mom's room despite it being obvious that the two suitcases that lay open on the bed would never hold them all. Marie had almost reached the point of despair as she cast the games, Rollerblades, and soccer ball to one side. "Jamie, stop it. Act your age. What are you going to wear? I've told you we may be staying with Grandpa for some time. You'll need some clothes, so go and get them right now. And you, Geoff. Put that airplane down and go and get some clothes. Otherwise, I'll choose what you'll be taking."

"Why, Mom? Why? You never said we were going to see Grandpa," whined Jamie.

"I've told you. It's a surprise. Grandpa called this morning to invite us to stay, and I accepted."

"I can't remember Grandpa. What does he look like?" was Geoff's contribution, followed by: "Why does he want us to go and stay with him?"

"Let's finish packing, then we'll talk about it. I expect he'll be here any minute now." The boys filed out of the bedroom and each returned with a selection of clothing. "Thank you Jamie, now get some shoes. You'll need some sneakers, too—there are some lovely walks in New Jersey."

Eventually the packing was complete, and Marie had managed to close the bulging suitcases. Her father would give her a hand downstairs with them. She sat the boys down, one on each side of her. "Now, I want you to be very brave because I have to tell you some terrible news. Something has happened to your father."

"Is he going to be a commander, Mommy? Is he?"

"No, Jamie, he's not. Do you remember going to his boat on families day last summer?"

"It's a submarine," said Jamie. "Uncle Geoffrey's the captain."

"It's all black," recalled Geoff.

"That's right. Well, there's been an accident, and it has sunk." There was a stunned silence. Geoff's jaw dropped, but he said nothing. "Pa has died." It was all Marie could do to maintain her composure.

The boys were quiet for a moment, and then Jamie said: "Is Uncle Geoffrey dead, too?"

"I'm not sure. I haven't been told. But there are still people alive in the boat. The Navy's going to get them out just as soon as they can. With any luck, Uncle Geoffrey will come home safe and sound and—" She was interrupted by the doorbell. She went over to the curtains and peeked through the window. There were rather fewer newshounds outside than earlier in the day. The bright ones must have realized that she wasn't going to play ball with them and gone home. Those who had stayed were huddled around her father, who was standing his ground by the front door. She could hear him shouting at them. She turned to the boys. "Come downstairs with me. Grandpa's here." Marie opened the front door and her father strode in. Incredibly, there were no flashing bulbs. He slammed the door behind him.

"I told them," he announced, "any more photographs and I'll see them in court. Vermin." He opened his arms. "How are you, darling? Let me give you a hug." Marie took a couple of steps toward him before being enveloped in a bear hug. Father smelled just like he always had, with just the faintest suggestion of Paco Rabanne. It felt so good.

CHAPTER

5

Monday, 1 November

Master Chief Steadman shook Lieutenant Raschello by the shoulder. "Sir . . ." Enzo rolled over in his bunk and reluctantly opened an eye. This was the second straight morning that somebody had come to wake him up.

"What is it, Master Chief?"

"Sir, I think you should come and take a look at the XO."

"What's wrong?"

"I've just started to change his bandage and his right arm looks real bad. He's not breathing too well, and I can't wake him up."

"OK, Master Chief. Give me five minutes, and I'll be right up." Steadman left and Enzo flicked on a battle lantern and reluctantly prepared to jump out of his bunk. God it was cold. Each time he breathed out, the vapor of his breath condensed immediately and formed a small cloud. It looked like he was smoking. He had been freezing cold in his bunk for most of the night and, try as he might, he couldn't get warm.

Shivering had woken him intermittently and eventually he had gotten up and put on an additional pair of socks, his sweats, and a skiing jacket. That had done the trick, and he had slept like a log ever since. Now that he was warm, he really didn't want to move—even to see the XO. His sense of duty prevailed, however, and he forced himself to get up. Out of habit, he tried to look at himself in the mirror, but it was covered with condensation, like just about everything else in the boat. Nothing was completely dry anymore. He picked up his coveralls and noticed that even they felt damp. At least what he was wearing was warm, so he decided not to change, and merely put some sneakers on. He wiped the mirror, and inspected the heavy growth of stubble on his chin. He had always wanted to grow a beard, but since beards had been banned in the Navy back in the mid-eighties, this had proved to be his first opportunity. He liked what he saw. By the end of a week, he would have cultivated something that could begin to pass for a full set. With his vanity satisfied, he made his way up to the XO's stateroom.

The smell hit him as soon as he opened the door. From a faint mustiness the day before, the odor had deteriorated to one of rotting flesh. It was powerful enough to make him gag. Clutching a handkerchief to his face, he made his way over to the master chief, who had laid bare Mitchell's right arm—or what was left of it. It was a shocking sight. The stump was swollen, the skin had a blue-gray discoloration, and it was decorated with blisters, some of which had burst. The upper arm looked no better. Even the shoulder was swollen but, at least, the skin around it was pink. The rattle that now accompanied Mitchell's every breath was, if anything, more pronounced than yesterday, and his breathing was now shallow and irregular. Enzo glanced at the IV that he had failed to get going the previous evening and then down at the catheter bag which contained a small amount of almost brown-colored liquid.

"Did he complain when you removed the dressing?"

"No, sir. He's not so much as batted an eyelid since I first saw him this morning," replied Steadman.

"I hate to say this, but I'm afraid that there is nothing more to be done."

"Do you want me to put another dressing on his arm, sir?"

"I really can't see that there's much point. . . ." Enzo stopped in mid-sentence because at that moment the XO stopped breathing. There was a long pause, one more breath, then nothing. The two of them just stood and stared at Mitchell and then at each other. Enzo broke the silence. "I suppose that's it." He felt the XO's neck for a pulse and couldn't find one.

"Poor man, what a way to go." Enzo looked over his shoulder at Steadman. He was somewhat surprised that the master chief sounded so dejected or, indeed, had showed any emotion. He so rarely did. Enzo reached out and put a hand on his shoulder.

"It's not, really. He won't have suffered, you know. He did more than his fair share of that two and three days ago. If I had a choice in the matter, I'd like to go peacefully like that. Did you know him well?"

"Yes, sir. We served in two commands together before the *Tulsa*. I've known him since he was a JG. He's always been a perfect gentleman. Even as the XO—and you know what they can be like, no disrespect, sir. The men liked him, too. He was calm, eventempered, and fair. They don't make many like that these days." Enzo decided not to respond to that comment. Apart from anything else, he didn't really know how to reply.

"The officers liked him as well. He had a good sense of humor. It makes a big difference to have an Exec with a sense of humor." This time it was Steadman who remained silent. "I'll leave you with him, Master Chief. I'm going to wash, take a look around the boat, and hand out the Valium. I'll tell the captain later. He won't be surprised."

0800A, COMJTFNON HQ, Bodø

Admiral Risberg called the meeting to order. Before they broke up into working groups he wanted to review the progress that had been made since yesterday's meeting. But first he wanted an update on the weather. Commander Larsson stood and walked over to a weather map that was now projected onto a large screen at the end of the room. He began to speak: "Good morning, ladies and gentlemen. This is the latest chart I have." He removed a laser pointer from his breast pocket and shined it at the screen. "Here's the front that I described yesterday and which is now well clear of the datum. Behind it, here, is an area of high pressure that will dominate the weather pattern over the *Tulsa* for the next day or two." He moved the pointer to the left. "And here's the next low-pressure area and its accompanying frontal systems that I also mentioned yesterday. You'll notice that its pressure has fallen to 965 millibars and it is still falling. I fear this is ominous. It's already packing gale-force winds. If the depression should deepen, these are likely to increase. With respect to sea-state, I am predicting five or more."

"Commander"—it was the admiral who had interrupted him—"as you are aware, it's the timing that will be critical here. Can you give me your best guess as to how long we can expect a sea-state of three or less?" He turned and looked at the British contingent. "That is the limit for *Salminster* to operate the LR5, isn't it?"

"Yes, sir," replied Lieutenant Commander Murphy.

"The sea-state should have approached that this morning. I expect it to remain at three or below until Wednesday morning, say until midday."

"And after that?"

"We're looking at two days, or possibly more, with a sea-state greater than three—at times considerably greater," replied Commander Larsson.

"Thank you, Commander. Does anybody else have a meteorological question?" There was no reply. "Well then, let's move on. What's the latest news from the *Salminster*?" He looked once again at the British contingent. Lieutenant Commander Murphy glanced down at the message that lay on top of the pile of papers in front of him.

"She's making good progress, sir, despite the poor weather. Her latest ETA at the datum is 0700A on Wednesday." A number of officers around the table eyed each other and mumbled a few words. It was blatantly obvious to everyone that no rescue could be started, let alone be completed, if there was just a five-hour window before the sea became too rough. There may not even be that long because the *Salminster* was going to have to travel through the frontal systems to reach the *Tulsa*. In any case, even these optimistic assumptions were only valid if the fronts behaved themselves. What if they arrived early? The admiral allowed the chatter to continue for a few minutes while he spoke to the Russian beside him.

"It would appear that the weather's going to make the use of the LR5 problematic much before Friday, by which time even the most liberal calculations with respect to the internal atmosphere in the *Tulsa* show that the survivors may be forced to escape. That's correct, is it not, Commander Selby?"

"Yes, sir. I estimate that they'll have used all their lithium by midday Wednesday. If they are to escape before the atmosphere becomes dangerous, they're likely to have to start on Thursday evening."

"What about the DSRV?" continued the admiral. "It can operate independently of the weather."

"The news there is a little more encouraging, sir," continued Selby. "The engineers estimate that they'll have it ready in a few hours. It should leave San Diego at 1400 local tomorrow. We estimate it will arrive in Murmansk and be fitted to the *Vindictive* by very early Wednesday morning, and the ETA at the datum is currently 0200 local on Friday morning."

"Would I be right in thinking that built into these estimates is an assumption that everything goes according to plan?"

"There's a little room in there for unexpected delays, but it's a pretty tight schedule, sir."

"It looks like this'll be a close-run thing. If they do have to escape on Thursday, what will we have by way of assets?"

It was Lieutenant Commander Murphy who flicked through his papers again and spoke up. "The *Wellington* should arrive at the datum at around 2300A tomorrow night. We discussed her capabilities yesterday. The *Centaur* is loading some additional stores and medical staff plus five compression chambers and divers to operate them as we speak. She should depart for the datum in"—he looked at his watch which was still in Zulu time—"just under two hours. At her best speed, she should arrive late Wednesday night. That should give her ample time to prepare for an escape."

The meeting went on to review the arrangements that were being made ashore to handle any casualties. There was a progress report on an advance party of American engineers who were on their way from San Diego to Murmansk, and they then went on to discuss any further assets that might be required before breaking up into the various working groups.

0900A, USS *Tulsa*

Having told Richter about the XO, Enzo was running out of things to say without asking him directly how he was feeling. He'd rather hoped that the captain would volunteer the information, but he'd showed no sign of doing so. "Enzo, would you ask Harvey to step in? I want an update on the atmosphere control. You'd better stay and listen in as well."

"Aye, aye, sir. I'll be right back."

Harvey had mixed news to impart. He showed the two of them the chart that he had drawn up of the oxygen and carbon-dioxide concentration and the pressure in the compartment. The CO_2 was holding steady at around 3 percent and the oxygen was also constant at just under 20 percent. Everybody seemed happy with that, despite all three of them feeling rather breathless. Even better news was that they still had sixty-five canisters of lithium hydroxide left and more than enough oxygen. Harvey was confidently predicting that the lithium would last well into Wednesday, which would be almost a week after the sinking. The only problem was the pressure. It had been gradually creeping up over the past couple of days and had now reached nine feet of seawater.

"Have you found out yet where the leak is, Harvey?" Richter asked.

"Yes, sir, I think it is coming through the ventilation trunking into the fan room."

"From the reactor compartment?"

"I think it has to be, sir. There isn't anywhere else it could be coming from."

"I've always wondered if those flapper valves would seal in the event of a sinking. Now we know the answer." Richter thought for a moment before continuing. "Enzo, you did a radiation survey yesterday and everything was OK. Did you check the fan room?"

"No, sir, but the upper level aft was clean."

"Better check it again to be sure."

"Will do, sir."

Although the discussion had lasted less than half an hour, Richter was looking tired. Enzo and Harvey glanced at each other and nodded. It was time to leave him to rest. Richter, unaware of how haggard he looked, was actually wide-awake. On his own once again, he returned to his younger days, to the party when he had first been ensnared by Marie. Perhaps it was a consequence of his head injury, but he had never before enjoyed such vivid recollections of that evening. She had changed into a small, bright red dress and wore matching shoes and little else apart from a fine gold chain around her neck and an even finer one around her left ankle. Despite all the beer that he had consumed during the afternoon, he could still not pluck up the courage to walk over and start a conversation with her. Instead, he had sat at a table with John and Phoebe discussing something of no importance and contented himself with just casting an occasional glance in her direction. Eventually, Phoebe had realized what was going on, and she got up and brought Marie over to the table.

That had proved to be the start of a romance that he had never entirely gotten over. The evening had passed by in a blur of one dance after another with Marie, all of them slow and erotically charged. His senses had been swamped by the music, her gentle touch, the sweetness of her breath, and the heady aroma of her perfume—Opium. All he'd wanted to do was whisk her off to bed, a proposition that he was convinced she would have agreed to. In the end, however, he had decided to return to the BOQ. This was not because he was afraid of rejection, but because he would have far better opportunities in the near future—Marie had agreed to accompany him on a tour of the Great Lakes and, even better, they would go in her beautiful car.

What an incredible vacation that had been. The following morning she had come to collect him in the Mercedes. Because it was really only a two-seater, they had decided to travel light. He had packed everything he intended to take into a canvas duffel. Marie's interpretation of "light" was somewhat different. She had filled the trunk with suitcases and assorted plastic bags and had even brought an umbrella and an overcoat, despite the temperature having already soared into the high eighties. She had insisted that he drive.

Despite many attempts over the years to do so, he had never been able to remember much about the journey to Dunkirk on Lake Erie. It had passed by in a blur. Although the top was down, they had chatted continuously, and it was only when he really put his foot down that the roar of the wind had made either of them shout. They'd got lost in New York and again near Corning but after a journey of over four hundred miles, they'd arrived in Dunkirk at just after seven. Marie had arranged for them to stay at her friend Chrissy's house, and it had taken another forty minutes to find it because Marie had forgotten the address.

Chrissy and her parents normally lived just outside Cherry Hill and had known Marie for most of her life. They welcomed her as one of the family. Richter had learned in the car that Marie had only befriended Chrissy five years earlier when they were both thirteen. Although Marie was still built like a pencil in those days, Chrissy had developed an almost Rubenesque figure and was the first of their year at school to start dating. Somewhat cruelly, she had acquired the nickname of "the significant udder," in a parody of the new, inclusive social terminology of the time. Marie had felt sorry for her, and their relationship had flourished. It had endured to that day.

As Richter had engaged Chrissy's parents in conversation, he'd gained the impression that they were impressed that he was a submariner, but at the same time he had the feeling that they were slightly reserved. Chrissy's dad was a plastic surgeon who had obviously made a considerable amount of money judging by the sheer size and opulence of their summer home. Like Marie's family, the Schoenfelds clearly moved among the upper echelons of New Jersey and Pennsylvania society. He had always thought that officers in the armed services occupied a socially neutral niche. That was before he had been drawn into this circle.

Although their hosts had eaten already, and despite Richter's protests, a meal was prepared. Marie and Chrissy talked incessantly. After the meal, and at Richter's suggestion, the three of them walked down to the lake to wander along the sandy shore and watch the sunset. It was a beautiful evening. They stopped at a bar for a quick beer before heading back, and all too soon it was time for bed. As he sank into the yielding warmth of the queen-size bed, all he could think about was his good fortune. He was infatuated with Marie. Just being with her was exhilarating. The prospect of a lasting relationship was too heady to even contemplate. Life had been tough up until now. If he played his cards right, he thought, things could be a lot easier in the future.

It had been a long drive, and Richter had already lost control of his eyelids. His breathing had become slow and regular. He was barely conscious. It was the smell of Opium that roused him. Marie had slid silently into the bed and was now beside him. She put her arm around him and snuggled up close. "I've never managed to find my way around this house," she whispered into his ear in a mildly complaining tone. "But then you know that navigation isn't my forte." Richter rolled over to face her and put an arm around her. She was naked.

"I think we can safely leave the navigation to me. I'm used to finding my way around in the dark. Oh, look! I've found a mouth." As they kissed, their petting became more exploratory and intense. "And map reading is second nature to me," he mumbled between kisses. He cupped one silky breast in his hand and gently massaged it. "Unless I'm very much mistaken, on top of this hill there's a trigonometry point. You know, they're used by surveyors to map the terrain?" Marie started to giggle as he played with her nipple. Using his index and middle fingers as legs, Richter started to walk his hand down her belly. "And what do we have here? Is it a forest? An orchard, perhaps?

No, it's marshland." She stopped giggling as Richter probed between her legs. "What's this, a railway cutting? No, it's a tunnel." He started to nibble the ear into which he had been whispering. "Mmmm, I think I'll explore it." He released Marie's ear and allowed his mouth to follow the trail blazed by his fingers only moments before. As he traveled south he delivered a series of light kisses and licks to Marie's breast and belly. He slowed his advance to build the excitement of the moment, but could no longer restrain himself and homed in on his target. Marie's giggles were soon replaced by deep sighs.

0900A, MV *Pelican*, Bergen Harbor, Norway

Due to the shortage of space, Simon Bannerman and Mick Russell had been forced to share a cabin—something they had not done before. SNN was generous with hotel expenses so, whenever they had worked together before, they had enjoyed separate rooms. But the *Pelican* was a small ship and with two full camera crews and all their equipment, there had been no alternative but to share. This had not been an issue overnight. They had both been so tired from the frantic preparation and transatlantic flight that sleep had come easily to them both. However this morning, being woken by the vibration of the main engines, a potential problem with this arrangement had become apparent.

Although it was not something he liked to discuss, Mick had some difficulties with digestion. He'd been teased about it at school, but had shrugged that off as the adolescent mischief of his school friends. As an adult he had managed largely to conceal it until his recent decision to become a vegetarian. Whatever the benefits of a high-fiber diet, and the ability to adopt the moral high ground with respect to animal welfare, the sad fact was that it had exacerbated his problem to the point that it could no longer be hidden. He let rip an explosive blast of flatulence, the third in the past half hour. Simon had ignored the first, registered a mild protest at the second and had now decided to confront his colleague. "For fuck's sake, what's your problem, Mick?"

"It's not my problem, it's yours. I can't help it." It was not a reply that was calculated to appeal to Simon. It was made worse by the fact that Mick had started to laugh, and that had caused him to release yet another noisy and pungent discharge.

"God above, Mick. Shove a cork in it or, believe me, I will!" With that, Simon had risen from the lower bunk with his pillow and struck Mick over the head with it. "We are going to be stuck in this miserable little ship for at least the next week. Unless you sort yourself out, you can sleep on the upper deck. Got it?" Mick had stopped laughing. He was quite a bit bigger than Simon and lowered himself to the deck to confront him. The two of them faced off wearing only their pajamas.

"If anybody sleeps on the upper deck, it'll be you, sunbeam." With that, Mick stabbed him in the shoulder with his index finger. "The only reason we're here is to get this fucking story covered, right? That's why I'm here, anyway. If you have a problem with that, you can complain to Max. In the meantime, can it. I'm going to take a shower."

1300C, Northern Fleet HQ, Severomorsk

Borzhov sat patiently at one end of a green leather sofa, trying to avoid the gaze of Meltzer, who sat at the other end. Both officers were in service dress blue without swords. The other occupant of the oak-paneled anteroom was a middle-aged secretary with graying auburn hair, who sat clicking away at a typewriter. The only other sound was the ticking of an old grandfather clock that dominated one corner of the room. Facing the two men was a door that led into the room

in which they were going to have to provide answers
to some searching questions.

Konstantin had trained and mentored Borzhov, they
liked and trusted each other. Consequently, Borzhov
had not been surprised that the admiral had been un-
guarded in his comments over dinner on Saturday. He
had outlined just how serious the situation was and
went on to recall his trip to Moscow. The meal had
concluded a very trying day for the admiral. He'd recounted how Gromyko had finally let him go to bed
at 0300. However, he'd enjoyed no more than four
hours sleep before the two of them were summoned
back to the Kremlin. His boss looked like he'd not
been to bed at all. They had spent the morning briefing
the defense minister on the extent of the support that
could be offered to help the Americans rescue their
submariners. It had been an ugly meeting because it
was obvious that the Russian cupboard was virtually
bare. There were precious few fully operational naval
assets that could be provided in the requisite time
frame, and none that would be of direct benefit to the
operation. The minister had appeared to be horrified
that the Russian DSRVs were not operational, and
only Gromyko, at his most persuasive, had managed
to deter him from placing a moratorium on further
submarine operations until they, and their MOSUB,
were repaired. The meeting had concluded with the
minister virtually incandescent with rage at having to
tell the president that, despite all the money that had
been squandered on defense, Russia was going to be
unable to help rescue the crew of the *Tulsa*. He had
made it clear that whoever was responsible for placing
him in this situation would pay dearly for it.

Borzhov was grateful that he'd only been put off
his dessert by this revelation. Had Konstantin mentioned it earlier, the whole meal would have been ruined. Over coffee by the fire, the admiral had explained
what was likely to happen. He would chair a preliminary
inquiry that would commence on Monday. Given the

political pressure, it was inevitable that a full court-martial would be convened at a later date. That Meltzer was history was beyond doubt. The only issue to be resolved was whether Borzhov would be burned as well. Konstantin had assured him that he would do all in his power to protect him.

Borzhov returned his thoughts to the present. After what had seemed like an eternity, the door had just opened, and Zerchev walked out. He was followed by a lieutenant who looked directly at him, and said: "Sir, please would you come through?" Borzhov rose to his feet, tugged at the hem of his jacket to straighten it, and approached the door. Despite having emptied his bladder no more than ten minutes earlier, he had to stifle an urgent desire to urinate.

0800R, Cherry Hill, New Jersey

Marie had forgotten just how enormous the house was. It wasn't just its size that was a surprise, but the interior was completely alien to her. Christine had apparently redecorated no fewer than six times since she had last been home, and she didn't recognize so much as a stick of furniture. The only place that had apparently been preserved was her father's office. She had not been able to confirm this because nobody, apart from him, was allowed in there. Marie didn't like what Christine had done to the place. It appeared that her taste had not benefited from the passage of time. With the expansion of available fashion options, she had selected different styles for almost every room, resulting in a place that had the coherence of a retail furniture showroom. It was a mercy that, as she had hoped, Christine was not at home. She had forgone the trip to Maui, visiting friends in Singapore instead.

Marie had slept remarkably well. Doubtless her new medication had helped in that regard. The rather late meal and her father's generosity with the after-dinner drinks had contributed as well. It was the first night since she had learned of the sinking that she hadn't woken at least twice to get the news. It was such a shame that there would be no news of the *Tulsa* that would be worth listening to—unless they were to announce that there had been a terrible mistake and John was still alive. But what were the chances of that? Infinitesimally small, she concluded. Marie lay in bed feeling rather hungover and decided that she would stay there for a while, at least until the boys were up and about. She reflected back on the previous day. It was one that she really didn't want to recall, but couldn't help doing so. She remained numb at the loss of John. It was almost as if she'd felt all along that he'd died, but had been unable to accept that it was true. Now that it was a harsh reality, it would take some time to sink in. The reason was all too obvious. Not having John at home was such a familiar situation that accepting the idea that he would never be coming home again was incredibly difficult.

Her mind drifted on to something that Jamie had said as they'd been sitting on the bed once the packing was done. "Is Uncle Geoffrey dead, too?" he'd asked. There had been no time for her to respond adequately to the question at the time. The more she thought about it, the more she realized that she desperately hoped that he wasn't. He'd been the very best of friends to both her and John since they'd been married, and particularly since the boys had been born. Maybe there was some news worth listening to after all—at least Geoff might survive. She lifted her head off the pillow and decided to get up. Securing her bathrobe with its belt, she made her way down to the kitchen. As she passed father's door, she thought she heard laughter, but there was not a sound from the boys. For the first time in their lives they had a bedroom each and the lack of fraternal influence had clearly allowed them to sleep longer than usual. What bliss.

Other things had changed at home apart from the decor. With Christine being away as frequently as she was, and father working crazy hours, somebody had to keep the house in some sort of shape. The solution was Carmen, a young and stunningly pretty maid from Costa Rica. Upon meeting her last night Marie had wondered, fleetingly, whether she was in the country legitimately. However, as far as she was concerned, it didn't matter. She cooked divinely and kept the house impeccable. After all, she wasn't responsible for the choice of furniture. It may be shit, but it was spotlessly clean shit.

There was a newspaper on the table. The front page was solemn and bordered in black. There was a stock photograph of the *Tulsa* and, below it, a list of those who had died. Presumably because of his rank, John's name was at the top. She couldn't bring herself to read the article, so she put the paper down. She heard the sound of somebody coming downstairs, and turned to see that it was Carmen. Her hair needed brushing, and she was adjusting her short, black dress. "So sorry, Mrs. Dowling. Would you like some coffee with your breakfast? I make it right away."

"Coffee sounds great, Carmen, but I don't feel like eating much. You fed us so well last night."

"No, no, no. You should have a good breakfast." Marie turned again, this time to see father storm into the room and take his seat at the kitchen table. "I've always believed it's the most important meal of the day. Your mother and I brought you up to believe that, too."

"Yes, Father. But a lot of water has flowed under the bridge since then."

"I know. We'll talk about all that tonight. Carmen, I'll have my usual, please." He turned back to Marie. "Are you sure I can't tempt you? Carmen's French toast is exquisite with some bacon."

"No thank you, Father. I'm not feeling hungry."

Her dad glanced at the front page of the newspaper on the table.

"No, of course. I understand." He changed the subject. "Unfortunately, I have to go into the office today. I've been away too long as it is. However, I'll be back as soon as I can, and then we must have a chat. How are the boys?"

"I haven't seen them yet this morning. No news is definitely good news in that department."

"Have you thought what you'll do with them today?"

"Not much. I think we'll just get settled around here."

"Well, there's more to the yard than you'll remember—I bought two more acres from the Simpsons, and I've put in a pond and stocked it with rainbow trout. The boys might like to try and catch a couple for supper."

"That's an idea." Her father hastily consumed his French toast and bacon, rose from the table, and made to leave, before turning and giving Marie a quick kiss.

"I must dash. See you later."

1700C, Northern Fleet HQ, Severomorsk

Borzhov was totally drained. As he left the inquiry and returned to the anteroom, he heaved a sigh of relief that it was all over for the day. But he was still going to have to come back tomorrow. He told Meltzer that he was free to go home for the night. The questioning had been thorough as well as exhausting. To begin with, things had not gone too badly. Actually, it was fair to say that they'd gone rather well. Borzhov presented, to the best of his recollection, the sequence of events that had led up to the collision and those that had followed, right up to the time that the *Gepard* left the scene. To his surprise, and despite his flagrant violation of international maritime law, nobody had criticized him for not reporting the accident earlier. They had even praised him for the way in which, by recovering the SLOT buoy, he had allowed the command the opportunity to consider the matter without undue pressure before action was taken.

His difficulty had been in explaining why Meltzer had been left with the conn at such a critical time. He'd been reduced to tap-dancing around his medical history. The dysentery he could not deny—it was right there in his medical records, as was his initially poor response to treatment. The reason he had not attended his follow-up appointments he had ascribed, quite accurately, to his commitments at sea. He had managed to avoid, at least so far, admitting that he'd not been cured. He would find out tomorrow how long that would remain the case. What concerned him more was the incredibly subtle way the board had gone about their inquisition.

Over dinner just two days earlier, Konstantin had led Borzhov to believe that he would keep the wolves at bay and manage the show so that the board wouldn't be able to hijack him. So much for promises, so much for friendship. The more he thought about it, the angrier he became. Having led Borzhov by the nose back through the sequence of events and given him confidence, the board had suddenly changed tack and started to ask pointed questions about members of his crew. They wanted to know all about Zerchev, about his competence, and how they got along. Next it was Meltzer. They grilled him on every aspect of his background and capabilities. They even reviewed each of his fitness reports that Borzhov had written. He thanked God that at least the system was so bent that he was expected to lie. Even a bad fitness report could sound like a citation for a Nobel prize. They had remarked on his observation, written only three months previously, that Meltzer was a man of "exceptional ability"—his very words. Mercifully, they'd missed the heavy irony with which that remark had been penned. The only exceptional aspect of Meltzer's ability was its limitations. Nonetheless, the impression given was that it was not unreasonable for Meltzer to be left with the conn. After all, he was an officer with substantial experience and exceptional ability.

Perhaps he should have smelled a rat when he had realized that Zerchev was to be interviewed before him, Borzhov mused. In retrospect it had made no sense, although it had not troubled him at the time. He and the XO enjoyed an excellent working relationship. Although they were not friends as such—he'd always tried to avoid anything other than a purely professional association with his men—they trusted each other. At least, until this afternoon. Borzhov was left wondering exactly what he'd told the inquiry about Meltzer and, more importantly, what he, the captain, thought about him. He'd not kept his views secret from his XO, there was no way he could. They both signed the fitness reports and discussed each man in detail. Zerchev had even witnessed his outburst after the collision. Borzhov was now 99 percent certain that he had reported all of this to the board. If he had, it would explain the unpleasant direction that the discussion of Meltzer had taken. Several members of the board had been stubbornly persistent in questioning his judgment in leaving Meltzer with the conn. The basis for this could only have been Zerchev's testimony.

Borzhov was overwhelmed with emotions. Exhaustion was the principal one, but through it seeped anger at what he saw as betrayal. He was frustrated at not knowing where he stood, and disillusioned because Konstantin had not been straight with him. Was he being set up? What alternative interpretation of his grilling could there be? He could think of none. All he wanted to do was hit the nearest bar and get completely drunk to the point where he no longer cared.

The young lieutenant who had earlier ushered him into the interview room marched smartly up to him, saluted, and presented him with an envelope. "With the compliments of Admiral Konstantin, sir." Borzhov looked the young man in the eye, returned the salute, and relieved him of the envelope.

"Thank you, that will be all." The lieutenant saluted again, turned on his heel, and marched away. Borzhov opened the envelope and read the brief, handwritten note inside before returning it to its envelope and moving off to find a shredder. Sympathy from Konstantin was more than he could stomach right now, no matter how he wanted to phrase it. The fact was that he had been badly let down, and nothing could change that.

1700A, USS *Tulsa*

Richter was shivering almost continuously. He rolled over onto his side and brought his knees up to his chest in an effort to get warm, or at least to stop himself from getting any colder. His head was still pounding, and he felt drained of energy. He was also thirsty, but just couldn't be bothered to get out of bed to fetch a glass of water. If he didn't know better, he would have diagnosed himself as suffering from a monumental hangover. What really concerned him was that he had developed a new symptom—he was short of breath. Much more so than earlier in the day.

There was a knock at the door. "Come in." Richter immediately regretted raising his voice as his head thumped with the effort. It was Enzo who opened the door and stepped in. To Richter's surprise, he looked breathless as well.

"Sir, I'm not sure what's going on right now, but I think something's wrong with our atmosphere control. I've been all around the compartment, and a lot of people have dreadful headaches and are short of breath. If it's OK with you, I've asked Harvey to join us and bring his records with him."

"Sure, I want to know what the problem is—" Before he could complete what he was going to say, Harvey stepped through the open door and stood gasping from the effort of climbing to the upper level. He was shaking his head.

"I've no idea what's wrong, sir. The numbers all seem OK." With that he advanced to Richter's bunk and laid his charts on the bed. "See? The oxygen level's only a bit lower than this morning and the carbon dioxide hasn't changed at all." Richter squinted briefly at the charts, but it was more of a gesture than a serious attempt to scrutinize the data. Harvey may not be the sharpest member of the wardroom, he thought, as he tried to focus on the charts, but he wouldn't show up with something that was glaringly wrong.

"Then why is everybody so short of breath?" he replied. "The only answer I can think of is that your numbers must be wrong."

"Which ones, sir?"

"I was hoping you'd tell me."

"Harvey," started Enzo, "it's pretty difficult to mis-read a Draeger tube unless you're using the pump incorrectly. I'm sure you've checked they're being used right, haven't you?"

"Well, yes. I even took the last two readings myself. I know the tubes aren't desperately accurate, but they shouldn't be wildly out."

"OK, I agree with that. You've read the atmosphere-control manual, just like me, and it's a high carbon-dioxide level that's supposed to make people breathless, isn't it?"

"That's what it says."

"But it also says that a low oxygen level can make the effect of a raised carbon-dioxide level worse. How confident are you of the oxygen readings?" Harvey didn't respond immediately, and so Enzo continued, "I suppose what I'm asking is whether the oxygen meter is working properly." Harvey's expression was a picture of perplexity. His forehead was furrowed, his right hand was now stroking his stubbled chin.

"Go and get the oxygen meter, please, Harvey,"

asked Richter quietly, "and bring the operating instructions back with you." Lieutenant Schwartz turned and left the stateroom.

"I can't think of anything else that could be causing the problem, can you, sir?"

"No, Enzo," replied Richter wearily, "I can't."

1900C, Northern Fleet HQ, Severomorsk

On his way out of the building, Borzhov caught sight of Zerchev and made a beeline for him. "Vladimir! I'm glad I caught you, we must talk."

"Sir, I'm under explicit instructions not to talk to any of the other witnesses."

"Nonsense. Come on, we're going out for a beer. Don't worry, we can talk about anything except the inquiry."

"If you insist, sir."

"I do." At the front of the building they hailed a cab and headed for Murmansk—there was little point in them being seen together too close to the base.

"It's a sorry business, sir. I mean, I am saddened that we're reduced to being puppets in a show. You realize it makes little difference what any of us say. The whole thing is an act to satisfy the politicians."

"Is that what you think, Vladimir?"

"Yes, sir. It is."

"Well, I think you're right to some extent. The only point of the inquiry is to satisfy a political imperative to identify the guilty parties. That there will be at least one is without doubt. But we have it in our power to limit the damage. There really is no need for us all to go down with the ship, as it were."

"I disagree, sir. I think the decisions have already been made, and this is a fishing exercise for excuses for the actions that will inevitably follow."

"You have made my point elegantly. It should be our business to ensure that they catch only old boots. I just wish I'd thought to discuss this with you before the proceedings opened this morning. You were in there for four hours. Did you offer them any fish?"

"Sir, that's unfair. I really can't answer."

"OK, Vladimir, then just tell me this: were you advised by anybody as to what to say?" Zerchev looked down and then out of the cab window. His expression was almost distant. "What's the problem? Are you under orders not to discuss even that?"

"Sir, I think you know how I feel about you. We've served together in the *Gepard* for two years now. They've been good years. I hold you in the highest regard. But you know I have a wife and now a son. The navy and submarines are all I know. Despite the irregularity of our pay, it's a secure job by the standards of civilian life. I can't afford to be without it."

Borzhov paused to collect his thoughts. "Has somebody been coaching you, Vladimir?"

"I'm coming to that, sir. While you were at dinner with Admiral Konstantin on Saturday, I was summoned by his chief of staff. The only thing that interested him was how good Meltzer was at his job. Naturally, I told him just what we'd agreed for his fitness reports. To have done anything else would have been foolish. However, he wasn't satisfied with that. He kept on at me to say more. It was only after quite some time that he put forward the alternatives that were open to me if I didn't tell him what he wanted to hear. They were not attractive." Zerchev swallowed hard and once again lowered his gaze. He had started to pick absently at a fingernail, a sign that Borzhov had grown to recognize as an expression of Vladimir under stress.

The cab had reached the bar, and they got out. Borzhov paid the driver and ushered Zerchev inside.

"What can I get you, Vladimir?"

"I'll have a beer, thank you, sir."

"That's what I was thinking, but I've changed my mind. I'll have a vodka." Once their drinks were in hand, Borzhov raised his glass. "To friendships past and future."

"To friendship," replied Zerchev. Borzhov put his glass to his lips, swallowed the clear liquid, and shook his head as the potent liquor reached his stomach. Zerchev gulped down his beer and placed his mug back on the bar.

"Bartender, the same again." The barman refilled the glasses. "Vladimir, I should explain that I'd always intended for us to have a few drinks together once we returned from patrol. After all, I need an opportunity to toast the new baby."

"Of course, sir." Vladimir's radiant smile was one of relief that their conversation in the cab was apparently over. It was also one of joy that his captain should remember his son.

"What's his name?" inquired Borzhov. Zerchev looked a little sheepish.

"We decided to name him Anatole."

"After me? I'm astonished." Zerchev didn't have the heart to tell his captain that the boy's maternal grandfather was also called Anatole.

"Yes, sir. We gave him your name."

"I'll drink to that." Borzhov raised his glass. "To young Anatole." With that, he drained his glass and thumped it back onto the bar. Zerchev struggled to down his beer, wiped his chin, and belched loudly.

"Sir, it's my round and if I am to keep up with you, I'll have to switch to vodka." He belched again, and they both laughed.

To Zerchev's disappointment, after they had consumed six drinks each, Borzhov returned to their discussion in the cab. "So the chief of staff persuaded you to admit to Meltzer's shortcomings?" Zerchev looked up somewhat disconsolately and nodded.

"Yes, sir, I am afraid that I did."

"And you did the same before the board this morning?"

"I've told you, sir, I can't answer that."

"Can't, or won't?" Zerchev was feeling very uncomfortable and it showed. He was picking at his nail again. "You understand why I must know, Vladimir? It will substantially influence how I react to the board tomorrow."

"I understand, sir. The fact is that I told them that you were planning to have him dismissed from the *Gepard* and, if possible, from the service."

"Because of his incompetence?"

"Yes, sir, and his arrogance."

"Thank you, Vladimir. That merits another drink. Will you join me in another vodka?" Zerchev nodded. "Good man. We can yet make this a night to remember."

1930A, USS *Tulsa*

"Oh my Lord, look at this," exclaimed Enzo as he studied the operating instructions for the oxygen meter. "We're supposed to calibrate it before use."

"What does that involve?" asked Richter, almost dreading the answer.

"Doc usually does this. I think he zeros it using pure nitrogen and sets the span using the CAMS readout of the boat's atmosphere. With the CAMS down, I don't think we're going to be able to calibrate this thing."

"But surely, it can't have changed that much from the last time Doc calibrated it," interrupted Harvey, who'd been checking the batteries.

"Do we know when that was?" asked Richter.

"I don't. Do you, Harvey?"

"No idea. I expect he wrote it down somewhere, but God knows where."

"Look at this," continued Enzo as he read further into the operating instructions. "I don't think it matters—this thing is temperature sensitive. You're meant to calibrate it at ambient temperature. Even if Doc calibrated it just before the sinking, it would have to be done again now that it's so cold." He read on.

"Oh, no! It's worse than just calibration. This thing's sensitive to humidity. With all the condensation in the boat, it's got to be close to 100 percent humid, and that will screw it up completely. I don't suppose it's been working properly for some time." Harvey let the instrument fall to the deck, where it landed with a thud. Richter and Enzo eyed each other, then glanced at Harvey.

"I'm sorry, this is my fault," he confessed, looking and sounding utterly dejected.

"No it isn't. It's pretty obvious this meter wasn't designed for DISSUB conditions. I expect it's only really supposed to be used in laboratories," soothed Richter. Nobody else had anything more to say.

It was Enzo who finally broke the ensuing silence. "Harvey, have you had to change the frequency with which you change the canisters in the hopper?"

"I don't think so. I'll check." He reached onto the bunk, picked up a sheaf of papers that were decorated with his characteristically untidy scrawl, and started to shuffle through them.

"What are you thinking, Enzo?" asked Richter.

"Well, if you think about it, the rate at which we use oxygen and produce carbon dioxide should stay roughly the same. If we haven't had to change the rate we use the canisters and Harvey hasn't had to change the bleed rate for days, we shouldn't have a problem."

"Forgive me for pointing out the obvious, Enzo, but even I can recall that we started down this track because we have got a problem, and one that's getting worse."

"OK, maybe I got it the wrong way around—"

"Right," announced Harvey, who finally looked up from his papers. "The last time I had to decrease the changeover frequency was midday Saturday."

"Did you change the oxygen bleed rate then?" asked Enzo intently.

"No, I haven't touched it since Friday. The oxygen readings have been rock steady."

"I smell a rat here," announced Enzo. "If we've been producing less carbon dioxide than we thought we would, surely we should have been using less oxygen."

"And, if we have," continued Richter, "the oxygen level should have been rising. Well done, Enzo. That confirms the meter's kaput, but I'm not sure it explains why we're all so breathless."

"Don't you see? We know that the oxygen readings have all been wrong, and we also know that a low level of oxygen will exacerbate the effect of too much carbon dioxide."

"So?" interrupted Harvey.

"So, my dear friend, there must be something wrong with the oxygen bleed. Have you checked it recently?"

"Well, no. There's been no need. The oxygen level . . ." Harvey's voice faded away and disappeared.

"I think it's time you and I went and took a look in the fan room." With that the two lieutenants rose and made to leave the captain's stateroom. "With your permission, sir?"

"Go ahead, Enzo. Tell me what you find."

1600R, Cherry Hill, New Jersey

The crunching of gravel outside, followed by the gentle thud as he closed the door of the Jaguar, signaled her father's return. Marie got up and went into the hall as he breezed into the house. He set his briefcase down on the Queen Anne table by the study door, opened his arms, and gave her a hug. "So how did it go today?"

"Well, if you were relying on us to catch supper, I'm afraid we'll go hungry. The fishing didn't go too well, and we lost the net."

"Oh, too bad. Didn't I give you my rod?"

"I tried setting up the one in the garage, but I had no idea what I was doing." She showed him a Band-Aid on the back of her hand that covered a puncture wound from the hook. "Looks like I'm the catch of the day."

"You can say that again. Thankfully, Carmen will have gone into town and fetched us something to eat tonight. I suppose I'm going to have to show you all how to catch trout. I'll do it tomorrow—I've decided to take the day off. Right now, it is time for a cup of tea. Will you join me?"

Marie declined, so her father vanished into the kitchen, returned with a porcelain cup and saucer, and settled down in his reclining chair. He took a sip and methodically placed the cup and saucer down on the Wedgwood coaster on the table beside him. He looked awkward and cleared his throat. "What I'm about to say is going to be as difficult for me to vocalize as it will be for you to hear. First of all, I want to assure you that all your mother and I ever wanted for you was the best. The best of everything. I, in particular, have worked hard to ensure that you could have it: the best schooling, vacations, hell, you'd seen more countries by the time you were eighteen than anybody I know. You always had fine clothes and a lovely car. Do you remember the Mercedes?"

"Yes, I do. It was very generous of you. It was a shame I had to sell it."

"When things started to go wrong between your mother and me, I think it's fair to say that you and I became closer. You meant everything to me—"

"Until Christine came on the scene," Marie interrupted. "I really can't imagine what you saw in her, and I still have no idea why you put up with her."

"It was my choice, and you must respect that."

"But it was obvious she was wrong for you—and she hated me."

"Look, Marie, with hindsight it is easy to pick faults in the way I behaved. As a matter of fact, I could do the same with you. Your language in front of Christine was, at times, unforgivable."

"I was provoked. You realize all she wanted to do

was come between you and me. I think she resented us being as close as we were."

"You may be right."

Father reached out, took another deliberate sip of tea and gently replaced the cup. "Is that why you took up with that first navy lad? What was his name? Godfrey?"

"Geoffrey."

"Geoffrey. Is that why you went off on vacation with him?"

"No, I liked him. He made me laugh, and I quickly grew to love him."

"I heard about that from the Schoenfelds. They were as puzzled as Christine and I were; and your mother, for that matter."

"So what's the point, Father? Where's all this getting us?"

"As I said, all any of us wanted for you was the best. We wanted you to go to a good school and train for a career. I was hoping you might choose my alma mater, Princeton. We didn't mind what you ultimately chose to do, but we wanted you to have the freedom in future life that a degree confers. At a university, you'd have surely met some fine young men with connections. Men who were going places." He paused. "We just wanted you to have the best. But you obviously didn't want the best for yourself. That Godfrey boy—his background was hardly—how shall I put it, top drawer, was it?"

"He's a nuclear engineer, Father, and a highly intelligent man. He couldn't help which family he was born into. In fact, the more I think about it, his achievement in doing as well as he has is far greater than something like another Kennedy being elected to Congress. Just because his father didn't have money, you turned your nose up at him. You all did." Marie was getting angry, and it showed.

"He was quite a bit older than you as well, wasn't he?"

"What's six years? How old is Christine? You've got at least double that over her, and the way she dolls herself up, it looks even more."

Marie was pleasantly surprised that her father looked a little nonplussed and had to compose himself before continuing. "In any case," he said, "what we did was in your own interest. To his credit, Godfrey saw the point and did the right thing."

"Father, his name is *Geoffrey*, and I don't think he did the right thing at all." Marie was lost for words. Bitter memories flooded back of how her father and Christine had refused to let her even invite Geoff home to meet them. Of how he had written and apologized for making what was clearly a difficult family situation worse. Of how he had returned to sea and not written again and, even when he eventually returned, of how he had made endless excuses for not seeing her. "I've never felt such pain as I did during those long months as he drew away from me," she continued, "until now, that is. Can you imagine how I felt, being punished because of the way you felt about him—you and that cow of a woman?" Marie reached for a Kleenex from the box beside her chair and dabbed at her eyes. Her father looked crestfallen. It took a few moments before he could reply.

"The way things turned out, it would seem that our actions weren't for the best. In fact, I deeply regret them now. What more can I say? I've invited you home so we could talk things over and see if we can't come to some sort of understanding. It's bound to be a painful process, but I know it's something we must do."

"In that case we'd better clear up what you did to John and me—it was dreadful. Why did you do it?" She paused momentarily. "And I don't want to hear anything about what you thought was best for me."

"Seeing as that was my motivation, I have very little left to say."

"Are you trying to tell me that excommunicating us

and leaving us to scrape by in navy housing, on a JG's pay, was best for me?" She raised her voice slightly. "How could it possibly be? Was depriving your only grandsons of their grandfather best for me? Or for them? Or even for you?" Tears had started to form again at the corners of her eyes, but she didn't feel like crying. She was still angry more than anything else. "Do you know that shortly after you called the other day and invited us to stay, I had to explain to the boys just who you were? They didn't even know what you looked like."

"Well, my treatment of you may have seemed harsh, because it was intended to be. How else was I to make you realize that you were throwing your life away? You'd made your bed, so to speak, and it was up to you to sleep in it."

"Look, Father, that doesn't cut it with me. You've just admitted it's my life, so why can't you be like any normal parent and let me live it my way? I chose to marry John. It couldn't matter less if you thought I should've done 'better.' It was my choice, wasn't it? What the hell did it have to do with you?"

"It had everything to do with me. I wasn't prepared to finance a venture that I considered to be foolhardy. In fact, I wanted to disassociate myself with it entirely—which is what I did."

Marie thought for a moment before replying. "Wait a minute. How could you ever consider that I was being foolhardy? Did you ever make any effort to get to know John? Before you respond, I'll save you the effort. The answer's no. How many times did you even talk to him, twice was it? Call yourself a lawyer? You're supposed to deal with evidence. On the basis of what evidence did you consider that I could have done better?"

"The man's background was working-class." Marie's jaw dropped.

"I beg your pardon, what did you just say?"

"His father was a truck driver, and his mother used

to wait tables in a streetside cafe. They were divorced as well. That's not the kind of background I expect for a son-in-law."

"Hello? This is twenty-first-century America, not Victorian England. How come you can be so judgmental? What's so special about the mighty Charles Goetschl, huh? What did your father do? Can't remember? Then I'll tell you—he was a storekeeper. Admittedly it was a big store, but size isn't everything, is it? Did his job in any way constrain *your* choice of a wife? No it didn't, and why didn't it? Because he wasn't a twisted snob like his son."

Marie's face was flushed, more from excitement than genuine anger. She sensed that she was in a winning position. Despite all the years of hardship, she had never really looked beyond her childhood impression of her father, one that had been founded more in idealism than objective reality. As she had just exposed, the root cause of their falling-out had been his dreadful snobbery, a trait that he shared with Christine. Was that what they had in common? She'd never really appreciated that before. Father was sitting motionless in his chair. Marie continued, "Divorced? I'm amazed you had the balls to raise that issue. You and Christine have both been divorced. Does that mean I should never get married? According to your argument, that should be sufficient to deny me a marriage license forever."

Father eventually composed himself and replied, "I don't suppose you'll ever know how it feels to have raised somebody like you. I was incredibly proud of you. You meant everything to me. You had the start in life that I'd never had. Dad's store wasn't big when I was a boy. Without working hard for a scholarship, I would never have gone to Princeton." Father reached into his pocket, withdrew a crisply ironed handkerchief, and touched it to his right eye. "Do you realize you could have ended up at the very pinnacle of society? A senator, even first lady, if you'd played your cards right. At eighteen, you didn't know how to play those cards. I wanted to show you, I wanted you to go to school and learn more. I wanted you to really make something of yourself. Instead, you started to dally with that Godfrey chap, and then you ran off and married John. Can you imagine how I felt? I was mad at you, truly mad. I even cut you out of my will."

"But why? What did you think you were going to achieve? Did you think I'd change my mind, dump John, come running home with my tail between my legs and enroll at Princeton?"

"Actually, I did. I was quite surprised that you held out for as long as you did. But you know me well enough. When I make my mind up about something I generally stick to it."

"And so do I," she replied emphatically.

Marie realized that they had fought to a standstill, and there was little point in continuing. It was time to cut to the chase. "So where do we go from here? Am I supposed to just forget the past fourteen years? All the pain, the misery, all the worries and anger. Just forget it all?"

"I don't expect you to forget it—I certainly won't. However, I think you should put it behind you. That's what I intend to do and, as far as I'm able, I'll try to make up for some of the hardship you've had to deal with."

"An apology wouldn't hurt."

"I thought I just had. Look, Marie, I am genuinely very sorry about the way things turned out. Can you accept that?"

"I suppose so. Does this mean I'm free to pick a future partner without fear of another thirteen years of exile—assuming I ever feel like doing so again?"

"Well," began her father, as he so frequently did, "I hope you'd listen to any observations I might make and take note of whatever advice I might choose to offer."

"I'd listen, sure. Actually, I always did. I just didn't always agree."

"No you didn't. Look, darling, I can't set myself up as any kind of paragon when it comes to partner selection. There's no point in pretending I know what's best for myself, let alone for you, no matter how much I wish that wasn't the case. From here on out, and as far as I am concerned, you can choose whoever you like. It's not as if you're still eighteen."

"Thank you, Father. I am so glad that you said that."

2000A, USS *Tulsa*

Harvey Schwartz looked at Enzo as they paused outside the captain's stateroom catching their breath. "Are you going to tell him or do you want me to?"

"What's the problem, Harvey?"

"I don't suppose it matters much. I'm going to look like a bit of a dickhead either way. I should have been logging the oxygen bank readings." Harvey knocked and they waited for a reply.

"Leave it to me, I'll tell him."

Harvey knocked again. "Do you think he's sleeping?"

"I'll take a look." With that, Enzo opened the door. By the light of the battle lantern which was still glowing dimly beside his bunk, Enzo could see that Richter was indeed fast asleep. "What do you think," he continued in a whisper. "Shall I wake him?"

"He said he wanted to know what we found, and I guess it's pretty important."

"OK." Enzo advanced and shook the captain by the shoulder. Nothing happened, so he shook him again. "Sir, we've got a problem." Richter stirred, rubbed his eyes, and opened them.

"What?"

"The oxygen-bleed manifold is frozen solid. It's literally a block of ice and it's not delivering any oxygen." Richter stirred and sat up slowly.

"How long has it been like that?"

"I don't know, sir, the oxygen bank pressure hasn't changed since yesterday's SITREP," admitted Harvey. "I'm very sorry, I should have checked it." Richter scratched his head and rubbed his eyes again.

"There's a manifold heater—isn't it working?"

"No sir," replied Harvey, "you've heard this before—it runs on AC."

"Perfect." Richter started to shiver. He slowly reached down for the quilted jacket that lay on the deck beside his bunk, picked it up, and wrapped it tightly around his shoulders. "What about Sparks? Can he fix it?" Enzo looked at Harvey, and indicated that he should reply.

"We thought about asking him, but decided against the idea. There's too much of a fire hazard. He only has to live up to his nickname, and we could have an explosion on our hands."

"Quite right, Enzo. Oh God! Why can't I think straight anymore?"

"We did come up with another idea," interjected Enzo. "We've got boiling water. We could thaw it out."

"I suppose it's either that or prepare the furnace and light off a few chlorate candles. No matter what, something has to be done right away," said Richter wearily. "I don't think I've ever felt quite so lousy."

"Let's do both then," said Enzo with an air of confident finality. "That'll be the quickest way to get the oxygen level back up. We'll let you know in the morning how we get on, sir."

"I want to know right away if it doesn't work. I've avoided saying this, but if you fail, we'll have to start escaping."

"Fail, sir?" replied Enzo breezily. "It's not in my lexicon. We'll fix it somehow."

"Say you can. How will you know when you've got the level back up to normal? I don't want it too high for obvious reasons."

"I'll use Harvey as my canary. I don't know if

you've noticed, sir, but his breathing rate is particularly sensitive to the atmosphere." With that the two lieutenants turned to leave. "Shall I leave the light on, sir, or would you prefer me to switch it off?"

"I'll manage, thanks, Enzo. Good night both of you."

"Good night sir," they replied in unison, and left the room.

Enzo reached his stateroom and automatically flicked the light switch as he entered and closed the door. "Shit!" he muttered under his breath as he groped his way to his bunk and switched on the battle lantern that stood beside it. He removed his sneakers and slipped under the blankets. It's only a matter of time before the captain loses it completely, he thought. It was obvious that Richter's normally nimble mind was well below par. Enzo's eyelids were heavy and he was being overwhelmed by a sense of exhaustion. He reached out, switched off the battle lantern and closed his eyes. Exhaustion was a sensation that he had grown used to ever since he had moved to New York. He had enjoyed virtually no social life in Brooklyn. He'd had a lot of catching up to do at school, and whenever he wasn't studying he was working in Uncle Alberto's laundry. That was hard, hot, physical work that drained him of any residual energy. It had also endowed him with remarkable stamina that had served him well in his choice of career. If he had thought, even for one minute, that he could end up in this situation, would he have still chosen the navy? He left the question unanswered and slid into a deep sleep.

2345C, Severnaya Hotel, Murmansk

Having half carried Borzhov to his room, Zerchev assisted him onto the nearest of the two beds, removed his shoes and tie, placed the room key on the nightstand, and walked over to the window. He'd asked the cab driver to wait and, as he peered through the net curtains he was still there on Profsoyuzov Street, standing by to take him back to his quarters on the base. It had become very cold, and the exhaust formed a large pale cloud that almost obscured the rear of the vehicle. It was time to leave. Zerchev crossed the room, closed the door behind him, and descended to the foyer and out onto the street.

"Your friend has had much to drink," remarked the driver.

"Yes, he doesn't do it often. When he does, it takes very little to knock him out. He's had a bad day."

"That is an expensive hotel. It's only used by tourists."

"I know it, but he wanted to stay there tonight. I expect he'll move back to the base tomorrow." Zerchev fell silent after that. His own head was far from clear, and he was troubled by the way the evening had turned out. Borzhov's mood had seemed to swing wildly. At one point he was laughing and making jokes. His mimicry of Admiral Gromyko was cruel, but hysterically funny. But his introspection as the evening wore on had become maudlin. It seemed that Borzhov had convinced himself that his naval career was over, and nothing Zerchev said could dissuade him from that view. The sad thing was he was probably right. He'd felt guilty about leaving Borzhov alone, but he'd insisted on it. Zerchev's conscience was salvaged by the realization that, with so much vodka inside him, Borzhov would sleep soundly.

Shortly after Zerchev had left, Borzhov rose from his bed. He wanted a shower. He removed his uniform, folded it neatly, and laid it out on top of the second of the twin beds. Surprisingly, he felt remarkably sober. His appearance of drunkenness had been largely for Zerchev's benefit. It was a convenient way to get rid of him. He'd become unbearably cloying as the evening progressed, undoubtedly because of a feeling of guilt that earlier in the day he'd betrayed his commanding officer. If nothing else, he was a good man, and it couldn't have been easy for him, thought Borzhov. Was it forgivable? Probably not—nothing about the present situation was forgivable.

After he'd showered he felt even more clearheaded. Having toweled himself off, Borzhov went over to the door, opened it, and slipped the DO NOT DISTURB sign over the handle. He didn't want any interruptions. He would even ignore the phone, should it ring. He then walked over to the window and looked out. The street was empty and there were no lights on in the building opposite. Nevertheless, he closed the curtains. He walked over to the desk, picked up the chair, and moved it over to the window. Once he was standing on it he reached up and tested the big brass curtain rail. It would take his weight easily. Next, he removed a wire coat hanger from the wardrobe and retrieved his black leather belt from his pants. He fed the end of the belt through the buckle to form a loop, before feeding it over the curtain rail and securing it by threading the coat hanger through two of the buckle holes. He then twisted the hanger wire to ensure that it wouldn't fall out of the belt. With his preparations ready, it only remained to write a note. He returned to the desk and removed a sheet of hotel letterhead from the drawer. He picked up the plastic ballpoint pen bearing the hotel logo and, sitting on the bed, started to write. In the absence of any close family, he addressed it to his men, the crew of the *Gepard*.

Borzhov put down the pen and slowly looked around the room. It was tidy. He walked over to the chair by the window and stepped up onto it. He slipped the makeshift noose over his head, tightened it around his neck, and rotated the buckle until it was below his ear. He reached up, grasped the curtain rail firmly, and balanced himself on the back of the chair. It wobbled beneath him and, for the first time that evening, he really felt the effect of the alcohol he had consumed. He was teetering on top of the chair and wanted to turn around, so that his backside faced the door. Clinging firmly to the curtain rail, he achieved this and was finally set. He looked up at the ceiling and then down at the floor. The fall should break his neck, at least he hoped so. A slow death from suffocation was not what he wanted. The chair wobbled again. It was time to put up or shut up. He checked the belt buckle with his right hand. The noose was tight. All he had to do was kick away the chair and release his grip with the other hand.

CHAPTER

6

Tuesday, 2 November

0500C, Murmansk Fjord

There had been many visits of Royal Navy surface ships to Russia since the thawing of the Cold War, but never a nuclear submarine, and certainly not a ballistic-missile boat. Even a few years earlier, the mere idea would have been out of the question. But times had changed, and the circumstances were such that saving lives took priority over security and operational considerations. Commander Philip Todhunter watched the reflection of the city lights as they danced and sparkled in the unfamiliar waters ahead of his submarine. And he contemplated how things had changed over the twenty years that he had been in the service. He thought back to the halcyon days of the Thatcher-Reagan era, with their vast military budgets and the high state of service morale, and made a mental comparison with the depleted coffers and limited horizons of today. The only reason he was in command of this fantastic weapon system was because of Maggie. He couldn't imagine Major or Blair being so bold as to order such an expensive item. Yes, so many things had changed and changed a lot.

His gaze shifted to the phosphorescence of the wash as the rounded bow of HMS *Vindictive* pushed effortlessly through the near-freezing water before taking a mental bearing of the z-berth that loomed in front of them. Although he gave the appearance of being absorbed with the spectacle, he felt obliged to keep an eagle eye on the pilot, who snapped occasional commands in somewhat broken English into the microphone he held in his hand.

Having never taken part in a DSRV operation before, Todhunter had spent last night reading all the documentation there was in the boat on how the thing worked and what was going to be expected of him and his submarine once they became the MOSUB. The principle was quite simple. As soon as the DSRV had been loaded onto the back of his boat, they would conduct a check dive and commence their surface passage out to the datum. Once there they would dive, maneuver as close to the *Tulsa* as safety would permit, and hover there. His boat was designed to do that, so it was not going to be too difficult. Finding the *Tulsa* should be quite a simple matter as well. Both the *Nordvik* and the *Wellington* should have solid fixes on her by now. The crew of the DSRV would then climb into their machine, detach from the *Vindictive*, and make their way to the *Tulsa*. They would then locate the forward escape hatch and lower the little craft onto the specially engineered ring around it, a process known as "mating." As soon as a good seal was established, the water would be pumped out of the mating skirt, the hatch of the DSRV would be opened, the area around the *Tulsa*'s hatch cleared, and then that would be opened, allowing free access from the DSRV to the DISSUB. People and stores would be exchanged and the whole procedure reversed. With the DSRV being able to transport up to twenty-four people at a time, it looked like five trips would be required. These would have to be broken up with two or possibly three breaks while the DSRV's batteries were recharged, but that should not present a problem. As soon as the first atmosphere-control stores were delivered there would be much less urgency over subsequent trips.

One thing that did concern him was a recent message that had indicated there was no means of establishing voice communications with the *Tulsa*. That was going to complicate things somewhat and cause delays. Would it also increase the chances of an accident? It could hardly reduce them. But as he thought more about it, his concern waned. After all, the US Navy had been operating this thing for nearly thirty years and must have ironed out all the wrinkles. Furthermore, there should be no safety threat posed to *Vindictive* because he would be able to talk to the DSRV at any time. So, to some extent, it wasn't his problem. But his unease would not evaporate completely. From his own experience, he knew only too well how easy it was to divorce military exercises from reality. It happened all the time. If problems were encountered at the planning stage that involved jeopardizing life, required unpalatable expenditure, or threw up questions for which there was no answer—they were archived in the "all too difficult" file and artificiality was introduced. If this was done often enough, it became tempting to believe that no problem existed. Since the DSRV had never been used for real, had it become the victim of exercise artificiality? he wondered. Had they ever tried to use this thing without UWT communications? A team of Americans would be joining *Vindictive* for the ride to the *Tulsa*. Todhunter made a mental note to ask them.

1000C, Severomorsk Harbor

The crew of the *Gepard* was assembled in two ranks at the dockside in front of their damaged boat. Despite the dock being covered, it was bitterly cold, and the men shuffled from foot to foot and slapped their hands together to keep warm. Rumors that something was wrong with the captain had spread like wildfire through the morning. His nonappearance had served only to fuel the more outlandish of the stories, despite some of the crew being aware that he was not expected on board anyway because he would still be attending the inquiry.

A car drew up at the end of the dock and the XO and Lieutenant Meltzer got out and made their way to the front of the group. They halted and turned smartly to face them. The Chief of the Boat brought the crew to attention. The tension was palpable. Lieutenant Commander Zerchev was feeling none too well after last night's excess in Murmansk and having to raise his voice to address the men was not something he was anticipating with any relish. Delivering the painful news of Commander Borzhov's death was even worse. He cleared his throat. "Officers and men of the *Gepard*." He paused for a moment to let the throbbing in his temples die down. "Some of you may be aware that the captain has been under a great deal of stress in recent days. It is my unfortunate duty to inform you that last night he took his own life." Zerchev had to stop at that point because the throbbing in his head was intolerable. The crew took the opportunity to mutter to each other. The thrust of most of the rumors had been that he was in custody and about to face a court-martial for the collision. This was a bombshell.

Zerchev raised a hand to silence the men. "Each of us has our own memories of the captain. I expect that mine are similar to many of yours. He was a man I held in the highest regard. He was a decent man and, above all, an honest one. These characteristics, as we know, are all too rare in today's navy. He was also highly intelligent, yet he was kind, and I know he cared about each and every one of you. His passing is a loss to us all." Zerchev was beginning to feel nauseated. The band of his cap had developed a vise-like grip around his head, that merely made it throb the more. He was going to have to get this over with quickly. He reached into his greatcoat pocket and retrieved a piece of paper. It was a photocopy of some handwriting on a piece of hotel notepaper. "Before he died, the captain wrote a note. As I expect you know, he had no close family, and so it is addressed to us all. It reads as follows:

My dear comrades and ship mates. I want you to know that what I am about to do is not intended to hurt you, quite the reverse. I therefore wish to apologize now to any of you who are grieving or feel a sense of loss. Although I would like to be able to sympathize and comfort you, sadly this is not possible. All I can say is that what you are feeling is nothing compared with the heavy burden that I have had to carry for the last few days. We live in difficult times. Both our great nation and its navy face very serious problems. In attempting to ameliorate these, there are people much higher in the chain of command than I, who appear prepared to abandon some of the principles and ideals that I hold to be sacrosanct. As a consequence, I feel that I can no longer continue to serve as an officer in this organization. Since, in the circumstances, my resignation would not be accepted, I have few options left open to me.

Leaving you in this way is the hardest part of this sorry business. I love you more than you will ever know. You, the men of the Gepard, are my family and my reason for living. It is to spare you the worst of the fallout from our last patrol that I am committed to this course of action. I blame nobody but myself for the way things have turned out and I believe that what I am about to do is for the good of us all. I will miss you very much."

There was no more chatter. The crew looked utterly shocked. A few looked saddened, and one, Lieutenant Meltzer, was in tears. Zerchev stared at the ground for a moment and said a silent prayer. There wasn't a sound in the cavernous building. "There's one more thing," continued Zerchev. "As you all know, the captain was a very private man, and I am told he has expressed a wish to be buried in private, so there will be no public funeral. Instead, Admiral Konstantin will lead a memorial service for Commander Borzhov on Friday at 1400. I will promulgate further details when they become available."

0800A, USS *Tulsa*

Enzo was concerned. Richter had not responded when he'd knocked at his door, nor had he moved when he entered his stateroom. It was only now, having shaken him by the shoulder for almost twenty seconds, that he appeared to be coming round. "Sir, are you OK?" Enzo shook him again. "Sir, please say something to me. Are you all right?" Richter finally stirred and opened an eye, then closed it again.

"Oh, it's you, Enzo." His voice was quieter than normal and he seemed to be slurring his words. "Yes, I'm okay. My headache's no better, and I'm thirsty as hell, but I'm fine otherwise."

"Harvey's done a great job with the atmosphere overnight; we both feel that the oxygen level's about right now. I made it up here without losing my breath, and I must say that I slept like a log."

"Yes, I'm breathing a whole lot easier, too. Well done, Harvey." Richter smacked his dry lips.

"I'll get you a glass of water, sir," said Enzo as he picked up the empty glass beside the captain's bunk and walked over to the sink in the head to fill it. He returned and replaced it. Richter reached out, grabbed the glass, and took a good mouthful.

"That feels even better. Thank you, Enzo." Richter

felt the all-too-familiar sensation of rising bile at the back of his throat. He started to swallow, but it didn't slow the process. Before he could even swing his legs round to get to his feet, he threw up onto the deck, narrowly missing Enzo. He reached under his pillow and retrieved a green-stained handkerchief, and wiped his mouth. "Oh God, not again," he complained. Richter's voice sounded strained and weak through his chattering teeth. "I couldn't keep anything solid down yesterday, but at least I managed to drink a little. It seems I can't even keep fluids down now. There's little hope for me, is there, Enzo?"

"Let's see how it goes today, sir. Just take a little at a time. I'll get you some orange juice. That might taste a little better."

"That's kind, but the problem isn't the taste. Water's just fine."

"Well, OK, sir, but you haven't had any calories to speak of for two days now. Would you like some chocolate? I'm sure it will make you feel better to have something sweet inside you, and it'll help you keep warm."

"Alright, Enzo, let's give it a try." He slumped back onto the bunk, and Enzo left.

For the first time since the *Tulsa* had been found, Richter was concerned that he wasn't going to survive. He couldn't recall ever having felt this way before. That may be because he'd never been in quite such a perilous situation before, but it really didn't matter why. The fact was that, for the first time in his life, he had a real fear of dying. Perhaps it was his single status and, consequently, the absence of family responsibilities that had allowed him to be so callous about it all up to now. Perhaps it was a sense of fatalism that's present, to some extent, in everybody who chooses a hazardous occupation. Whatever it was, even in the closest of scrapes, and there had been quite a few, he had never experienced either a sense of his own mortality or a powerful urge for self-preservation, until now. There was a knock at his door. "Come in." Even Richter was now aware that his voice was not as strong as usual, but Enzo must have heard him because he entered.

"Here you are, sir, two Hershey bars. I'll leave you in peace now. If it's OK with you, sir, I'll look in every few hours."

"That's fine, Enzo, and thanks again."

Richter returned to thinking about why his attitude had changed. Why was it he was so scared that he would die before being rescued? It didn't take him long to think of one reason: Marie and the boys. Over the past five days he'd gradually accepted some kind of role in their welfare and wanted an opportunity at least to offer it. That he wanted to do so for John went without saying. What he now realized was that it was something he also wanted for himself. He was amazed at the change that had come over him in just five days, five days of introspection more intense than anything to which he had ever subjected himself before.

Richter rolled over and opened the top drawer of the locker beside his bunk. He retrieved two framed photographs and settled back to look at them. He adjusted the battle lantern to throw more light on them and closed one eye so he could concentrate on a single image. In any other situation he would have had these pictures on open display. But, with John as his engineer, he'd decided to keep them hidden. The first photo was of Marie. He'd taken it fourteen years earlier when they were on the outskirts of Toronto on their first, and only, vacation together. He'd taken one of her as she'd come out of the shower and had wanted to keep it. But she had demanded that he gave her both the print and the negative of that one. This was his second favorite shot of her. She was wearing tight denim shorts and a skimpy T-shirt. She wasn't wearing a bra—in those days she never did. She was lying back on some grass, propped up on her elbows, with her legs slightly apart. Her nipples were obviously erect and she was wearing an impish expression of pure beguile. He must have looked at it a thousand times since he'd taken it, and it still aroused him. The second photograph was much more recent, taken by John's father at Christmas only two years earlier. There was John and Richter seated in front of a highly decorated tree with Marie standing between them. Jamie was on John's lap and Geoff was on his. He liked it because everyone in the picture looked so happy, and Marie's expression was radiant. The years had been kind to her. She still looked youthful and vaguely mischievous.

He'd been concerned that she might refuse his offer of a greater involvement in her life and, of course, the boys'. That might yet be the case, but a far bigger problem was her family. Her father was an arrogant, supercilious man who was convinced that he knew what was best for his daughter. The way things turned out, that had resulted in her virtual isolation from the rest of her family. Richter had seen a major conflagration coming if he had continued his relationship with Marie, which is why he'd backed off. He'd warned John that the same would apply if he went ahead and married her. However, he wasn't sure whether John hadn't believed him or if he'd just thought it would quickly blow over. Either way he'd been wrong and, at times, he was aware that John had regretted his decision. He'd never been able to provide Marie and the boys with the standard of living that she'd been used to, or that he'd wanted for them all. Navy pay, although adequate, was far from generous, and John's biweekly paychecks, even as a lieutenant commander with submarine pay, were still less than what she used to receive from her father as a teenager. Marie, to her credit, apparently never mentioned money—not even when they were at their most destitute. To some extent, no doubt, she blamed herself for the Dowlings' lack of funds. Although John was never willing to say so openly, Richter knew he was haunted by the idea that he was a less-than-adequate provider. After all, they didn't even own their own house.

Although he'd only been awake for half an hour, he was tired. Despite doing little but sleep for the past two days, he felt exhausted. His headache was so bad he thought his skull was about to explode. He reached out and opened a Hershey bar, snapped off a piece of chocolate, and popped it into his mouth. It was so dry that he had to wait until some of the chocolate had melted before he could really chew it. But it tasted good. He washed it down with a couple of sips of water and rested back on his pillow. With his eyes closed he was asleep again in moments.

0400R, Cherry Hill, New Jersey

Marie woke with a start, sat up in bed, and screamed. She felt sweaty, her heart was pounding, and she was shocked by just how vivid her dream had been. Commander Thompson had told her what little was known about the sinking, but her brain had obviously taken over and imagined the rest. She was still trembling at the horrifying, ghoulish creation of her mind. The dream was about John. There he was thrashing around in the water with his face pressed against the overhead, gasping for air. He was pale, shivering, and obviously scared, his eyes open wide with terror. His thrashing became more violent as the water advanced until it covered his mouth and nose. Despite his best efforts, he couldn't avoid inhaling it and had started to choke. That was the point at which she'd woken. She was more scared than saddened by what she'd imagined. So scared that her mind had seemingly rejected these horrible thoughts and had awoken her before John had reached the point of death in the tragedy that she'd just created. Would this nightmare keep coming back until it played right through to its inevitable conclusion? Oh God! That

would be too much to bear. She couldn't handle any
more reruns of that sequence or anything like it. It
dawned on her that she'd forgotten to take her sedative last night. She would not forget again.

Marie was wide-awake and didn't want to go back
to sleep. She decided to go down to the kitchen and
raid the refrigerator. Her appetite had deserted her at
dinner the evening before, but the rumbling in her
stomach told her that now would be a good time to
nibble at something and maybe even have a drink.
She'd break the habit of a lifetime and pour herself a
Scotch whiskey. It was a remedy for almost any unpleasant shock in all the old movies.

With her bathrobe wrapped tightly around her,
Marie made her way downstairs to the kitchen. The
refrigerator was vast and filled to the brim with food
of just about every description. Her first thought was
to have a chunk of cheddar cheese, smeared with English mustard, and an apple. It was an unusual combination, but one which she had grown to enjoy. Then
she spotted the cream-covered sponge cake, layered
with fruit, that her father had bought to welcome her
and the boys home. It was too tempting. She cut a
generous slice. After a quick visit to the liquor cabinet
for her whiskey she went into the library and settled
herself down in a red leather recliner and raised the
footrest. It had been well over a day since she had
watched any TV or listened to the radio, and she was
curious to know what was happening with the rescue.
She wanted to get news of the survivors and, of
course, Geoff. Marie wanted him to get out alive so
badly it hurt. However, if they kept going on about
those who had died, she'd turn it off. She clicked
the remote.

Much as she expected, all of the major networks
were running the story, even though it was just after
four in the morning. She selected SNN. It looked like
a repeat of an interview from the previous day because the people involved would surely be tucked up

in bed at this time of night. Three men were seated at a semicircular table. The anchor was flanked on one side by Senator Sorenson, chairman of the Senate Armed Services Committee, and on the other by an assistant secretary of defense. The anchor was speaking: "Mr. Secretary, we've just seen some training video footage, supplied by the US Navy, showing how it is possible for submariners to escape to the surface from a submarine. Why is it that nobody from the aft end of the boat was able to escape on this occasion?"

"Well, Bernard, we're still gathering information, and we won't know all the answers until we've interviewed the survivors and salvaged the boat. But if I had to guess, I'd say that the escape trunk, or its hatch, was damaged in the collision."

"Have you not been able to get any information from the survivors in the front end of the boat?"

"Very little, unfortunately. The conditions are making communication extremely difficult."

The senator butted in: "But there are surface ships directly over the *Tulsa* right now, aren't there?"

"Yes, there are. There's a Norwegian Coast Guard ship, the *Nordvik*, and a British warship, the HMS *Wellington*, is expected shortly."

The senator continued: "These ships are equipped with underwater telephones, aren't they—surely they must be able to talk to the men in the *Tulsa*?" The ASD was beginning to look a little flustered.

"I'm sure I don't need to tell you, Senator, that underwater telephones are not the most reliable pieces of equipment. They're very sensitive to the sea-state and thermal layers, to mention but two problems. As you know, it's been stormy around Bear Island for the past few days, and I expect that's been the main problem."

The senator was on a roll and was not about to quit. "Are you telling me that we can communicate with spacecraft on Mars but not a submarine in water that's only five hundred feet deep? I mean, the weather and thermal layers can distort sound waves, but they don't destroy them. I thought there were codes that could be used in poor conditions."

"Senator, with all due respect, I'm not qualified to answer questions on the technical aspects of underwater sound transmission. All I know is that it has proved very difficult to communicate with the *Tulsa*."

It was the anchor who interrupted this time. "The men in the *Tulsa* know that a rescue is under way, I presume?"

"Oh, yes. The surface ships can use small explosive charges to let them know that they are above them, and that's already been done."

"But if communication is so difficult," continued the anchor, "how will they know when to expect the DSRV?"

"The DSRV will be carried on another submarine. It should be a lot easier for one submarine to talk to another than it is for surface forces." With the communications issue exhausted for the moment, the anchor changed subjects.

"Mr. Secretary, you've mentioned that the DSRV will be carried to the *Tulsa* by submarine. I understand that this will be a British submarine."

"Yes, Bernie, you're quite right, it will be. For many years we've had an agreement with the British on sharing our submarine-rescue capabilities. As I expect you know, the British are also sending their rescue vehicle to assist in recovering the crew of the *Tulsa*."

"Why wasn't an American boat available for this?" interrupted Senator Sorenson.

"Well, one was. The issue here was one of time. It just so happened that the British could get a submarine to the accident site before we could. It's not that surprising, as they're located much closer to the Norwegian Sea than we are."

"Am I not right in saying that the number of American submarines that are equipped to carry the DSRV has declined in recent years?" the anchor inquired.

"Yes, that's correct. But we've also reduced the size of our submarine fleet, so the chances of an accident have fallen as well."

"That may be so, Mr. Secretary. But isn't it true that a consequence of the reduction in the number of submarines is that now each one has much more work to do? They spend more time at sea, and the intervals between maintenance periods has increased. So it could be argued that the risk of an accident hasn't fallen." The ASD paused a moment to collect his thoughts. This was getting tricky.

"The US Navy has been operating nuclear submarines to the highest safety standards for over forty years. We have easily the largest operational submarine fleet in the world, and this is the first boat that we've lost since the *Scorpion* in 1968. I think that record speaks for itself. If you're trying to tell me that corners are being cut, I would deny that."

Senator Sorenson butted in again: "Jim, you know as well as I do that potentially hazardous events are not uncommon in the submarine service. Groundings, fires, and collisions happen all the time. If you don't believe me, just inquire at the Naval Safety Center—they keep records of these things. I know that the safety record of the navy is good when it comes to the loss of boats. But it's easy to be complacent. Just below the surface there's a tide of mishaps, any one of which could have resulted in a sinking. This time the *Tulsa* had the misfortune to roll snake eyes." The anchor wanted to take this line of inquiry further, but the producer was telling him to break for commercials.

"Thank you, gentlemen. We'll be right back after this." The image cut to a healthy-looking woman in her late forties. "Some nights I can't get to sleep because of pain. So I tried Somwel KO. It's not just a pain reliever, it aids restful sleep naturally, without drowsiness the following morning. . . ." Marie hit the remote. Why don't they advertise something really useful, she wondered, something to relieve the pain of losing a husband? She downed the rest of her whiskey and headed back to bed.

1000A, COMJTFNON HQ, Bodø

Like most of his colleagues, Mike Selby was sick of his phone ringing off the hook. He had been cautious about giving out the number shortly after arriving in Norway, quite rightly as it turned out. Now it had obviously been distributed around the fleet, and everybody back home seemingly wanted to know what was going on. The six-hour time zone difference didn't help that much. Although his mornings were reasonably peaceful, callers had kept him up until well past midnight with endless requests for information that was just not available. The Pentagon was the worst offender, followed by NAVSEA, COMSUBLANT, and Group 2 in Groton. Everyone, it seemed, had an urgent requirement to know what was going on. Doubtless much of this was because of the need to keep a voracious press well fed, but it went beyond that. He'd received calls from friends and colleagues of survivors in the boat, even a chaplain in Groton had called him, wondering what to say to distressed relatives. The kicker was that he had nothing to tell them.

The phone rang yet again. "Selby."

"Mike, it's David Sangster. Look, I've just had a meeting with the admiral, and he's asked me to go over a couple of things with you. Have you got a moment?"

"Sure, do you want me to come over?"

"No, we'll do this by phone. There's no point getting lost in this rabbit warren again." Mike flushed briefly at his embarrassment at getting so lost in the mountain, that he'd arrived nearly thirty-five minutes late at the last briefing in the admiral's office. "The thing is, I've looked into the problem of the way the Brits scrub CO_2, and you're right. They use totally different equipment than us—different hoppers, their canisters are a different shape and even contain a different absorbent."

"So all the stuff they're carrying in the *Salminster* will be incompatible with what they have in the *Tulsa?*"

"Dead right. It's not all bad news though—MAC will be flying a load of canisters into Hammerfest this afternoon. We'll then get them helo'd out to the *Salminster* before they use the LR5."

"What about a hopper or two with a DC motor?"

"I'm sorry, that wasn't possible at such short notice, although DEVRON FIVE has found an inverter and a cable that'll let them tap into the emergency lighting circuit. It'll travel with the doctors on the first DSRV run."

"Do you mind if I go to Hammerfest and check out those canisters? You know how the supply system can screw things up."

"OK, but make sure you get back here as soon as you can. It grieves me to admit it, Doc, but we couldn't have managed here without you." Selby raised an eyebrow. He and Sangster had never been close, and in the past he'd detected some jealousy over the fact that his paycheck was quite a bit bigger than the RDO's. This admission of his value was therefore something of a surprise, although a most welcome one. He wouldn't rub it in though.

"Alright, Dave, I'll come straight back."

Mike Selby sat back in his chair and stared at the ceiling. Although it was coffee time again, he was reluctant to subject himself to another toxic Norwegian interpretation of the beverage. The locals had been delightfully welcoming in so many ways, but when it came to coffee they had really dropped the ball. One tip he would pass on to his hosts was the idea that it was acceptable to make a fresh brew before the previous one had been reduced to a tarry deposit in the bottom of the pot. His desire for caffeine eventually overpowered his reticence, and he got up and wandered over to the coffeemaker. To his surprise the warm, brown liquid smelled relatively fresh, and so he poured himself a generous mugful. He returned to his desk, booted up his computer, and rechecked the numbers in his spreadsheet. By now he estimated that they had just forty-five canisters of lithium hydroxide left in the *Tulsa*, and those would be used up sometime tomorrow night, after which the atmosphere would gradually deteriorate until it became lethal, probably sometime on Saturday.

1430A, USS *Tulsa*

Enzo had invited Master Chief Steadman to take a look at the captain. He'd tried to rouse him and failed, and was looking for moral support more than anything else. "I'll try if you want me to, sir, but if you can't wake him, I don't suppose I'll be able to do much better."

"All right, Master Chief. I'll have one more go." With that, Enzo shook Richter firmly by the shoulder and moved closer to his ear. "Sir, please wake up. Just open your eyes if you can hear me." The two of them stared at Richter's face, but there wasn't so much as a flicker of movement. "He's got a pulse, and it's not even very rapid—feel for yourself." Steadman felt Richter's wrist and nodded.

"What are his eyes like?"

"Let's see." Enzo reached into his pocket for a flashlight and opened the captain's left eye. The pupil was constricted quite tightly, but still reacted a little to light. The right one looked to be a more normal size and reacted as he expected. "Looks okay to me. I guess he's just out of it. You realize we'll have to establish an IV and get a catheter into him?"

"I was afraid you might say that, sir. Do you think we should move him down to the wardroom?"

"I don't think so. I don't want the men to see him

like this. It wouldn't be good for morale. I'll stay here and keep an eye on him." Another thought had occurred to Enzo. "I suppose this means I'm in command."

"I think it does, sir. Congratulations."

"In any other circumstances I'd be pleased to accept them, Master Chief, but the way things are, I'm not so sure. I just hope I can see us through all of this until those lazy bastards topside decide it's convenient to come and get us." Steadman didn't know what to say. "Sorry, I shouldn't have said that. It's just that the captain . . . well he's so smart, so knowledgeable. I feel somewhat second-best."

"Sir, you're the best we've got right now. I know that Commander Richter has every confidence in you and, if it's any consolation, so do I."

"That's very kind of you, but I'm going to need all the help I can get."

"Sir, I'll support your every move, and you know it. Yours isn't a job that any sane man would ask for. I'm sure you'll find that the whole crew's glad it's you who'll have to make the tough calls, and I know they'll be right behind you." Enzo looked at Steadman, a man almost twice his age. The stubble on his chin was flecked with gray and the crow's-feet beside each eye were etched deeply into his pale skin.

Steadman continued. "Just one thing, sir. If I may make a suggestion, I think it would be best to involve the other officers, the lieutenants at least. A problem shared is a problem halved, and I think they would respect you for seeking their opinions."

"Thank you, Master Chief. You're right, we'll pull through if we pull together. Now let's see if we can't persuade somebody, anybody, to come and get us. After that we will see to the captain."

In the chiefs' mess, Santana had become serious. He'd persuaded his colleagues to play for $100 per point in a blatant attempt to reverse his losses. He'd also been given the deal after Bill Hicks had accused Lehner of dealing from the bottom of the pack. Hicks's losses were tiny compared with Mitch's, but he had become optimistic about his survival and desperately needed every penny to maintain his family. "Dealer's dealing, no passing this hand, $100 per point, all agreed?" announced Mitch. There were nods around the table. "What's the score?" he asked.

"Do you really want to know?" asked Czapek.

"Why do you think I asked?" Hicks looked down at the piece of paper in front of him. It was damp and though he had found it increasingly difficult to write on, the totals were still clear for all to see. "Mitch you're in the hole to the tune of $34,753, I'm down $3,664, Larry's up $12,092 and Carl's got $26,325 in the bank." Mitch couldn't conceal his disgust at Lehner's expression of complacency.

"Dealer's dealing and fuck the lot of you, I'm going to get you bastards this time. See if I don't." The door opened, and Master Chief Steadman poked his head into the mess.

"OK, Larry, it's time for another smoke."

"I'll be right with you, Stan." Chief Czapek rose from the table. "You're going to have to wait a few minutes, Santana, but I'll be right back."

Mitch was doing his best to play the desperate gambler, and replied gruffly. "OK, I'll clock you."

Sonarman Evans lay on his bunk, dead to the world. The Golden Dreams award was his for the taking. He was miles away in his home state of Kentucky walking through a wooded valley, arm in arm with his girlfriend, Kate. He stooped and tossed a pebble into the babbling brook by which they had been walking for the past hour. Kate picked up a larger stone and did the same. It didn't travel far before it plunged into the water, splashing both of them. They laughed. The front of Kate's white T-shirt was wet and had become almost transparent in places, revealing her left nipple.

He wanted to see more. He picked up a small boulder and hurled it into the brook. Water splashed everywhere. He checked to confirm that Kate's breasts were now displayed in their full glory before he wiped his face with his handkerchief and licked his lips. That was odd, he thought, the water tasted salty. He felt more cold water on his face and it definitely tasted salty. He woke with a start and realized that water was splashing out of the air vent in the bulkhead immediately beside him. It was seawater. Where's that coming from? he asked himself.

"What the fuck . . . ?" cried STS3 Ballard in the bunk above him.

"Hey. Where's all this water coming from?" screamed another voice farther down the compartment. Evans rolled out of his bunk and looked up at the overhead. Water was dripping out of just about all the vents. The blue curtains that provided what passed for privacy in the bunks began to shake along the length of the lower-level berthing space as the men realized they had a choice of getting up or getting soaked.

Enzo and Lieutenant Trost soon arrived to survey the scene. It looked like a rainy day at the Wimbledon tennis tournament. Wherever they looked, water was cascading down from the ventilation trunking in the overhead. The same thing was happening in the auxiliary machinery room. Both of them were wet through, and Enzo's long, normally curly hair was plastered to his face. He reached up and smeared it away from his right eye. "Right, Paul, we need to get everybody out of here. Get them to take their mattresses and any valuables, including warm clothing, to the upper level. . . ."

"OK, Enzo."

"Wait a minute, I haven't finished. Get somebody up to the fan room to open up the trunking leading forward from the flapper valve. We're going to have to jury-rig a drain that'll take the water away and down to the AMR or the auxiliary tank below it."

"Consider it done."

"Let me know when you're through. We'll then need to get a team down here with mops and towels to clear the water away from the battery compartment. I don't want to cook that sucker."

"Right."

Enzo had started to shake with cold. His teeth were chattering, and, even if he wanted to say more, he would have difficulty making himself understood. He made his way up to his stateroom to find some dry clothes—or at least, some that were drier than those he was wearing. The thought of flooding the battery compartment terrified him. If seawater came into contact with the battery, the boat would be filled with chlorine gas in no time. That would drive them to make an immediate escape. The alternative was choking to death on the pungent, green-colored gas like so many had done in the trenches of World War I.

0930R, Cherry Hill, New Jersey

Having had so little sleep the previous night, Marie took one of her prescription tablets and returned to bed. She'd left the boys to go fishing with her father. It was a good thing for them to do—they needed to get to know one another. If things between her and her father really were on the mend, that was great, especially right now. Father could never replace John, he couldn't even begin to fill the gaping chasm that had been left in their lives, but he was a lot better than nothing.

She was beginning to feel drowsy and closed her eyes. What about Geoff? If Father wasn't going to mess things up, would she let him back into her life? Would he want to try again? Marie thought about it a bit more. If she hadn't been feeling quite so sleepy, she might have felt a twinge of embarrassment at the brazen way she'd behaved when they had first met. But she didn't feel embarrassed. A smile briefly

creased her face as she recalled their only vacation
together all those years ago. She remembered the jealousy she had felt when she'd noticed Geoff eyeing up
Chrissy over dinner that first evening in Dunkirk.
More than anything else that had spurred her on to go
to his room—she didn't want to lose him to Chrissy, or
anybody else for that matter. Another smile flicked
across her face. Had she regretted it? Hell no. He was
a fantastic lover, better than anyone she'd been with.
The only thing she'd regretted was the reaction of her
father and that witch, Christine. Simply put, they'd
been merciless. All they had achieved was to solidify
her intention to throw herself into the arms of the
next man that came along, just to spite them. Poor
John had never really known what hit him. She'd had
a hard time trying to explain her family to him, but
he'd seemed to understand and accept the situation.
Of course, he'd wanted to get married. She'd never
really got the feeling that Geoff did. Maybe she was
wrong, it was just a feeling she'd had. Would that have
changed over time? Did she even want to find out?
The tablet was working too well, and she really
couldn't think straight anymore. There would be
plenty of time to mull this over. It was all so confusing.

1430A, MV *Nordvik*

The past two and a half days had been little short
of hell for Steve Marchant. He had lived and relived
the period leading up to the drop a hundred times,
and on each occasion he had questioned his own judgment. Last night he had done nothing else. He had
now convinced himself that the board of inquiry would
find him liable for the death of two of his men and a
subsequent court-martial would issue him with, at
best, a severe reprimand and dismiss him from the
service. He was profoundly depressed about the whole
thing. He had responded as best he could to the request from the embassy in Oslo to explain what had

happened in Hammerfest. It had all happened so fast
that neither he, Percival, nor Jock Sharples had any
clear recollection. Then he'd started to draft a letter to
the parents of the missing men, expressing his regret at
their loss, and trying to explain how it had happened.
It was impossibly difficult and he had given up in disgust at his inability to write anything coherent. He had
therefore decided to wait until his boss showed up in
the *Wellington* this evening. It was an encounter he
was dreading. Tremble was a nice enough guy until
things went wrong. Then he could explode spectacu-
larly. And when he did, the target invariably suffered
severely, and there was frequently collateral damage.

By way of thanking his hosts, and giving himself
something different to think about, Steve had offered
to take watches on the bridge. Commander Jonsson
had been most appreciative, but declined on the
grounds that there might be language difficulties and,
in any case, he should take some time to recover
from his ordeal. The captain had been disarmingly
charming about it but, in so doing, had denied him
the distraction that work would bring. So, instead,
Marchant stood on the port side of the bridge staring
out through the thick, slightly green-tinted glass, watching the world go by as the *Nordvik* slowly circled above
the *Tulsa*.

The weather had moderated considerably. Gone
were the whitecapped mountains of waves, and in
their place was a languid swell, the surface of the sea
being little more than rippled by the gentle breeze.
The sun had set below the horizon to the southwest
before lunch; since then the twilight had slowly disappeared as if some lighting technician had exercised
exquisite control over a celestial dimmer switch. The
high cirrus clouds had held on to the light for as long
as they could before getting lost in the deep aquama-
rine sky that had gradually lost its color. The sea was
now lit by a black sky, speckled with millions of stars.
If he were in almost any other mood, he would have

regarded the scene as one of majestic beauty. Instead, he drew a parallel between this day and his naval career. To all intents and purposes, both were almost over.

As he studied the scenery, he suddenly noticed a red glow in the water about half a mile away on the beam. He picked up a pair of binoculars and studied it before turning to the officer of the watch and pointed. "Sven, there's a smoke candle on the port beam."

Lieutenant Nordvahl reached for the binoculars that were hanging from his neck, aimed them in the direction that Marchant was pointing, and fiddled with the focus. "Thank you, Steve," he said hastily as he picked up the bridge telephone and called the captain.

Over the next few minutes the *Nordvik* altered course toward the smoke, lowered the sea boat, and recovered the spent signal and its attached message. As soon as it had been delivered to the bridge, Commander Jonsson invited Steve to read it and interpret what might be going on in the *Tulsa*. The news was not good. They were running out of lithium and had started to use oxygen candles. The pressure was still rising and there was now flooding, the death of the XO and the captain's illness meant that a junior officer, Lieutenant Raschello, was in charge. It also seemed that morale was suffering because of the delay in mounting a rescue. However, Lieutenant Raschello was clearly no dummy. In requesting an estimate of when the rescue might commence, he'd had the presence of mind to propose a code for the explosive charges: three for less than four hours; four for less than eight; five for less than twelve and so on. He wanted two charges to indicate that the message had been received, followed by a single charge five minutes later to indicate that the *Tulsa* should wait for a reply if one was not going to be forthcoming immediately. The question was how many charges to let go? Commander Jonsson was in no doubt. They would release two now and one more five minutes later. In the meantime the contents of the *Tulsa*'s second SITREP would be forwarded to COMJTFNON HQ by immediate message. He'd let them work out how to reply.

1445A, Hammerfest Airport

The clattering of the Norwegian Army Lynx slowly died away as it set down, the chop of the blades drowned out by the high-pitched whine of the engines. From the rear of the cabin Commander Selby could see a US Military Airlift Command C130 unloading by the main terminal and wondered if it was early, if he was late or if the extra canisters of lithium he had ordered would arrive on a different aircraft. He asked the pilot to stay put until he had clarified the situation.

Once in the terminal Selby looked around for somebody that might be able to help him. After a few minutes he realized that he was wasting his time and decided to go out to the plane and find out what it was carrying. No sooner had he reached what he assumed was the right door than through it marched the aircrew. The senior officer among them, an air force captain, advised him that the sergeant had a copy of the manifest and in no time Selby was poring over the list of supplies that had been delivered. As he neared the bottom his heart sank. Instead of canisters of lithium hydroxide, two hundred chlorate candles had just arrived in Norway. Just about the only thing that the crew of the *Tulsa* seemed to have in abundance was oxygen. These candles would be about as much use as a fur coat on a nudist beach. "Jesus Christ!" he exclaimed in frustration.

"Is something wrong, sir?" asked the sergeant.

"You bet, but it's not your fault." He thought quickly. There was not much point in hanging around the airport. He'd get back to his desk and burn up a few telephone lines. If he couldn't persuade somebody Stateside to fly the right fucking stuff over here, he'd see if someone in Naples, Rota, or even the goddamned Azores would be more obliging. "Thank you Sergeant." The sergeant snapped off a crisp salute, which Selby returned before hurrying back to the helicopter. He was furious.

1500A, COMJTFNON HQ, Bodø

Admiral Risberg had gathered together the meteorologist, the American and British staff, and Captain Smetana. Once they had all read the latest message from the *Nordvik,* Risberg asked for a weather forecast. Commander Larsson got up and moved over to the screen on which the latest weather map was displayed. There wasn't much change. The British contingent reported that the *Salminster* was expected at the datum around 0800 tomorrow morning. It would take a little time to prepare for an LR5 run and so it was unlikely that one could be completed before bad weather precluded further operations. On the plus side, at least the DSRV was on time and would arrive in Murmansk in about two hours' time. Captain Smetana reported that a route from the airport to the harbor had been cleared of traffic. So, provided the loading of the DSRV onto the *Vindictive* went smoothly, she could put to sea around midnight, with the first rescue run possible sometime early on Friday morning.

Admiral Risberg summed up: "So, gentlemen, it boils down to a possible, weather-vulnerable rescue in eighteen hours or a weather-independent one in, say, fifty-five. The question is what should we tell the *Tulsa?* I should point out that we mustn't take all day over this. Those people are expecting a prompt reply."

There was some muttering around the table. The British and American contingents were particularly vocal before the discussion died down. "So, gentlemen, will it be seven charges or fifteen? I am going to suggest seven. Does anyone disagree?"

"It's more of a psychological point than anything

else, sir," started Lieutenant Commander Murphy. "If
we go for the earlier attempt and fail, what's that
going to do for morale in the DISSUB?"

"A fair question. I look at it another way. It will
take some time for the bad weather to seriously alter
the sea-state. If we can get a first run in before the
weather deteriorates, we can resupply the boat, get
medical attention to the injured, retrieve the more seriously ill. The list of benefits is tremendous, not to
mention what it would do for young Lieutenant"—the
admiral paused to glance at the message—"Raschello.
I don't believe that we really have any alternative."
There were nods around the table. "It's agreed, then,
we'd better let the *Nordvik*, *Salminster*, and *Wellington* know immediately, with priority messages to the
usual copy addressees. Good. I think, gentlemen, we
are about to enter the final bend—to use a middle-
distance running metaphor." Or a bathroom plumbing
metaphor, thought Murphy. He still harbored serious
reservations about wisdom of an LR5 run in marginal
conditions. The admiral rose from his seat. "I'd like
to move tomorrow morning's meeting forward to 0700.
By then, everything should be in place for what I hope
will be a successful rescue." The other officers rose to
their feet as the admiral left the room, before the
British and Americans formed a huddle to ensure that
everything that was going to be needed for the rescue
would be flown out to the *Nordvik* overnight.

1430Z, HMS *Wellington*

Commander Muggeridge settled back in his chair
on the starboard side of the bridge and passed the
latest message from COMJTFNON HQ to Surgeon
Commander Freeman, who was standing beside him.
"It looks like they're shooting for an early rescue with
LR5. Is everything ready for that?" Freeman was
somewhat taken aback. He and his men had been so
absorbed preparing for an escape that they had given

little thought to the possibility of a rescue. After all, the *Salminster* was not yet even at the datum.

"All that we can really do is provide medical manpower to travel down to the DISSUB on the first run. They'll be able to triage the survivors and deliver some fresh atmosphere-control stores. I propose sending Lieutenant Commanders Stemple and Sheppard. We can rustle up some medical gear for them in no time. What I don't know is whether the *Salminster* has the necessary stores. I'd better get in touch and find out."

"OK, do that. If they don't have the right stores, I'm just wondering if it's worth doing a first run—particularly if the weather is marginal."

Freeman thought for a moment before replying. "I have little doubt it would be. The LR5 can carry up to nine people. Taking them out of the *Tulsa* would serve to prolong the life of any remaining scrubbing material. We could recover the more seriously injured and get them flown ashore—it sounds like the *Tulsa*'s captain needs to be in a neurosurgical unit. We could deliver medical assistance, the relevant tap and charge codes, and, possibly, an underwater telephone. That's a lot of pluses even before the morale issue is thrown into the equation. I don't think we would have any option but to try it if we get an opportunity."

"You'd better get ready then." Freeman left the bridge and made his way down to the sick bay. Leading Medical Assistant Harper was sitting at the desk annotating medical records.

"Harper, would you be so kind as to gather together the medical staff. We need to plan a submarine rescue. I think you'll find most of them in the hangar training the first-aid parties and boat crews."

Freeman didn't like using the LMA as a messenger, but he needed a few moments to himself to gather his thoughts. He was going to ask Sheppard and Stemple to do something that was potentially very hazardous.

They would have to remain on the *Tulsa* either until the weather blew over or the DSRV could rescue them. That meant at least two days and, if no atmosphere-control stores could be delivered on the first run, they would be forced to survive in an increasingly toxic atmosphere. They will have to volunteer for this, he thought. He really couldn't order them to go. His mind raced on, what if one, or both, of them refused? Things could go pear-shaped rather quickly. Would he have to go himself? Jesus—that would be a tester. He could claim that he was required to coordinate the medical resources topside and, having taken part in more SMASHEXs than anybody else here, the claim could be justified. The trouble was that it was transparently an excuse not to go. How could he ask anybody to volunteer to do something that he wasn't prepared to do himself?

The sick-bay door opened and the other medical staff filed in. Sheppard ended up standing next to Stemple, and they both noticed the anxious look on Freeman's face. He held his hands grasped together behind his back and was rhythmically rising up and down on the balls of his feet. He cleared his throat and brought them up to date on the situation. There were no interruptions. Once he had finished, his audience looked at each other and exchanged a few barely audible remarks. Surgeon Lieutenant Commander Sweeny, who was on the other side of the overcrowded sick bay, spoke up. "Unless I missed something, sir, you are saying that two of us will have to take a one-way trip down to the DISSUB."

"Not exactly. It will be a round-trip, but with a two day layover between the legs." In any other circumstances such a clumsy phrase, so loaded with innuendo, would have provoked gales of laughter. But there was none.

"Have you anybody in mind to go with you, sir?" Sweeny replied. Sheppard was amazed by his impertinence. Freeman looked stunned. His mouth moved but nothing much came out before he composed himself:

"The reason I brought you all in here is to ask for volunteers."

"Sorry, sir, but before anybody commits themselves, why send two people down there?" Sweeny shot back. "Wouldn't one be enough? I mean, sending two will just add more carbon dioxide to the atmosphere, won't it?" Freeman stopped rocking on the balls of his feet, his expression changing to one of aggression.

"Do you imagine that I haven't given this some thought, Dr. Sweeny? The effect of one more person on the atmosphere will be negligible. I don't think we need worry about that. Would you like to do this alone?" Before he could answer, Lieutenant Commander Stemple broke his silence.

"Look, it's my fellow countrymen down there. I'll go and, before you ask, I'm perfectly happy to go alone. I don't see why any of you should put your asses on the line. Can we just get on with deciding what I'll be expected to do and what I'll need to take with me?"

"Does anybody want to accompany Dr. Stemple?" Freeman looked around the room.

David Sheppard felt he had to break the silence. "Sure, I'll go with him. I don't suppose we'll be able to think of every eventuality down there, and two heads are better than one. Count me in." Freeman looked relieved. It had been rather obvious that he wasn't willing to go, and David's opinion of his boss hit a new low.

1800A, USS *Tulsa*

"Good evening everyone." The response was not as exuberant as Enzo had expected. "I know you want to chow down, but I thought you'd like to know that the flooding is just about under control, and it's not a threat to our survival at the moment. Okay? I mean

that. We're going to be all right and get out of here
alive, are you with me on that?" There was a low
register series of grunts from the audience, many of
whom were now so cold they had concluded that survival for hours, let alone days, was most unlikely.
"Furthermore," continued Enzo, as cheerfully as he
could, "you all heard the seven charges earlier this
afternoon." The atmosphere seemed to lighten a bit
as people nodded. "The good news is that we can
expect the first rescue run by eleven o'clock tomorrow morning."

"How sure of that are you, sir?" asked Chief
Czapek.

"As sure as I can be, Chief. The seven charges were
in response to a message you kindly sent up earlier
this afternoon in which I asked that specific question.
Now, I can't tell you which rescue vehicle will be coming for us, but I don't think that matters. Whichever
it is, we'll surely receive more atmosphere-control
stores, another scrubber or two, and maybe a few doctors to take care of the injured."

"Thank you, sir. Let's hope it happens," replied the
chief. Enzo looked around the mess. It looked more
like a sauna than anything else. The air was thick with
steam that rose from the personnel who were still wet
from tackling the flood. The expression on the faces
he could see was one of concern more than relief.

"Now, I know all of you who live on the lower level
had a rude awakening today. I see most of you have
found someplace to lay down your mattresses. I hope
you'll be comfortable." Enzo looked down at the
soggy, dog-eared scrap of paper on which he had jotted down some brief notes. "Now, I'm sorry to report
that the captain's no better. I've been thinking about
what Sonarman Evans said yesterday and decided it
makes a lot of sense. I will therefore make sure that
he gets off on the first run tomorrow." Approval swept
the room, and there was even some applause. "That's
agreed then." Enzo smiled. It looked like he'd re-

stored the balance. He wanted the crew to be optimistic without being exuberant. That way the chain of command would remain intact yet they wouldn't be running around exhausting the dwindling reserve of lithium. It was time to quit and let them eat.

Master Chief Steadman was concerned that the officers would want to take over the chiefs' mess, and it was time to bring the game of cards to an end. He approached Chief Czapek. "Larry, I'm going to have to shut down the game and I want the four of you to get back to your bunks."

"What?"

"The officers need somewhere to plan the rescue and, seeing as the wardroom's full of the injured, our mess is where they'll do their business."

"Right, leave it with me."

2000C, Murmansk Harbor

According to the last message he had received on the subject, the DSRV had landed in Murmansk over two hours ago. Commander Todhunter paced from one side of the bridge to the other, slowly freezing in the subzero temperature. Where had the bloody thing got to? he wondered. His thought was interrupted by the sound of sirens wailing in the distance. This must be it, he thought, as he lifted a microphone to assemble a working party to receive his passengers. He just hoped that the Americans had sent some engineers who knew how to mount this expensive toy on the back of his boat, because if they hadn't, it was going to be a very long, cold, and frustrating night.

Within a few minutes the wailing of the sirens had intensified and then an assortment of motorcycles and cars boasting an array of flashing lights appeared at the end of the jetty and slowly advanced toward the *Vindictive*. Shortly afterward a large red tractor appeared with what looked like a shiny black cylinder mounted on the trailer behind it. This presumably was

the DSRV. Having never taken part in an Exercise
SEDGMOOR, an event that took place every six
years in which the rescue submersible is operated from
a British MOSUB, he had only ever seen pictures of
it before. It presented an almost surreal image as the
reflections of the massed flashing lights bounced off
it. With much hissing of brakes, the convoy came to
a halt and Todhunter prepared himself to go down
and greet his guests.

As he arrived at the brow, the jetty floodlighting
had been turned on, throwing a harsh white light over
the scene that resembled, in terms of activity, an ants'
nest. A small group of American naval officers appeared from among the crowd, and one of them
shouted in Todhunter's general direction: "Permission
to come aboard, sir!"

"Yes please, it's good to see you at last." He nodded to the bosun's mate to pipe the men aboard. They
might be short of time, in an unfamiliar port, and on
a totally alien mission, but the captain was determined
that the niceties of naval etiquette would be observed.
Officers of foreign navies were entitled to be piped
over the side, so piped they would be.

After a brief round of introductions, he led the
Americans through the sail hatch and down to the
wardroom, where the XO and engineering officer
joined them. A steward poured coffee and left the
room. Todhunter began. "To business, gentlemen. I
expect you're all tired from your journey, but I'm
under a lot of pressure to get out of here as soon as
possible. Those of you who will be sailing with us will
have ample opportunity to sleep once we are at sea—
at least I hope you will. We'll be making a surface
passage to the datum, and I'm sorry to say that the
forecast isn't too good. It might get a bit lumpy."
There were smiles around the table. "Anyway, I
thought it would be a good idea for us to get together
so that we all understand what's going to happen over
the next few hours while the DSRV is being loaded

on board. Perhaps you should start, Commander Tyson." The commanding officer of the Deep Submergence Unit started to explain the procedure in his characteristic, deep Southern drawl. Those around the table listened attentively. Todhunter issued an almost silent sigh of relief. The Americans had, indeed, brought all the expertise they would need with them.

1820A, USS *Tulsa*

Enzo sat at the head of the table in the chief's mess. On either side of him were Lieutenants Gallagher and Trost. Harvey Schwartz would join them as soon as he had completed the atmosphere-control log. Enzo wanted the four of them to eat their evening meal together in peace and begin to get his colleagues involved in making the decisions that would be necessary in the next few days. He had resolved to use his casting vote only to break a tie. Although the military was normally a strictly hierarchical system, this was not a normal situation—anything but. The COB was right: a little democracy was desirable.

The meal wasn't particularly appetizing to look at. It was a sort of Irish stew made with beef rather than lamb. However, it was hot and tasted good with a little extra black pepper. The four men attacked it with gusto. "That was a really neat idea to suggest a code for the 'start rescue' time, Enzo," began Paul Trost. "It's resulted in the first piece of really positive news in six days."

"It took them a while to let us know, though. Do you think the seven charges were just to keep our morale up?" was the typically negative contribution from Gallagher.

"Shove a sock in it, Tim. Why would they do that?" riposted Paul. "They've nothing to gain from lying to us. Think about it. They've had six whole days to mount a rescue. I find it completely believable that somebody will be here to get us out of this mess tomorrow morning. Actually, I'd be disappointed if they weren't."

"Do you remember the calculations the captain made shortly after the sinking about how soon we could expect to be rescued?" asked Enzo.

"Yes I do," replied Paul. "He reckoned on six days and guess what? He was close to being right on the money. How is he, by the way?"

"He's no worse than he was earlier this afternoon. Then again, he's no better. I'm going to make damned sure that he gets out on the first run. I really don't want him to go the same way as the XO."

"Is it that bad?" asked Paul.

"I fear it is. I've read all the medical books we've got on board, and I wouldn't mind betting that he's bleeding into his head. If he is, it'll kill him eventually if he stays here. He's been going steadily downhill ever since the collision."

"That would be too bad. He's the best skipper I've ever served with."

"Enough of that," interrupted Enzo. "He'll make it if we can get him out of here tomorrow. We need to get a team together to operate the trunk and receive the DSRV. Paul, will you take charge of that?"

"Sure, what do you have in mind?"

"Read through the relevant sections of the Ship's Systems Manual, then check out the trunk, remove all the spare gear that's stowed in there, and make sure all the valves are lined up ready for a rescue. Then run the team through the routine until they can do it in their sleep. Pick whoever you want for the job, except the COB—he's working with me. Oh, and I nearly forgot, make sure that they don't swallow any more Valium. I want them thinking straight tomorrow."

"OK. I'll plan a familiarization this evening and we'll practice from first thing tomorrow until whoever arrives to get us out of here." The door opened, and Harvey made his way to the table, carrying the sheaf of papers that was now his constant companion.

"Take a pew, Harvey," said Enzo. "Hungry?"

"Oh, I'll get some in a minute. I thought you should see this." He selected a sheet of paper and placed it on the table in front of Enzo. "The pressure's rising faster than it has been."

"How much faster?"

"I can't be precise—it's too soon. But certainly three feet per day, maybe even four." There were concerned faces around the table. "I've been doing some calculations and it looks like the flooding's likely to cover the battery compartment some time on Thursday."

"Assuming which flood rate?" asked Enzo, trying to suppress the urgency in his voice.

"The lower one."

"We'd better seal it then," announced Gallagher. "I've got a mountain of silicone sealant and duct tape in the store."

"Hold on, I don't want to do anything in haste. If Harvey's calculations are anything near to being right, we'll have the whole of tomorrow to work out what to do. By then we'll also have a better idea of the flood rate."

"Give me a single example of Harvey's calculations that have been right so far. I think we should seal the thing right away."

"I can only assume you get some kind of a kick out of gratuitous insults, Tim." Enzo was seething with anger. "If I thought you could do any better, I'd have you take over from Harvey and see how you manage on as little sleep as he's had over the past six days. The trouble is, judging by your recent performance, I wouldn't trust you to boil a four-minute egg, let alone provide us with breathable air. Tim, I'm warning you. Any more shit, and you're out of here. You can twiddle your thumbs in that septic tank you refer to as your stateroom. Do I make myself clear?"

"Absolutely. You'll get no more opinions from me. I'll just sit here and cheer from the stand."

"I'll ignore that. You know exactly what I mean. Harvey, thanks. Is the rest of the atmosphere control holding up?"

"Yes, I think so. As you know, carbon dioxide's the other major issue. It's going to be close, but I think they'll turn up just as we're down to our last few cans of lithium hydroxide. That's what I call a really neat piece of timing."

"Good. Anything else for right now?"

"I don't think so, Enzo."

"Well, go and get something to eat. To my surprise, I must congratulate the supply officer. I think this is definitely a recipe for your best-seller. Who did the cooking?"

"As a matter of fact, I had a hand in it myself," started Gallagher, pleasantly surprised by Enzo's change of attitude.

"I wondered what all those small bones were," interrupted Paul in a further attempt to defuse the tense atmosphere. There was a mixture of laughter and groans around the table.

"So why don't we play in here?" Santana gestured to their berthing space, which contained four bunks, some lockers, and little else.

"You don't seem to get it, do you, Mitch? The COB made it pretty clear to me that he wanted the game over."

"How convenient." Santana had raised his voice. "There you are sitting on seventeen thousand dollars of my money and now you're basically saying that I can't get it back. That's not right, and it's not going to happen. We'll play on the bottom bunks." He reached into his pocket, retrieved the pack of cards, and started to shuffle them.

"Put them away, Mitch. I'm fucking wiped, and I'm going to get some shut-eye. I suggest you do the same."

"That's great. Thanks Carl. Thanks a bunch. Haven't

any of you got the guts to let me win some of my money back?" There was no reply. "Look, I can't afford to lose the best part of $50k." The tone of his voice had changed, and tears now formed at the corners of his eyes. He quickly wiped them away with the back of his hands. "Come on, guys, don't do this to me."

"Maybe your wife'll pay up," replied Chief Hicks. "Go to sleep, Mitch, and if it's any consolation, I'm down almost $10k that I can't afford either."

"You're all assholes. I'm not going to lie down in here with a bunch of jerks."

"I can't stand a sore loser," growled Chief Lehner, as Mitch got up and left. "He's the jerk and deserves to be taught a lesson." He shivered and pulled the blankets tightly over his shoulders. "Fuck, it's cold. See you guys in the morning."

Mitch closed the door and stood for a moment in the passageway. He was utterly exhausted and deeply depressed. What was his future even if there were a rescue tomorrow? Could he live with an unfaithful wife? Hell no. What about that bastard boy? Thirteen years old and already an accomplished, violent criminal. He no longer felt up to disciplining him for fear of violent retaliation, perhaps in bed at night when he was defenseless. What was there to live for? If there was no rescue, all he faced was a slow, suffocating death. Not attractive. If he chose to take his own life, he could at least make it painless, and if he made it obvious that it was a suicide, his life insurance wouldn't kick in and Paula would face a substantial debt. There could be no better way of leaving her.

2320A, HMS *Wellington*

The Merlin had returned from the *Nordvik* and had been hovering over the port quarter for a full minute before moving to its right and setting down onto the flight deck. Airmen scurried around securing the aircraft as the engines shut down. The cabin door opened and the remaining members of the SPAG team, led by Lieutenant Marchant and Surgeon Lieutenant Ward, filed out of the rear. Once in the hangar they reported on board to the master-at-arms before dispersing. Richard Tremble approached his colleagues and shook them by the hand. "Welcome home, Steve, and you too, Simon."

"Thank you, sir," replied Marchant. "I can't tell you what a long time it's been since we left Fort Blockhouse, even though it's not even four days ago."

"I know. Come along to the wardroom, we need to talk." Marchant and Ward hastily removed their helmets and immersion suits and followed Tremble along the main passageway and into the wardroom. It was almost deserted. With the evening movie over everybody, except the middle watch keepers and Surgeon Commander Freeman, had turned in. There was another round of greeting handshakes and they settled down around the wardroom table.

"Anybody fancy a drink?" asked Freeman. The two junior officers looked at each other before Freeman continued, "It's all right, you know. After what you went through, you deserve one, and it is not every day that I offer to pay. Alternatively, you can have a coffee on the house. What's your poison?"

"Well, sir, seeing as you put it like that, I'll have a Scotch please," replied Ward.

"I'll have the same. Thank you, sir," said Marchant.

"Large ones, I presume." It was rhetorical. "Richard?"

"Why not, sir? Thank you." Settled once again around the table, this time with large measures of Glenlivet in front of them, the informal debriefing began. They went over every step and reviewed each decision up to the point of the drop. With their glasses refilled, they discussed the subsequent events in the water, the rescue, and finally the wonderful hospitality of the Norwegians. By now it was almost one in the morning. Everybody was tired. Freeman relaxed onto the backrest of his chair and clasped his hands behind his head.

"Steve, I expect you've been blaming yourself for what happened. It's a natural reaction, but I don't think you should. From what I've just heard, you deserve a bloody medal. You all do. I think what you did was nothing less than heroic. What do you think, Richard?"

"I agree. We haven't heard how all of this is playing at home, but I'd be utterly amazed if there was anything but praise for what you did so selflessly. In the highest traditions of the naval service, I think they generally say."

Steve Marchant was overwhelmed. Over the past few days he'd managed to convince himself that his career was over, all but an inquiry and a court-martial. He blamed himself directly for the death of two of his men. Indeed he was responsible for the whole fiasco. He had expected fireworks from Tremble, and this expression of comfort and support had surprised him. He started to shake his head from side to side, and tears began to roll down his face. He folded his arms on the table, bent forward, and rested his head on them. He then released a groan that developed into a deep, mournful wailing over which he had no control. The surprising thing was that rather than making him feel better, his boss's kind remarks served only to release the misery that he had bottled up since the search for the missing members of his team had been abandoned. Tremble patted him on the back. "Come on, old chap, we must find somewhere for you to get your head down. You must be exhausted."

There was a knock at the door. Freeman got up to see who it was. It was one of the communicators. "The captain asked me to show you this, sir." Freeman scanned the message and annotated that he had read it. It was the first time he'd seen a message detailing the current movements of a ballistic-missile submarine that had not been marked TOP SECRET.

"Thank you, Leader." He returned to the group around the table and checked his watch. "Well, gentlemen, things are looking up. The *Vindictive* left Murmansk two hours ago."

CHAPTER
7

Wednesday, 3 November

0100A, COMJTFNON HQ, Bodø

Commander Selby put down the phone, sat back in his chair, and rubbed his eyes. He bitterly regretted agreeing to sort out the problem of getting more lithium hydroxide canisters. It was properly the task of the material working party and would have remained so if he hadn't opened his damned mouth at the last plenary session. His search for the canisters that would be needed if the LR5 was to make a worthwhile visit to the *Tulsa* had led him through an endless series of phone calls throughout Europe and the States. The problem hadn't been limited to finding where the stuff was stored, but establishing how it could be delivered to Hammerfest in time to get it out to the *Salminster* before the Brits commenced their LR5 run in the morning. Despite his annoyance he felt a distinct sense of achievement that one hundred canisters were now in a fast jet over the middle of the Atlantic and would arrive in sufficient time to be picked up by the *Wellington*'s Merlin at 0400.

Selby looked at the sheets of paper on his desk

that seemed to have multiplied in number during the evening. Each of them was covered in his barely legible scrawl. As a mark of his frustration there were some names on the pieces of paper, circled in copious quantities of ink. He would make it his business to ensure that each of them would be in receipt of a less-than-flattering letter from COMSUBLANT. It was a delicious prospect that almost compensated for an otherwise dreadful evening.

He checked his watch. It was undoubtedly time for bed. Selby had considered returning to Hammerfest to ensure that, this time, the correct canisters arrived. But even if they didn't, there was really very little he could do about it. Furthermore, he'd failed to persuade either Commander Sangster or Admiral Risberg that he could be spared to ride the LR5 down to the *Tulsa*. So there was really no point in going to Hammerfest. His case for the LR5 trip had been wrecked by a message from the *Wellington* indicating that an American medical officer was on board and would be transferring to the *Salminster* for that very purpose. In the small world of undersea medicine, he was a little surprised to learn that the man involved was a guy called Stemple, whom he'd never heard of before. Still, the man had apparently earned the badge and must surely know his job. Selby made a deliberate effort to stem the flow of thoughts that were swirling around in his head. Tomorrow was going to be a nail-biting one. Since sleep would be essential, it was time to return to the hotel and grab the remaining few hours of the night.

0630A, MV *Salminster*

Since the little *Salminster* didn't boast a flight deck, the two doctors and the atmosphere-control stores from Hammerfest had to be winched down to the ship. A small reception committee was gathered at the stern, stamping their numb feet and squinting up at the giant, brightly lit helicopter that was hovering fifty feet above them. At just thirty-five degrees Fahrenheit it was a cold morning, but, in the prevailing stiff breeze, the windchill made it feel a lot worse. The downwash from the rotor chilled the group to the core.

David Sheppard, who had been winched into and out of helicopters more times than he cared to recall, had volunteered to go first. He sat in the open doorway with his feet dangling over the side of the helicopter, with a strap secured tightly around his torso under his armpits. There was a powerful smell of jet engine exhaust. He surveyed the scene below as the aircrewman to his right chattered into the microphone mounted on his helmet. Apart from refreshing his memory of just how far fifty feet can seem from a bird's-eye view, he could see that the *Salminster* was rolling all too ominously.

He turned to Stemple, who was just behind him. "Hank, what do you reckon the sea-state is?" Stemple cupped a hand to his ear and raised his eyebrows to indicate that he hadn't heard. David repeated the question at the top of his voice and pointed to the *Salminster*.

"No. It's not a big ship at all," Stemple howled back. In the prevailing bedlam generated by rotor blades and engines, there was no point in attempting further conversation. Sheppard looked down again. He was indeed going to be winched down to a rather small target. He began to feel a slight hollowness in the pit of his stomach. He felt a tap on his shoulder. The aircrewman raised a gloved thumb, and Sheppard nodded. The strap around his back tightened and he was lifted off his backside and swung out of the open door. He resisted the urge to grasp the cable above his head and let his arms hang down naturally. He couldn't resist the urge to look down. He had started to twist on the end of the cable, and his view of the *Salminster*'s brightly lit quarterdeck disappeared under his left shoulder. All he could see ahead of him was the blackness of the sea below, broken only by occasional whitecaps of breaking waves as they reflected light from the ship. A sudden jerking indicated that he was, at last, being winched down, and as he twisted back in the opposite direction, his target came back into view. He hit the deck with a thud and the strap went slack. Sheppard quickly stepped out of it and looked up at the aircraft. Moments later he saw Stemple's face peering out of the door. He was wearing an expression of sheer, wide-eyed terror.

No sooner were the two medical officers and atmosphere-control stores on board the *Salminster*, and the immersion suits and bone domes returned to the helicopter, than it turned away and clattered off into the darkness. Sheppard and Stemple were greeted by a junior officer and quickly escorted to attend a meeting in the officers' mess. Around a table were Frank Williams, a Royal Navy commander from SM 514, who was responsible for chartering the LR5; Susan Alderdyce, a senior representative of Cable and Wireless, the LR5's owners; Henry Dawson, the master of the *Salminster*, and Michael Formby, his chief engineer. With the introductions complete, Frank Williams assumed the chair and got down to business. "Gentlemen, we've made excellent time and will shortly be at the datum. We now have to make a decision. Do we go or not?" He paused to loosen his tie and unbutton the collar of his shirt. "At its simplest, the issue boils down to one of risk. Attempting to use the LR5 in these conditions could result in damage to it and this ship as well as injury to the LR5 crew and riders. If the weather worsens, which it's forecast to do this afternoon, these risks will increase. On the plus side, well, we all know about the plus side—it's why we're here. Any opinions?"

There was a pause during which Sheppard studied the faces of the people around the table. There was little sign of levity. Henry Dawson's face was that of a classic seadog who looked to be in his late fifties. His face was deeply tanned, the skin broken up by deeply etched lines. He sported a generously proportioned, well-veined nose that betrayed an affection for strong liquor. His hair was quite long and an unusual silvery white color. Sheppard guessed it had been like that for many years. He glanced down at the table and noticed that Dawson's hands were large, worn, and obviously powerful. Having visited a number of RMAS vessels in his time, Sheppard had concluded that their masters were generally in one of two camps: those who were proud of their ships and maintained them to a very high standard, and others who saw them as workhorses that were owned by the government. From what he had seen on the upper deck, Henry Dawson was firmly in the first camp.

The engineer was quite a bit smaller than his skipper and was younger, probably in his early forties. He had a pale complexion that was accented by an overnight growth of stubble. He sported a stud in his left ear and appeared to be rather deaf. He had delivered the few words he'd uttered with a perceptible stammer. When combined with his continually shifting gaze, Michael Formby gave the impression of a man who was none too sure of himself. Susan Alderdyce was a totally different kettle of fish. From what he could see, she was dressed in a white, woolen, polo-necked sweater and was well made-up. In any other circumstance, he thought, she would surely be wearing a business suit. She looked athletic and was probably no more than forty. She wore expensive rimless glasses and had recently visited a competent hair stylist.

Frank Williams looked the way he always did—somewhat on the disheveled side of what might be expected of a British naval officer. He had clearly enjoyed little sleep overnight and was wearing the same shirt as the day before. It was now open at the neck, and his tie hung limply at half-mast. He had yet to shower. His dark, curly hair was rather oily, and his body odor was perceptible, if not pungent. His only concession to personal hygiene appeared to have been a halfhearted sweep along his jawline with a shaver. Despite that, his posture at the table made it clear that he was in charge and was not going to postpone a decision for a moment longer than was necessary.

During the passage from Aberdeen, many of the issues pertaining to poor weather conditions had been visited, but at a rather superficial, almost theoretical level. The die was now cast and a decision was required. Williams had no doubt as to what the outcome should be. Disappointed by the lack of response to his previous question he tried a different tack. "OK, I'll phrase it another way. If I were to say we're going for it, does anybody object?" This approach produced results.

"I should bloody well say so!" responded Dawson brusquely in his broad Yorkshire accent. "I'll risk none of my men, nor this ship, for an operation which is outside the laid-down specifications. If it is above sea-state three, and the last time I looked it was, you can forget it."

"Perhaps I should point out," added Susan Alderdyce in more moderate tones, "that the company would take a dim view if the LR5 was damaged in anything other than an accident which occurred within its normal operating envelope. I have no doubt that the MoD would be billed for any repairs and would be liable for any worker's compensation in the event of injury."

Commander Williams felt an urge to thump the table. Given the way he was feeling, he would relish the opportunity to thump Dawson if not Alderdyce. However, he realized that if he did, Dawson would certainly thump him back, and there was no doubting who packed the bigger punch. He resisted the urge to thump anything and responded as calmly as he could manage. "Lady and gentlemen. We've steamed over one thousand nautical miles, through some unpleasant and very uncomfortable weather, for the sole purpose of getting the survivors out of the *Tulsa*. I, for one, have not come all this way to bicker over the small print of contracts which were drawn up by lawyers who have only a nodding acquaintance with reality. I am sure the doctors here can tell you the unpleasant details of what is likely to happen in the *Tulsa* if we don't act right now." He ignored the nods from the new arrivals because his urge to thump the table had got the better of him. He hit it forcefully with his index finger to emphasize the last two words and did so again as he repeated them, "Right now. I don't give a tinker's damn who pays for what in this operation. Accountancy is the last thing that should concern us. We are here to rescue some very brave and seriously imperiled men. The possibility of scraping or bending painted metalwork is equally irrelevant. That can be repaired. If those men down there die, that can't be undone, and I, for one, don't want to find out if I can sleep at night with the knowledge that I didn't do everything I could to keep them alive."

He turned and stared directly at the skipper. "Mr. Dawson, if you like, I'll sign a piece of paper making it clear that I accept full responsibility for any damage to your ship." He avoided the urge to add a disparaging adjective. "Ms. Alderdyce, I will do the same for the LR5. Alternatively, I'll get on the blower to the RMAS and Cable and Wireless and get them to persuade the two of you that we'll do what has to be done. I'd rather not because it would waste valuable time." He paused to let the message sink in. Dawson and Formby took the opportunity to exchange hushed whispers. Susan Alderdyce fiddled with the hair just above her left ear. The tension was palpable. "So, lady and gentlemen, I'll ask the question again. If I say let's go for it, will anybody object?" Inevitably, it was Dawson who piped up.

"What about injuries? My men could be injured." Commander Williams's eyes had narrowed to slits, his face had reddened, and the veins in his neck were bulging.

"Mr. Dawson, the same applies."

"Look, Frank." Susan Alderdyce had been studying the commander and realized that the situation desperately needed defusing, "I wish it were that simple. Let's just say we launch the LR5 right now. It'll take at least half an hour to get down to the *Tulsa* and locate the hatch. It could take longer—it'll depend on the visibility down there. I believe there's a rocky bottom covered in fine silt, and there are no nice white markings on the DISSUB as there are in some exercises, so let's say forty minutes. Mating and opening the hatch could take an hour—it could even take two or more if there is any significant damage to deal with. The transfer of personnel and stores will take another three-quarters of an hour and the ride back will take, say, fifteen minutes. Then there is the hookup and hoist on board. Let's add another twenty minutes but, seeing as the weather's not too good, maybe we should double that. By my calculation that totals well over three hours, and could be over four. What will the sea-state be by then? The weather in these latitudes is unpredictable—even the most recent forecast last night had not anticipated this frontal system arriving so soon. We could be faced with a situation where it will be more hazardous to hoist the LR5 aboard than leave it in the water. Just imagine what it would be like in the vehicle, being tossed around in an angry sea, with the most severely injured of the *Tulsa*'s crew on board, and no medical expertise—because the doctors will have stayed behind in the boat. Throw in the fact that there will be very limited power and life-support resources to keep them going for two days until things calm down sufficiently to recover it. I've no doubt that everybody would be better off where they are right now."

Williams's attitude had moderated while he was listening to Susan Alderdyce. She was an articulate woman with a rational point of view. "I had thought of that," he replied. "We're going to have to play this by ear. We have excellent communications, so the LR5 can be recalled at any time. I know the current conditions are marginal but, in my view, they're acceptable. If they don't change over the next three hours, we can do something really important."

"What if they do?" It was Dawson who spoke up. Williams had got to know him sufficiently that he could imagine what was going through Dawson's mind. He was a man who was determined not to be outdone by the slick businesswoman across the table from him. "If the weather deteriorates as predicted," he continued, "we could launch the bloody thing, recall it before it's done it's business, and bugger it and my ship trying to recover it. What will that achieve except a bloody huge bill?"

"Thank you, Mr. Dawson. I expect you imagine that I'd not considered that. Please leave accountancy out of this. It may be difficult for a Yorkshireman, but please crave my indulgence."

"It isn't just the money, Commander. If we bugger the LR5, it'll be useless even when the weather settles in a couple of days, when it could be used safely and to some purpose." Williams had also thought of that, but was surprised by Dawson's dour perspicacity.

"By then, we'll be a sideshow to the DSRV. I don't think it should concern us. Look, if we spend a moment longer playing what-if, we'll miss our window, and the entire issue will become moot. Are we going or not?"

There was an uncomfortable silence. Even Sheppard was confused about the best course of action. If things turned out the way Dawson was proposing, he and Stemple were in for a rather uncomfortable experience, at best. He just thanked God he was not in command of this operation. Frank Williams was paid the big bucks—not big enough in his view—so it was really up to him. He was actually somewhat surprised that he wanted agreement from the group. Sheppard changed the direction of his thoughts to a rather more selfish one. Since, of those around the table, he and Stemple were going to be the most directly at risk, he felt obliged to comment. "I came here to do a job. I knew it wouldn't be easy, but it's something I volunteered to do, and so I'll do it. Hank, do you agree?"

Stemple looked at him quizzically. He'd not joined the US Navy to embark on harebrained adventures. He'd joined to get a free medical education and a subsequent life that was as devoid of hassle as possible while wearing a uniform and practicing medicine. However, he'd never predicted a situation like this, even in his wildest dreams. Seeing as he'd also committed himself to this course of action, he could hardly back out now. He nodded in agreement. Eventually Susan Alderdyce, Dawson, and his chief engineer also nodded their consent. The rescue was on.

0710A, COMJTFNON HQ, Bodø

"Ladies and gentlemen," announced Admiral Risberg, "I've just received this message from the *Salminster*." He waved the piece of paper in his hand. "Despite marginal weather conditions, they will very shortly commence a run with the LR5." A few of those gathered around the long table looked at each other. The remainder, except Commander Larsson, broke out into a spontaneous round of applause. There was an almost tangible sense of relief in the room. "Now to business," continued the admiral. "Commander Larsson, it has become traditional to begin with you, but today it is essential. Please tell us what to expect from the weather." Larsson rose to his feet as the latest weather map was projected onto the screen at the end of the table.

"Thank you, sir. I wish I had some better news to impart." He removed the pen-sized laser pointer from his pocket and fiddled with it until a bright red spot appeared on the screen. "This is the weather pattern that we've been tracking for the past few days. The first front will be upon the *Salminster* within the hour. The wind has been increasing overnight and is now southwesterly at Force 6. It will increase to a severe Gale Force 9 by midday. The sea-state is currently four and will increase to six or even seven by early afternoon. I regret that this is not ideal rescue weather." Larsson felt the joy that had been so freely expressed only moments before drain from the room. He felt obliged to issue his customary meteorologists' apology. "Please don't blame me, I merely report on the elements. I am powerless to alter them."

"Thank you, Commander. Has this been sent to the *Salminster*?"

"This forecast is hot off the press, sir. It should be sent anytime now. Unfortunately, I had no idea that they'd started a rescue and gave it only a priority precedence."

"That's what these meetings are for. You'd better make it immediate and send it right away. We may be able to stop this before any damage is done or people are hurt."

0710A, MV *Salminster*

The LR5, a gray, twenty-eight-foot-long minisubmarine with a large Plexiglas dome, an array of lights, and a pair of manipulator arms at the front, was loaded and ready to launch. Inside, David Sheppard and Hank Stemple were forced by the limited headroom to crouch rather than sit. The bulkhead separating the pilot's position from the main cargo area was open, allowing both of the young men a good view of what was happening outside. The bright lights that flooded the *Salminster*'s fo'c'sle spilled through the dome and supplemented the subdued glow of the LR5's internal lighting. They could both feel the ship heaving beneath them as she pointed her bluff bow into the prevailing wind, an effort to reduce her rolling to a minimum in the increasingly choppy conditions. The wait for something to happen seemed interminable.

Stemple groped around for the canvas holster at his right hip and felt the cool metal of the Colt .45 that he'd borrowed from the *Wellington* and had insisted on wearing. He had no idea what to expect once they reached the *Tulsa*, but he considered that it might be necessary to impose some order. Those men had been cooped up in what must feel like a fancy coffin for nearly a week. They would surely be more than mildly interested in getting out. Although he had no intention of actually using it, just wielding a pistol might be useful if the rush to leave became disorderly. If there were stretcher cases, as seemed likely, very few would be leaving on the first run. He just hoped that somebody had explained that to the survivors.

All of a sudden there was a sharp jerking motion, and the LR5 was airborne. The twenty-two-ton submersible gradually began to swing at the end of the cable that suspended it from the boom of the fo'c'sle crane. The movement became more pronounced as the boom swung around, taking the LR5 over the port guardrail and out over the open sea. David's knowledge of seamanship would not cover a single piece of letter-sized paper. However, he was increasingly concerned that unless they were lowered into the water pretty damned soon, the LR5 would assume a life of its own. The direction of its oscillation only needed to change slightly and it could smash into the side of the *Salminster*. Dawson's nightmare would then become a reality. There was a series of violent jerks that left David's heart adjacent to his tonsils, and then the LR5 splashed down into the water. Within moments, an inflatable was alongside and a crewman unshackled the minisubmarine from the crane. At last, they were on their own. "Everybody okay in the back?" asked the pilot in a lilting Glaswegian accent, twisting in his seat to glance over his left shoulder. "Sorry about the ride so far, it should be a lot smoother from here on, especially once we're below the surface."

There was no reply from the doctors, but the crewman who was crouched next to Stemple piped up, "All OK back here, Peter. Let's go to work."

"All right, everybody, we're diving." There was a roar from the ballast tanks, and in moments they had slipped below the surface. A steady whine from the electric propulsion motor gradually replaced the hissing of compressed air, and the LR5 gained forward momentum. The pilot lifted the receiver of the underwater telephone and spoke deliberately and slowly into it: "*Salminster, Salminster, Salminster*, this is LR5, LR5, LR5. Comms check, comms check, comms check, over." He switched on the loudspeaker so that everybody could hear the reply. It was distorted, but intelligible. They were receiving.

It had become dark, and the pilot flicked a switch to energize the array of lights just above the dome. Even so, there wasn't much to see except for particles of silt and small bubbles that seemed to dance and glitter in the bright lights. One thing was clear—finding the *Tulsa* by eye would take a very long time because the visibility was little more than ten to fifteen feet. However, the designers of the craft had anticipated the problem and installed a sonar. The pilot was studying the display carefully. They took a spiral course down to the bottom so that they could take a good look around both visually and with sonar. There was an almost surreal silence. Sheppard was aware that his heart was thumping away in his chest and his breathing was rather more rapid than usual. He glanced at Stemple, who just raised an eyebrow and let a brief smile flicker across his face before returning his gaze to the dome. Sheppard shivered. It was getting colder in the diminutive submersible, but it was also getting tense. He had no idea what to expect. There was nothing to see through the dome except for the shaft of light that just seemed to vanish into the near distance.

Once they'd reached four hundred feet, the pilot looked up, twisted in his seat again, and announced over his left shoulder, "I have the *Tulsa* on sonar. We're just about 150 feet from the stern. As we approach, I'll take some video footage of the damage. I expect somebody in the Pentagon will be interested in that." The descent continued until the bottom was visible through the dome. The pilot leveled out and the LR5 crept forward at two knots. Fifteen seconds later the *Tulsa* became visible through the murky water. The first thing they could see was that two of the crescent-shaped, bronze blades of the vast propeller were missing and just about all of the others were badly bent out of shape. The rudder was similarly mangled, as was the port horizontal stabilizer. The pilot steered up and over the damaged stern. The superstructure looked like the wrapping of a Christmas present that had been torn open by massive fingers. There was a line of destruction that extended from about ten feet forward of the screw for what must be thirty feet or more. The pressure hull, which was just visible in places through the gaping hole, still looked to be intact. As they approached the after escape trunk, something dull red in color, but with a bright white stripe on it became visible. As they got closer David gasped in horror as its identity became all too clear. It was a Steinke Hood that covered the torso of a submariner. It appeared to be flooded, and through the clear, plastic window a pale face stared blankly at the lights of the LR5. It looked like the poor man had been almost cut in half by the hatch. One of his arms was still stuck in the hatch, the other was held out and wafted gently in the slight underwater current. Wrapped around the hand was a large spider crab that appeared to be breakfasting on the macerated flesh. The scene was grotesque.

The eerie silence that had descended on the submersible was broken by the pilot. "Seen enough, gentlemen, or should we go around again?"

"No, let's get on with it," Sheppard replied, visibly shaken by what he'd just witnessed. "We need to mate and get this thing back to the surface as soon as possible. There's nothing to be gained by hanging around."

"Very well. I can see the forward trunk just ahead. I'll see if I can't set her down right on it, first time." No sooner had he completed the sentence than the underwater telephone broke into life.

"LR5, LR5, LR5, this is *Salminster, Salminster, Salminster*. Do you read me, over?" The pilot replied in the affirmative in his uniquely monotonous, deliberate and repetitive style. "LR5, LR5, LR5, abort, abort, abort."

"Do you hear that, gentlemen? We're being called back," announced the pilot somewhat unnecessarily. Under any other circumstances, David would have regarded the transmission as a dreadful disappointment. However, the way he was feeling right now, he was slightly relieved. That old bugger Dawson had called it right, thought Sheppard.

"It can only be because of the weather. You'd better acknowledge," he remarked.

"Aye, I'll do that. Hang on tight, everybody, we're going home."

Although the rescue mission was only half an hour old, and they were heading home empty-handed, Sheppard was painfully aware that the morning's entertainment was far from over. The recovery had the potential to eclipse any amusement-park ride in terms of sheer, white-knuckled terror. After all, everybody knew that amusement parks were inspected endlessly and certified as safe. Returning to the *Salminster* carried no such guarantee. As they rose through the water, it became lighter to the point that, just below the surface, the pilot was able to switch off the floodlights. Even before they broke the surface they could

all feel the ocean's swell. Sheppard was quite convinced that it was worse than it had been only forty
minutes before. As they surfaced, large waves broke
repeatedly over the submersible and the neatly
stacked columns of canisters of lithium hydroxide in
the rear of the craft started to collapse. In no time
twenty or thirty of them were rolling around on the
deck colliding with each other and the fixtures in the
craft. They could hear an outboard engine, belonging
presumably to the inflatable that would hook them up
to the crane. The presumption was confirmed by the
soft sounds of somebody clambering aboard and the
harsher clanging tones of a shackle being secured in
place.

Sheppard had started to feel really unwell. It had
begun when he had seen that poor man trapped in
the aft escape trunk hatch and had become distinctly
more pronounced as the LR5 was being tossed around
in the choppy water. He was on the verge of praying
for the strength to resist vomiting. The hoist from the
water was almost imperceptible when it happened. If
he had closed his eyes, Sheppard doubted if he would
have noticed. As it was, the Plexiglas dome cleared
the water and the familiar image of the *Salminster*'s
horned bow filled the right side of the field of view. It
was a comforting sight. Maybe he'd been unnecessarily
pessimistic about returning on board.

Commander Williams had been in two minds as to
whether he should witness the recovery. He was irritated that things had turned out the way Dawson had
predicted, and he really couldn't face being anywhere
near him in case he should start to crow. However,
he was nominally responsible for the LR5, as well as
the unfortunate people inside it, and he couldn't stay
in his cabin for the whole evolution. Apart from that,
if anything should go wrong, he wanted to witness it.
If it was serious, he might have to recall the events
before a board of inquiry. It was therefore with some

reluctance that he stood on the port side of the bridge, staring out over the fo'c'sle. His view was not improved by the heavy, wet snow that was falling from a leaden sky, driven against the windows by winds approaching gale force. He reached out, flicked a switch, and immediately a wiper blade began to make silent, horizontal passes across the armored glass.

The boat's crew was clear of the LR5 and Williams could see the master, his silver-gray hair whipping wildly in the wind, give a signal to the crane to start hoisting. Williams's heart sank as, no sooner had the LR5 broken clear of the water, it started to oscillate. Two other lines had been secured to the shackle. One led forward to the *Salminster*'s bow and the other aft toward the stern. Their function was to limit the range through which the LR5 could swing. They appeared to work well in limiting the extent of any forward/aft movement, but they could do nothing about movement toward the *Salminster*. Denied the opportunity to oscillate in any other direction, that is what the craft was trying to do. It began to swing toward the ship and stopped only inches from the *Salminster*'s side. It then swung back, away from the ship, only to be brought up short by the stay lines. It stopped abruptly, a shower of water drops shaken loose from its hull. Then the cycle started again. Williams could only imagine what it must be like inside the LR5.

With the next swing there was a loud crash as twenty-two tons of submersible thudded against the *Salminster*'s hull. Williams picked up a pair of glasses and rapidly focused on the LR5. As it swung away from the ship he scanned its side for evidence of damage and was relieved to observe that there appeared to be none. However, the impact had not been as benign as he had initially imagined: the LR5 began to twist on the end of its cable. As it reached a shuddering halt over the water and started back toward the ship, the Plexiglas dome now pointed directly at the *Salminster*. Williams couldn't bear to look, but felt compelled to know what happened next. He could see the pilot leap out of his seat and disappear toward the stern of the craft just seconds before the crunching impact. The tremendous blow was accompanied by an explosion of small pieces of Plexiglas. As the LR5 swung away from the ship, Williams didn't need binoculars to assess the damage. The dome, its surrounding metalwork, and the array of lights above it were smashed beyond recognition. The LR5 would not dive again on the *Tulsa*.

Williams was crestfallen. He buried his face in the palms of his hands and only gradually lowered them. The scene below him had possessed a horrible inevitability. Deep down, he'd known that Dawson was probably right, but he'd felt a moral obligation to try to get to the survivors in the *Tulsa*. He looked out of the window and saw to his horror that the same thing was about to happen again. Why didn't Dawson hoist the bloody thing? What in blazes was the man waiting for? After all, they'd reached the point of no return. Leaving the LR5 in the water was no longer an option, it would sink. It had to be hoisted aboard. There was an even louder impact as, once again, the LR5 smashed into the side of the *Salminster*. He began to wonder what the collisions were doing to the ship. As he thought about donning some foul-weather gear and going down to the main deck to take a look, he saw Dawson stride across the fo'c'sle and bend over the guardrail. He recoiled rapidly and began to gesticulate wildly to the crane operator and the men minding the stay lines. The hoist was apparently on. The LR5 had just shuddered to another halt over the water and disgorged a load of gray canisters of lithium hydroxide into the sea through the broken dome. It now commenced its return journey. As it gathered momentum it also began to rise as the crane winched it up. Dawson took one more look at the

LR5 and scurried back across the fo'c'sle. This time, as the LR5 approached the side of the *Salminster,* it was just clear of the hull and instead smashed into the guardrail with tremendous force, just two feet from where Dawson had been standing only moments before. The wood-and-sheet-metal structure was demolished in a split second.

If there was a plus side to what had just happened, it was that the impact had served to slow the violent swinging of the LR5 and, in response to more wild gesticulation from Dawson, the crane operator released the brake, sending the submersible crashing onto the deck of the *Salminster*. Another load of lithium hydroxide canisters and a cloud of white dust spilled out of the shattered dome. The canisters clattered to the deck and started to roll randomly across the fo'c'sle. Then there was silence apart from the wind howling through the rigging and the low purr of the main engines, which, at slow ahead, were barely able to keep the ship pointing into the oncoming weather.

Dawson made his way over to the open end of the LR5, bent down, and peered in. "Is everybody all right in there?" he asked in his usual, no-frills approach to problems. All he could hear by way of a reply was a series of groans mingled with violent coughing. The occupants had been tossed around like beads in a rattle and were nursing cuts and multiple bruises. One of the canisters of lithium hydroxide had broken open, but it appeared that nothing more serious had occurred and, thankfully, nobody had been injured by the flying shards of Plexiglas. As soon as he felt able, Sheppard struggled to his feet and groped his way forward and out onto the fo'c'sle. His eyes were smarting, the collar of his shirt was soaked with blood from a gash on the back of his head, and he was unprepared for the icy blast of driving snow that greeted him. So he nodded briefly toward Dawson and trotted away, emitting a series of staccato coughs, to seek refuge in the warmth of a shower. Hank Stemple, who was nursing a nasty cut on his forearm, limped after him and, finally, the crewman and pilot left their craft. Their reddened eyes were barely open as they groped their way to cover, convulsing with bouts of coughing.

Williams marched up to Dawson and patted him on the shoulder. "I must admit you made the right call this morning. But you know the way I felt. As far as I was concerned, it was the people down there"—he was pointing toward the sea—"who come first." Dawson stared back at him with a faint smile on his face—or was it a smirk?

"Unless we fix the hole in our side, we'll be joining them shortly," he replied. Williams, shocked by what the older man had just said, hastily made his way over to the port side to take a look. "Be careful," continued Dawson, "I don't want to have to throw a life belt to you. Enough of my gear's already gone over the side today." Given the movement of the ship and the absence of a guardrail, Williams realized that Dawson's warning was probably well intentioned. So he lowered himself onto his hands and knees to complete his journey to the side. As he peered over the gunwale he could see what Dawson was worried about. There was indeed a hole in the side of the *Salminster*. However, it looked worse than it was. The hole was only a foot in diameter and was located well above the waterline. More impressive was the effect of the impacts on the paintwork. Large areas of the shiny, black finish had been stripped away to reveal a mixture of rust and red-lead undercoat. He turned and crawled a short distance inboard before rising to his feet.

"Look, I'm really sorry about this, but it looks worse than it is," started Williams. "Which space is holed?"

Dawson's smirk broadened. "I might be wrong," he replied, "but I think it's your cabin."

0900A, USS *Tulsa*

"How many times do I have to say this, Tim? If you don't have something positive to contribute, I'd much rather you said nothing." Enzo's irritation showed both in his face and the terse tone of his rebuke. But Gallagher was not prepared to be silenced that easily.

"This isn't a fairy tale, Enzo. It's real. Things have gone wrong, and they'll surely go further downhill in the future. All I'm trying to do is inject a little realism here. We could all sit around this table and grin at each other and try to kid ourselves that everything is just great and wonder why all patrols aren't this much fun—" He was interrupted by Harvey Schwartz.

"Why do you have to take everything so far? You're not content just to make your point—every one has to have barbs attached. Do you get some kind of a kick out of that, Tim?"

"I don't see what you are driving at. All I said was that the rescue's late, and I bet it won't happen. That's the way I feel, and I thought we were encouraged by the captain to offer up our ideas. I thought that was why Enzo took the chiefs' mess over—so that the four of us could eat together and express our views. Anyhow, where is the barb in that observation?"

"I want to inject a little common sense here," began Enzo. "Tim, the first thing is that the rescue won't actually be late until after 1100. But that's not my point. I really don't appreciate your endless stream of bad vibes and negative thinking. It gets us nowhere, and I thought I'd made my position pretty darned clear last night. By all means express a contrary opinion, but you'll have to be able to defend your position if you want to keep me interested in what you have to say."

"What do you mean?"

"You've just provided an excellent example. So you don't think we'll be rescued. What's your reasoning? There's a growing number of people up there with an

increasing capability. Do you know something I don't?
Come on, Tim, what the fuck's wrong with you?" Gallagher furrowed his brow and thought for a moment
before responding.

"It took over two days for them even to find us and
confirm that we were down. The DSRV has less than
one hundred percent availability these days, because
there is only one left. I'll bet the thing is still being
screwed together in San Diego."

"Then why did the people topside tell us yesterday
afternoon to expect a rescue within twenty hours?"
riposted Harvey.

"As I said at the time, they just want to keep up
our morale." Enzo realized that Gallagher had not
been privy to the early discussions on the probability
of rescue and was probably unaware of the alternatives to the DSRV. This was probably as good a time
as any to inform him, he thought.

"Did you know that there are other rescue vehicles available?"

"Yes, the British have one."

"So do the Russians, the Swedes, the Italians, the
Japanese, the Australians. . . . The list goes on. If
we just assume for now that you're right about the
DSRV, can you think of any reason why any of the
other rescue vehicles couldn't be ready to come and
get us?"

"It wouldn't surprise me if the weather is too bad.
Of the group you mentioned, I think only the Russians
use a MOSUB."

"Thank you, Tim. Do you see? We're getting somewhere now."

"No I don't. Not to put too fine a point on it, we
are still stuck in this leaky, goddamned coffin." Enzo
was irate, but was prepared to have one more go with
Tim before he acted on his threat and banned him
from these gatherings.

"What we have just enjoyed, prior to your most
recent outburst, was reasoned debate. Everybody here

had an opportunity to assess whether there was any value in your remarks. Each will have made his own judgment, and I've certainly made mine. It was an intelligent process, not just the ritual throwing of cold water over every positive thought that has characterized your contribution to our debates up to now. Do you understand?"

"Sure, rather than just saying that we are all going to die in this fucking hellhole, you want me to tell you how and when."

"That's the idea. Then, if we think your opinion is a load of bullshit, we can tell you so."

"Fair enough." He changed the subject. "You know, I was going to open a book on when we'll get out of here. You know, spread bets? Do you know why I didn't bother?" Gallagher looked around the table. Since nobody looked like they were about to reply, he continued. "Then I'll tell you. I couldn't win. Even if I won the bet, I wouldn't live to spend my winnings."

"Stuff it, Tim." It was Paul Trost who had spoken up. Enzo was aware that Trost had never liked Gallagher, and the tone of his voice had made it clear to all in the room. Enzo pushed his empty cereal bowl away and made to leave the table.

"Just before I go and take a look at the captain, I'd like an update on the flooding. What's the story, Harvey?" Schwartz looked up from his precious stack of papers. The dark rings under his eyes betrayed the fact that he had enjoyed little sleep overnight.

"It's just about as I figured yesterday. The pressure's up to fourteen feet of seawater and the lower auxiliary tanks are filling up. I expect there will be free water over the lower-level deck plates by tomorrow night."

"OK, Harvey, so we've still got some time, and if this rescue happens soon, it shouldn't be an issue. Look, guys, while I'm gone, I'd like you to do something constructive. I'm going to send up another SIT-

REP and I want to include some explosive charge codes so the folks topside can give us a better idea of when we can expect to receive a rescue vehicle and which one to expect. If it's anybody other than the Brits or Italians, we may have some major language problems. And, while you are at it, think about any other codes that might be useful. We'll discuss them when I get back. Paul, I expect you want to do some more trunk practice. Feel free to get on with that whenever you want."

Master Chief Steadman had become concerned that nobody had seen Chief Santana since the previous evening. His nonappearance at breakfast had alerted him to a possible problem. Santana missing a meal was about as likely as finding an Eskimo out hunting with his fly unzipped. As he entered the berthing area and sat down on Mitch's empty bunk, he looked up at Chief Hicks. "I think you'd better tell me what's been going on."

"Look Stan, he had a run of bad luck and got angry about it. That's all there is to it."

"Does anybody have anything else to say?" He looked at the other two men.

"There's no big deal, he was just a sore loser."

"Carl's right," added Chief Czapek. "He was just being stupid."

"If that's the case, you'll have no difficulty finding him. I've got to get back to the wardroom. Let me know when you've located him."

0900A, COMJTFNON HQ, Bodø

There had been a break for half an hour to allow people to attend to any e-mail or faxes that they had received, then the meeting had reconvened. The message from the *Salminster* was about as depressing as any that had been received at the HQ. The only consolation was that nobody had been seriously injured.

A flag lieutenant had just delivered another message and, for the first time in two hours, the admiral smiled. "Ladies and gentlemen, I am pleased to report that, following the highly successful loading of the DSRV, the *Vindictive* has been making excellent time and has been able to maintain a speed closer to twelve than ten knots. It seems that her ETA at the datum could now be as early as 1400A tomorrow." He turned to Commander Selby. "What sort of state is the atmosphere in the *Tulsa* likely to be in by then?"

"Using the data from yesterday's SITREP, sir, they will have run out of lithium hydroxide and the CO_2 concentration will be rising. They'll be uncomfortable, but it looks like the cavalry might just make it in time."

"Sir, excuse me for interrupting," said Commander Larsson. "I don't understand much about DSRV operations, but is the reason that the *Vindictive* has made such good speed have anything to do with the sea-state?"

"Commander Sangster, would you like to explain?"

"Yes, sir. The DSRV is held on the superstructure of a MOSUB by a cradle made of tubular steel that was fitted to the *Vindictive* in Murmansk. Depending on the class of MOSUB, it may be well clear of the water or rather close to it. What you want to avoid, if possible, is exposing the DSRV to heavy waves that could knock it off its cradle."

"So the speed of the *Vindictive* will depend on the sea-state?"

"Yes. The *Vindictive* has a rather odd shape. The diameter of the hull aft of the missile compartment is considerably smaller than the rest of the boat, which means that the cradle will be quite close to the water." Commander Larsson was clearly concerned.

"There are times when I do not like my job, and this is one of them. I expect that within three hours, the *Vindictive* will hit the same weather system that caused so much trouble for the *Salminster* this morning. From what you've said, it will inevitably reduce her speed. We may need to plan for a later arrival."

"How bad is it likely to get?" asked the admiral.

"Well, sir, just about what I said this morning. Sea-state six or seven could be in the cards. That's waves as high as six to seven meters, or about twenty feet." There were concerned looks around the table. Lieutenant Commander Murphy spoke up.

"If it gets that bad, the *Vindictive* may have to dive and ride the storm out. Needless to say, that will delay her considerably. Commander Larsson, when is this due to blow over?"

"By midday tomorrow it should be largely over."

The admiral spoke next. "Okay, any estimates of the latest ETA?" Lieutenant Commander Murphy had been jotting some numbers down on a piece of paper.

"Probably around 1000 local on Friday."

"Can they last that long, Commander Selby?" Selby had powered up his notebook computer and was studying the screen.

"They will be sick as hell by then, sir, but they should still be with us. I reckon that by noon on Friday that CO_2 will be up to about 7 percent. We'll have to get to them very soon after that."

"Thank you, everybody. It would seem that, as always, we are in the hands of the Almighty. Let us pray that, on this occasion, He is merciful." With that, Admiral Risberg got up and left the table.

1000A, USS *Tulsa*

Enzo had examined Richter and was saddened to see that there was little change in his condition. However, he recognized that his skills were, at best, rudimentary and this was not a conclusion that he was completely comfortable with. The IV was behaving well, and the catheter looked like it was working, the color of the contents of the bag was a satisfactory pale yellow. He studied the notes that Master Chief

Steadman had made, and it seemed that the captain was in just about neutral fluid balance—what they had poured into his arm was a reasonable match with what had arrived in the catheter bag.

Enzo turned to Steadman. "If this rescue doesn't happen this morning, the captain's the one who'll be most disadvantaged. We can muddle through with the atmosphere control for a day or so, but I really don't know if the captain can."

"I know, sir, it's been weighing on my mind. Do we know if they're still planning to come and get us?"

"I'm afraid not." Enzo saw that Steadman had dark bags under his eyes and was looking even more pale than usual. "Did you get any sleep last night, Master Chief?"

"A little, sir." Enzo knew that he was lying.

"I'm just going to prepare a new SITREP and then I'll be back to relieve you here. I want you to get some rest." Steadman nodded, and Enzo left the stateroom and made his way back down to the chiefs' lounge.

Gallagher and Schwartz looked up as he entered. The table was covered with pieces of paper, all but one of which Schwartz quickly shuffled together into a neat pile. "Just the atmosphere-control data, Enzo. I've abstracted what they need to know topside, and it's in the SITREP."

"Good. What about the explosive charge signals?"

"We've taken a stab at them. Have a look." Schwartz pushed the remaining single sheet of paper on the table toward Enzo, who sat down to study it. It read:

CHARGE SIGNALS FROM SURFACE TO DISSUB

Charges	Pattern	Meaning
2	30-second interval between them	Alert, message to follow.

Charges	Pattern	Meaning
4	In series	Rescue aborted
5	In series	Rescue not possible, start escaping
6	Two groups of three charges	The number of minutes between the groups is the number of hours until the rescue will commence.
6	In series	Rescue starting now, prepare to receive a rescue vehicle.

"That's pretty good, guys. I like the flexibility of the time to rescue signal—it'll cut down on the number of charges they have to use. I'm going to suggest that the 'start escaping' signal should be repeated after, say, five minutes, because that is a major deal. It would only take one charge not to go off in a 'rescue now' series of six for some truly horrible mistake to be made. I had wondered about asking for which rescue vehicle we might expect. I guess it doesn't really matter so long as they use our tap codes and bring the right stores with them. I can't believe that hasn't been sorted out." He studied the rest of the message, then looked up and passed it back to Gallagher. "Tim, if you just make the one change I suggested, it's time for Chief Czapek to earn his pay again. I'm going to relieve Master Chief Steadman in the captain's stateroom. He is one very tired man."

1200A, MV *Pelican*

The VHF receiver was set to channel 16 and crackled into life. "Ship on my starboard bow, ship on my starboard bow, this is Warship *Wellington*, Warship

Wellington, over." The master looked at Simon Bannerman for instructions.

"We'll have to reply sooner or later," he said. "This is the fourth time they have tried to raise us. What do you want me to do?"

"How far away are they?" asked Bannerman. The master moved over to the radar, twiddled a couple of knobs and replied:

"Ten miles."

"It's obviously a British ship—reply in Norwegian. That should stall them for a while. How many other ships are there?"

"Two," replied the master in his characteristically parsimonious manner.

"Not quite the reception committee I was expecting," said Mick Russell to his colleague, as the two of them stared through the bridge windows at the storm-tossed sea in front of them.

"No," replied Bannerman. "I think we both expected there to be rather more than this."

"What if he comes back in Norwegian?"

"We'll just play it by ear. We have every right to be here. There's nothing they can do about it." Bannerman changed the subject and spoke to the master again. "I wasn't expecting the weather to be quite so bad. What are the limits for launching the submersible?"

"As you have seen, we have an 'A-frame' at the stern. We can launch in anything up to Force 6. But the wind now is over forty knots. That's just too much. We'll have to wait until things calm down a bit."

"Damn. I really want to get that underwater footage and see if we can't contact the survivors. When will that be possible?"

"It's hard to tell," replied the master. "Could be later today, could be tomorrow." No sooner had he said that than the *Pelican*'s bow headed down into a deep trough and buried itself in the following wave with a thunderous boom and an explosion of spray that the wind swept over the starboard side. The whole ship seemed to stop and quiver. Slowly the bow began to rise and rivers of water scurried along the fo'c'sle and against the white superstructure. The master smiled. "I think you'll agree, this is no weather for submersible operations." Bannerman nodded reluctantly. He didn't fancy being tossed around in this lot with only a minisub to protect him. He was quite happy to hold on until things improved. They would wait until the rescue flotilla was in sight and then set up a broadcast. They would not mention the submersible yet, but there could be some good shots of the other ships. He would need to identify them. He had a copy of *Jane's Fighting Ships* in the cabin, and knew that they should all be in there. They could also interview the master about the weather. That should keep the folks in New York quiet for a while.

1400B, HMS *Vindictive*

Commander Todhunter was worried. He had already reduced speed twice and was now making barely eight knots into the worsening weather. The *Vindictive* was rolling through an arc of about fifteen degrees which, apart from anything else, was increasingly hard on his stomach. He stared out over the port bow in the direction of the oncoming weather for the slightest sign that it was going to moderate, but could see none. The sky was slate-colored and looked like it was about to disgorge large quantities of snow. It was certainly cold enough. He turned and faced aft again. Waves were now breaking over the stern with some regularity and, when the boat rolled to port, they washed over the DSRV. That would have to stop. Given the bad news from the *Salminster*, if they lost the DSRV the men in the *Tulsa* would be condemned to death.

Two choices presented themselves. He could alter course directly into the weather. This would serve to offer his little passenger a large measure of protection by putting it in the lee of the massive missile compartment. The disadvantage would be that such a maneuver would substantially increase the distance they would have to travel to reach the datum. The alternative was to dive. Their speed of advance would be slowed to about five knots, but they would at least be traveling in the right direction. Either way, they were going to be delayed, and he regretted sending his last SITREP in quite such optimistic terms only four hours earlier.

It had finally started to snow. Large, wet flakes were being driven almost horizontally by the biting wind and it made the decision easy. They would dive. A periscope watch would be considerably more comfortable than standing on the bridge, slowly being turned into a snowman. He spoke briefly to the officer of the watch and headed down into the warmth of the control room.

1400A, MV *Salminster*

Just about everybody had eaten lunch and returned to their duties. Frank Williams sat alone pretending to read a dog-eared, four-day-old copy of the *Telegraph*. Although he didn't normally drink at sea, he had decided that today would be an exception. Beside him was a tumbler containing a generous measure of Cutty Sark and two ice cubes. Today had already been a very long one, and he didn't really care what happened during the rest of it. He had considered the idea of returning home rather than sitting around in the frozen north being tossed about in this godforsaken little rust bucket by weather that seemed to be capricious even by English standards. His humor had not been improved by the state of his cabin. His collection of family photographs, his beloved boom box, and his duvet had all been ruined by being doused in liberal quantities of seawater that had washed in through the large hole made by the LR5. His gloom had not been relieved by the prospect of moving to a smaller cabin once the engineers had finished patching up the ship's side. He reached out, grasped the tumbler and took a good mouthful of the fiery, amber liquid and marveled at the warm glow it generated in his stomach. On balance, he decided, the *Salminster* would stay on task. It still carried a functional ROV, a remotely operated, unmanned submersible, that might be of use in guiding the DSRV onto the *Tulsa*.

Williams looked up to see that Hank Stemple had appeared and was casting somewhat disapproving looks in his direction. Commander Williams got to his feet and approached the young American with an outstretched hand. "I don't think we had time for a proper introduction this morning. I'm Frank Williams."

"Nice to meet you, sir," he replied somewhat furtively. "Hank Stemple. I'm the US Navy exchange medical officer at the Institute of Naval Medicine." They shook hands briefly.

"I've known a good many of your predecessors," Williams replied. "Quite an illustrious bunch. Have you been over here for long?"

"No, sir, just six months."

"Quite a change from the States, isn't it?"

"I've been surprised by the many similarities, actually. Driving on the wrong side of the road has taken me longest to get used to."

"You seem to have managed okay. You're still in one piece."

"Sure, but you should see my car. It's taken several good hits at those infernal circles you stick in the middle of every intersection." Williams smiled.

"Look, I'm sorry about this morning. You must have been pretty shaken up. Would you care to join me in a shot of something?"

"No thank you, sir, I don't drink in the day."

"As a matter of fact, I don't normally either. Today, however, I simply felt like one. November 3 will not shine out in my memoirs as being one of my best days.

In fact, I can't think of a single thing that I would wish to remember about it." He walked over to the bar and freshened his glass. "Are you sure I can't tempt you?"

"Quite sure, thank you, sir. Actually, the worst thing about this morning wasn't the launch or recovery or even being covered in lithium hydroxide. Unpleasant as all of them were. Do you know that we saw the *Tulsa*?"

"No—I'm surprised you had time to see much of anything."

"Well, we did. The *Salminster* must have been directly over the wreck. We found it in just a few minutes. I'm no engineer, but it wasn't tough to work out why it sank. The stern's a real mess."

"I'm not surprised. Those Akulas are big boats. Not the sort of thing you want to have run into you."

"The worst thing was that there's a man trapped in the after escape trunk hatch. It looked like they'd tried to pump it shut and his pelvis was in the way. What a dreadful way to go—drowning in excruciating pain." Stemple's face looked drawn, and there was a suggestion of a tremor in his lower lip.

"You will join me in one of these, no more excuses." Williams poured a second glass of whiskey and handed it to Stemple, who accepted it with a reluctant nod. "I know you doctors are trained to handle death and disease, but it can't be easy to deal with something like that."

"No it's not." He took a liberal sip of his drink and decided to change the subject. "Do you know, you've just shown me one of the other big differences between the UK and the States?"

"What do you mean?" replied Williams.

"You're a lot less puritanical over here. What we're doing now would be unthinkable in an American ship."

"More's the pity," replied Williams. "I should make the most of it while you can, if I were you. There is a new puritanism sweeping through our own navy that started with the integration of the Wrens into the service and the introduction of women at sea. We're now the victims of political correctness and just about every other social scourge that you guys dream up across the pond. It may not be quite so obvious, but it's there and, I fear, growing like a cancer." Williams studied the young man in front of him. He was fresh-faced, slim, and obviously very astute. "One thing I can't stand is that nobody's supposed to say what they really mean anymore in case somebody is offended. I mean, if anybody doesn't like what I say, they can bloody well lump it, as far as I am concerned. I hold the view that I have the right of freedom of speech and that ranks well above the sensitivities of anybody who happens to enjoy the privilege of hearing my opinion." He took another mouthful of his whiskey. "Across the Atlantic, your founding fathers had the wisdom to enshrine that in the Constitution. It's a great shame we don't have the same thing over here. However, you'd best not get me started on this subject. I've been known to get quite agitated about it."

The wardroom door opened and David Sheppard came in and glanced at the two men standing at the bar.

"What's this, an early happy hour?"

"Sort of," replied Williams. "What on earth happened to you?" Sheppard's normally cherubic complexion was gone, his face swollen and bright red. His left eye was half-shut and was watering profusely.

"I'm afraid it was that lithium hydroxide. I must be really sensitive to the stuff. It's why I'm here actually—I'm going back to the *Wellington*. There isn't much in the sick bay here, and I want to put some steroid cream on my face and hands. I was wondering if you need anything, Hank?" Stemple glanced down at Sheppard's hands and noticed that they looked just as angry as his face.

"No, I'm OK. Thanks, David. Do you want me to come with you?"

"No, that won't be necessary. I don't know what

Führer Freeman has in mind, but if he needs you, I'll let you know. Can you keep an eye on the LR5 crew? They seem to be okay right now, but chemical burns can take some time to develop."

"Sure thing. Have a safe trip."

1410A, USS *Tulsa*

"Don't bother to get Tim, it's you two I wanted to talk to," said Enzo in somber tones as the three young officers sat round the table in the chiefs' mess. "I think we have to accept that the rescue we were expecting may not happen anytime soon."

"It's just so frustrating!" exclaimed Trost as his fist crashed down onto the table. "If only they would let us know what the hell's going on."

"We all feel the same way, Paul." Enzo reached over and patted him on the back. "The three of us, above all, must remain positive. The problem we've got is that, with the delay we're facing, we've got no choice but to look at ways of keeping water away from the battery compartment. I thought about what Tim suggested yesterday, and I don't think sealing it will work. If we do an imperfect job and there's some electrolysis, an explosive mixture of oxygen and hydrogen will be released as well as chlorine. If that gets too hot or there's a spark, we can kiss this life goodbye and look forward to the next. I, for one, am not ready to do that yet, so we need to come up with an alternative. Any ideas?" The three of them sat and thought for a moment.

"Do you think Sparks could build a cofferdam around the access?" asked Schwartz. "He'd need to get started soon, because it would have to be both watertight and robust. It may have to withstand quite a pressure of water if the topside crew leave it a whole lot longer. If the rescue takes a day or two to complete, there could be two or three feet of water to hold back by the time everybody's out of here."

"Hmm, what do you think Paul?"

"There's not a long list of options. I suppose we could try to discharge the battery so that even if the compartment did flood there would be minimal electrolysis. The way I see the problem, it's not just the battery we have to deal with—it's the distribution panels that'll have to be protected as well."

"Good point. Though it'll mean going back to cold food . . ." groaned Schwartz.

"Better than going onto EABs. That would mean no food or drink," riposted Trost.

"Well, thanks, both of you. I think we have the answer. We'll do both; I'll have a word with Sparks right away."

1430A, Northwood, Middlesex

Admiral Patterson was sitting at his desk when his chief of staff knocked at the door and entered. He presented the admiral with two messages. "Sir, I think you should read these." Patterson scanned the first piece of paper. It was from the *Salminster*, and included a lengthy description of the damage to the *Tulsa* that had been seen from the LR5. The video footage was being digitized in the *Wellington* and would be sent on as soon as possible. The second message was from the *Wellington*. It was bad news. The press had arrived on the scene in the form of the *Pelican* and, although the weather conditions prevented Commander Muggeridge from confirming it, there was the possibility that they were equipped for submersible operations. He looked up at the chief of staff, who nodded. "The press are definitely there, sir. SNN has just aired a broadcast from the *Pelican*."

"Oh God!" replied the admiral. "I don't think any of us had anticipated this."

"Perhaps we should have after that scene in Hammerfest."

"Maybe. What on earth are we going to do about it?"

The chief of staff raised an eyebrow and thrust his hands into his pockets. "There's not a whole lot that we can do. They're in international waters."

"Surely the Vikings can come up with something. Can you check that out? I'm going to phone Gerry Talisker and see what he has to say."

"Yes, sir. I'll get the staff legal adviser onto it as well. If we've got one thing going for us right now, it's that the weather is pretty foul up there. I'll be surprised if they can launch their minisub until things settle down a bit."

"Good." The admiral reached over to the telephone, picked up the receiver, and waited for a moment. "Yes, get COMSUBLANT for me please. It's rather urgent."

1500A, USS *Tulsa*

Enzo looked at Richter again and satisfied himself that nothing had changed. The IV bag was almost empty, and he would have to change it in the next half hour. He was also growing concerned about his patient's pressure points and, when Master Chief Steadman returned, they would have to turn him. The last thing he needed right now was pressure sores like the ones he'd seen in the nursing manual.

Enzo was feeling at a loose end. The four charges that they'd heard just a few hours earlier, indicating that the rescue had been aborted, had dealt a dreadful blow to morale and, worse, it had served only to fuel Tim Gallagher's atrocious attitude. It was not a feeling that he had experienced with many previous colleagues, but Enzo really didn't want to serve with him ever again. Indeed, he'd go out of his way to refuse appointments if there was even a suggestion that Gallagher would be within a day's drive. Perhaps that was putting it a bit harshly, but Gallagher was not the sort of man he would wish to go to war with. It was inevitable that there would be serial inquiries once they got home. He would make it his business to cast the supply officer's performance in the least charitable light that was consistent with accuracy.

Enzo had noticed before that the captain's diary was open beside his bed. He'd obviously not had an opportunity to put it away before he lost consciousness. He was sorely tempted to pick it up and read it and wondered if the master chief had thought the same way. Eventually his curiosity got the better of him and he did just that. It should be more interesting, he thought, than the medical texts that had been his almost exclusive literary diet for the past week. He flicked the pages back to 28 October and read from there. He was immediately struck by Richter's thoughts about the loss of John Dowling and of his past relationship with his wife, Marie. He had no idea that anything like that had occurred and that, as John was dying, he'd agreed to look after her and the boys. His admiration for his captain grew the more he read. He resolved to get Richter out of the *Tulsa* alive or perish in the attempt.

There was a knock and after a brief pause the COB stuck his head around the door. "Sir, I'm sorry to bother you, but I think you should come and see this."

"What's up, Master Chief?"

"I'll explain when we get to the freezers." Enzo wanted to ask just exactly what was going on, but thought better of it and followed the master chief down to the freezers. They were met by Chiefs Hicks, Lehner, and Czapek. He could control his curiosity no longer.

"OK, so what's going on?"

"I think you should look in here, sir," and with that Chief Hicks opened the freezer. Enzo's jaw dropped in disbelief. Curled up in the far corner, wearing nothing more than a pair of boxer briefs, was a body. He could only see the back of the head and didn't immediately recognize who it was.

"Can somebody explain what the hell's going on? I

thought the deceased were being stored in body bags in the torpedo room."

"It's Chief Santana, sir. It looks like he walked in here and froze to death."

"Why should he do a thing like that?" Enzo turned round to face the chiefs. "You all berth with him. Was something wrong?"

The COB replied, "I think you should know, sir, that he lost a game of cards yesterday evening. It seems he was pretty sore about it."

"Do you expect me to believe that losing a game of cards would cause a sane man to do this?" He paused for a moment. "There was more to it than that isn't there? You were playing for money, weren't you?" He looked each of the chiefs in the eye. They didn't have to say anything. "How much did he lose?" Chief Hicks looked at Lehner, who glanced at Czapek. It was Lehner who replied.

"Almost fifty thousand dollars."

"What? Did I hear that right? Fifty thousand? Are you all stark raving mad? What on earth got into you? This is a court-martial offense!" Enzo's mind was reeling. What on earth was he going to do about it? The first thing was to keep it as quiet as possible. "Right. Get Santana into a body bag and take him to the torpedo room and keep this to yourselves. Is that clear?"

"Yes, sir!" the chiefs replied in unison.

"Good, I'll think about what's to be done and let you know my decision. Master Chief, please come with me."

1800B, HMS *Vindictive*

The past four hours had been agonizing for Commander Todhunter. All he wanted to do was surface, speed up, and get to the datum, but the weather had remained atrocious. The only good news was that the wind had veered to the northwest and if he were to try to resume his passage to the datum on the surface, he would be able to do so with the DSRV in the lee of the missile compartment. It would be a little risky because there was a rather confused sea up there. The swell from the west would still threaten his diminutive, piggyback passenger. Todhunter weighed the odds. No matter what, he couldn't afford to lose the DSRV. With the LR5 damaged beyond repair, the American rescue vehicle was the only way the survivors were going to get out of the *Tulsa* without getting wet. The wind speed was forecast to have fallen to below twenty-eight knots, and the storm was surely blowing over. He decided that he'd surface and see just how fast he could safely make headway into the weather. If it was anything less than five knots, he'd dive and try again in another two hours. It had also stopped snowing. That would make it a lot more comfortable on the bridge than it had been earlier in the day.

CHAPTER

8

Thursday, 4 November

0700A, USS *Tulsa*

Despite being dressed up like a Michelin man and covered by blankets, Enzo was chilled to the bone. He'd not slept well, having been woken in the night by a series of messages and sporadic bouts of violent shivering. Between spells of fitful slumber he had occupied his mind trying to work out what was going on topside. As far as information was concerned, the situation had gone from one of famine to one of feast. During the night they had received no fewer than two updates on the estimated timing of the rescue. Two thoughts had occurred to him. The first was that the surface weather conditions were probably difficult; otherwise, the estimates wouldn't keep changing as they had. The second was that the most recent estimate was sooner than the previous one, which could indicate that the weather was improving, or was expected to get better. However, he was still puzzled as to why the rescue that had been promised yesterday morning hadn't materialized. He'd reached the conclusion that a rescue vehicle was on-site but, for some

reason, it was not operational. Was it the weather or
had there been some kind of mechanical failure? Were
the delays due to repairs? In his experience, engineers
were notoriously poor at predicting when they would
finish a job—particularly if they weren't certain as to
what was wrong in the first place. Could that be the
explanation, or was something else wrong?

He had been churning such thoughts over in his
mind in a search for a way forward. He desperately
wanted to give the crew some good news or, failing
that, a positive spin on what was known. The blow
to morale that had been delivered by the failure of
yesterday's rescue had been savage—even in the wardroom. Although Gallagher's response had been pre-
dictable, he was concerned that Schwartz and Trost
were noticeably gloomy. Even the irrepressible COB
had felt moved to comment—not just to express his
concern at the delay in getting the captain ashore, but
that a feeling of abandonment was widespread among
the enlisted men. The potential for the flood to ruin their
day had caused further concern. He'd been unable to
conceal the extent of the problem from the crew. All
the bulbs had been replaced in the emergency lighting
circuit as part of the drive to discharge the ship's main
battery so that, compared with earlier, the forward
compartment looked like it was lit up for Christmas.
Despite the improved illumination, the sense of depression in the boat had seemed to deepen with each
passing hour. If only he could work out what was
going on, he could provide some rationale for assuring
his people that next time they really were going to get
out, and that their rescue would happen before they
choked to death on chlorine gas.

The other matter that had been troubling Enzo was
Santana's apparent suicide. How could normally sensible chiefs gamble so wildly? It didn't take him long
to realize that they, or Santana, at least, must have
reckoned on never getting out. The irony of Santana
killing himself because of the increasing likelihood of

being rescued wasn't lost on Enzo. What was he going to do about the situation? What was he going to tell the crew? More importantly, what would he tell the inevitable court of inquiry? There was no doubt that Santana would be autopsied. Trying to claim that he'd died in the collision or fire wouldn't work, because there wasn't a mark on him. Furthermore, the whole crew had seen him at mealtimes, so they knew that he'd survived the sinking. He might be able to get the three chiefs and the COB to sing a new tune, but there was no chance of getting the whole crew to do so. What on earth was he going to do? He'd talk it over with the COB after breakfast.

0800A, COMJTFNON HQ, Bodø

Having bounced between the British and Norwegian Ministries of Defense and a number of other departments in Oslo, the idea of arresting the *Pelican* in order to undertake a full pollution inspection had gathered momentum and was now being debated in Bodø. Only a minority of those in Oslo, or around the table, understood why it was so important to get the ship away from the *Tulsa*. Just about everybody had seen the television that morning and, on it, clips of the *Pelican* and its minisub. The sentiment that had been expressed by some was that filming the *Tulsa* would be tasteless and intrusive, but not grounds for an arrest on a trumped-up charge—particularly as she was a Norwegian ship. The press was likely to become antagonistic unless a more acceptable reason could be found or, at least, some evidence provided to support the charge. Admiral Risberg was beginning to regret opening the issue for discussion. After fifteen minutes of debate, Lieutenant Commander Murphy decided that it was time to enter the discussion.

"Sir, I think I should explain that unless this minisubmarine is removed from the area, there will be no

rescue by the DSRV." The chattering around the table
stopped abruptly.

"Can you explain why?" asked one of the representatives from the Norwegian Health Ministry.

"I can't go into details, but it's unacceptable from
the British perspective to have our submarine filmed
or observed in any way underwater. We've been here
all week with one objective in mind—to get those
people out of the *Tulsa*. I assume that remains our
primary objective. It is still the objective of my government. As I see it, we can settle this peacefully
and arrest the ship or, subject to the approval of
the Norwegian government, the *Wellington* will be
instructed to disable or sink the *Pelican* and its minisubmarine before the *Vindictive* arrives. The latter
course of action would inevitably have unfortunate
consequences. Not least, somebody could get hurt.
However, I want to make it absolutely clear that
either the *Pelican* is removed or the men in the *Tulsa*
will be forced into an escape which, as we have discussed before, will mean that some of them will inevitably be injured or die. I'm sorry to be so brutal
about it, but those are the only alternatives. A pollution inspection strikes me as being the ideal way out
of this."

"That puts a rather different complexion on the
matter," replied the female health executive. "However, we'll have to address the public-relations aspect
of this."

The exasperation that Lieutenant Commander
Murphy was feeling now showed on his bearded
face. "Madam, I don't minimize the importance of
PR but, quite frankly, it's a sideshow to the matter
at hand."

"You see, this is where we differ," she replied. "The
Pelican is carrying reporters, and not just any reporters, but SNN reporters. These people are not noted
for their diffidence or timidity. Furthermore, it will
have cost a great deal of money to put them on the

scene. The local media could well turn antagonistic if strong-arm tactics are used to gag the press, but I hate to think what SNN will do."

"They can do as they please as far as I am concerned," replied Murphy, who paused because Captain Eistvig of the Norwegian Coast Guard had raised his hand.

"I am perfectly happy to arrest this ship under the circumstances. You may be interested to know that it has been arrested before—not for pollution, but for drugs. It would not surprise me if more are found when she's searched again. The first mate keeps some unsavory company." There was a babble of conversation around the table which, as it frequently did, died quite quickly. Admiral Risberg concluded this section of the meeting.

"Thank you, Captain Eistvig. I'll direct the OSC immediately to task the *Nordvik* to that effect. The sooner the *Pelican* is removed, the better. We'll break for coffee now and reconvene"—he checked his watch—"in twenty minutes, ladies and gentlemen."

The admiral leaned over the table and whispered to Captain Eistvig, "Thank you so much for that—when was the *Pelican* found to be carrying drugs?"

"Nineteen seventy-three. I was a young lieutenant, and it was the first ship I arrested. I'd have to check, but I don't think it's even the same vessel and, even if it is, it would be incredible if she still has the same first mate. He was quite old then and would have retired by now." Admiral Risberg grinned from ear to ear and only just stopped himself from laughing.

"You realize, of course, that once you've arrested the *Pelican* it'll be the Coast Guard that will have to deal with the press."

"Of course, I fully expect that. In any case, these things happen all the time."

"What happens all the time?"

"We make mistakes. To err is, I believe, human," replied Eistvig.

"It is also true of computers. Blame it on them—I do. Frequently."

0800A, USS *Tulsa*

Enzo and Master Chief Steadman were sitting at Richter's desk, munching mechanically on their cereal. "I asked you to join me in here because I don't want us to be overheard."

"I suspected as much. It's about Santana, isn't it?"

"Yes, Master Chief, it is. We need to come up with a plan pretty quickly, and I'm at a loss for good ideas at the moment. I don't think we can rely on the truth, do you?" Steadman looked up from his bowl, put down his spoon and swallowed.

"The way I see it, sir, we've got two audiences to satisfy. The crew and one or more inquiries once we're out of here."

"I agree with that."

"The fact is that Santana committed suicide."

Enzo stopped eating and looked directly at Steadman. "Are you certain of that?"

"Pretty much. The only other possibilities are that he went into the freezer and couldn't get out, or somebody somehow locked him in there. I don't think either of those theories would stand up to serious scrutiny. The door mechanism works perfectly, and if he'd tried to raise the alarm, or attempted to break out, it would be reasonable to expect him to have damaged his hands. There's not a scratch on them. I think he must have done it himself and done so deliberately."

"So the only question we have to answer is why? The only people who know about the cards are the three chiefs and the two of us. That's right, isn't it?"

"Yes, sir, it is."

"You do realize that if the gambling angle ever gets out, all five of us will be canned?" There was no need for Steadman to reply. A fresh thought came to Enzo.

"By the way, did you know about the game before Santana died?"

"Yes, sir, I did. However, I didn't know about the gambling. There was never any money on the table. I just thought they were playing for points."

"I believe you, but do you think that would wash at an inquiry?" He paused; they were drifting away from the main issue. "No, we have to find another reason why he committed suicide. Any ideas—you knew him better than I did."

"The short answer's no. He was a completely normal guy. A bit sullen perhaps, especially on this deployment, but happily married I believe. Successful career—as you know he was shortly due to be promoted to senior, and he had no money worries that I'm aware of."

"Nothing in his medical records?"

"Not that I'm aware of, sir, but I'll dig them out and check."

Enzo was desperately searching for a worthwhile line of inquiry. He chewed another mouthful of cereal and suddenly stopped munching. "Did he leave a note?"

"No, at least I haven't seen one."

"Rather odd, don't you think?" Steadman wasn't too sure what to make of that remark.

"Not really. Then again, I'm no amateur sleuth."

"Nor am I, but I believe suicides generally do leave a note. If he did, we need to know what's in it. Look, Master Chief, I need you to get on this right now. I'd appreciate it if you'd have a word with Hicks, Lehner, and Czapek. We need to find a reason why he did this. We'll talk again this afternoon."

"Aye, aye, sir."

1000A, HMS *Vindictive*

In order to accommodate the whole DSRV team, as well as all the key players in the MOSUB, Commander Todhunter had called for the meeting to take place in the junior rates' dining hall. As soon as everybody was seated he began: "Gentlemen. In about twelve hours we'll be at the datum and ready to commence the rescue. I thought it would be a good idea if we all got together and discussed just what will happen. Many of the Brits here will have been wondering what all the equipment that was brought on board in Murmansk is for, and why white lines have been painted on the superstructure. Doubtless some of our visitors are wondering if it'll be possible to operate from a British boat. I can reassure you on that score. Some of you must have been involved in the 1996 exercise which proved that you could. Nonetheless, an exchange of ideas at this point can only be helpful, and hopefully it will result in things going smoothly later on." He went on to introduce the members of his crew who were seated in the room, before looking to his right to the leader of the American delegation. "Commander Tyson, is there anything you'd like to say before introducing your people?"

"Thank you, Captain. I'll keep this brief and just say that I would like to express my personal thanks to the British navy and the whole crew of the *Vindictive* for being so willing to help us out with this rescue. We've been made to feel very welcome on board despite the fact that I know some of you had to be recalled from leave and others have had to revise your vacation plans. I can assure you that it's really appreciated, and I just hope that we can find some way to make it up to you all." He went on to introduce his people before concluding. "I'll now ask Lieutenant Commander Sheridan to give you an outline of the DSRV. That is what you wanted, isn't it, Captain?"

"Yes indeed, go ahead."

Lieutenant Commander Sheridan rose to his feet and walked over to a bulkhead where a cutaway diagram of the DSRV was displayed. He reviewed its construction, which was based around three steel

spheres—the forward one containing the two pilots
and all their navigational and control equipment, the
center and after spheres being mainly for passengers.
He moved on to explain how the mating skirt, with
its shock-absorbing outer ring, worked and some details of the pylons that secure the DSRV to the
MOSUB. In sequence, he reviewed the intricate trimming system and ballast-control unit used to maintain
the DSRV at neutral buoyancy, regardless of whether
there were passengers aboard. He concluded with
some of the operational limitations of the rescue vehicle, such as it having a top speed of only four knots
and a limited battery life. "I know some of you are
interested in how this thing maneuvers and is navi-
gated. The main propulsion unit is the large shrouded
screw at the stern, although she also has two vertical
and two horizontal ducted thrusters that allow the
pilot to position her with great precision. There are
four pan-tilt cameras with lights and additional lighting around the skirt to facilitate mating, and a variety
of sonars permit accurate navigation at short and
longer ranges. He concluded by asking if there were
any questions. There was a brief pause before one of
the British petty officers raised a hand.

"Sir, with a speed of only four knots, isn't this thing
going to be limited by underwater currents?"

"Yes, to some extent. However, we've had some
good news from the *Salminster* that there's a negligible
current at the datum, and so that should not be a
problem."

The next questioner followed immediately. "I've
been trying to work out how you can recharge the
DSRV's batteries without having both hatches in the
escape tower open—a situation we try to avoid for
obvious safety reasons."

"Your after escape trunk—sorry, tower," he cor-
rected himself, "contains a power outlet. Obviously,
the upper hatch has to be open, but the lower hatch
can remain shut throughout the process. There's no

need to be concerned about safety. We conducted a successful skirt-seal-integrity test dive just after leaving Murmansk. The pylons are doing a great job of holding the DSRV over the escape trunk nice and tight."

"Sir, I know it's not directly relevant to us in the *Vindictive*," started a British chief, "but what do the crew of the *Tulsa* have to do? I mean, if they're all sick because of foul air, as is quite likely, can you get them out if they can't cooperate?"

"Sure. They really don't have to do anything. As you know, there are two hatches in the escape trunk—the basic design is just like yours. Under normal circumstances, both the upper and lower hatches will be shut. The upper hatch opens right onto the superstructure and is designed as an access for salvage purposes. If need be, it can be opened from the outside. The DSRV is equipped to do that. Once into the trunk, opening the lower hatch is not a problem. If the *Tulsa*'s crew is able to assist, there's a routine for them to perform, basically to speed things up. It's pretty simple, and they'll have a copy of the relevant instructions on board." Lieutenant Commander Sheridan looked around the room. There appeared to be no more questions.

"Thank you." After a brief pause Commander Todhunter continued. "We now have to consider how we're going to get the survivors adequate medical care." He glanced over at his medical officer, Surgeon Lieutenant Ferguson. "No disrespect, Doc, but I think even you would admit that we're not really equipped to provide that here. It's clear to me that on the first run, we'll need to recover the most seriously injured and provide as much help as we can for the others. It therefore strikes me that Doctors Samways and Kellman should travel down to the *Tulsa*—"

"That's already agreed, Captain," interrupted Commander Tyson. "But we may have to discuss rescue policy briefly. The fact is there are no regulations covering this so, to a certain extent, we can do as we please. My take on this is that unless one of the survivors is in real trouble, we should aim to get as many people out as quickly as possible. That means taking only those who can walk on the first three or four runs and only then taking the stretcher cases. Commander Samways, do you agree?"

"Well, for the first run I have no doubt you're right. It'll take Pat and me some time to assess the injured, and it would be downright crazy for the DSRV to wait while we do that. I'd like to suggest, however, that we play it by ear after that. Once a satisfactory atmosphere-control protocol is established, there's really no limit to how long the fit survivors can remain in the boat. On the other hand, there may be a limit to how long some of the injured can."

"Looking at the figures," interrupted Pat Kellman, "I estimate the DSRV is probably going to have to do at least nine runs, no matter which way we cut the pack. That's going to take us well into the weekend. I agree. I think we should be flexible."

"How long do you plan to remain in the *Tulsa*?" asked Commander Todhunter.

"As long as we have to. We'll certainly not leave until the last of the injured is recovered."

"I'm a bit concerned about what we'll be able to do for the injured once they're aboard *Vindictive*. Obviously, I'd like to get them off as quickly as possible, but that'll require rather better weather than we've enjoyed recently. Doc, can you manage them here?"

"Well, sir, the POMA and I can only do our best. We should be able to keep them alive. Once we've got an idea as to what injuries we're dealing with, I'll give you a better idea. Obviously, the *Centaur*'s equipped to deal with them definitively, so we should aim to get them over to her as soon as it is safe to do so."

"Right. Agree with that." Todhunter looked at Commander Tyson. "Unless you've got anything more, I think we've covered the important issues."

"I don't think so. I'd just like to reiterate my thanks to you all. Now let's get these guys out alive."

1030A, USS *Tulsa*

Enzo descended to the lower level and walked aft to where the inspection hatch for the auxiliary tank was open. Sparks stood next to Lieutenant Trost, who was aiming a flashlight at the rippled, oily surface of the water. The level was only just below the deck plates, and the roaring of the flood sounded like a waterfall. "No sign of it slackening I suppose?" began Enzo, more to break the tension than because he was hoping for a positive response.

"No, sir," replied Sparks. "It won't be long before we can sell tickets for the lower level Jacuzzi."

"I don't think you'll make your fortune with this enterprise, Sparks. The water's a bit cold, isn't it?"

"It'll warm up when it hits the battery, sir," he replied dryly.

"How's your cofferdam?"

"Come and see, sir." The three men turned and moved forward. "I've done my best with what there is, but without power tools and a more generous supply of wood there's nothing more I can do." They reached Sparks's polythene-and-timber creation that surrounded the access hatch to the battery compartment.

"It looks pretty robust to me, Sparks, well done." Lieutenant Trost sucked in some air between clenched teeth before commenting.

"He's not been able to test it, Enzo. It's going to have to work first time."

"Sparks's record speaks for itself—look at the hopper." Sparks looked a little sheepish.

"Actually, sir, it took me two goes to make that work properly."

"Well yes, but it's worked flawlessly since then."

Enzo wanted to change the subject. "What about the battery? When do you think it'll be discharged?"

"I'm draining it as fast as I can, sir. We'll be able to tell by the lights. Once they start to dim we'll be close to our goal." Enzo looked up at the nearest bulb—it was still burning brightly.

"So it'll be a while yet."

"Looks that way, sir. There's one hell of a lot of amp hours down there."

"Hmmm. Well, you can only do your best, Sparks. Keep it up." Enzo turned and made to leave. Almost as an afterthought he turned to Lieutenant Trost. "I suppose the trunk's all ready to go, Paul?"

"Sure is, Enzo."

"Good."

"Just one more thing, Enzo—Harvey asked me to tell you that the last canisters are in the hopper."

"Why couldn't he tell me himself?"

"You were busy with the master chief at the time. He's turned in now."

"I don't blame him; he's worked very hard on the atmosphere. Thanks for letting me know, Paul."

0800R, Cherry Hill, New Jersey

There was only an inch of air between the surface of the water and the overhead. John had wedged himself in place and tilted his head back as far as it would go so that his nose was just above the surface. He was gasping for air. Suddenly he seemed to lose his grip because his nose slipped below the surface just as he took another breath. His eyes bulged with shock as he felt the cold water enter his nose, followed by a burning sensation as it irritated his nasal passages and caused him to sneeze explosively. He inhaled again involuntarily. This time more water flooded into his nose. . . .

Marie woke with a start and sat up. Her pulse was racing, and she felt sweaty. She swung her legs round and sat on the side of the bed trying to calm down. Something was going to have to be done about these nightmares. She couldn't stand them anymore, and it seemed that she couldn't rely on her sedative to do the job anymore. She tried to work out what was going on inside her head. Each dream was similar to the one before, if not exactly the same. Furthermore, they all reached a similar point just before she woke. They were all about how John had died. But the weird thing was that she didn't know what had happened, not exactly. He might have died as a result of the collision, there could have been a fire, perhaps he fell and hit his head—who was to say he drowned? The trouble was that her subconscious obviously needed to know what had happened and, in the absence of the facts, her mind was making something up. How was she going to get the facts? That was the question. There was no point in phoning Group 2 in Groton again. Even if she got through, they wouldn't know until the survivors had been rescued.

Marie emitted a deep sigh and began to wonder what she was going to do today. She didn't really feel like getting up yet, but didn't want to go back to sleep just in case that horrible nightmare returned. In fact, she really didn't feel motivated to do anything much. Despite saying that he was going to take a break, Father had said just last night that he was going into work again today. Carmen could look after the boys— they seemed to like her a lot, and she obviously enjoyed their company. So, not only did she not feel motivated to do anything, there really wasn't anything that had to be done. It was a weird feeling—one that she'd not experienced since before Jamie was born.

The temptation to think about John was powerful. Although deep down she knew he was never coming home again, she was still not completely certain. After all, the news had been sparse and of questionable quality. Furthermore, she was so used to him being away that she really hadn't missed him in the same way she would if they lived a normal civilian life. The absent spouse was a way of life in the navy. As time went by, and the rest of the crew was rescued and he wasn't among them, his loss would surely become more real. The boys had been incredible. There had been a minimum of tears or questions about death. She had no idea how children should react to bereavement, but doubtless they would deal with it in their own way and in their own time.

She didn't want to dwell on John since it would surely end in tears again, so she turned to her altercation with her father—if that was the right word for their most recent exchanges. What was he up to? He didn't normally behave like this. He'd been brutally distant for so many years and now, all of a sudden, he'd altered course and wanted to forget about it all. He might be able to do that, but could she? And what about Christine—how was she going to react to Father's change of heart? None too well, in all probability. Having returned to the fold, Marie would now represent a threat—a competitor for Father's affection and wallet. Given the situation with Carmen, and who could say how many others over the years, she was unlikely to have ever enjoyed exclusive access to his affection. The real threat would be if the flow of funds into Christine's coffers were to slacken or stall because of Father's restored indulgence of his estranged family. That she was a selfish, scheming bitch was a given. Spiteful and vengeful could be added to the list of adjectives, unless Father managed the situation very carefully. She began to wonder who he would side with if trench warfare erupted once again between Christine and her. The precedent wasn't good. The situation would then revert to the status quo ante whether Father wanted it that way or not. The only way to prevent the situation would be for Marie to avoid claiming so much as a penny from her father.

She mulled that idea over for a while and, as she was doing so, another problem presented itself. How was she going to manage financially without help from her father? Doubtless she would be entitled to a widow's pension from the navy, but it would be a poor replacement for John's salary. Then there was the problem of somewhere to live. She would surely have to leave her navy quarters, but where would she go? John had some money put aside for the boys' education, but that was the sum total of their savings. What on earth was she going to do? Staying with her father indefinitely wasn't the answer. Christine would see to that.

1330A, MV *Nordvik*

With the handover of OSC between the *Wellington* and *Centaur* complete, Commander Jonsson was mentally bracing himself for the order that would surely arrive very shortly. The arrest of the *Pelican* was inevitably a task that would fall to him. He just hoped that she didn't make too much of a fuss over it. Would its master turn and run? He thought about it for a moment before concluding that he wouldn't because it would achieve nothing. Not only would it deny the reporters on board the opportunity to film what they wanted, but the *Pelican* wouldn't be able to outrun the *Nordvik* and certainly could never escape from the *Wellington* or *Centaur*.

Although he didn't know the *Pelican*'s master, he knew he would be reluctant to end this charter because the owners would be earning a great deal of money and he was almost certainly going to be in receipt of a fat bonus. So he might try to tough it out and insist on his right to innocent passage. The more he thought about it, the more he realized that it might take some harsh measures to persuade him to heave to and receive a boarding party. He looked out of the forward bridge windows at the 57 mm Bofors gun that dominated the foc's'le. There would be no arguing with that, he thought. Although he had very rarely been called upon to use the weapon, he would do so if necessary. It could lob fifty-two pounds of high explosives almost ten miles. In this weather, that wouldn't be achieved with great accuracy, but the effect should be sufficient to put the wind up anybody on board the *Pelican*. If it came to it, he'd put a shot across her bow.

1400A, HMS *Centaur*

"Immediate message from Bodø, sir." Captain Temple eased round in his chair and eyed the radio supervisor, who was standing just behind and to the left of him. He reached out and grasped the message. It was the order to arrest the *Pelican*.

"This should be interesting," he announced somewhat blithely to nobody in particular and, on a fresh pad, scribbled out a message to the *Nordvik*: "Arrest the *Pelican* and escort to Hammerfest for drug inspection. Authorized to use any necessary, nonlethal measures."

"Send this right away please, RS." Temple swung back round in his chair and stared out of the bridge windows. The *Pelican* was a small speck in the water about six miles off the starboard bow. "Officer of the Watch."

"Yes, sir?" A young lieutenant looked up from the radar plot.

"I think we'll get a little nearer the action. Close to a mile off the *Pelican*."

"Aye, aye, sir. Starboard ten, revolutions 120," he announced and, moments later the large, gray warship heeled as she answered the helm. "Midships."

"Wheel's amidships," echoed the quartermaster.

Captain Temple reached down to the pocket on the side of his chair for his binoculars and focused them on the *Pelican*. She was not a particularly good-looking vessel. Her design was rather too practical for that. Her red hull had a high freeboard at the bow

that stepped down to a much lower one at the stern,
rather like a tug. Her oversize, white superstructure
was topped off with a small helicopter deck located
above the bridge. At her stern was a large A-frame.
He estimated that she displaced no more than 4000
tons. Her top speed was probably something like fifteen knots. He panned round and saw that the *Nordvik* was now some three miles off his starboard beam.
As he studied her he realized that she must have just
received his message. She broke out of her patrol pattern, which had been intended to deny the *Pelican*
access to the water above the *Tulsa*, and steered directly toward her. There was a puff of black smoke
from her funnel, and the water at her stern started to
boil as she increased speed. The VHF radio crackled
into life, and he could hear the two ships in conversation over channel 16. The initial challenge from the
Nordvik had been in English but, characteristically,
the reply had been in Norwegian. Now both parties
were chattering away in Norwegian. He had no idea
what they were saying to each other, except that it
gradually became more forceful. He focused once
again on the *Pelican*. She appeared to have altered
neither course nor speed. There was another staccato
command from the *Nordvik*. Was that an ultimatum?
wondered Temple. There was no response from the
Pelican either over the radio or with an alteration of
course.

1410A, MV *Pelican*

Simon Bannerman left his cabin and raced up to
the bridge in response to the message for him over
the main broadcast. "What's up?" The master was
speaking into a microphone that he held in his right
hand, and with his left he pointed through the port-
side bridge windows at the gray, Norwegian Coast
Guard vessel that was bearing down on them. The
master stopped speaking. "They want me to heave to.

They're going to send over a boarding party," he replied in his heavily accented English.

"What are you going to do?"

"I'm going to obey him."

"The hell you are! You'll take your orders from me. Have you any idea how much SNN is paying the owners of this tin can each day?"

"Mr. Bannerman, I am responsible for the safety of this ship, its crew, and passengers. That includes you. I don't know if you noticed, but that ship has a gun—quite a big one. He is threatening to use it unless we heave to and allow their boarding party to come aboard. Over there is an aircraft carrier." He pointed to the *Centaur*. "I don't intend to argue with that."

"What the fuck's going on here? We're in international waters, and neither the British navy nor the pissant Norwegian Coast Guard have any right to tell us to do squat. Do I make myself clear?"

"Perfectly. However, they're claiming that we're carrying drugs, and they do have a right to inspect us for that reason."

"That's bullshit! There aren't any drugs on board—are there?" inquired Bannerman, who momentarily sounded a little less sure of himself.

"Not that I am aware of."

"Well tell them, for Christ's sake! Insist on your right to innocent passage."

"Do you think for one moment . . ." The master was interrupted by another radio message that even Bannerman couldn't mistake for anything but a threat. "What do you want me to say? They're insisting that we heave to."

"Give me that thing." Bannerman strode across the bridge and grabbed the microphone. "This is Simon Bannerman of SNN; I am chartering this vessel. We are in international waters and have an absolute right—"

He was interrupted by a dull thud followed by a high-pitched shriek. He spun his head round to see a puff of smoke rapidly being blown away from the muzzle of the *Nordvik*'s gun. The shriek reached a crescendo and a large, white plume erupted in the water just two hundred yards ahead of the *Pelican*. "Fucking hell!" screamed Bannerman.

"All stop," announced the master calmly to the quartermaster.

"No, this is ridiculous!" objected Bannerman at the top of his voice. "Let me speak to New York. They'll have something to say about this. At least they can get on to the Norwegian embassy and put a stop to this nonsense." The quartermaster looked nonplussed, unsure how to react to the chaotic scene on the bridge.

"I am sorry, Mr. Bannerman, there's no time for that. I'm going to heave to before they hit us."

Bannerman clicked the button on the side of the microphone and spoke into it once again. "This is Simon Bannerman of SNN. I must advise you that we are filming this act of piracy and will have no hesitation in broadcasting it around the—"

There was another thud, this time rather louder, as the *Nordvik* was drawing ever closer. The shriek of the shell was earsplitting as it passed low over the bridge and plunged into the water just fifty yards on the starboard beam. "All stop!" yelled the master.

"Aye, aye, sir. All stop," repeated the quartermaster as he reached to his right and moved both main engine controls to the STOP position. The way came off the *Pelican* quite quickly and in no time she was wallowing in the choppy sea. The *Nordvik* slowed to a couple of knots and lowered a rigid inflatable boat over the side containing a crew wearing bright orange immersion suits. In no time it was speeding its way toward the *Pelican*. Simon Bannerman stared out of the port-side bridge windows with a look of misery and resignation on his face. The opportunity for one of the greatest scoops in television news history was evaporating before his eyes. The only issue he could concentrate on was how he was going to get his revenge. Mick Russell's film of the arrest would be the start of it. Next he would have to see if he could get a court in the US interested in the case.

0930R, Cherry Hill, New Jersey

Breakfast was later than usual. Carmen was busily beating eggs for the Spanish omelet that Marie's father had requested, and the boys sat silently at the table, munching away on cereal. Marie sat down opposite them. The bags under her eyes betrayed her lack of restful sleep. No sooner was she seated than her father breezed in. "Morning all," he announced as he lowered himself into his seat at the head of the table. "How's everyone today?" He glanced round the table and Marie answered for the boys.

"Just fine, thank you, Father."

"Hmmm," was all he could say before the kitchen was filled with a loud sizzling as Carmen poured the eggs into the pan.

"Would you like an omelet, Mrs. Dowling?" inquired Carmen gently.

"No thank you, just some toast, please."

"You are not eating enough," diagnosed her father. "There are sparrows in the garden with bigger appetites than you."

"That may be so, but I just don't feel like food at the moment." He decided to change the subject.

"Well, boys, what are you going to do today?"

"We haven't discussed that yet," interrupted Marie. "There's a new Disney movie at the theater. Would you like to see that this afternoon?"

"Only if Carmen comes too," replied Jamie.

"What about it, Carmen?" She looked up from the pan.

"I'd love to go. I'd be pleased to take them if you want to rest."

"Why, thank you, Carmen. That would be wonderful." With the afternoon's entertainment agreed, a fresh silence filled the room. Eventually, it was broken by her father.

"I've changed my mind—I'm not going into the office today. I've got something I need to discuss with you, darling. Will you have a few minutes after breakfast?" Marie didn't respond immediately and took a small nibble out of a piece of toast. What on earth did he want to talk about? she wondered.

"Sure."

For the first time in her life Marie was ushered into her father's study. What she saw surprised her. Since he was the only person ever to use the place, and knowing his ambivalence toward housework of any kind, she had expected it to be a mess and knee deep in dust. In fact it was remarkably tidy and, if not spotless, it had obviously been cleaned quite recently. It was an impressive room. The walls were covered in a rich oak paneling, and two of them contained rows of leather-bound books. A vast, antique, mahogany desk was set at an angle near the full-length, south-facing window, which admitted a remarkable amount of light. Beside the desk, and in front of one of the bookshelves, stood two occasional chairs finished in polished red leather. The wall opposite was decorated with large oil portraits of his parents and, between them, a break in the paneling revealed a huge HDTV television screen. The floor was covered in an intricately patterned Wilton carpet. Father beckoned to the closest of the empty chairs and invited her to take a seat before moving round to the far side of the desk and sitting down. "I expect you've been wondering what I want to talk to you about."

"It had crossed my mind."

"One of the things I've been doing these past few days is sorting out your financial future."

Marie was at a loss for words. Had he been reading her mind? "John was signed up with the navy's life-insurance program and you'll receive a reasonable chunk of change from that. I think it should be roughly a quarter of a million dollars as a lump sum. There will also be a small pension and one or two other minor benefits—the navy will cover the cost of the funeral, for example, and he's entitled to be buried in Arlington Cemetery with full military honors if you wish. I know it sounds incredible, but you'll have to apply for these benefits, and the necessary forms are in this envelope." He opened a drawer at his side of the desk, retrieved a large brown envelope, and passed it across the desk to her. "I've filled out all the parts I can. I think there are two or three that you'll have to deal with yourself. The thing is, I realize that this won't be sufficient to provide for you and the boys, seeing as you have no house. In view of our discussions earlier this week, I've decided to round up the lump sum to a million, and I'll also buy you a house. You'll find a check in that envelope, but no title deeds, because you should choose the house, and I don't know where you'd like to live. That's what I wanted to discuss."

Marie was completely dumbfounded. Her father broke the silence. "I know this has probably come as a bit of a shock, so I don't expect an answer right away. Sleep on it, as they say. Do you think you'd like to live around here? I'd love it if you did."

"Ummm," she replied, somewhat hesitantly, "I really don't know. I've no idea." Confusing waves of emotion began to wash over her. The first was relief. She had managed to work herself into quite a frenzy over her finances earlier this morning, and it looked like that had been unnecessary. The second was a sense of total emptiness. For the past twelve years, where she had lived hadn't been a matter of choice. She'd gone wherever John had been sent and done so willingly. Subconsciously, she'd expected that would always be the case—at least until he retired from the service. And all of a sudden, she felt exposed by the need for a decision about something she'd never even considered. All of a sudden the loss of John became much more real and immediate. Where was she going to live? After their tour at SUBPAC, she and John had always wanted to return to Hawaii. Would she want to go back there again without him? Probably not, and certainly not to Maui—that was now Christine's stomping ground. She felt completely lost. In no time tears were welling up again in her eyes. Marie reached into the sleeve of her cardigan, retrieved a tissue, and blew her nose. She really didn't want to cry in front of her father after he had shown such kindness and generosity. "I'll sleep on it," she sniffed, and paused to compose herself before continuing. "How's Christine going to react to this?"

"What do you mean?"

"In the early days, I think she was jealous of our relationship. Since it seems that's on the mend and, particularly with your generosity, don't you think she'll begin to feel that way again?"

"She might. However, that's for me to deal with. She's always had everything she could ever have wanted from me, and she always will. I really can't see that she has a case for objecting. Nonetheless, I think it would be prudent for her not to know about either the money or the house. There's no sense in provoking her, is there?"

"I'll say. Let's hope she'll believe that my future standard of living is thanks to the indulgence of Uncle Sam and a guilt-ridden nation."

"Indeed."

1000R, Atlantic Fleet HQ, Norfolk, Virginia

Admiral Talisker had gathered together his remaining staff officers to plan how to respond to the imminent congressional inquiry. He had barely managed to conceal his outrage that the bastards on Capitol Hill were going to embark on a witch-hunt for purely political reasons, before the survivors had even been recovered. The task they faced was one that nobody sitting at the table was going to relish. "The way I see it," he continued, "we'll have to review every aspect of submarine rescue and escape policy and capability from the *Thresher* onward. The cupboard is far from bare. It's fair to say that we've led the world in submarine rescue systems; I expect it's our escape capability that will come under greatest scrutiny."

"That's the problem, sir," interrupted the chief staff officer. "It's been a joke for years and one that's been shared by just about the whole submarine community in the US and overseas."

"I think that is a bit harsh," replied the admiral.

"Sir, I think that's the view we'll have to defend. It won't take Congress more than a morning to elicit testimony to that effect from submariners and engineers alike. I have little doubt that's where Congress will be coming from."

"I have a rather different perspective than most of you," announced the staff supply officer. "My background isn't rich in submarine folklore like most of you. Can anyone explain why submarine escape has been treated as such a joke?"

"Well, I suppose there are a couple of strands to it," replied the admiral. "The first is that the only two modern submarines we have lost went down in deep water, water far too deep for escape or rescue. So nobody's really taken the matter of escape too seriously. The other thing is that with such a good rescue system escape has always played second fiddle."

"I find that rather puzzling," replied the supply officer. "If the precedent for the current policy is a submarine sinking in water that's too deep for escape or rescue, why has so much money been spent on the DSRV?"

"Simple. That was mandated by Congress after the *Thresher* disaster."

"I think there's more to the 'joke' issue than that, sir," interrupted the chief staff officer. "It's an attitude that feeds on itself. No sooner had the escape training

towers in Pearl Harbor and New London been shut
down in the mid-seventies, than doubts about the capability of the escape system began to creep into the
service. If you don't believe that escape's possible because you've got no experience of anything like it, you
ignore it. If you ignore it and don't upgrade the system, or train people realistically how to use it, guess
what? It does indeed become impossible. Interestingly
enough the Brits and many other nations that use their
technique—the Canadians, Australians, and Norwegians to name a few—have upgraded their systems and
train their men almost religiously. And of course, they
believe that submarine escape is perfectly possible."

"We are upgrading our system," responded the admiral gruffly. "The problem is it's a slow process, and
the *Tulsa* has yet to receive the upgrade."

"Congress will want to know why it's been such a
slow process, of course," the CSO continued. "No
prizes for an answer to that."

"Thankfully, that's not my territory," responded the
admiral. "N87 and NAVSEA will have to explain that
to our political masters. I have a record of support for
submarine escape going back many years, which is
more than can be said for some." He looked at his
CSO, who busied himself fiddling with the briefing
notes in front of him.

The ops officer broke the awkward silence. "We'll
have to defend our almost exclusive reliance on rescue
though. I mean, if you study the data from the safety
center, just about all the near misses—by which I
mean the groundings, collisions, and fires that could
have resulted in a submarine sinking—just about all
of them have occurred in shallow water. Furthermore,
I've studied how long the survivors of a sinking will
be able to maintain a breathable atmosphere with the
stores they have available. In 688s in particular, escape
becomes not just a remote possibility, but a certainty
in most scenarios. Look how long it's taken us to get
the DSRV up to the Norwegian Sea. By rights, the

men in the *Tulsa* should have escaped and died of hypothermia in the water days ago—assuming they got out successfully in the first place. That they're still with us is, frankly, something of a miracle rather than a triumph of planning."

"Yes, we're going to have to defend the policy," admitted the admiral wearily.

"You know, it's been my impression," remarked the supply officer, "and correct me if I'm wrong, but most of those who I've met in the service don't believe our submarines can be sunk. It strikes me there's almost a state of denial about that possibility. Of course, I can understand why. Nobody's going to volunteer to go to sea in a death trap. So if you believe that escape's a joke and you want to be a submariner, you have to believe that our submarines can't be sunk."

"Like the *Titanic*, you mean?" noted the CSO, somewhat sarcastically.

"Nicely put. That's exactly what I mean."

"Look," interrupted the admiral, "much as I'd like to sit here all morning discussing the philosophy of service in submarines, we must put some structure into our deliberations. I think we've made some useful progress in defining some of the directions we're liable to be attacked from. I'd like some detailed study of the following. . . ." He went on to allocate the subjects on which those around the table were to prepare position papers with talking points for the next meeting. They had only forty-eight hours in which to do it.

1800A, MV *Pelican*

Lieutenant Nordvahl entered the officers' mess and sat down at the chair that had been left unoccupied for him. A slight wrinkle of his nose was the only outward sign that he had noticed the sulphurous aroma in the room that was a consequence of Mick Russell's second helping of lentil and carrot stew the previous evening. "The first thing I want to say," he began in heavily accented English, "is thank you to you, Captain Petersen, and your crew for cooperating as you have with my men. We have completed a preliminary search—"

"And did you find any drugs?" interrupted Simon Bannerman.

"Mr. Bannerman, there is a limit to what we can do at sea."

"That's not my point. Did you find any drugs?"

"We have found a number of substances that will be sent for laboratory testing. I am not prepared to say more."

"I don't think you can get away with that," interjected Russell. "We have been prevented from engaging in perfectly lawful activity by this arrest and I, for one, insist that you tell us whether it was justified by what you have found or not. You realize that if it isn't, it will become a serious international incident very quickly. I am certain SNN would make damned sure of that."

"Mr. Russell, all I and my men have been able to do is a very preliminary visual search of the ship. We are heading for Hammerfest, where a more detailed search will be conducted. Only once that is complete, and we have the results of the laboratory tests, will I be in a position to answer your question. I can understand your frustration, but please be patient."

"When will we know then?" demanded Bannerman.

"It will take about twenty-one hours for us to reach Hammerfest, another day, at least, for the full search, and up to a week for the laboratory results." He removed a diary from his jacket pocket. "Let's see, today is the fourth of November. You should know sometime on . . . Monday the fifteenth."

"This is intolerable!" Bannerman replied, tapping the table firmly with his index finger. "Absolutely intolerable. I've never known anything like it outside a third-world dictatorship. You should know that I am highly suspicious as to why this has happened and intend to get to the bottom of it. If you think for one millisecond that you will be off the hook as soon as we get into Hammerfest, you'd better think again."

"Mr. Bannerman, I am merely following my orders—"

"That was tried as a defense at Nuremberg, and look where it got the Nazis. It just won't do, Lieutenant. I will speak with my producer now, who will, I am quite certain, take the matter further."

"You are perfectly free to do so, Mr. Bannerman. I, too, must speak to my superiors, so if you will excuse me, I must take my leave."

2230A, HMS *Vindictive*

Commander Todhunter initialed the message he'd just read and returned it to the yeoman. He then turned to Commander Tyson, who was standing next to him in the control room. "Well, Philip, that's it, we're cleared to dive and get this rescue under way. Is your team set to go?"

"They sure are. Ready when you are, Captain."

"Okay then. The next stop will be the USS *Tulsa.*"

The dive was uneventful and, over the following half hour, Todhunter brought the vast ballistic-missile boat to the hover just fifty feet from the bottom and a hundred yards off the starboard beam of the stricken boat. The *Vindictive* was headed directly into a gentle, half-knot current and presented her stern to the *Tulsa.* Since the DSRV was going to have to head into the current on either the outbound or homeward leg, this was as good a position to be in as any. Todhunter eyed the plot. "I think this'll do. I'll keep us at a steady range and bearing from the *Tulsa.* It's up to you, Philip, to get her crew."

"Thank you, Captain. We'll get going right away." He looked up at Commander Todhunter. "With your permission?"

"Go ahead." Commander Tyson lifted the intercom

and spoke briefly to one of his staff in the engine room.

"Launch the DSRV."

"Switch the periscope video to the casing camera," ordered Todhunter.

"Aye, aye, sir," came a reply from somewhere in the control room, and the video screens blinked. Todhunter turned to his American colleague. "We might as well watch this, seeing as you people went to the trouble of fitting the camera in Murmansk." An American petty officer, wearing the single chevron of a third class, sat at a small console that had also been loaded in Russia, from which the camera and external lights were controlled. Within moments the screens showed a crisp image of the rounded bow of the DSRV, which was still mounted on its white pylons over the after escape trunk.

In the forward sphere, the pilot and Lieutenant Commander Sheridan were sitting in the only two comfortable seats in the craft, confronted by an array of instruments that would not look out of place in the space shuttle. In the center sphere the third crewman and two medical officers sat on the circular seat that surrounded the access to the hatch and mating skirt, through which they would deliver themselves and their supplies to the *Tulsa*. The center sphere seemed quite full with just the three of them sitting there. Just how another nine personnel were going to fit in was not immediately obvious. That an additional twelve were going to occupy the after sphere stretched Kellman's credulity to the limit.

Without warning, the underwater telephone crackled into life and the order to lift off was delivered. "There they go," exclaimed Commander Tyson, his voice conveying tones of both relief and pride. "I expect they'll be away for at least two hours. Those guys have a lot of work to do."

"Let's hope it all goes smoothly," replied Todhunter. "There's not much more we can do until they return except wait." He thrust his hands deep into his pockets. "It's at times like this I can imagine how Barnes Wallace must have felt once the Dam Busters had taken off to strike Germany in World War II. Did you ever see the movie?"

"Years ago. It was an old black-and-white production, wasn't it?"

"Yes, with Michael Redgrave as the inventor of the bouncing bomb. It was a great favorite in the wardroom of HMS *Courageous* some years ago. I almost got to memorize it."

"Yeah, it's funny how movies catch on. Back in the mid-eighties there was a group in the *Boston* who watched *Flashdance* almost continuously. I couldn't work out why." Todhunter eyed his colleague quizzically. He could think of at least two very firm reasons for a repeat viewing of that movie but decided to keep his thoughts to himself. Instead he looked at his watch. It was almost twelve o'clock and the night had only just begun.

2350A, USS *Tulsa*

Although Enzo had retired to bed three hours earlier, and despite his exhaustion, he'd found it impossible to get to sleep. There were two reasons for this: he was shaking with cold and couldn't take his mind off the rescue that was now surely imminent—if the latest charge signal was to be believed. It would have to happen soon. Sparks's cofferdam was still holding, but it now had almost nine inches of water to retain. Much more and the walls would surely start to bulge. When would they give way? The lights had begun to dim, but not by much. There would still be quite a reaction if seawater got to the battery.

His bunk was already piled high with an assortment of damp blankets and resembled an igloo, with just his head protruding from the small opening at one end. A cloud of steam hung above it that appeared to grow slightly each time Enzo exhaled, which he was doing a lot more frequently than normal. He clenched his teeth again to stop them from chattering. With the prospect of being rescued now a virtual certainty, it was the perpetual, bone-chilling cold that he liked least about the present situation. Paul Trost had exercised his trunk team so frequently that he was quite certain they'd be able to receive the DSRV without a problem. He rolled over onto his left side, tucked his knees up to his chest in an attempt to get warm, and tried to concentrate on the solution to the Santana predicament. He desperately wanted to get some sleep but, more importantly, he wanted to be certain that he'd not missed anything.

The good news was that Chief Czapek had found a suicide note in the storekeeper's office. What was amazing was that it contained no reference to the game of cards. It had obviously been written by somebody who was shivering violently and, in places, it was barely legible. In it Santana had complained about the conditions in the boat and his growing despair at the failure of those topside to launch a rescue mission. He'd written quite a long passage about how he loved his wife and son and how he couldn't face the prospect of never seeing them again. It was a pitiful letter in many ways, one totally lacking in any sense of hope. The COB felt that Santana's atheism had probably played a part in his mental state. A belief in God had apparently provided so many of the crew with a source of strength. Enzo had some doubts about that theory, but couldn't refute it. So there it was; everybody was off the hook and there was no need to invent anything. The three chiefs had agreed to nullify all debts arising from the game and had sworn never to mention it to anybody. The issue was over. He'd decided not to announce Santana's death to the crew, just in case it gave anybody else a similar idea. As far as they were concerned, Chief Santana wasn't well. That was credible because just about everybody was feeling the same way. They were afflicted by increasing shortness of breath, pounding headaches, and waves of nausea. It was directly attributable to the carbon-dioxide level in the atmosphere that, with no more lithium hydroxide available, was out of control and rising inexorably. Enzo's own head was buzzing, and it was becoming very difficult to concentrate. Had he missed anything? He didn't think so. He started to shiver again.

Master Chief Steadman knocked lightly on the door. He'd been in two minds about waking Lieutenant Raschello. He'd not done so on the two previous occasions that a death had occurred at this time of night, but this time it was special. He knocked again a little more forcefully.

"Come in." The COB put his head around the door and shone his battle lantern into the dark stateroom. All he could see was the igloo.

"Sir," he began somewhat diffidently, "I need you to take a look at the captain." The igloo convulsed as Enzo rolled over.

"What's the matter, Master Chief?"

"Sir, I think he's dead." Enzo didn't reply immediately. As the news sank in, he felt as if a trapdoor had opened in the pit of his stomach, and the very core of his being had just fallen through it. It was a feeling he'd felt only once before, when his grandmother had died. Although they'd been very close, even the news of her passing away hadn't felt quite so gut-wrenching as the sensation he was experiencing right now. She'd been old and ill and had been expected to die. Richter was not. Sure, he'd not been well since the sinking, but Enzo had steadfastly refused to believe he would die.

"All right, Master Chief, I'll be right up."

With that Steadman turned, closed the stateroom door, and headed back up to the captain's stateroom. He too felt utterly dejected. He'd never really had any effective means of altering the course of his condition and, as soon as Richter had lost consciousness, he'd devoted much of his time to nursing him to the highest standard that his limited abilities and knowledge would permit. He'd changed the sheets and remade the bed using only the two driest blankets. He'd maintained a near-perfect fluid balance, washed him, turned him and massaged talc into his pressure points. It had been a labor of love. Although Steadman had not really considered his task in quite that way, as he looked at the motionless figure of the captain, he realized that was exactly the way he felt. He'd not cried since childhood and had no intention of doing so now but, for some reason, his vision had become blurred, and instinctively he wiped his eyes.

In just a few moments Enzo arrived. Having opened the door he paused at the threshold and stood staring at Richter as he tried to catch his breath. It was a few moments before he eventually stepped inside and closed the door behind him. "He's not moved, sir. I can't feel a pulse, and he doesn't seem to be breathing." Enzo slowly walked over to the captain's bunk and stared down at him. He looked peaceful. The master chief had tidied the bed, and it wouldn't have looked out of place in a hospital. Enzo felt Richter's brow. It was cool, almost cold to the touch. It was fairly clear that he wasn't breathing because there was no cloud of condensation around his nose. He reached down for Richter's wrist and felt for a pulse. His heart leapt as he thought he felt something, a slight movement beneath the skin, but it couldn't have been anything because it didn't happen again. Enzo looked Steadman in the eye and then glanced away.

"I suppose you checked his pupils?"

"Yes, sir. Not a flicker." They both knew there was nothing more to be done.

"I think we'll leave him here. I don't want the men to know. Morale's rather fragile at the moment. All it would take to set things right back is for the rescue to be delayed again or for news of this to get out. Even if the lazy bastards topside do arrive as promised, it'll be at least another day before we can get everybody out of here, so keeping morale up will be important." Enzo paused, because he was a little unsure of himself. "So we'll keep this strictly between the two of us, okay?"

"Yes, sir. What do you want me to do with the body? Shall I take down the IV and remove the catheter?" Enzo considered the matter.

"No, just secure the drip. Might as well disconnect the catheter bag as well; it'll only get in the way. It's going to be tough enough to get him up through the trunk and into the rescue vehicle as it is without that getting snagged and covering everybody below with piss." He thought for a few more moments. "You know what? I'm still determined to get him off the boat on the first run. I know it means he'll take up a lot of space and fewer fit ones will be able to go, but with the additional canisters of lithium that will arrive, we can easily survive for longer in here, despite the flooding. If the men think he's alive, they'll expect him to go with the first run, so let's not disappoint them."

"Sounds like a plan, sir."

"I'm glad you agree. While we're on the subject, I want you to be in the first group to leave. I want you debriefed as soon as possible. I think you've got as good a grasp of what's happened here as any of us."

"With all due respect, sir, I'm the COB, and my place is right here."

"Objection noted but denied, Master Chief, and I'm not going to change my mind on this one."

"Very good, sir. You're the boss." That remark had a peculiar effect on Enzo. Steadman was right—he really was the boss. The *Tulsa* was now indisputably his command.

CHAPTER
9

Friday, 5 November

0045A, DSRV

Finding the *Tulsa* had not been difficult, and maneuvering to mate with the forward escape hatch had gone smoothly. "Nice piece of driving, Petty Officer Avila," remarked Lieutenant Commander Sheridan.

"Thank you, sir. After all the practice we've had, it was a piece of cake." The high-pitched whirring of a pump stopped abruptly, and Sheridan studied the dials in front of him. The conduit linking the center sphere and the superstructure around the *Tulsa*'s escape trunk hatch should now be free of water. If the pressure in the skirt was holding steady, any leak was going to be small.

"Skirt dewatered. Looks like we have a tight seal." He looked over his shoulder. "Okay, let's open the hatch and take a look." In seconds Petty Officer Loeffler had opened the hatch and the three men in the center sphere were peering down at the wet, black fairing that covered the *Tulsa*'s forward escape hatch. A fine jet of water was squirting horizontally from a small blemish on the submarine's mating ring, but it was insufficient to cause a problem.

"Looks good, sirs," announced Loeffler. "I'd better let them know that the cavalry has arrived." He grabbed a large wrench and lowered himself through the hatch and onto the hull of the submarine. "This is going to sound like music to those poor bastards' ears," he continued as he raised his hand and struck the fairing eight times.

0100A, USS *Tulsa*

Enzo had been trying to fight the urge to supervise the proceedings in the trunk access compartment because he had delegated the task of receiving the DSRV to Paul Trost. He'd always resented the unnecessary interference of senior officers in his responsibilities and was not about to upset Paul by doing the same thing—no matter how great the temptation was to do so. He would wait until the hatch was open and then introduce himself to his visitors. It wasn't going to be easy, but that was his decision. He had also decided that further trips down to Sparks's cofferdam would not be productive. It was performing brilliantly, keeping well over a foot of water away from the battery compartment, and Sparks would surely tell him as soon as it failed. Further comments about the battery would also be unnecessary. Sparks had done all he could to discharge it and the dull glimmer that now issued from the emergency lights was testament to his success. Enzo managed to stifle a shiver and returned his attention to the rescue instructions in a slender volume of the Ship Systems Manual that was open on his desk. He had lost count of the number of times that he'd read it over the past two days, but something was nagging at the back of his mind. He was certain that he'd overlooked something and was irritated that he couldn't see what it was.

The trouble was that he was finding it increasingly difficult to concentrate. The unremitting cold was sapping his energy, and the rising carbon-dioxide level in the atmosphere didn't help him think. He'd felt thickheaded for well over twenty-four hours and just couldn't seem to shake it off. The persistent headache and shortness of breath only made matters worse. He tried to stifle another shiver, but failed. His teeth began to chatter. The situation reminded him of the account he'd read as a child of Captain Robert Scott's last days. He and his colleagues had died of hypothermia in a tent in the Antarctic, having been beaten to the South Pole by the Norwegian explorer Amundsen. OK, he conceded to himself, so it wasn't quite as cold as that in the boat and, unlike Scott, at least he now had a realistic chance of being rescued. Perhaps the situations were not comparable after all, Enzo thought as he wrapped his ski jacket tightly around his shoulders. Why had he even thought of it? He gave himself a mental kick and tried once again to focus on the page in front of him. What was he missing?

Chief Czapek heard the tap signal at the same time as the others who were gathered around the ladder leading up to the escape trunk. His drawn expression changed instantly to a broad grin, exposing his immaculate teeth. "Hey, the triple A have made it!" The silence that had engulfed them all for so many days, which had been broken only by the incessant bleating of the sonar distress pinger and sporadic conversation, had been replaced by the bumps and thumps of the DSRV as it had settled onto the mating ring, and now the clanging on the hull. There were whoops of sheer joy from the small group gathered to receive their visitors. Lieutenant Trost waited while they blew off steam for a moment before raising his hand to silence them.

"Okay, guys. It's our turn now." He glanced down at the limp, dog-eared piece of paper he was clutching, on which were the detailed notes he'd made of the rescue procedure that they'd practiced until they were all utterly bored with them. "As soon as the DSRV gives us the go-ahead, we'll open the lower trunk hatch," he continued. The whooping died away, and Chief Czapek spoke again.

"Excuse me, sir, how are they going to do that?" Lieutenant Trost looked up from his notes.

"What do you mean?"

"How will they tell us to open the lower hatch?"

"Tap signals, I expect. They could shout as loud as they like up there and we wouldn't hear them."

"But . . . ." An awful realization gradually began to dawn on Paul Trost.

"How on earth did we miss that? There's no special tap signal for this. . . . Wait a moment, I'll see what Lieutenant Raschello has to say about it." He turned and made his way forward to Enzo's stateroom and knocked. He was angry with himself. With all the rehearsing they'd done over the past two days, why hadn't he noticed that there was a problem? Why had nobody done so? Why had Chief Czapek waited until now to point it out?

"Come in." Enzo looked up from the manual. "What's up, Paul?"

"You know all those codes we sent up with that smoke on Wednesday?" he gasped.

"Yes, is there a problem?"

"Well," Trost swallowed and waited a moment while he caught his breath, "we didn't include any tap signals for the rescue."

"They're in the manual, there wasn't any need to."

"Well, we're waiting for the go-ahead to open the lower hatch," Paul paused as he fought to control his heaving chest, "and I've no idea how they'll do that. There's no code." A horrible realization hit Enzo like a speeding truck. That's what was missing, he thought. He was furious.

"God damn it!" he exploded, and thumped the desk with his clenched fist. "Damn, damn, *damn*!" He punched the desk with each utterance and the effort left him breathless. "I knew there was something missing in these instructions, and that was it!" Enzo paused and tried to calm down. "What are the options, Paul?"

"The only thing that's occurred to me is to use Morse code. But it'll slow things down a bit, it can't be accused of being an efficient communications system."

"Do you know Morse code?"

"Hell no. I know SOS is dot-dot-dot, dash-dash-dash, dot-dot-dot."

"Whoopee! That's going to make interpreting 'open the lower hatch' a real breeze," replied Enzo sarcastically as he shook his hand again and clenched and unclenched his fist. "I'm sorry, Paul, it's not your fault. Look, one of the ETs should know it. If not, it must be in one of the comms manuals. Go back to the trunk and make sure that somebody writes down any taps they hear. I'll see if Chief Baxter knows Morse. You never know, when he trained they may have still used it for real."

0130A, DSRV

Things were no easier in the DSRV. The absence of any reply to the eight taps had them all thinking. Petty Officer Avila looked up from yet another manual that he'd studied. "If you read this, they're not expected to reply with eight taps until they drain the hatch cavity. And they're not meant to do that until we've told them it's OK to open the lower hatch. How do we do that?"

"I don't know. How come this problem hasn't been spotted before?" asked Lieutenant Commander Sheridan of nobody in particular.

"Well, we've always used an underwater telephone in exercises."

"Hell and damnation! I guess we'll have to use Morse. Even if they could hear our transmission on UWT, we could never pick up their reply." Sheridan swiveled round in his seat and addressed the occupants of the center sphere. "Anybody know Morse code?" There was silence.

"We can still speak to the *Vindictive*, why not ask them?" suggested Avila.

"Could do, but transmitting the whole code would take forever. Come to think of it, so would returning to pick up a hard copy." Frustrated by the delay, Petty Officer Loeffler had climbed back into the center sphere.

"Why don't we just go ahead and break in? The worst we can do is empty the contents of the hatch cavity into the trunk. Anyone standing underneath it will get a cold shower, but that's about all."

"I'll vote for that," announced Commander Samways.

"Me too," added Lieutenant Commander Kellman.

"I'm just concerned that the guys in the *Tulsa* won't do anything stupid, like pressurize the trunk just because they've got no idea what's going on," said Sheridan. "Opening the hatch of a pressurized trunk wouldn't be a good idea. It would crush Petty Officer Loeffler, blow us off, and sink us. At the very least, the pressure would wreck our instruments."

"Wouldn't do us much good either," replied Samways. "I hadn't thought of that possibility."

"They wouldn't do anything dumb like that. No submariner would." The certainty in Loeffler's voice concealed a sudden doubt in his mind that had been sowed by the prospect, albeit a remote one, of being crushed by more than a thousand pounds of fast-moving hatch.

"I wouldn't be so certain," replied Kellman. "They'll be cold down there and high as kites on carbon dioxide. Conditions like that can play havoc with even the smartest brain. There's no telling what they might do." Nobody had anything else to say.

It was a while before Lieutenant Commander Sheridan broke the silence. "OK, I'm going to call up the *Vindictive* and see what they have to say. Let's hope we can find an answer to this before the problem becomes moot. The *Tulsa* needs our cargo right away."

0145A, HMS *Vindictive*

Commander Todhunter listened to his American colleague and couldn't believe his ears. It seemed incredible that the DSRV had been in use for more that twenty years and the basic tap codes had apparently not been completely worked out. His mind drifted back to his thoughts about exercise artificiality—what a perfect example. However, this was no time to gloat. The situation in the *Tulsa* would be bordering on dire, and a solution had to be found more or less immediately. "Look," he began, "given the weather and poor reception conditions, transmitting the whole of the Morse code via UWT would take an age, especially since the DSRV will have to repeat each letter back to avoid mistakes. So that really isn't an option. Then again, do they really need the whole code? Which message is missing from the tap codes?"

"Something like OPEN THE LOWER HATCH," replied Commander Tyson. "Once that's open, the rest of the tap codes should be sufficient."

"Well, that more than halves the problem. They only need twelve letters to send that."

"Are you prepared to maneuver closer to the *Tulsa*? It might improve UWT conditions." Todhunter didn't want to get any closer. If anything went wrong, there would be no time to correct it before possibly hitting the DISSUB or, even worse, unseating the DSRV. It was too risky.

"Not unless I absolutely have to." Both men were deep in thought. The DSRV was capable of remaining on task for five hours before the battery would need a recharge. It had already been away for nearly two of them, and they still had to dismantle the upper hatch fairing—four pieces of steel weighing almost 250 pounds in total. If the bolts that secured them were either rusted or painted into place, removing them could easily take another two hours. There would be very little time to unload the atmosphere-control stores, take on board a group of survivors, and get back to the *Vindictive*. A solution was required right away. "You know, I can't believe that they'd pressurize the trunk if the DSRV crew started to break in. What would it achieve?"

"Good point," replied Tyson. "Also, they would hear the trunk being pressurized in the DSRV, and that would alert them."

"Hmm. Of course they may already have done so. I can't think why, but it is a possibility. Can you sample the air in the trunk?"

"Sure."

"Well, that's the answer then," announced Todhunter triumphantly. "Get them to sample the air first. If the pressure isn't raised, they can break in safely."

"You're right, I'll tell them to go ahead and remove the fairing. Let's hope the survivors just ignore what's going on and go back to sleep."

0200A, USS *Tulsa*

Lieutenant Trost looked at his watch. The wait for another tap signal had already seemed interminable. This was an absolutely frustrating situation, he thought. "I'm sorry, guys, we'll just have to wait. I don't want to do anything to confuse the situation." He stamped his feet in an attempt to coax some warmth and feeling back into them, but without success. All of a sudden, there was some scraping followed by a fresh series of taps. Chief Czapek started to jot down what he heard. It must be a long message, thought Trost, as the banging continued before it stopped just as suddenly as it had begun. Chief Czapek handed over the piece of paper he'd been writing on to the young officer.

"It doesn't make much sense to me, sir."

"I thought you said you didn't know Morse code, Chief."

"I don't, sir. It's just that they don't seem to have broken the message up into letters."

"Well, just give me a few moments to look at this." Trost squatted on his haunches to avoid soaking his pants on the wet deck and studied the code in front of him. The chief was right. The first entry was what Czapek had interpreted as a series of nine dots followed by a dash. Trost looked at the Morse code he was holding in his other hand and wondered what it could possibly mean. It could be the number 54, he thought, but that didn't mean anything—at least, not in this context. He scanned down the list of letters. It had to be some combination of E, H, I, and S, he thought, and end with either a T, U, or V because each of them finished with a single dash. The only word he could make out of it was SHIT. How appropriate, he thought, as he went on to look at the next sequence that contained a few more dashes. He looked up briefly as another series of blows was being delivered to the fairing and then struggled to write them down. God this was difficult, he thought. All the taps sounded alike. How was he supposed to tell the difference between a dot and a dash?

The tapping stopped again, and Chief Czapek studied the face of the young officer as his brow became more furrowed with puzzlement and he scratched at his sodden hair. "Sir, I don't think these are tap signals."

"What . . . ? Wait a moment, Chief, there's another word here—SHIT BEST. What the hell does that mean?"

"It doesn't mean anything, sir. I think they've decided to go ahead and remove the fairing. They're coming to get us." Paul thought for a moment. He might be right. If he was, what should he do? Should he open the lower hatch and drain the hatch cavity? "I think it would probably be best if we just stay put and let them get on with it. Sure we could speed the process up, but we could also cause a disaster."

"I think you're right, Chief. I'll just let Lieutenant Raschello know what is going on."

0300A, DSRV

Petty Officer Loeffler was breathless from the effort of trying to break into the *Tulsa*. His coveralls were sodden with sweat, and he was close to exhaustion. He'd managed to remove just two pieces of the hatch fairing, but the bolts securing the other two stubbornly refused to budge. There were obviously just too many layers of paint covering the thread. He climbed back into the DSRV and opened his coveralls in an effort to cool down. "I'm sorry, sirs, I'm just going to have to take a breather for a few minutes."

"You're doing a great job," replied Kellman. "Would you mind if I had a go?"

"Help yourself, sir."

"Right. Time is marching on, and we really can't afford to waste any." With that he advanced to the lip of the hatch and eased himself down into the skirt, applied a wrench to the nearest stubborn bolt, and delivered a series of blows to the other end of it with the two-pound lump hammer that Loeffler had been using. The fifth blow was the telling one. "F . . . f . . . fuck!" erupted Kellman as he dropped the hammer and wrench and started to shake his left hand up and down. "Jesus, that hurt." He stopped shaking his hand and inspected it carefully. The hammer had landed squarely on the thumb which was already turning a slightly bluish tinge and had started to swell. "I hope I haven't broken the darned thing," he continued, and started to shake it again.

"Sir, I think you'd better leave that to me," observed Loeffler somewhat reluctantly as he realized that his much-needed rest would have to be curtailed. "I'll take it from here." Kellman and Loeffler swapped

places, and the rhythmical clanging of hammer on
wrench resumed.

0345A, USS *Tulsa*

Pat Kellman tried to hold his breath as he descended into the boat, to stop himself from gagging.
The smell in the *Tulsa* was utterly repulsive. It wasn't
too tough to work out why. The acrid quality to the
stench obviously had its origins in a fire. On top of
that, about a hundred men had been trying to survive
in the place for well over a week with no opportunity
to shower. They'd been unable to flush the heads, the
burners hadn't been operating to remove contaminant
gases from the atmosphere, and thirty-three bodies
were slowly decomposing somewhere in the compartment. Somewhat to his surprise, the crew was apparently oblivious to the fetid odor. He exhaled, took a
deep breath through his mouth, and tried to hold his
breath again until he'd reached the bottom of the ladder. It was a pointless effort. The high carbon-dioxide
level forced him to take another breath right away,
and then another. In moments he was puffing away as
if he'd just run half a mile.

The scene that greeted him was like nothing he had
ever seen before. Everybody in the reception committee sported a beard, although they varied in terms of
color and completeness. The array of different outfits
the men were wearing was extraordinary. All but one
had improvised some kind of warm headgear, and
most had wrapped themselves in many layers of
clothes. Two of them looked a bit like Viking warriors,
wearing an outer layer of blankets that had been fash-
ioned into a long cloak. All their ensembles lacked
for authenticity was a sword and a horned helmet. The
atmosphere was cold yet steamy, being thick with the
water vapor that the crew blew out with each of their
rapid breaths. That gave the trunk access compartment
an almost claustrophobic feel as it severely limited the

visibility and caused each of the battle lanterns and dim emergency lights to be surrounded by a multicolored halo of refracted light. Condensation ran down the bulkheads and dripped continuously from the overhead. The men were all smiling. As Kellman advanced a couple of steps to allow his colleague room to leave the ladder, Enzo pushed his way through the crowd and grasped Kellman by the hand. "Dr. Livingstone, I presume?" he announced, grinning like a Cheshire cat.

"Pat Kellman, actually," he replied and turned to look over his shoulder, "and this is Commander Samways. You must be Lieutenant Raschello."

"I am, and I can't tell you what a joy it is to see you guys. Is anybody else with you?"

"Yes," gasped Kellman. "Petty Officer Loeffler will give you a hand unloading the stores we're carrying. We need to get the scrubbers we've brought with us up and running right away."

"We'll talk about that in a moment. This is Lieutenant Trost." Enzo glanced at Paul. "He'll arrange for the stores to be unloaded. Come along to the wardroom and we can discuss what happens next. Come to think of it, we'll use my stateroom." Enzo spun on his heel and led his visitors forward and into his stateroom. "Sorry about the mess, I haven't had a chance to do much housework recently."

"Don't worry about that," replied Samways, hungry for air. "I'd have been more surprised if you had." The three of them squeezed into the stateroom, and Kellman shut the door. Enzo waited a moment to catch his breath.

"Perhaps I should start by explaining what I want to happen. I'm sorry to report that the captain died a few hours ago, but the crew doesn't know about it. They just think he's sick. As you might imagine, morale has been somewhat volatile with all the delays over the past few days, and I don't want to upset everybody. So I want him taken off first."

"Wait a minute," replied Samways. "We're short of

time and are going to take as many of the fit ones as
we can carry on the first run. The wounded will go
next and the fatalities will—"

"I don't think you understand me," interrupted
Enzo sharply. "I'm not going to debate this. The first
person to leave the *Tulsa* will be the captain. Do I
make myself clear?"

"You've made yourself perfectly clear, but that's
not the game plan. There are good reasons for getting
the fit ones out first. The DSRV can carry a total of
twenty-three ambulatory survivors, plus the crewman.
If we have to take a stretcher that will reduce the
total to about fourteen. It makes obvious sense to get
as many men out as soon as possible. Apart from anything else, the fewer that remain in the boat, the easier
it will be to manage the atmosphere." Enzo was reaching the end of his fuse. These officers were senior to
him, but this was his ship. He was not in a mood
to argue.

"You obviously don't understand me. Either Commander Richter leaves on the first run or none of us
does. You can just turn around and go back empty-
handed. That's my final word on the matter."

Samways was baffled. Lieutenant Raschello looked
exhausted. He had obviously been under considerable
stress for the past week. Was he cracking up? His
response to a perfectly rational argument had been
less than cogent. What on earth was he to do? His
own head was beginning to thump with pain, and he
was unable to control his gasping for air. Perhaps it
was hardly surprising that Raschello wasn't thinking
too clearly. He'd try another tack. "There's one other
thing to consider. We've only got a very short time to
load the DSRV. Its batteries are low and need charging. Trying to maneuver a stretcher down to the second level and then up through the trunk and into one
of the spheres will just be a waste of valuable time."
Enzo didn't reply. He just stood his ground staring
back directly into Commander Samways's face. His

expression was one of grim determination. "Fair
enough, these are your men," Samways continued.
"You'll have to explain to the crew why more of them
can't leave on the first run."

"I won't have to. They're expecting the captain to
leave first. As soon as he's in the DSRV, I would like
your opinion on the wounded. Master Chief Steadman
will brief you on their condition. After that I'll get
Lieutenant Schwartz to go over the atmosphere-
control logs with you. I assume you'll be staying to
help us out?"

"That's the plan, if you'll have us."

"Good. I think we're going to have a problem with
the atmosphere. Have you brought some hoppers
with you?"

"Sure have, and we'll be able to tap straight into
the ship's main battery. We've brought some inverters
with us."

"Great. The problem is that, as you can see from
the lights, there's not a lot of juice left in it anyway."

"You never mentioned that in any of your messages," replied Samways in exasperated tones.

"I told you about the flooding, can't you see what
we've had to do?" Without waiting for a response
Enzo continued. "The battery compartment could be
flooded any moment now and that'll kill it anyway.
We've discharged it as far and as fast as we can so
that it won't generate chlorine when that happens and
kill us in the process."

"But if we can't scrub the atmosphere we're stuffed
anyway. We must be really close to the limit as it is."

"Right, so we'd better get a move on. Now, if you'll
excuse me, I need to brief the master chief before
he leaves."

0410A, HMS *Vindictive*

Commander Tyson glanced anxiously at his watch
again. The DSRV was on the return run but was hav-

ing to head into the current. Would the batteries hold out? All he could do was pray. The silence in the control room was broken by the crackle of the UWT. Lieutenant Commander Sheridan and the first batch of survivors were at the hover, forty feet above the after escape hatch and were ready to commence the mating sequence. "Look," said Todhunter, "you handle this. Just let me know when you're ready to open any hatches and shout if you need anything from me."

"Thank you, Captain. Let's reel it in."

The American contingent went through the routine of recovering the DSRV with slick professionalism. The pylons were made ready, and, using the vertical thrusters, the little submarine sank onto them. The shock-mitigation ring cushioned the contact with the *Vindictive* and then the pylon latches were activated. With the skirt once again dewatered, they were ready to open the hatches and receive the first survivors. It was Schwartz who was first down the ladder. Commanders Todhunter and Tyson had formed a reception party at the bottom of the ladder.

"Welcome aboard." Todhunter took a step forward and extended his hand as Schwartz reached the deck and turned to greet his hosts.

"Thank you, sir. I can't tell you how pleased I am to be here." Commander Tyson was next to shake his hand and couldn't help wrinkling his nose at the repulsive stench that emanated from his compatriot.

"I expect you'll be looking forward to a shower and a change of clothes," he remarked as he surveyed Schwartz's less than regulation ensemble. "You'll be pleased to know that we've brought some fresh clothing with us."

"There'll be quite a line for the showers. None of us have so much as looked at a piece of soap for the past eight days. I expect you can tell, sir."

"I had noticed."

"Sir, there are a couple of rather urgent matters that I need to discuss with you before I wash up. Is there somewhere we can do that?" Schwartz inquired.

"Sure, we'll go forward to my stateroom—sorry, cabin." Tyson eyed Todhunter and smiled. "Must get the terminology right, mustn't I? When in Rome . . ."

0420A, USS *Tulsa*

With the DSRV well clear of the boat, Enzo decided it was time to visit the wardroom and hear what the visitors made of the condition of the injured. The COB was in deep conversation with the two doctors. "Master Chief, I thought you were leaving on the first run."

"That was the plan, sir, but I also had to brief the doctors. There wasn't time to do both."

"You had absolutely no intention of leaving the boat, did you?" Enzo tried to resist the urge to smile and failed.

"I had every intention to do so, sir," he lied. Enzo was pleased to see that his mood had obviously improved, and the twinkle had returned to his eye. In the corner of the crowded room one of the new hoppers was laboring away. Even with so little power available, it had made a noticeable difference to the atmosphere. It even felt a little warmer. The five canisters of lithium hydroxide were reacting vigorously with the carbon dioxide that was being drawn through them and were kicking out a good deal of heat. Enzo noticed that his breathing was almost normal again and, for the first time in days, his headache was tolerable.

"What's the story here, Doctors?" Commander Samways looked up from a chart and replied.

"I think you and your men have done an incredible job given the circumstances. There's nobody on the critical list. However, I would like to get Lieutenant Gallagher into surgery as soon as possible. He should leave on the next run, as should ET1 Toynbee. Unless Gallagher has his zygoma elevated soon, he could face permanent paralysis in his face. It looks like Toynbee's burns are infected, and they need to be cleaned up. Otherwise, from what I've heard so far, the stretcher cases can all wait until the ambulatory survivors are out of here."

"Okay. As I said before, I am quite happy for you to determine the pecking order now. Just remember that I won't leave until the last run."

"That's your call, Lieutenant—or should I call you captain?"

"I don't know, and I don't really care. My name is Enzo."

"Enzo's fine by me."

Raschello turned toward the COB again. "If you've not left on the first run, who has?"

"Lieutenant Schwartz went, sir. I passed on your message, and he left the atmosphere-control logs here with me."

"Fair enough. I'm going to see if Lieutenant Trost has arranged some tap signals with the DSRV crew. I want the next run to go smoothly. If we get it right, we might be able to get two in before the next battery recharge."

0430A, HMS *Vindictive*

Commander Todhunter looked concerned as a group of officers took their seats at the wardroom table. "I've asked you to this meeting because the situation in the *Tulsa* is rather worse than we imagined. Lieutenant Schwartz, would you like to outline the problem?"

"Thank you, sir. The main problem is the flooding. It's only a matter of time before the battery compartment is compromised, and that will mean that there's no power to scrub the atmosphere. When I left, the carbon-dioxide level was nudging 6 percent and I can tell you, it wasn't pleasant."

"They can always go on to EABs," suggested Commander Tyson. "That would buy them some time."

"Yes, sir, it would," remarked Surgeon Lieutenant Ferguson, "but we have to consider the pressure. What was it when you left?" Ferguson asked Schwartz.

"It's already twenty feet of seawater and rising at something like four feet per day."

"Hell, what's that in sensible units?" muttered Ferguson as he pulled a piece of paper out of his back pocket and jotted down some numbers. "I make that 1.6 atmospheres and even without EABs, it'll be 1.7 by this evening. Much more than that and we'll start to bend the survivors unless we're careful."

"Bend them? What on earth do you mean?" inquired Commander Tyson.

"They'll get decompression illness, sir—the bends."

"Oh."

"That'll mean that we'll certainly have to put them into a chamber. Let's put it this way—it's going to make the logistics of the rescue a whole lot more awkward."

"OK, thanks, Doc," remarked Todhunter appreciatively. "The bottom line is that we're going to have to turn around the DSRV a whole lot quicker than we planned. I'm no expert in this—any suggestions?" It was Commander Tyson who responded.

"Well, at a push, we can cut back the battery recharges to three hours. There's one more thing we can do. There's a current down there, isn't there, Mike?"

"Yes, sir, there is," replied Lieutenant Commander Sheridan. "Over the *Tulsa* it's just about a knot, I reckon."

"Now this is going to take some doing, but I'd like to suggest that we launch the DSRV upstream of the *Tulsa* and recover it downstream. There are two advantages as I see it, it'll save time, the DSRV will be able to transit at close to five knots in both directions, and it'll reduce the load on its battery."

"I think we can do that," replied Todhunter in as reserved a tone as he could manage. "Let's say we do all this—how long's the rescue going to take?" Commander Tyson exchanged whispers with Lieutenant Commander Sheridan as he started to jot down numbers on a piece of paper.

"It's nearly five now. At a push we could have them all out by fifteen hundred."

"Right, let's go and do it." Commander Todhunter rose from the table, and the others followed.

Harvey Schwartz looked around and called out to Surgeon Lieutenant Ferguson as he was about to leave the room.

"Doctor, can I have a word with you?"

"Sure, what can I do for you?"

"I know he's dead, but have you taken a look at the captain yet?"

"No, I'm just going to. Would you like to come with me? You can tell me what happened."

"Okay." The two of them left the wardroom and headed for the sick bay.

Commander Richter was lying on the examination couch in the sick bay. Ferguson had searched unsuccessfully for a pulse and was now examining the eyes. His left hand was resting on Richter's forehead. It felt cold to the touch. Both pupils were dilated, but was there a suggestion of a reflex? He turned to Schwartz. "When did he die?"

"I believe it was about eleven o'clock last night."

"You mean," Ferguson looked at his watch, "six hours ago?"

"That's right."

The medical officer turned to his assistant. "Petty Officer Clifford, can you find our low-reading thermometer?"

"I'll have a look for it, sir." Ferguson's mind was racing. It was just possible that his patient was profoundly hypothermic rather than dead. Apart from how the head injury had happened, Harvey had only been able to provide a very sketchy idea of what had been wrong with him before he'd lost consciousness. The laceration to the left side of his head was obvious enough—he had clearly hit it hard against something. If he'd sustained a subdural hemorrhage, that would account for the apparently progressive nature of his condition. An arterial bleed would have been more rapidly fatal.

POMA Clifford returned from the medical store with the low-reading thermometer, and they rolled Richter over onto his side and introduced it into his anus. "We'll give it a minute or two," said Ferguson more to break the silence than for any other reason. This was not a procedure he practiced with any regularity. While he was waiting he noticed that no spigot had been placed in the end of the urinary catheter and there was a sizable wet patch on the blanket underneath him. This looks promising, he thought. Dead men don't urinate. The wait was over, and the three of them stared at the thermometer. "I think he's probably alive," announced Ferguson. "His core temperature is 25 degrees Celsius. Given the temperature in the *Tulsa* and the fact that he will have been cold for some days, it wouldn't be that high now if he was dead."

"That's absolutely incredible!" exclaimed Schwartz. "I'll get the DSRV crew to relay that to the boat. What fantastic news!"

"Hold on a minute," said Ferguson. "This is one very sick man. I really don't rate his survival chances very highly at all. I'd hold off with any news until we can get him over to the *Centaur* and they've taken a look at him there." Ferguson paused. "I just hope getting him to the *Centaur* isn't going to be too tough. The weather's been pretty damned awful up to now.

Have you ever tried a helo transfer from a submarine in rough weather, Harvey?"

"Can't say I have."

"Well, trust me. You don't want to."

0100R, Cherry Hill, New Jersey

Marie had woken up some minutes earlier and now sat, bleary-eyed, in front of the television in her bedroom. Quite why she had woken so soon was a mystery to her. It must have something to do with the rescue, she rationalized. She had just sat through three ads for different antacids and was wondering if the nation really was in the grip of a heartburn epidemic. She was at the point of deciding to go back to bed when the news anchor returned. "We've just learned that the first survivors from the USS *Tulsa* have been transferred to the British submarine *Vindictive* by the DSRV. Our defense correspondent, Robert Cross, is on board the HMS *Centaur* . . . Robert?"

"Thank you Sam. I'm here on the flight deck of HMS *Centaur*, a British helicopter carrier. She is the command ship for Operation Deep Hope here in the Norwegian Sea. With me is the commanding officer, Captain 'Bull' Temple." The camera zoomed out to show the two men side by side. The captain was dressed in a dark blue sweater with four gold stripes on each shoulder. He was also wearing a dark blue beret and was squinting slightly into the camera lights that were positioned to augment the natural tones of the early dawn. A slight breeze ruffled the correspondent's wispy, brown hair. "Captain, can you tell me what's happening at the moment?" The reply was delivered in a clipped, public-school accent.

"Yes. The situation is that the rescue vehicle has just completed its first run. It went very smoothly, and the DSRV is now recharging its batteries before going back to the *Tulsa*. Fifteen survivors were transferred to the *Vindictive* and I expect they're taking showers and getting ready for a hearty breakfast."

"Is there any news of the condition of the survivors?"

"Not much at the moment. I understand that one of them is unwell, but I've no more details at this time."

"What about the other fourteen?"

"As I understand the situation, they are all just fine."

"Captain, can you tell me what is going to happen next?"

"Well, the DSRV's batteries will take several hours to recharge. So not much more will be happening for a while."

"What about the injured man? Will he receive treatment in the *Vindictive*?

"Yes, the *Vindictive* carries a doctor, so he'll be managed there initially."

"Thank you, Captain." The camera zoomed back to the correspondent. "That's all I have for you at the moment, Sam." The producer cut back to the studio, where the anchor had turned to look at a screen displaying an image of the correspondent. Captain Temple was now out of the shot.

"Robert, the captain has just told us that the first run of the DSRV went smoothly. Has he provided any explanation for the delays? I think we were all expecting it to be completed sooner than this."

"Sam, I've received no explanation for the delays. I understand that communication with the *Vindictive* has been difficult at times. That may be the reason."

"Thank you Robert, we'll be right back to you if there are further developments." He swung around and faced the camera. "In his address to the nation on the *Tulsa* rescue this evening, the president repeated his assurance that everything possible was being done to ensure that the entire crew of the disabled submarine would be recovered. . . ."

Marie had seen the broadcast live and had no wish

to see it again. She'd grown weary of the sanctimonious crap that characterized so many public utterances on the *Tulsa* by government officials and politicians alike. It was late, and it looked like there was going to be no more real news for a few hours. She would try to get some more sleep. She picked up the bottle of pills and read the label. It advised her to take one before retiring. She felt like swallowing the lot, but settled for one more. No more nightmares, please God, she thought before she downed it.

0700A, HMS *Vindictive*

Commander Todhunter stood on the bridge and eyed the horizon. The sky had cleared to reveal a myriad of stars, and the weather had improved considerably. Sunrise wouldn't be for another couple of hours, but to the south there was the first glimmer of twilight. It was clear that the sea had lost much of its savagery overnight. The wind had died down to a gentle Force 3 and was struggling to add anything to the swell that formed the only remaining evidence of the recent storm.

He turned to look aft at his diminutive passenger sitting astride the after logistic escape tower on its white pylons, rapidly charging its batteries before returning to the *Tulsa*. Todhunter checked his watch. As soon as this evolution was complete he'd have to dive and get ready for the second run. In the meantime it was one of the DSRV's recent passengers that concerned him. He'd waited until now to surface and transfer Commander Richter to allow the weather to abate as much as possible. He couldn't wait any longer because he didn't want to delay the next DSRV sortie. For the first time on this cursed mission, it looked like the weather wasn't going to screw up his plans. He returned his gaze to the bow of his enormous submarine. With just enough headway to maintain his circular course around the datum, the bow wave was well clear of the forward hatch that would be used to bring Richter out onto the superstructure, and he concluded that it would be safe to attempt a helicopter transfer. He lifted a microphone toward his mouth and depressed a button on its side. "What's the ETA of the *Centaur's* helo?"

"Wait one, sir," came the reply via a speaker to his left, followed by a pause. "Should be here in one-five minutes, sir."

"Roger. Alert the sick bay. They need to get their patient onto the casing—use the forward LET."

"Aye, aye, sir."

Surgeon Lieutenant Ferguson and the POMA had been working feverishly to prepare Richter for the brief flight. They had wrapped him in several blankets, the outer of which was a shiny, metallic space blanket that was intended more to keep out the wind than reflect what little body heat Richter was likely to radiate. Next, they had placed him in a Neil-Robertson stretcher. Although of antiquated design, being made of little more than bamboo and canvas, it was by far the easiest means of maneuvering a body around the cramped confines of the submarine and up through the LET. They would simply place the stretcher into whatever container the helicopter lowered to receive the casualty and strap him into place. They were ready to move.

The speaker to Todhunter's left crackled into life again. "From *Centaur*, sir, the helo's on its way."

"Roger." He peered over to the eastern horizon again. He could see the lights and shadowy outline of the flat-top three miles away on his port bow. A flashing light rose almost silently from her deck, then turned and headed toward him. The noise from its blades started as the dullest thudding and gradually grew into a distinctive clatter, accompanied by screaming engines. The hatch of the forward LET had opened, and a group of sailors in white jerseys, amber life vests, and blue pants emerged. Among them was Sur-

geon Lieutenant Ferguson, who had chosen to wear
full foul-weather gear and a beret. The helicopter
slowed to hover just above and in front of Todhunter.
He clasped his hands to his ears in an attempt to dull
the deafening noise emanating from the Sea King and
to protect them from the freezing downwash from the
massive rotor. Slowly the helicopter swung round to
a westward heading so that its starboard cabin door
was facing him and was directly over the party below
on the fo'c'sle. An orange-suited airman and cradle
were lowered, and in no time Richter was secured and
winched up into the aircraft. Todhunter watched the
helicopter crew swarm around him near the cabin
door. Moments later, a single strop was lowered, and
Surgeon Lieutenant Ferguson was on his way up to
join his patient. There was a wave from the navigator,
then the helicopter dipped its nose and clattered away
toward the *Centaur*. Thank God, thought Todhunter. If
only all helicopter transfers went so smoothly.

0710A, USS *Tulsa*

There was a sharp series of knocks at the wardroom
door, and Enzo got up to answer it. Sparks stood in
the dark passageway with an anxious look on his face.
He was shaking with cold and his chest was heaving.
"Sir, the cofferdam's broken," he gasped. "It collapsed just a minute ago. There's nearly three feet of
water in the lower level now." Enzo looked up at the
emergency lights in the passageway—he could barely
see them. The hopper in the wardroom had stopped
working half an hour ago.
"With any luck, it won't matter, Sparks. It did a
fantastic job, and I think you've bought us the time
we needed." As he was speaking the dull, amber glow
in the emergency lights suddenly disappeared and only
the shaft of light from the open wardroom door lit the
passageway. Enzo turned, disappeared into the wardroom, and reappeared holding a flashlight. "Here, take

this and go back down to the lower level. Don't get too wet, but come back and tell me if you smell chlorine. If anything's going to happen, it should do so in the next half hour."

"Aye, aye, sir."

"And Sparks."

"Yes, sir?"

"Be sure you're on the next DSRV run. I want you to have a nice hot shower. There'll be nothing more for you to do by the time it arrives." Sparks's face was creased by a broad grin.

"Yes, sir!"

1000A, HMS *Centaur*

Ferguson patted Sheppard on the shoulder to indicate that they should leave the operating room. "Look, David, I hadn't planned to stay this long," he started as they entered the recovery room and removed their masks. "I need to get back to the *Vindictive*. She'll be surfacing very shortly."

"Well, I am glad you could stay for as long as you have. That man owes his life to you, Donald. You realize that, don't you?"

"What do you mean? I believe the lieutenant and master chief in the *Tulsa* have a better claim to that honor than me."

"Sure, they did a great job with what was available to them, but you spotted that he was hypothermic rather than just accepting he was dead. I don't know many of us who would have been so thorough."

"Well, that's very kind of you. I don't really know what to say—except that he still has a rocky road ahead of him."

"You're right. Just because they've managed to evacuate all that blood from his head doesn't mean he'll live or even be able to thank you. He's still damned cold, and I expect it will be some days before they'll establish if there's likely to be any permanent brain damage." Ferguson was looking a little embarrassed and was clearly keen to get moving. Sheppard changed the subject. "I won't hold you up, old buddy. I'll keep you posted on how Commander Richter does. If you get a moment, why not come over again tomorrow? I have a feeling the man will be transformed."

"Okay. But only if the weather's like this. I don't feel up to a swim in the Arctic Ocean."

"Pussy!"

"You say the nicest things, David."

0700R, Cherry Hill, New Jersey

Marie woke somewhat reluctantly. The tablets she'd swallowed had worked rather too well and she felt thickheaded, but at least she had endured no nightmare. It took a few moments for her to gather her wits. She glanced at the clock on the nightstand beside her and realized that there might now be more news of the *Tulsa* rescue. In moments the TV was on and she was watching the same channel as the night before. Robert Cross was reporting once again from the deck of the *Centaur*. The wind had died down, and he was standing in bright sunlight.

"I've just received more news of the injured survivor that was recovered on the first run of the DSRV last night." He glanced down at whatever he was holding. "The injured man is the captain of the *Tulsa*, Commander Geoffrey Richter. He's had to undergo emergency surgery to remove a blood clot on his brain that was a result of a head injury he received during the collision with the Russian submarine, *Cheetah*." Marie was stunned. None of her mental images of Geoff were of an invalid, they were all of an attractive man in fine health. More often than not they were of him smiling at her or playing with the boys, or in deep discussion with John. Earlier ones were of him as an Adonis, the man she had so desperately wanted to marry. The man who would take her away from the misery that life in her family had become. She remembered the nights by Lake Erie and the mornings, waking up beside him, feeling loved. A blood clot in the brain? That sounded serious.

"I am also told," continued the reporter, "that it's very cold in the *Tulsa* and that he is hypothermic—which means that his body temperature is low."

"Robert?" The female voice-over was from the anchor. "Have the medical personnel given you any idea of how Commander Richter is likely to do?" The reporter squinted toward the camera and pressed the index finger of his right hand against his earpiece. He was clearly having difficulty hearing.

"Well, Stephanie, they're not prepared to commit themselves on this—although it would appear that there is an irony here."

"What's that, Robert?"

"It seems that the hypothermia might have saved Commander Richter's life."

"How is that?"

"I've been told that the cold substantially reduced his brain's need for oxygen and that this reduced the effect of the blood clot. It's all very technical, but it would seem that his prospects for recovery are quite a bit better than if he'd remained warm."

"That sounds like good news then?"

"Everything has a downside, Stephanie. I'm told that he's become so cold that warming him up isn't going to be easy. However, I detected a note of distinct optimism in the medical people I've been talking to. It seems the medical staff on board have considerable expertise in this area."

"Robert, some more of the *Tulsa*'s crew have arrived on the *Centaur*. How many have been rescued now?" Robert Cross looked down again before looking straight into the camera.

"Yes, a total of sixty-three have been brought out. . . ."

The exchange between the anchor and the reporter

became fuzzy, and Marie was absorbed with her
thoughts. Was this good news or bad? Was he going
to live? If he lived, was he going to be OK? She
couldn't begin to imagine Geoff as a vegetable. Her
thoughts ran on. Nobody had said that the casualty
list was wrong. She could have missed that, of course,
while she was asleep. Nonetheless, she knew instinctively that John was dead. The thought of losing the
two men in her life who meant the most to her was
almost too much. But she hadn't lost Geoff . . . yet.
She refocused on the screen.

". . . Yes, Stephanie, the *Vindictive* has dived again
and the next DSRV run is under way as I speak."

"We'll be back to you shortly, Robert. Thank you."
The screen blinked, and there was the anchor sitting
at a desk with a laptop computer to one side of her.
"So, to summarize, the casualty list in the *Tulsa* is
confirmed and it now looks like the remainder of
those alive in the submarine will be rescued by mid-
afternoon local time, which will be about eleven
o'clock Eastern Standard Time. Yesterday evening
Admiral William Ballantyne, the Chief of Naval Operations, paid tribute to those who had died in the
Tulsa. . . ."

So that was it. She had lost John and might yet lose
Geoff. Marie was aware that she was not thinking
straight and still felt incredibly tired. She also felt utterly
miserable. She'd take another tablet and go back to
sleep. After all, what was the point in waking up today?

1620A, HMS *Centaur*

The last rays of twilight had disappeared two hours
earlier, and the flight deck was now illuminated by the
ship's floodlights augmented by those of the camera
crews assembled adjacent to the large island on the
starboard side of the ship. The transfer of the last
members of the *Tulsa*'s crew was almost complete. A
Sea King touched down, and the main cabin door

opened. A crowd quickly assembled in front of it, composed of members of the press and the crew of the *Tulsa*. There was a roar as Lieutenant Commander Kellman and Commander Samways exited the aircraft and louder ones followed as Master Chief Steadman, Lieutenant Trost, and finally Enzo stepped out onto the deck. They'd had time to change into clean coveralls, but remained unshaved. They all sported broad smiles and waved to the crowd and the cameras. Enzo looked up, nudged the master chief, and pointed to the sky. "Look at that—isn't it beautiful?"

"What, sir?"

"The sky, the stars. Smell the fresh air, isn't it wonderful?" Paul Trost looked up as tears started to form at the corner of his eyes.

"I'll be honest, Enzo, there were times when I never thought I'd see the sky again. But we made it." He slapped Enzo on the back just as he was turning to embrace Paul in a bear hug.

"Yep. We made it." A reporter had reached them, and he thrust a microphone toward Paul Trost.

"Lieutenant Trost, what does it feel like to be out in the fresh air?" Enzo felt he should reply.

"I'm Lieutenant Raschello, and I can tell you it feels great." The reporter moved the microphone toward Enzo.

"How did the final stages of the rescue go? I understand the *Tulsa* was flooding."

"Yes it was. We also had no power to scrub the atmosphere. The pressure was increasing, and it was getting pretty hard to breathe."

"Did you have to use breathing apparatus?"

"No, we made do with the air in the boat." Commander Roberts, the executive officer of the *Centaur*, made his way toward the gaggle of reporters that now almost surrounded Enzo.

"Look, ladies and gentlemen, there will be an opportunity for you to ask your questions later. These men need to get cleaned up and have a good meal,

I'm sure you understand." With that he shepherded his new guests towards a door in the island. The other *Tulsa* survivors followed them. They were led down to the hangar, where Captain Temple was waiting to greet them.

"Gentlemen, it's my privilege and great pleasure to welcome you all aboard. I'm not going to take up much of your time—I know a lot of you have yet to take a shower and have a meal. We've brought you over from the *Vindictive* because we have a lot more room, and you'll need to be given the once-over by the medical team here. As I say, we have plenty of room for you, and we'll do all we can to make you as comfortable as possible."

It suddenly dawned on Enzo that he should say something and he made his way forward to stand next to Captain Temple. "Thank you for your welcome, sir. Believe me, it's our pleasure to be here." His audience erupted into applause, and the hangar echoed to cheers and piercing wolf whistles. Enzo waited a full minute before raising his arms to quell the noise. As he did so, he winced as an aching sensation gripped his left shoulder. The noise died down. "Unlike the captain, I do have more to say to you all, but it will keep until we have eaten. Is there somewhere that we can use to meet a little later on, sir?"

"By all means. Assemble your men in the junior rates' dining hall after dinner."

"Thank you, sir." He turned to his audience. "I'll speak to you all again later. Eat well." Commander Samways eased his way through the crowd and tapped Enzo on the shoulder.

"Enzo, I saw you wince a moment ago, is anything wrong?"

"No, sir. Things have never been better," he lied as the twinge in his shoulder had developed into a persistent, throbbing ache.

"You know, shoulder pain is a pretty classic symptom of bends. Are you sure you're okay?"

"I'm fine. If I start to get any aches and pains, I'll come and see you. Right now, I want to see Commander Richter before I clean myself up."

"Be sure you do. Limb pain can progress to involve the nervous system, you know. Shame to screw that up when it can all be fixed by spending a few hours in a compression chamber."

"I'll bear that in mind, sir."

2030A, HMS *Centaur*

The cheering that had accompanied Enzo's earlier remarks were repeated as he rose to address his fellow survivors. "Look, you'll have to quiet down. I'm not going to shout." The cheering subsided. "The first thing I have to say is that Commander Richter is doing well. He's still unconscious, but he's warm, and the operation went very well." The last few words were drowned out by a fresh outbreak of cheering. Enzo resigned himself to the fact that this was going to take rather longer than he had expected, and it would inevitably postpone yet further his going to see Commander Samways about his shoulder. It now felt like much of his left forearm was tingling, and he was clearly going to need some treatment. Sitting in a compression chamber for the next few hours, having just got out of the *Tulsa*, was not the way he had planned to celebrate. Commander Richards's kind offer of a glass of Chianti would have to wait.

Enzo continued. "Now the next thing I must do is congratulate each and every one of you. The past nine days have not been easy for any of us. They would have been impossible if you hadn't behaved like the professionals you've proved to the world that you are. You were simply amazing, and that made my job bearable. If you hadn't all racked out and stayed that way, we would not be enjoying the hospitality of the Royal Navy." There was another cheer, and the men raised the cans of beer that they had been given by their hosts. "This brings me to the Golden Dreams award. So many of you would make worthy winners! However, there can be only one, and I am delighted to ask Sonarman Evans to come and collect his prize." There was another outbreak of applause and Sonarman Evans, blushing bright red, walked up to Enzo. "Here, take this. I'm sorry there's been no time to make the trophy; I'll give it to you as soon as it's finished." He reached down and handed Evans a case of beer.

"Thank you, sir," beamed Evans.

"Don't drink it all at once!" Evans returned to his seat and was immediately surrounded by thirsty colleagues. "There are many others I'd like to thank but two people in particular deserve a mention right now. Sparks, I really can't thank you enough for all you did. What with fixing the hopper and keeping water away from the battery. . . . None of us would be here without you." The air was pierced by the loudest cheering so far. Enzo raised his voice. "And Master Chief Steadman, not everybody here will know what an incredible job you did looking after the injured. They are all in professional hands now, but they wouldn't be without your tireless efforts." He reached down, picked up two more slabs of beer, walked over to their table, and placed them in front of Sparks and Steadman. "This is a wholly inadequate way of expressing my gratitude, but it's the best I can do at the moment."

"Can't think of a better one," joked Sparks, and the cheering was now accompanied by the stamping of feet.

Enzo returned to the front of the group and let the noise die down spontaneously. "The last thing I have to say is that you'll all need to get a good night's sleep." There was an outbreak of hysterical laughter, as most of them had spent the last nine days doing nothing but trying to sleep. The laughter abated. "The reason is, I've been notified that a team of officers from the Judge Advocate General's office will be flying out to the ship tomorrow." Enzo's audience fell completely silent. "You'll all need to be on your toes. They will be here to begin their investigation."

EPILOGUE

Friday, 17 December

1230Z, Institute of Naval Medicine, Alverstoke, United Kingdom

Surgeon Commander Freeman dropped his bags on the floor of his office and indicated to his guests that they should do the same. "Right. Richard, Steve, time for a quick beer and some tapas in the wardroom. Thank God they had the Christmas lunch here yesterday; otherwise, we'd be roped in to serving turkey and trimmings to the rest of the establishment." He led them out of the office, down some stairs, and out onto the lawn. "I expect that David and Roger will be right behind us." They walked across the lawn and into the wardroom. There were already half a dozen officers present. As he advanced to the bar, Freeman noticed the medical officer in command standing in the corner. "Sir, you've met Lieutenant Commander Tremble and Lieutenant Marchant?"

"Yes, indeed. Welcome, gentlemen. How was San Diego?"

"Busy, sir," replied Tremble wearily. "It was productive though. There's going to be more than enough work for SCOSER for the next ten years. Mark you, the Yanks have even more to do."

"SCOSER?"

"Oh, sorry, sir. That's the Standing Committee on Submarine Escape and Rescue."

"Right." The MOIC continued, "I expect you'll all be ready for some leave. You've had a busy time recently."

"Incredible. It just hasn't stopped since we got back from Norway."

"Well, you all deserve a break, and I shouldn't be too apprehensive about work that's over the horizon. After every accident and operation it's always the same. Endless inquiries into events that nobody expected and multimillion-pound systems that either failed or underperformed. They rarely come to much. In the end it's the ingenuity, guts, and hard graft of individuals that usually wins the day, and I expect that'll always be the case." Everybody nodded sagely. "By the way, I believe congratulations are in order. Complete exoneration of the SPAG by the board of inquiry? Great news, you must both be relieved. What can I get you?"

"Well, thank you, sir. I'll have a pint of bitter," replied Tremble.

"I'll have the same thank you, sir," added Marchant. "And it was a relief. I'd reached the point where I didn't really know if we'd done the right thing. I'm just glad it's all over."

"I wouldn't be so sure it is. I've rarely read a report that was so effusive about the courage of individuals without there being further recognition."

"Do you know something, sir?" asked Freeman.

"No I don't. What can I get you, Eric?"

"Thank you, sir, a pint would be most welcome." He paused for a moment before continuing. "One thing that came out of the San Diego meeting is a proposal for a new exchange appointment between DEVRON FIVE and Fort Blockhouse. There's a real need for us and the USN to coordinate our efforts in submarine escape and rescue rather better. If it's approved, Steve here's a hot bet for a couple of years in the sun." Marchant beamed as the drinks were served.

"Well, good luck with that, Steve, it would be very well deserved." The group was joined by Roger Stemple and David Sheppard. The MOIC ordered drinks for them. "How are you feeling, chaps?"

"Knackered understates it, sir. I've never been able to sleep in aircraft, although I must say the front of a 777 is a whole lot more comfortable than the back of a Hercules," replied Sheppard.

"The cabin service is rather better as well," added Stemple with a twinkle in his eye and a barely suppressed grin. "Young Tanya was remarkably attentive."

The MOIC coughed and raised his glass. "Here's to a good Christmas leave. Relax and enjoy yourselves. You should all be very proud of what you did. Be assured that I certainly am."

Sunday, 19 December

1000R, Bethesda Naval Hospital

Richter woke abruptly and opened his eyes. A nurse was gently shaking his shoulder. "Commander Richter, you have a visitor," she said.

"Who is it?"

"Mrs. Dowling, sir." Richter thought for a minute, the name was familiar. The nurse studied him. "Surely you remember, her husband died in the accident?" Richter tried not to look too confused. "She says she's an old friend, sir, this is the third time she's tried to see you."

"Yes, yes, sure, please show her in," he slurred in reply. As he slowly struggled up to a sitting position, he watched her leave the room and walk over to the nurses' station. She spoke briefly to a woman with mousy hair, who was wearing a long black coat. The visitor nodded and looked up in the direction the nurse was pointing. He saw her smile as she started to walk toward him, a smile that widened as she approached his bed and embraced him.

"How are you, Geoff?" She released him, stepped back, and studied his face. She was still smiling. Richter returned the smile a little crookedly because the right side of his face still didn't move quite as well as the left.

"I'm fine . . . tired, but fine. They make me work pretty hard here—physical therapy twice a day, swimming, speech therapy."

"The nurse tells me you're doing really well, she said you'll soon be walking unassisted."

"Can't be soon enough for me. It feels like I've spent a lifetime in bed."

There was an uneasy silence. Marie was beginning to wonder how well Geoff really was. He looked OK, if rather thin, but he was obviously not his old self. "Look," she began, "I've brought you some fruit." She groped around in the carrier bag she'd been holding. "There are some grapes, satsumas, kiwi fruit— you love those." She looked up and offered him a few grapes. A lopsided smile flickered across his face.

"Thank you," he replied as he popped one into his mouth and started to chew. "I'm in trouble," he continued. "The court of inquiry's in recess until the engineers have finished their work. They've raised the *Tulsa* and, as soon as it's back in Groton, Electric Boat will go over it with a fine tooth comb. But I'm really worried about what'll happen once the court reconvenes. My counsel thinks it'll turn into a witch-hunt, and I'm the obvious target."

"Come on, why should they do that? You're all national heroes."

"For the moment we are. I'm delighted that Enzo's to receive the Navy Distinguished Service Medal."

"That's not all, I just heard on the news that Master Chief Steadman and Petty Officer Cotton are going to be decorated as well, and I'm sure there will be a whole lot more."

"I expect you've noticed that I'm not on that list. The *Tulsa*'s crew may be flavor of the month right now, but when all the hoopla dies down the knives will be out. The navy doesn't like to lose submarines. It was my command, so it was my fault. It's as simple as that." Richter paused for a moment and looked at Marie. His eyes betrayed his fear. "The trouble is that I'm defenseless."

"Why? I've never heard you talk like this before."

"I've lost my memory. I can't remember a damned thing about the collision or anything after it until I came around in hospital in Tromsa. Two weeks of my life are missing completely, and my recollection of some things prior to the collision is patchy. How can I defend myself if I can't remember what happened?"

"Surely Harvey and Enzo will support you?"

"I expect they will, but they've got to cover their own asses. . . ."

"Well, one of the things I wanted to say was that Father has offered to defend you, and he'll bring in any heavy guns that are required to make sure you get out of this all right."

"That's very kind of him. I can't really refuse, can I?"

"I don't think so." It was Marie's turn to pause. "Geoff, they're going to let you out of here soon. Where are you going to live?" Richter popped another grape into his mouth and chewed rhythmically.

"I've no idea. What with my therapy, the court of inquiry, and the congressional hearings I'm going to have to be based in Washington for the time being. There are some bachelor quarters on base here. I expect they can make room for me there."

"The thing is, Geoff, I'm going to have to leave Groton. There are just too many memories of John there, and in any case, I'll lose the quarters. I've been staying with Father in Cherry Hill, but I'm going to have to move out. Christine's back, and although she's trying to be nice, it's all a sham. And the boys don't like her. So I've been looking around for somewhere to live. It's taken me a while because I couldn't decide on a location until I was sure what I'm going to do." She reached onto the bed, plucked a grape off the bunch and started to chew it thoughtfully. "You know, being involved with the *Tulsa* sinking as I have been has made me think about going into politics. Father's all for it; it's what he always wanted. What do you think?"

"It's an idea. Quite a challenge. What do you want to do, run for election or just work on the Hill?"

"Not sure yet. One thing's for certain. If I'm going to be successful, I'll have to go to school, so I'm thinking about Georgetown. They offer a world-beating major in Political Economy."

"You mean you're thinking of living in Washington?"

"Well, Chevy Chase. It's a very nice area, and Montgomery County has great schools. I'm thinking about buying a house there."

"There? It's just down the road, isn't it?"

"It sure is."

"We'll virtually be neighbors then."

"That's right, and if you find yourself going mad in the Q, you can always come round for a meal."

1200R, New London Submarine Base, Groton, Connecticut

Enzo plunged into the pool, swam a width underwater, and surfaced next to Lieutenant Schwartz. "Hey, Harvey, so you didn't fancy a run either?"

"Too darned cold. I don't know why, but I seem to wheeze if I run in cold weather these days."

"Have you seen the doctor?"

"No, can't see the point. I prefer to swim anyway."

"I'm off to Norfolk tomorrow, COMSUBLANT wants to see me again."

"Any idea why?"

"No, Harvey, although I wouldn't be surprised if it wasn't the decorations I've recommended."

"I thought the squadron and Group 2 had sorted all that out."

"So did I, but there's still a whole lot pending." Enzo paused. "I'm thinking of stopping off in DC on the way back. I want to see the captain."

"Are people allowed to see him now? He wasn't seeing visitors for ages."

"Yes he is; I spoke with him on the phone just yesterday."

"How is he?"

"Hard to say, Harvey. He's still slurring his speech, and he hasn't a clue about what happened. He sounds rather depressed as well. I'll see if I can't cheer him up a bit, poor guy. None of us would have survived without him; it's high time he understood that. I also want to return some things I rescued from his stateroom. I've got his diary and a couple of photographs. I expect he'll be glad to see them."

"Enzo, you don't think COMSUBLANT wants to discuss Chief Santana do you?" Enzo raised an eyebrow.

"Why should he? It was a straightforward suicide. The man just couldn't take the situation any longer. I feel very sorry for him and his family."

"Don't you think it's a bit odd that he was the only one to crack like that? I heard that a group of chiefs were gambling, and Santana had lost a lot of money."

"What?" Enzo had raised his voice and quickly looked around to see if anybody might have overheard the conversation. "Where on earth did you hear that?" he continued in a hoarse whisper.

"Paul Trost mentioned it."

"Where did he get it from?"

"I've no idea, I didn't ask. Is it true?"

Enzo took a moment before replying. "Harvey, I've got no hard evidence of anything of the kind. But obviously I'm going to have to have a word with Paul and the COB. This would make a very ugly rumor if it was spread around. You'll keep it to yourself, won't you?"

"Sure, Enzo."

"Right. Fancy a race?"

"OK, four lengths. Loser buys the beer."

"You're on."

GLOSSARY

ABS Antilock braking system.

AC Alternating current electricity of the kind that is used by most domestic appliances. Most devices that run AC are incompatible with DC power and vice versa.

ASD Assistant secretary of defense.

BNQ-13 A small battery-powered sonar used to indicate the location of a disabled submarine. Also known as the sonar distress pinger.

BOQ Bachelor Officers' Quarters.

C130 Also known as the Hercules, this is an all-purpose military transport aircraft.

C5 A very large military transport aircraft capable of carrying the DSRV.

CAMS Central air-monitoring system. This machine samples air from around the submarine and maintains a log of its composition and major toxic pollutants.

Cavitating	When propellers turn very fast they generate bubbles in the water by a process of cavitation. These are noisy and can be detected by sonar.
CBNSW	The Commander British Navy Staff, Washington. Part of the British Embassy, this organization is staffed mainly by naval officers. Its purpose is to support collaborative projects between the British Royal Navy and the USN.
CINC	Commander in Chief.
CHINFO	The chief of Naval Information.
CINCLANT	The commander in chief, US Atlantic Fleet.
Civvy	A slang term for a civilian.
CNO	The Chief of Naval Operations.
CO_2	Carbon dioxide.
COB	Chief of the Boat.
COMSUBLANT	The commander, Submarine Force, US Atlantic Fleet.
COMSUBPAC	The commander, Submarine Force, US Pacific Fleet.
COMJTFNON HQ	The NATO headquarters in northern Norway.
CPA	The closest point of approach of one vessel to another.
CPR	Cardiopulmonary resuscitation.

Crabs	An irreverent reference to the British Royal Air Force used by the other two British armed services.
CSO	Chief staff officer.
Datum	Military term for a particular location or objective. In this book it is used to refer to the position of the wreck of the *Tulsa*.
DC	Direct current electricity of the kind that is delivered by a battery.
DDMO	The Royal Navy duty diving medical officer.
DEVRON FIVE	Submarine Development Squadron 5, a group responsible for overseeing submarine escape and rescue. It's based in San Diego.
DISSUB	Abbreviation for a disabled submarine.
Draeger tubes	Glass tubes containing a chemical which changes color when exposed to a particular gas. One sort is used for measuring CO_2 levels in the atmosphere. They can only be used once.
Duff	A Royal Navy slang term for dessert.
DSRV	The Deep Submergence Rescue Vehicle is a US Navy minisubmarine that is air-transportable and designed to rescue submariners from a disabled submarine.
EABs	Emergency air breathing apparatus. These are masks which provide clean air from the ship's compressed-air banks.

EMT	Emergency medical technician.
ETA	Estimated time of arrival.
FOSM	The British Royal Navy's Flag Officer Submarines, broadly equivalent to the US Navy's COMSUBLANT.
HP air	High-pressure air, usually stored in groups of bottles, known as air banks.
IMF	The International Monetary Fund.
INM	The Institute of Naval Medicine located in Gosport, United Kingdom.
IV	An intravenous infusion.
JAG	US Navy's Judge Advocate General.
LET	Logistics escape tower. This is the normal conduit, containing the escape tower, into a Vanguard class submarine, which can be removed in dock to provide greater access to the boat.
LMA	Leading medical assistant in the Royal Navy. Equivalent to a petty officer corpsman third class in the US Navy.
LR5	British submarine rescue vehicle. Owned by the Cable and Wireless Corporation and leased by the Royal Navy.
JG	Abbreviation for the rank of lieutenant, junior grade.
MC	This is a generic term for internal communications circuits. The number preceding "MC" indicates which circuit. 1MC is the ship's main broad-

cast; 31MC is the circuit for talking to the occupants of the escape trunk, etc.

Merlin   The naval version of the EH101: a large, multifunction helicopter built by a European consortium.

MIA   Personnel listed as missing in action.

MOSUB   A full-sized submarine, normally a 637 or 688 class, which has been adapted to carry the DSRV on a cradle located over the after escape trunk. The MOSUB can recharge the DSRV's batteries and receive survivors as they are recovered from the disabled submarine or DISSUB.

MV   Motor vessel.

N87   A two-star officer on the staff of the Chief of Naval Operations responsible for deep submergence systems, including the DSRV.

OSC   The on-scene commander. The senior officer at the site of a submarine sinking. This may be the pilot of an aircraft or the captain of a ship.

Overhead   US Navy term for ceiling.

P3   A naval reconnaissance and anti-submarine patrol aircraft. Also known as the Orion.

PAO   Public affairs officer.

psi   A unit of pressure in pounds per square inch.

PDQ   Pretty damned quickly.

Planesman	Enlisted man who responds to commands from the diving officer to control the angle of the hydroplanes and, thereby, the depth of the submarine.
POMA	Petty officer medical assistant in the Royal Navy. Equivalent to a petty officer corpsman first class in the US Navy.
RDO	Rescue and diving officer.
RFS	Russian Federation ship.
RMAS	The Royal Maritime Auxiliary Service. A civilian-manned organization that provides support vessels to the British Royal Navy.
ROV	Remotely operated vehicle. This is an unmanned minisubmarine equipped with television cameras, lights, and manipulator arms that can be used for underwater exploration and salvage. The one used by the British Navy is called Scorpio.
RS	Radio supervisor.
SETT	The British Royal Navy's submarine escape training tank located at Fort Blockhouse, Gosport.
SITREP	Abbreviation for a situation report.
SLOT buoy	An emergency radio-transmitting buoy. This has a range of approximately ten nautical miles for a surface ship or one hundred miles for an aircraft. It transmits the signal "SOS SUB SUNK" repeatedly in international Morse code on the

aeronautical distress frequency for about eighteen hours.

SMERAT   Submarine Escape and Rescue Advisory Team. A group of experts in the field of submarine escape and diving who fly out to the first-reaction vessel and serve to advise the on-scene commander. The group contains some specialist medical staff who are trained to provide care to the crew of the submarine after they have escaped or been rescued.

SOSUS   The Sound Underwater Surveillance System. A global network of hydrophones designed to detect and track submarines.

SPAG   The Submarine Parachute Assistance Group. A group of submarine escape trainers who parachute into the water at the site of a submarine sinking. Equipped with inflatable boats and life rafts, they are trained to provide first-aid care to those who have to escape from the DISSUB. They also have an underwater telephone and radio which allows them to relay the conditions on board the submarine to the commander of the rescue forces.

SRC   Submarine rescue chamber. This is a specially designed diving bell that is lowered from a support vessel to the DISSUB and located over one of the escape trunks. Survivors climb through the escape trunk and into the SRC, after which the escape trunk is closed and the bell is raised to the surface. The SRC can rescue six personnel at a time.

Steinke Hood An inflatable life vest with a hood that is worn over the head when submariners have to make an escape to the surface. It traps a large bubble of gas that the escaper can breathe from while he is underwater. Since they are very rarely required, they have to be checked for leaks before being used.

SUBLOOK An operation to establish contact with a submarine with which communication has been lost. The submarine is not yet considered to be missing.

SUBMISS A submarine is significantly overdue with a required report. SUBLOOK procedures have been completed and no contact has been made. This normally results in a more intensive search.

SUBSUNK A submarine is known or presumed to be disabled and unable to surface. This generally results in a full rescue operation to recover the crew.

USNA US naval attaché.

UWT Underwater telephone.

Z berth A harbor berth that is equipped to support a nuclear-powered vessel.